HERO'S BEST FRIEND
AN ANTHOLOGY OF ANIMAL COMPANIONS

HERO'S BEST FRIEND

AN ANTHOLOGY OF ANIMAL COMPANIONS

EDITED BY
SCOTT M. SANDRIDGE

 SEVENTH STAR PRESS

Cover art and design: Enggar Adirasa
Cover art in this book copyright © 2013 Enggar Adirasa & Seventh Star Press, LLC.

Editor: Scott M. Sandridge

Published by Seventh Star Press, LLC.

ISBN Number: 978-1-937929-51-0

Seventh Star Press
www.seventhstarpress.com
info@seventhstarpress.com

Publisher's Note:
Hero's Best Friend: An Anthology of Animal Companions is a work of fiction. All names, characters, and places are the product of the author's imagination, used in fictitious manner. Any resemblances to actual persons, places, locales, events, etc. are purely coincidental.

Printed in the United States of America

First Edition

Copyright Acknowledgements

DEDICATION

To Killer, Baby Jr., White Sox, White Sox II, Lucy, Loki, and all the other fuzzbuckets, featherheads, and scalybutts out there that keep life from ever getting boring.

To Stephen Zimmer and Seventh Star Press for giving me the opportunity to edit this anthology. And to all the writers, for without you there would be no anthology.

Last but not least, to my family for having the patience to put up with my ornery arse.

FEATURED IN HERO'S BEST FRIEND

FOREWORD

When I first read *The Two Towers* I thought Shadowfax was the coolest thing ever. And the best thing about *The Beastmaster* was the animals, especially the ferrets. Outside of Fantasy, were the two novels that sealed my love for animal stories: *Black Beauty* and *White Fang*.

Short of *Watership Down* and old fairy-tales there were very few Fantasy-based stories done from the viewpoint of animals or even had animals be the main characters. The human heroes always managed to somehow get all the credit despite all the sacrifices their faithful animal companions made. And Disney always managed to ruin it for me by making the animals way too human. *The Lion King* was the only one that ever came close, and that got ruined by all the singing and dancing.

So when I sent my anthology proposal ideas to Seventh Star Press, an anthology about animal companions was on my list. And the rest is, to borrow a cliché, history.

At first I was worried if there were enough writers out there who'd be up for the challenge. Crafting a good tale is difficult enough—let alone one where the animals get central stage. But not only were there writers, both aspiring writers and seasoned pros, willing to accept the challenge, but I was pleasantly surprised by the sheer quality of the stories that landed in my inbox. Stories that made me laugh, that made me cry, that made me laugh while crying. It was an emotional rollercoaster ride the entire time.

And not just the fictional stories themselves, but also the real stories that some of the writers shared with me regarding their wonderful furball friends: like Frank Creed's heroic little tuxedo who was on his little death bed as Frank was finishing "Dusk."

R.I.P. little fella. Your fictional alter ego will forever be immortalized in print and electrons.

It is said that losing a beloved pet is almost as traumatizing as losing your own child. I've never had any children, but I did lose both my parents, and the pets I've lost—B.J., Lucy, White Sox, Loki, and even the ones that weren't technically "mine"—hurt about as bad, and for just as long. Some days, I still miss them, right along with my parents.

Making this anthology brought back memories of old

friends long gone, and I have no doubt that it'll do the same for whoever reads it.

Because our pets are more to us than just pets. They are loyal allies, valiant heroes, and lovable rogues with hearts of gold. And sometimes, on occasion, adorable fools.

They are companions in this journey we call life. And life would not be anywhere near as interesting if they weren't around.

So curl up with your lovable companion and enjoy the adventure. Just be sure your adorable fool, if you have one, doesn't mistake this anthology for a snack....

TOBY AND STEVE SAVE THE WORLD
BY JOY WARD

Toby officiously tripped down the wooden-floored hallway, his almost tailless bunny butt proudly swinging from side-to-side. Yes! He had saved the day once again! The red and white Pembroke Corgi grinned to himself. If he could have reached his little white left front foot around he would have been patting himself on his back. Toby couldn't do that so he pranced down the hall. He felt like the biggest baddest Corgi in the world (or at least in North America)!

And so he should. Toby had just saved the world one more time. Okay, Toby hadn't actually been the one doing the saving, but he had made sure his human, Steve, had done it. Steve with his voice, human form and opposable thumbs carried through the actions, but Toby knew that Toby was the one in charge when Steve did his best. Steve was well known for being in the right place when someone was in danger and showing up at the right time to oh, catch the baby falling out of a tenth story window, block the entrance of an armed schizophrenic from entering a grade school, or even intercept a confirmed sex offender from climbing in a ten-year-old girl's bedroom window.

Yes, Steve had been the human doing those things but nobody knew that, without Toby, Steve would never have shown up at the right time for any of those deeds. Toby was the one responsible for getting Steve to the right spot at the right time. Without Toby, Steve was just a really big, strong human male with good intentions.

As Toby sat congratulating himself on their most recent success over evil, he felt that pricking in his huge triangular ears that meant it was time to jump into action again. He sat quietly for the merest moment as he listened to find the potential bad guy or girl. At first all he could hear was the large, brownish dog down the alley barking at two obnoxious male human teens as they strolled down the alley. One of them was making a pain of himself by slapping a stick across the fences along the alley. Were these the humans about to cause serious trouble? The question went out to Toby's friend, Blaze, the dog who was barking.

"No," Blaze sent back. "These old pups walk this was

every day, doing the same useless tricks. No real danger here."

Toby turned his fuzzy head this way and that, looking for the danger to address.

All of a sudden, Toby caught the mental scent. Sweetie, a two-year-old Pomeranian a few streets over, was frantically sending a call for help. The young bitch was jumping up and down calling for Toby's help and attention.

"Defender! Defender! Help! Help! Bring your human! Need you next door!"

"This is Toby. What is the need? How can we help?" Toby sent his thoughts back to the obviously panicked young girl.

"Fire! Fire! Fire next door. No adult humans nearby. Two human pups in back room. They are sleeping and don't know. Help soon!"

Toby leaped up, making sure he knew exactly where the Pomeranian lived. It was mid-afternoon, so Steve was in his office typing on his metal box. It could be hard to get Steve moving in that case, but Toby was the area Defender, charged with keeping his area safe by working with his human. Okay, time to make Steve think Toby HAD to go walkies.

Toby prepared himself for a performance as he zoomed into Steve's office. Sure enough, Steve sat in his big, rolling chair moving his fingers across the metal case on his desk. The speed of the taps told Toby that Steve was deeply into this piece. Toby would just have to pull out all his tricks to get

Steve moving!

Toby started with his opening gambit by placing himself directly behind Steve's chair. He braced himself and let out a series of piercing barks. "Bark! Bark!" He stopped a second and then started barking again. "Bark! Bark! Bark!"

Steve almost fell off his chair as the barks hit with full force on the immense, twenty-seven-year-old man with curly brown hair tumbling to his shoulders. "Whoa, Toby! What the hell is your problem? We just got in a few hours ago. Surely, you don't have to pee again this soon. Shut up!"

Toby backed up a foot or so to let Steve know that he really did have to go walkies.

"Can't you wait? You're not an old dog, and I'm really into this article now. It's going right where I want it to go."

Yeah, but I have somewhere else for you to go RIGHT NOW! Toby thought as hard as he could at Steve with another increasingly sharp bark to punctuate the thoughts. "Now, now, now!" Like a drummer pounding out notes, Toby pushed each "now" with stronger and stronger barks.

Steve looked disgusted as he hit a key on his metal box and pushed his chair back from the desk. "Dang, Toby. You just have no respect for my time, do you?"

Toby redoubled his efforts to get Steve moving by jumping up as he barked. Steve was moving now but not fast enough. Toby had to get him moving faster. Okay, let's put this into high gear, he told himself.

Toby started gagging. It wasn't hard since he could throw up at will. A bit of bad grass here or decayed bird there and there sat a little pile of stomach contents. "Ack!" Toby let the sound and the sight of potential vomit fill the room. Just to make sure Steve got the message Toby hit it again, hard. "Ack, ack, ack!"

Now Steve started moving! "Hold that, Toby! I'm moving! I'm moving!" Toby knew Steve hated cleaning vomit off the beautiful wooden floors. He would do almost anything to keep Toby from throwing up on his beloved floors. Toby didn't understand it, but he did know how to use that fear to motivate Steve. And right now Toby needed Steve to get really motivated, and fast!

Steve shoved his huge feet into the boots sitting next to the desk, grabbed his denim jacket and pulled Toby's blue leash out of the closet behind him. "Let's go, pukey!"

Toby hated to be teased, but he would do what he had to save the little humans. He was the Defender! Let Steve call him pukey or even stinky like he did when Toby had eaten too much dog food if Toby could do his job.

As Toby was getting Steve out of the apartment and down the front steps he could hear Sweetie's frantic barks. "Help, Toby! Fire faster, bigger! Come! Come! Now! Now!" He could sense her jumping up like a cotton ball blown by a mad wind as she bounced against her glass front door. Toby had to get Steve moving faster!

There! Toby could smell just a whiff of the fire. But he knew Steve's puny nose would not help him recognize the danger. Toby had to get Steve within a human's smelling range.

Steve and Toby got down the front steps when Toby hit the end of his leash hard. "Come on, Steve! Come on, Steve! Move! Move! Move!" Once again, Toby was frustrated by how deaf humans were, including his mostly wonderful Steve. Somehow Steve could only hear wordless barks instead of the messages Toby tried so hard to mentally push to him. How could humans be so deaf?

"Toby, not so fast. You'll pull me down. Just pick a spot to urp and do it! One place is as good as another. Come on!"

Toby mentally shook his head and continued massive pulls on the leash, oh so slowly hauling his reluctant hero behind him.

Foot by foot Toby leaned against the leash as he moved Steve closer and closer to the endangered children. "Please let us be on time," Toby prayed to Sirius, the dog god. All Toby could hear was the blood pounding in his head and Sweetie's frenzied barks.

Finally, Steve realized he was needed a block ahead. "Do you smell that, Toby? I think I smell fire up ahead. Let's speed up!" Now the tables turned and Steve led the way as he pulled on Toby's leash. Steve was almost dragging Toby down the dry sidewalk.

Then Toby could hear Sweetie. "Sweetie, we're here. We're here."

Sweetie's barks got faster. "Yay! Yay! Children still in house and asleep! Humans lock front door but not back. Go to back door, Defender!"

Steve was running faster now. Toby was having trouble keeping up with the human. Toby's short dwarfed legs were not meant to move this fast but he did. They flashed like white rabbit paws right behind Steve's long strides. An onlooker might only have seen the flash of red and white at Steve's denim-covered legs as they raced, man and Defender at his heels.

Toby knew which house so he had to get in front. He put on a burst of speed, throwing himself at Steve's feet to make him stop in front of the right house. Toby could smell the fire, and he had Sweetie's help, but Steve could wander around until the flames emerged and the children were dead. Toby had to move Steve to the right house immediately.

"Toby, what the hell are you doing? You almost tripped me up." Steve yelled at Toby, but Toby had stopped him in front of the right house.

Steve turned around, sniffing the air. How did they use those tiny noses? The thought flashed across Toby's mind. No time for that thought. Toby had Steve at the right house, but he still had to get Steve in the house.

Steve ran to the front door, simultaneously pumping the door bell and pounding on the metal door. No way to get in here. Toby had to pull Steve to the back.

Toby pulled violently towards the side of the house. Steve looked at Toby then back to the invincible metal door in front of him. "Let's see if there's another way in." The leash suddenly went slack as Steve followed Toby around the house to the back door.

By now, the smoke was starting to leak under the slightly raised windows next to the back door. Steve wasted no time knocking on the stained metal door. "If this door is locked, Toby, I'm not sure what we can do." He grabbed the handle and yanked the door open. Smoke almost knocked him over.

Toby could hear the two humans screaming one room over. Steve obviously could hear them but not tell where they were. He was coughing up smoke as he tried to see through the smoke. Toby grabbed his leash in his mouth, forcibly leading Steve to the children. Steve dropped Toby's leash and swept up a child in each arm. Within a moment or two Steve, the children and Defender Toby were out of the house and on the grass across the street. The humans fell on the ground coughing up black saliva. Everyone was safe thanks to Steve and Toby, though only Steve would get the credit they both deserved.

TOBY AND STEVE SAVE THE WORLD

Sweetie was right! Would anyone know she shared this victory? Probably not. Humans tended to look around for human heroes. She had called the Defender and his human. So often the Defenders and their fellow dogs were the real heroes but humans, head blind as usual, didn't see that. Oh well.

Later as Toby laid on his doggie bed in the family room, munching on one of his favorite crunchy treats, Toby thought about how funny humans were. Steve is a good man but even he doesn't suspect he has help being in the right place at the right time. But what the heck? Toby loved defending his neighborhood, his world. He didn't need the humans' appreciation. He could hear Sweetie's contented barks as she slept on her human's couch. She dreamed of her part in the day, her tiny legs moving in the air above her. He could also sense Blaze's nightly intention to make his daily stand against the two obnoxious boys, along with all the thoughts and wishes and loves of the other canine in his area. He didn't care that the humans didn't know he was the Defender and Steve got all the credit. Toby had Steve, a warm home, and these oh so tasty treats. Who needs fame when he could sleep on The Bed with Steve and help Steve defend their area? Toby loved his life! Life was good!

Toby crunched his treat and waited for the next call to save the world.

DUSK
BY FRANK CREED

"After dark all cats are leopards."
~ Native American Proverb

Whisp and I strode the reds and golds of Chicago Chinatown with its pointy flared roof corners. My being a 55 kilogram tuxedo-cat drew the usual stares. That's just a little smaller than a small mountain-lion. I have to mind my tail to keep from hitting faces when sidewalks are full. My genetic size modification makes a big first impression.

Ethnic cuisine scenting thick in my snout, I caught our reflection in a store window—I'm a looker you know. Black on top, my front paws and back legs are white, like pants. Whisp says the black on my white face looks like lipstick but being a fine male specimen, I think of it as a moustache and goatee. He's a sandman in the Underground who raided the lab where I was born and caged. Saved my life and raised me. Whisp is short for whisperer. That's what folks came to call him. Folks ignorant of my own capabilities. I like that it makes Whisp smile, though, so I just purr.

A steady warm summer rain fell on rush-hour pedestrians who sprouted umbrellas as they streamed. An unmarked showroom-fresh 2038 navy Crown Vic with a light-bar in the back window rolled down Cermack slowly to disappear in traffic. We reached the worthless property along the rail-lines where, in this neighborhood, clay brick buildings sprang up without permits. Like the weeds that grow here.

The time of day for which I'm named arrived—dusk—when shadows' contrast trick eyes and my camo works best. If we need to prowl, it's at dusk. Dawn if we have to, but I like sunbeaming while my sandman takes his coffee.

West Cermack Road's traffic whooshed behind us as we stalked into a narrow packed-gravel lane with weed-grown shuttered storefronts. Three buildings down lie the train tracks and beyond, the Chicago River's South Branch. Two- and three-story clay brick shanties glimmered barely lit windows in upper stories. Candles.

I stalked the right wall, tail level behind me, as far as the second building. It opened in a ground floor half-full parkade.

No motion or sound besides the usual rush hour noises. Motor oil and garbage tainted the air.

Whisp eased down the left wall of shuttered shops, toward fluorescent lighting that flickered from inside the only open shop. The soles of his smart-boots made little sound. An unbuttoned dark olive shirt covered a black tank-top, and hid the straps to his gear. Rain fell on the stubbled hair and beard on his tanned head. He squinted faint crow's feet that put him in his thirties.

I trotted across the packed gravel, tail up, eager to get out of the rain—wet fur doesn't insulate. A sun-rotted awning covered trays of bulk foods displayed on barrels. We faced the end of two aisles, hand-built shelves displaying items in colorful oddly marked wrapping. The shop's right-front corner featured a brief scarred kitchen countertop across two barrels in front of a doorway with stairs up behind it. There stood the shopkeeper, an elderly balding Chinese man in a faded t-shirt and shorts. Rubber nubs covered the soles of his flip-flops. He nodded a polite smile at my partner but his eyes kept darting to me.

I flicked my tail while half-lidding a gaze, not trusting him until I had good reason—a good policy I find.

Whisp checked the street a last time before facing the man and palming his hips. "Virtual-e. I have bitcoin." That was pirate's gold to these people.

The Body Surfers had scanned chatter about a dozen Virtual-e units in Chinatown, the new hot not-yet-available entertainment device.

Problem was the tech could kill you.

Users were dying across the rest of the world in an addiction scandal but Calamity Kid had sabotaged production plans for North America, delaying an advertised release.

Our orders were to get these off the street before someone died, but word had it our hacks wanted to modify the devices as well.

The old man chattered sing-song words.

A cough sounded just inside the stairwell.

A teen next-gen of the family, also in faded shorts and tee, descended the stairs. "After you open an account, I'll take you."

I sniffed the alien scents on the shelves in my aisle — and also the faint charcoal bouquet of expensive whiskey — while Whisp did what they wanted. From the back of the shop I eyeballed inside the stairwell where sat a thin middle-aged yellow-skinned man on a stool. He wore suspenders over a plain white stained tee and held a cup. He looked at me, but it felt wrong.

Other eyes saw through his eyes, and the fur on my spine spiked.

Through parted lips I breathed air over the roof of my

mouth, sniffing and tasting in a feline sense humans lack... this man's sweat tanged whiskey-flavored. I walked closer... beneath that hovered something inorganic...a combination of smells I call robotic. I growled.

And then Suspender Man's ears *heard* for others.

Spyrus! I hissed an alarm and sprang at the doorway, claws extended.

My prey fled up the stairs. The teen and grandfather cowered in the counter's corner.

I lay belly-on-paws at the counter's end, jerking my tail every few seconds and watching Whisp.

He stayed level. He understood my reaction. We'd faced Spyrus before—nanobots in the bloodstream that tap an organism's senses. Turns a being into a walking security-cam. Whisp just gave me a nod and calmed the locals while I bathed a shoulder of raindrops. We would carry on even though someone knew we were coming. Spyrus is a tool of powerful men, not something immigrants in clay brick buildings use for security. We'd be out in five minutes. I hoped we'd have that long.

When they finished their biz the lad said, "Follow me."

"No." Whisp pointed at me. "Walk next to Dusk. Don't turn your back on a big cat. Their instincts can take over."

The lad's eyes rounded but he nodded.

Across the gravel lane and through the parkade, a straight

slender alley ran behind the buildings. A square of chain link fence cut off the Cermack end but we headed left to follow a footpath through weed-grown back doorways and garbage cans, the latter rank from the early summer heat. Before we reached the train tracks, a gap between the last two buildings cut right. My whiskers brushed both sides of the entrance and instinct froze me.

Spyrus had us rushed, so Whisp disobeyed his own advice and pushed ahead, angling his shoulders.

I followed. I really can be trusted behind you. You may get a Tigger bounce but I'm very good about not using my claws. If I like you. Usually.

Unshuttered shops bathed the street in light. Pneumatic tools shrieked from a half-open overhead door at the tracks. These storefronts leased stalls to vendors, and signboards hung thick over the lane, above shoppers with plastic sacks and umbrellas.

"There," said the teen, and gestured across from the garage to a bright yellow entrance and door frame. Its hand-painted signboard read *Drag-on Inn.*

A wide hallway lobby of exposed brick stubbed into the building with stairs up and a small desk at the end. I shook off rain. A stocky ginger-haired Anglo in blue and white Hawaiian print manned the desk. That same charcoal whiskey scent trailed smoke-like from behind the counter.

DUSK

I cornered eyes at Whisp, who shared my glance. A connected outsider this deep in Chinatown? Unusual. Chicago was a city of neighborhoods. My head dipped below my shoulders and I watched this one. He was a big soft man, flavorful to bite.

The boy spoke sing-song with the desk clerk before Hawaiian Print handed him a key and said, "Room twenty-one."

We followed the teen to the door at the top of the creaky stairs where he unlocked the knob, pushed open the door, and sing-songed with someone just inside. A man poked his head out and googled eyes at me.

Then the boy squared shoulders before my sandman.

Whisp fished a bit of circuitry from his pocket and dropped it in the boy's outstretched palm.

We live in Chinatown because I can't hide from sec-cams the way humans can. Chinatown is a place in the city where sec-cams are stolen, despite harsh rehab sentences, faster than they can be installed. The cams are gutted to be used as street level black market currency.

The door guard, a meaty Asian, watched me enter. Street noise and dusk's overcast light filtered in through the room's single open window. Cheap throw pillows sat around the walls where eight motionless humans wearing bandanas reclined. They reeked of urine and worse. Virtual-e users don't unplug for anything. If they have enough money to keep using, they eventually starve. Whisp called Virtual-e the prophesized famine of the last days.

I sat and feigned interest in washing a paw while staring down the door guard, who closed the door before being intimidated like good prey and sitting in a chair. Fear's sweat is distinct, and his lingers on the roof of one's mouth.

Whisp walked to the nearest user and toed the man's ankle. No response. He raised an arm, one of his pistols in hand from a Quick-Draw sleeve holster. He shot the door guard in the forehead and the pistol disappeared again.

No wound showed but the slumped guard's forehead trickled with gel from a tranq round. Whisp is called a sandman because while he will take you down, he'll only put you to sleep.

My dew-claws were genetically altered to give me crude thumbs so I helped Whisp raid the room of twelve bandanas, which he stuffed in a sack that got tucked inside his tee.

On the way out, my sandman touched Hawaiian Print on the arm and discharged his Executioner shock-glove. The man collapsed like prime rib. I gave him a bite on the thigh for flavor, and we were back in the lane, the rain a drizzle —

Something crashed across Cermack — a tanker truck on its side — could barely see the top of it around the corner. It cut off both directions, locking traffic.

DUSK

It had to be because of the Spyrus. Fast response time. Probably a Federal Bureau of Terrorism ready-team. Or was this a trap and agents were already around us?

The truck ignited in rolling flames. No explosion…yet.

A pair of flat-black Goliaths filled the alley's mouth. These metal monsters were humans in brainwave operated power-assisted battle armor. Strong, fast, armed, armored, and can leap short buildings in a single bound. We run from just a single Goliath.

"Up, Dusk," said my sandman and angled an arm at the top of the three-story building, over the garage. A dark blur launched from his sleeve. When his molecular bonding grapple struck, he'd reel in cable and shoot to the rooftop.

I laddered jumps on three street signs and finished with a one-story rooftop leap. Basic strategy still applied and there was likely a sniper or drone posted high, but nothing moved on the flat rooftops. The Goliath's flat-black coloring struck me — these units were not FBT. Who was behind the spyrus?

I bounded ahead of Whisp, zig-zagging my way toward Cermack, in case a targeting system was trying to get a bead on me. I leapt down to a two-story roof in the middle of the block, then back up to a three-story on the corner. The pair of Goliaths remained in position in the lane and four more strung down the block along Cermack. We'd have to — .

One of them spotted me.

A bullet zinged above from ahead.

Motion on a sixth-floor rooftop across Cermack.

Cloth and flesh collapsed behind me. "Backup's en-route, Dusk," breathed Whisp.

I ran back to my unconscious sandman who bled from two holes in the side of his neck. *Nooo!* Blood already pooled. I yowled, singing that Whisp was my world.

Molecular bonding grapples slapped brick. They were coming.

By the back of his collar, I dragged Whisp back to the two-story roof to dangle and drop him over the edge. *I'll protect you, my friend.* His legs worked like shock-absorbers to absorb his fall.

My ear stung and another bullet sounded loud. I crouched low facing the shooter, flattening my ears. *My territory.*

When the metal-plated humans climbed as a team onto the rooftop, I bounded in their direction to show them why the housecat is nature's most efficient predator.

Bouncing off the chest of the first, I ricocheted at a second and teetered them both. Their treads found no purchase on the wet ledge and they tumbled to the pavement. Their suits would protect them but would need a tune-up.

The remaining three spun chain-guns from shoulder mounts—Goliath's primary weapons and almost always loaded with armor-piercing rounds to shred anything.

DUSK

I held my territory by leaping into the middle of them. They now risked hitting each other if they shot at me. Head below my shoulders, I kept moving, writhing, to watch them all, leaving the next move to them. Blood flow tickled my ear. No more sniper shots either—I guessed he had AP rounds loaded too.

All three snapped long blades from forearms and closed on me.

The rooftop groaned, shuddered, and I leapt on instinct. The weight of three Goliaths on a single not-to-code panel proved too much and the street-corner quarter-rooftop disappeared with puffs of dust.

I landed on the edge of the yawning hole. Screams sounded from inside. The too-thin-corrugated-metal-smeared-with-concrete did not completely crush the contents of the room. Nobody could have been trapped. Good thing too, because I was busy.

The Goliaths jumped to the remaining rooftop without bunching up this time.

I sprung to the side of a woman closest to Whisp's hiding spot, and clawed.

Virago LTD was stenciled on their armor. Meant nothing to me but Whisp would know. If he lived.

She swung a blade hard.

I darted back with cat speed and her blow whiffed past.

Whisp had found my records when he saved me from the lab so when I bit the back of her robotic-tasting arm I knew that my genetically altered jaw torqued with jaguar strength, the strongest of any mammal. Armor crunched satisfyingly. I even bent the suit's frame to pinch her arm, and she recoiled.

My ears laid back, I tried to lead them away from Whisp, but they circled around from me, toward him.

They thought to ignore me? My back arched.

I kept out of their blade's reach with a flicking tail, tight, ready to spring. I attacked when they jumped to the lower roof. My victim poked a blade at me as he fell and I crunched his forearm, spitting flat-black fragments.

They surrendered the high ground so I leapt ten meters onto my remaining prey, the only unbitten Goliath. The man yelped when I crushed the neck of his suit, and this time the tips of my teeth found extra flavor.

One of his buddies sliced my left haunch as I sprang to Whisp. I pawed at his belt and came away with an electro-magnetic pulse grenade on my dew-claw. I lay down.

Eyes saucered behind face-plates when they realized I had pierced their EMP shielding. They had no prayer of outdistancing my pulse but turned to run anyway.

Instinct flinched me, and I almost leapt after them when they gave me their backs. *Good prey.* Instead of springing, I licked my shallow wound. Were it not for Whisp I'd have taken them one by one. The grenade was the quickest way, though.

When its light turned red, Goliath circuitry fried. They statued and toppled forward stiffly, trapped in their suits.

I shook my head rapidly and lay on my belly — I'd protect him. If the agents in the Goliath exited escape hatches I'd be here. If their friends in the street came up, I'd be here. Dusk had faded and night covered us. I leaned in so my whiskers touched Whisp's face.

His fingers brushed at my tickle.

I bathed his bullet holes. There wasn't *too* much blood. A paw slowed my sandman's bleeding, and I rested my chin on his chest.

* * *

Footsteps. Two men dressed like Whisp appeared on the garage's rooftop. One in a floppy wide brimmed hat pointed at us. That took more than human vision.

I stood them down, my flank aching, but I arched my back anyway.

They drew no weapons — a good sign. When they rushed to Whisp's side I moved to his feet and lay down with a purr. It felt good to pay back my best friend who'd done so much for me. I placed a paw on his ankle. I'd saved him. *My sandman.*

THE HUNTER'S BOY
BY CASSIE SCHAU

Most mothers, even the best, would have given up on a kitten like Grith by now. Something was undeniably wrong with him. Teffa acknowledged that without pride or derision, too tired for either. All that mattered was the dirt beneath her paws and the dead bird she dragged behind her. A night avoiding ogling alley toms and defending her kill from scavengers left her relieved when dawn shone glowing and orange on the the stone-quarry.

The thin, hunt-weary queen made her way to the collapsed entryway of the abandoned stables, checking for predators at every step. Clear. Thank goodness. Her load made clambering towards the sagging hayloft difficult, the still-warm feathers bumping against her legs with each step along half-fallen beams, until she reached a the only remaining floorboards and their warm, dry hollow, one corner stuffed with fur and grass.

"Mima! Mima!" A bundle of coppery fur hurled from this bed, sending leaves skittering like rabbits. Teffa dropped their feathered meal to welcome her kitten, meeting him purr for purr while sniffing him over for any harm suffered in the night. Grith danced around her, a flurry of energy with a red tail, which made the check a bit difficult. Teffa didn't mind.

It had been hard, yes, with her others barely born, when she'd found Grith huddled in the marketplace road. Hard to take him in, to feed him when it might have starved her own, and it certainly cost her several pounds. It was unarguably prudent to leave him to starve. Prudence could choke on a hairball. Grith was hers.

He was hungry but would not say. Teffa batted the bird forward, tearing off chunks for him. His teeth were still small for the task.

Grith waited with more patience than she'd have preferred. "Was it a good hunt, Mima?"

She dropped a chunk at his feet, moist with heady warmth. "Eat, and have your answer."

Her hint was too blatant to ignore, and he certainly was hungry. Grith fell on the bird-meat like a fighter, tearing it, inhaling it as if he were four weeks old. He needed every bite he could get, and she prepared three quarters, only reserving the toughest and stringiest bits for herself.

Still, he was so small, barely up to her chest. She perpetually overestimated his stomach. All too soon, sated, stuffed, he hesitated, nudging the white shreds fretfully. He drew back in shame, the poor thing. How many times had she told him he must eat to grow big and strong? He tried, she knew he tried. But until he grew bigger, he could eat no more.

Teffa soothed away Grith's mutters with an affectionate tongue, cleaning the residue off his chin. Gathering the leftovers, she clambered down to ground level and buried them for later.

Grith was waiting for her when she returned, paws together and tail curled in. Exhausted from the hunt, Teffa only shared a short nuzzle before curling up in the nest, lifting a paw so Grith could snuggle up next to her. She would have to hunt again later in the day.

"Mima...." Grith never pronounced "Mama" as a kitten ought. Thinking she heard hints of a long night's loneliness in his tone, Teffa tangled whiskers with her kit, rubbed his cheek until his purr met hers.

But that did not placate him. Grith shifted against her belly, little feet kicking soft fur. "Am I old enough now to come on the hunt?"

Teffa carefully did not bristle. Old enough was a loaded

phrase. Two years too old, for any ordinary kit. His brothers and sisters, long departed to their own lives, had been old enough since their twelfth week of life.

Yet at three years old Grith was no bigger than his siblings had been at six weeks. He developed at a frighteningly slow pace, sometimes living weeks before Teffa could discern a change.

"I would like to learn, Mima."

She could hardly bear the thought of taking so small a kit out there, to a world he was still unready for. She would go hungry, ignore the slow contraction of her skin, if only she could keep him safe until he was grown. Until he was strong enough to survive. It could not be much longer. No cat spent four years a kitten.

"Grith, I do not think—."

"I am four times as old as Tito or Maka were." He stood up, fur bristling and legs straight. "I will never make decent a hunter, Mima, if I don't practice." His voice was firm, even with that speech impediment mangling his "Mama."

He was so small. So very, very small. Yet so old, more experienced than any of her children, now grown and gone. He had been older, bigger than them when she'd found him, before they outgrew him.

"Mima, please…?"

She tried to be hopeful. He must grow up soon. He must.

Much as the idea appalled her, reality could not be ignored in all its mundane, cold particulars. Her strength would not long last an eternally dependent kitten. He had to hunt, or else one day she would starve, and him with her.

"Very well."

* * *

Grith knew the mechanics of hunting. Always intelligent, he'd learned from his younger and bigger siblings, in a time when his mother's optimism was not worn so thin. Strength and coordination he still lacked, but he wished so deeply to make her proud, to be *old enough*, that today he persevered against each distraction. A flashing purple butterfly wing, charmless. The new scent of strange, hunched mushrooms, passed unnoted.

Teffa saw, and spared a moment for pride, for her determined, wise son. If only he were bigger. He might then have a chance at success. As it was, any meal they were to have must come from her.

Content, however, that his focus kept him out of trouble, she zeroed in on the unwary vole rustling up ahead. Its footsteps pattered against her ears, like its warm-fast heartbeat would against teeth. She flattened to the ground, shoulders tense, drawing the warm, salty scent across the roof of her mouth. This would sate Grith, if not her.

Something farther back breathed, disrupting her cone of attention. She swiveled her ears sharply, fur bristling. Human. Awkward two-feet steps in the gravel froze her in alarm. Humans never came to the stone-quarry. For that reason she'd kept this hunt close to home, despite lessened prospects of success.

The sound startled the vole into bolting, and she had no time to question, only to lunge, claws scything out. The human was not so close that they could afford to go hungry. She had to maintain strength, or Grith would starve.

But bad luck or apprehension landed her short. Eyes wide with terror, the vole skittered across the loam unscathed. Teffa stifled a hiss of frustration, crouched low to the ground amid the dust. The echo of dislodged pebbles ricocheted in her ears, muffling the intruder's steps. Where was Grith?

The sound of scrabbling of paws on stone threw her into a run, because she could hear her kitten keening. No, no, no!

Rounding a sharp corner she saw a kneeling female human, quartz-dust clinging to her sleeves and knees, offering a scuffed hand. Mere arm's length from her, Grith flattened against the mined remains of a boulder, the shelves of long carved away stone digging stark and white against his back.

Yowling in rage, Teffa threw herself between the human and her kit—fur bristled like quills, lips drawn back from gleaming teeth. The stones grabbed her hiss and reverberated it, making the quarry echo with a thousand snarls of hatred. Grith pressed his body against her, trembling.

The human started back violently at Teffa's appearance, attention now fixed on her, where Teffa wanted it. She twisted to block Grith from view, trying to look bigger, fiercer.

The human, unfortunately, showed no further alarm. She broke into a tight smile. "Ah, there you are, madam. I'm glad; he wasn't listening to me." Teffa was old enough to understand human speech, even if Grith wasn't, but the placating tone and familiar address did not calm her. She gnashed her teeth, snarling to cover a sidestep. She only had to rotate far enough for running space.

The human had sharp brown eyes that seemed to move towards Grith even when he was blocked from sight. She smelled so thoroughly of dust that she must have been out here for a day, at least. "Honest, I don't want it. Here." She nudged something with her knuckles, closing the distance between them uncomfortably. Teffa only just curbed the reflex to lunge.

Not taking her attention from the human, Teffa tested the scent. It smelled like a chunk of fresh meat before her. The human's smell clung to the offering, meaning she'd carried it for some time.

Teffa did not trust it. The human used it as ruse, leaning

close towards them as she offered it. Teffa would not be fooled.

"I brought it for you. I thought he might be hungry." Again, the human leaned, inching a little closer. "I just want to look at him. Just a look, I promise."

Lies. All lies, she could hear them on that human tongue, see it in the lines of that furless face, thin lines of deceit and motive between the eyes. Teffa pinned her ears back flat, prepping her claws, and subtly nudged Grith. The human reached forward, a nonsense-soothing sound in her throat.

That was all Teffa needed. She sank in teeth. A grunt of pain, the human reeled back, and Teffa hurled herself upwards, vaulting off the extended hand. Red-salt-taste in the air told her success as she clawed her way up the offending arm. But only a moment's victory: with swift reflexes the human blocked her vicious kicks at the face, batted her to the ground. Teffa twisted in the air and landed low, the fur along her spine standing straight up like a bear's ruff.

The quarry was abandoned except the two of them. Good kit, Grith. Keep running.

Two angry red scratches ridged the human's cheek. Her stance was tight, too. It probably stung. Good. The woman's face drew and clenched, until Teffa could see the wind-cracks on her cheeks. "I'm not trying to fight you, ma'am."

Teffa licked the blood from her teeth. She waited,

heartbeats telling time. No, no, she wasn't trying to fight either. She didn't care to fight anyone with such a size advantage. Yet, to her displeasure, even with Grith gone the woman showed no hint of losing interest. She took a step, Teffa stepped away in return, and they turned a half-circle in this manner.

She only had to stall long enough for Grith to disappear. He was still small, he could do so easily. She'd taught him almost as soon as he could walk.

"You don't believe me, but I only want to help." The woman's hands were lined and rough, dirt scuffing her broken nails. They spoke differently than her words, tense and curled. Urgency, enough to make her movements jerky. Liar.

"Your son seems rather unique." And her mouth turned down at one side.

Teffa lost count completely, everything in her bristling. Something sharp, birdlike, in this human's face had told her before, but this confirmed everything: this was no idle attention drawn by Grith's smallness. This woman had aimed for her son, sought him specifically. Teffa wished she were within reach to scratch her face again.

That changed plans. Stalling wouldn't cut it, not if this human was *hunting* her son. Teffa gnashed her teeth, patient, waiting for the human to gain confidence, step forwards again.

"Madam Taleffa—."

Shock—how did this human know her name?—but not a breath wasted. Only two feet, one in the air, off balance. Teffa bolted. She heard the human scrabble on the quartz sand, the imbalance of seconds allowing Teffa a burst of speed. The mazes and caverns of this quarry were hers; she'd spent her whole life twisting in their overgrown confines. No one could catch her here.

Pounding footsteps echoed jaggedly after her, pebbles clattering in chorus. But she wasn't concerned. The human was determined, she'd concede that, hearing the echoes of pursuit longer than expected. But she was watching for a dusty cat on stone slabs, in brushy crevices and afternoon shadows. Humans weren't meant to hunt.

Inevitably, the sounds of chase faded. The woman, whoever she was, however she knew Teffa's name, gave up. Motionless in the thicketed shadow of a stonepile, Teffa tested with nose and ears. The scuttling of little creatures, the hiss of the wind across rock, the brush of the little shrubs lodged in the crannies. No two-foot steps among the gravel paths.

Still, such quick disappearance did not solely reassure her. Most humans were loud, clumsy beasts, trudging along in strange foot-coverings that shouted their movements and frightened away all game. That this one had so quietly vanished from her ears, while her scent lingered about in shreds on the wind, was a matter of unease.

Time to breathe, to settle her fur, to think, brought all the alarm back again, more logically arranged in her mind. This human sought her son, clearly, knew her name, smelled so much of the quarry as to have wandered there all morning. Finding them could be coincidence, but knowing her name required some form of spell. Dread flared her whiskers, but Teffa controlled herself. There was no hint of magic in the air. Do not panic.

It was probably a fluke. An interested human. No human was wise or determined enough to find a cat who didn't wish to be found. She'd evaded plenty such fools in her day, who'd taken it into their heads to consult her for aid or some other stupidity. They could chase a less busy queen if they wanted help with a hunter spell.

But, all the same, she waited a little shorter than perhaps she should have, goaded by the silence to move, darting from bush to bush across the quarry. She'd been gone too long. Grith must be home by now. She kept her distress at bay by making herself remember how well he could conceal himself, having had years for practice. He was smart, and she'd taught him well enough; he would not lead danger home. He would be fine. He was safe, waiting for her, disappointed by the interruption of his hunt.

She forced herself to detour and backtrack, snaring her tracks across the sun-scorched rocks and under the thornbushes, until tracking became near impossible. Then, and only then, with the sun far lower in the sky, and knowing that there would be nothing for them to eat tonight, she finally felt calm enough to walk to the southern end.

She only reached the central, man-carved shelf of stone where nothing could grow, when out of place sounds bounced from the high walls towards her. Voices. Voices hummed in the stones. Then closer, snapping. Smoke, sour in the air. Fire. No!

She didn't even think of stealth, throwing herself down the path, pebbles screeching as she knocked them into gaping crevasses. No, no, no!

Three humans loomed from the unnatural edges of the stone-shelves, their scents heavy and thick in her throat, their heavy robes crackling in the dried air. She could see them, their backs cast black by flames that scorched her eyes and cast the whole world in strangled white. Her pupils contracted to slits, and the world darkened, the fire leaping to stark relief, twisting savagely.

They'd set the back of the stable on fire. The beams hissed and screamed as sparks gnawed them, but it was the smoke that stopped her heart, set her coughing in desperation as she ran. Her baby! Her baby was in there!

A sudden flurry of motion, two humans leaping forward, sharp elbows flailing. "He's out! He's out, catch him!" A terrified, high-pitched scream tore into Teffa's ears. Grith!

The screech broke off in a hoarse yowl as one of those robes lunged to the ground, its human hunched and pounding with harsh, huge hands. "I have him. Quick I have him—Yagh!" A sharp, hard word spat from his lips, and his arm moved sharply, cruelly. The thump of flesh turned her world red as Grith yelped. "The little bastard bit me!"

She lunged toward that monster, thinking nothing of size difference, of the fire blinding her right eye, of the stifling smoke hazing the entire world. Only of her baby, dragged up in the man's hands, smothered in thick gloves.

"Control that thing and get moving." A sharp, heavy strike to her side sent her flying, an instant of fear as the fire swooped close. Stone crags slammed into her like a dog's bones. Her ribs ached. Boot-tips. Metal. She spat dirt from her mouth, heaving for the wind knocked out of her. The crackling of the stable was deafening.

"Mima! Mimaaaaaa!" Another thump, a cry, and his voice stopped. She felt something, a sudden tense prickling in her whiskers, a flaring of power. Magic. All her hair stood on end as if shocked by static.

"We're done here." Flame-shapes flashed across her eyes. She heard the voice but could not see. Teffa stumbled to her feet, limping, spitting and hating. No! Still unseeing, pupils driven to blind lines by the light, she lunged again.

"Enough, fleabag." Batted aside again, as if she weighed nothing. This kick was aimed, sent her straight towards the fire. Racing adrenaline screamed in her ears, twisted her in midair, just enough to hit the sagging beams first. Teffa jumped, the smell of burnt fur smothering the world, but she could run when she hit the ground.

Good thing, too. A deep, shuddering groan barely warned her before the back support beam gave, bringing the entire rear of the stable tumbling down, sparks sailing airborne like showers of ravenous, deadly crickets. She only just managed to roll from their path, tearing through smoke-corridors until she found open quarry.

Her throat burned, her eyes stung, half-sightless from the light, but she was alive, and running. Grith's scent lingered thick in the burning air, stronger away from the smoke, his fur and fear and warmth. Teffa did not need her eyes. They'd hurried to the quarry gates, past the withered metal fixtures standing sad guard. The stones still echoed the sounds of their steps, as if directing her. She flew through the ledged alleyways and cat-sized shortcuts faster than she ever had before.

But not fast enough. Too soon, a new echo joined the steps, the sharp snap of pebbles kicked against the flagstones by great hooves. Wooden creaking—a cart. It didn't matter. She kept repeating that, it didn't matter, she would chase, she would follow them to the ends of the earth, she *would* find Grith.

Night was slow in falling. Cool air soothed the smoke from her throat, the setting sun behind spared her light-bleached eyes, and she loped along the old road as fast as she could limp, mouth half-open to catch Grith's scent. They had not moved so fast as to obliterate his smell. The dirt was packed and newly turned by cart tracks, and she trotted in their wake, hoarsely calling his name. He never answered.

Then, after dark, with Teffa shelterless and alone on the road, Grith's scent ceased. Utterly, entirely ceased. As if, right on that spot, her kit had disappeared.

A mournful cry tore from her throat. Even dead—they had taken him, he wasn't dead, he couldn't be!—even dead, scent lingered. She should be able to find him. She had to find him. He couldn't have just…stopped.

Teffa wandered the road aimlessly, calling his name until she grew too weary for voice. Too weary to see the cart tracks, her night vision yet to recover from the onslaught of a fire's burn. It all blurred, all merged into a dull, empty grey. She stumbled a few steps onward, feeling the grooved dirt with her paws, until that, too failed her. Exhausted, aching, limping, Teffa could only shuffle back to the last trace of her son's scent, and lay down in the dirt.

* * *

"Madam Taleffa? Is that you?" The voice was aghast, human, female.

Teffa had been squinting up at the sun, marking the white ball's slow drift through crooked branches. She wasn't sure when she woke. Sometime before dawn, she'd opened her eyes and again found herself at the end of Grith's trail.

Nothing. Still nothing. So she'd laid there, because if his scent ended here, he must be here too. Somewhere beyond her ability to sense, beyond those fading spots the fire had left on her eyes last night. She could feel the particular stiffness of magic in her whiskers. She could not undo magic. She'd wait until something changed, until she could find him.

Footsteps in the dirt. Two feet. A shadow across her, and the soft jangling of metal. Humans were so loud when they walked.

"It is you." Teffa looked up, and found that woman crouched beside her. Those brown eyes seemed less sharp with the sun behind them. The human frowned, skin pulled in as if trying to pin back ears she couldn't move.

Teffa had been exhausted a moment before, but seeing

the monster who'd distracted her while they took her baby, she felt her pupils contract in rage, all the ache from the day before forgotten. She was tired, dirty, the scent of soot clung thickly to her fur and whiskers and tongue, but a night's rest had restored her strength, and it would be enough. As the human reached out, Teffa curled in a taut twist of sinew, braced on the dirt.

The human froze, but awareness came an instant too slow. Teffa was faster. Snarling, she sprang upwards. This time they were close, no time for reflexes, and she buried her claws in cloth and launched herself. Teeth to bare skin, a bark of pain and the blood on her tongue was a small comfort, because someone would pay, she could make someone suffer.

Her prey reeled back, Teffa carried with her, the sun wheeling wildly as she leapt and kicked and scratched. Two leather bracers thwarted her back paws, the woman parrying her with surprising agility. Teffa hated gloves, hated leather, wanted only to scratch and screech and *hurt*.

"Shit, calm down, panther!" A snatch at her scruff yanked her teeth loose, a satisfying defeat in that it certainly hurt. Unlike those rat-biters yesterday, this woman dropped her to the ground without force. Teffa had ages to twist and land feet first.

The woman retreated, fresh blood on her arm and cheek, hands raised defensively. "Stop! I didn't take your kit!"

Teffa snarled, furrowing her entire face at the lie. She *had.* She had distracted her. If Teffa had been there, if she hadn't been across the quarry, she'd have been able to protect Grith! She'd have stopped them, scratched until their eyes bled! Fire and metal boot-toes be damned!

The woman pressed a hand to the bloody marks on her cheek. "I swear. I didn't know anyone else was in the quarry. I didn't realize what had happened until this morning." She hurried on, giving no time for Teffa to spit on the words. "I came looking for you. To help. They went ahead to market, I know that, but the farmers have come in already. Even I can't track them by the wheels now."

Of course she couldn't. She was a cruel, lying, useless human. Humans could track nothing, find nothing, do nothing but take and wreck and kidnap! Teffa was glad she'd opened those red scratches on this woman's face, proud of the scabbed and darkened marks from yesterday.

The woman wisely heeded her gnashing claws, crouching at a safe distance, hands loose. "Please, Taleffa, hear me out. You stopped. I assume your kitten's trail ends here." She did not wait for answer, as humans often did when speaking to those they could not understand. Dark lines of fur above her eyes drew together. "They can't have gone far. If you help me, I can cast a hunting spell, and we can find them in time."

Teffa ground her claws into the dirt. Grith's scent was already thinned and scattered by the wind, faint, as if he'd never been. She could not follow. But this human was a liar too. Teffa could practically smell the tension twisting off her. The way she sat was all tight ligaments, and her leather glove, that had rebuffed Teffa's vengeful claws, creaked and shifted, never still. She could not offer aid for Teffa's sake, for Grith's.

"I can't hunt without your help." The woman's bracers winked in the light as she pressed her hands on her knees. "And I don't see you finding him on your own. I won't ask you again, I promise." Restless movement made Teffa tense, but the woman did not approach, merely pulled something from a belt across her shoulder. The bundle of frayed, dark cloth was grizzled with tiny clinging quartz crystals. The human set it between them, an offering.

"We don't have much time. Please. You'll need strength for the spell."

Teffa recognized the scent immediately, the slight change a day made to meat. The same this woman had offered her son.

Grith hadn't eaten yesterday. Neither had she. Hunger hit like another blow to the side, her stomach shrunk into a painful knot. She needed to get him food. He was too small not to eat.

This human was lying, but why should she offer to help if working with the others? They had what they wanted. No scent of horse or donkey clung to her, nothing but coated dirt and sweat and dust, and a sense weary tension, days in the making.

Narrowing her eyes, Teffa forced her fur down, though a ridge remained tense along her neck. She stepped cautiously forward and nudged the tatters. The meat was raw and thick, richer by far than she'd had in days. Its scent filled her throat. Bird, chicken? Hunger overruled pride. She inhaled it.

The woman shifted, her fists uncurling as she watched Teffa eat. Relief, a dim smell, a release. "My name is Len. I apologize for scrying for your name...I did not think you'd believe me otherwise."

Teffa hadn't believed anyway, as those bite marks on Len's chin must remind her. Teffa swallowed loudly, flicking her ears to show she did not care. Hungry though she was, she would not finish bribe-meat, stepping back with shreds still left. Len's head moved sharply, surprised. Teffa knew bone showed around her hunger-thinned shoulders and hips, but she flicked back her lips, showing teeth.

Len took the bundle back. "We had better get off the road. If you're ready...?"

Teffa wished the human would speak less, or remember she spoke to an intelligent being. Shaking herself off, she noticed dark bits of soot flaking off her coat with sharp cracking sounds. She'd come...closer to that fire than she remembered. Her right whiskers stung, the tips singed. That was why she felt off balance, her senses blunted.

Len followed at a wary distance. Her tanned skin was crossed and ridged by Teffa's claws now, and small spots of blood glowed on her jerkin and in her long black head-fur. Still, despite distrusting her, Teffa was glad Len deferred to her choice of location. She was not so young that she'd never managed a hunt spell before.

Her mother had taught her, long ago. Teffa had meant to teach Grith when he was ready. When he was old enough. Some quiet part of her muttered that she'd waited too long, lost her chance.

No. She *would* teach him still.

A safe distance from the road, Teffa halted, giving Len a hard look. Obediently, the human set down her dirty pack. Heat was mounting, the air beginning to press heavily around them, and Teffa could not sit still. Each moment the human ordered her accessories was longer her baby spent with those monsters, who had somehow made him *stop*, made him nothing, made him disappear. She could not bear it.

Finally, Len dug into her belt, and scattered a few blue-tinged crystals in the dirt. They winked in the sunlight like frozen rain. With a larger fragment, she drew lines connecting the stones, all converging in a central mark like the trunk of a tree. The roots of this earth-tree, conjured by her deft human fingers, twined together into a ring.

Forcing herself to calm, Teffa claimed her place inside this circle, setting her paws at the roots' prongs. Len freed a small cord from her wrist and Teffa gazed hard at the human before allowing this pendant to be placed over her ears. Len's anchor-stone, orange, smooth, about the size of an acorn, settled heavily against Teffa's chest, and she could feel its warmth through her fur.

Len settled cross-legged beyond the crystals, still holding the long, thin fragment. It looked like a claw, like a needle, and Teffa fixed her eyes on its winking tip, forcing her spine-fur completely flat. They could afford no distractions.

Len's face relaxed, scratches glinting, and she cupped the bluish splinter in her hands. A rush of focus thinned the air. Teffa felt more than heard, "Begin."

She drew a deep breath.

Distrust or no, a hunting spell demanded cooperation by nature. She felt the woman's energies thread slowly between the crystals, twining in intricate patterns along the lines of the tree. A chill brushed her claws as the roots flared to magical life, the strands hesitating there briefly. Contact was tentative, wary. Teffa could hardly blame Len. She was impressed despite herself with the woman's ability to ignore the red scratches on her face, the puffed up teeth gouges near her ear.

The orange stone at Teffa's neck hummed softly, warmed as she reached out. She could only work in claws and bristling bolts of power, hooking sharply into the framework Len set in the earth. The woman never flinched. Even so, Teffa felt the buzzing, the distracting stinging of the scratches; tangling together like this brought unavoidable consequences. Hearing thoughts and feelings always unnerved her. She did not trust Len, but she dulled the sharp edges of her power as she could, so as not to prick. No distractions, nothing to break focus.

A flickering light awakened within their scattered crystal tree, pulsing in waves through the earth. It twined and glowed orange at Teffa's feet, as she felt Len catch her wild, untempered energies and direct them along her human threads. Teffa took this spell as a hunter took prey, made it hers in sharp strikes of tooth and claw. The tree's branches stretched her beyond this place, every sense and instinct magnified. With the flared perception of a huntress, she opened her eyes far beyond her body, and took air into her throat, testing for scents, for presences, as the village flashed before her eyes.

But she'd known this answer before she started. Grith's

scent had *ended* in the road. Disappeared. And now when she cast about for some hint of her son, for the familiar crook in his left whiskers and that tawny patch between his shoulders, for the smell of red, of purrs and pricking only-just-grown up teeth, she found the world empty. Nothing. Her hunting spirit aimlessly roamed the hills, finding no trail, roaring like a lioness. All traces of him ended.

He wasn't there. And she had nothing else to track them by, no thread to follow those who had taken him. Smoke and fire had obliterated all sense of their presences from her, and she could not trace them.

Teffa did not move, did not yowl, betrayed no grief. But Len, tangled up as they were, clearly sensed it. The first and third fingers of her right hand brushed the crystal, and the spell's weave tightened. The tree branched farther. She spoke softly, barely moving her lips. "Maybe not his scent."

A strange notion. But the series of garbled concepts flitting through their patchwork attempting explanation. Len spoke cat dismally, but Teffa could mostly translate human. Len seemed, for some reason, to think that even if Grith's scent had ceased, he, and the other things he stood for, must still remain. The idea of "son." Different. Changed. Yet enough for Teffa to find.

Ridiculous. But Len seemed certain, and whatever her ulterior motive—one hidden far deeper than Teffa could catch by magical proximity — her sincerity was loud. Perhaps too loud. But Teffa could not let this fail. She could not cast a hunting spell alone, the structure was too complex. They only had one chance. She concentrated.

Grith's eyes were green. As he'd grown, their baby-golden edges had faded, until they were green, all green. She'd pitied him when he'd lain alone on that road and looked up at her with those eyes, terrified, but willing to hope.

He was small, but he was so willing to try. He grew so slowly that he frightened her. He knew he did. Too old and wise — and young and small — not to know. And she loved him for trying to eat, trying to hunt, to be a cat.

Her son. A red, red cat. Her son.

A thread. Her hunting spirit snarled and pounced. A familiar sense of green, splashed carelessly in the marketplace. She dug in claws before it could fade. Teffa tensed, eyes narrowed, and surged along the branches of Len's tree, flying through the streets of the village like a ghost, following that trail.

Red tufts, trying and hoping, and golden-green and fear sharp on her tongue, setting her sinews grinding, her claw gouging the dirt. And still no scent, no physical trail, only instinctive knowing that this was her son. She'd never followed so dim a trail before.

Close now, the hunt building to an indelible sense

of "found", of quarry caught. But there Teffa skidded to a sudden stop. She'd reached a branch of Len's tree that was red, frayed and burnt, turned black and shriveled in the earth. Teffa snarled in alarm and rage. She could follow no further. Magic. More magic, curse them. She would claw out their eyes.

She could see enough, though. Her huntress-spirit could taste the closeness of prey, tense and ready to pounce beyond the force halting her. The jumbled contours of the dockyard roofs were familiar; she'd killed rats there before kits. That was all she needed.

Hissing defiantly, Teffa retraced the twisted path Len kept for her, returned to that clearing. She was too rushed to pull back gently, heard the woman' tight little breath as she unhooked her claws from their tangled weave. No time for sympathy. She did not need Len's help anymore. The human had served her purpose.

Len was careful. Teffa had gained little information, but she sensed that buried motive somehow meshed with her son. She did not want Len anywhere near him.

Cats recovered swiftly, whether from falls or from spells. Teffa kicked dirt across the tree as Len tensed, still withdrawing into herself. The cat grabbed the orange stone in her teeth, tongue curled back from it, to twist off her neck. She hated wearing a human's anchor, the connection it required of her. She tossed it in the dirt and turned to go.

Len settled quickly, for a spell caster. Her hand — the one Teffa had clawed — closed on the stone as it hit ground. "Wait. You can't go by yourself."

Teffa paused just long enough to arch her back, fur along her spine rigid, and flash her teeth. She did not need a connection to know the threat translated, the wounds she'd gouged in the woman's skin stinging sharper. She was grateful for the aid, but gratitude extended exactly so far as staying her teeth. If Len touched her son, Teffa would hurt her.

Then, before Len could react further, Teffa disappeared into the net of dirt and trees and dead leaves. Len's scent was soon lost behind her. She would cut through the inn yards. She could be there in an hour.

Memory of that tingling, awful brush of magic set her fur on edge, her burnt whiskers aching more sharply. Please let an hour be fast enough.

* * *

The dockyard sat in the shadow of the storage sheds, hedged by bobbing fishing boats and the ferry unloading cargo and passengers. In an out of the way corner, away from the bustle of the newly arrived ship, the darker shade of a crate concealed a dusky form. Teffa flattened herself against the damp wood, forcing herself to stay still.

She could see the man there, mere steps from her. Leather boots that clinked with heavy buckles. Him. The one who caught Grith. Who hit him. She saw small, scabbed teeth marks on the man's thumb, and felt a ruthless swell of pride.

But now the man paced back and forth amid the crates, grating her nerves as she waited for him to show the way. A shielding spell, the one that had burnt Len's tree, still hummed about, she could feel it tingling at the edges of her toes. There was still no scent of Grith here.

"You're late!"

"I am here now." A man's voice, calm, soft. A walking-stick carved like a griffin clunked down a whisker's length from Teffa. She froze, making everything in her small and grey, a shadow within a shadow.

He loomed like a tree, smelling of the river, whitish skinned with a cold blue glint worn at his wrists. Spell crystals, the tingling in her spine told her. Magic user. Two magic users, in a rural fishing village?

"You come prepared to buy, I hope."

She would not be grateful to the sentry, wanted to make him suffer in many creative ways. But she was glad he turned the stranger away. The walking stick clunked forward, its owner moving with a surety and command that nearly masked his limp. "I mean to inspect first."

The cruel man smirked. "I think you'll find this one's the real deal. He'll make you a pretty penny." They threaded among hills of crate, slipping away from the bustle of the ship. Teffa waited, tracking by smell when they left sight, keeping herself still by imaging her claws buried in the upturned corner of that sentry's mouth. As her patience began to fray, she saw the stranger ushered through a small entrance to a bowed shed, hidden at the far end of the yard by the grander buildings above.

The guard moved back out into the cargo, glancing around as if to check for stray eyes. He stayed on that side, away from the ships and their activity.

More than enough for Teffa. She followed on silent feet, darting past the bustling sailors until their movements became dim white noise. It was quiet on this side of the yard, away from the ferry. Her fur prickled upwards, the hunter awake, claws out in readiness. Grith had to be hidden here, somewhere.

The guard's boots moved again, and Teffa grew still, invisible as only a cat can manage. He could not see her, she was hidden too well. He clinked so loudly, it was incredible he thought he could catch anyone.

A board creaked, far too close, making every joint in Teffa's body clench. She twisted, claws snapping out. She had smelled nothing, sensed nothing!

Then she stared at Len crouching behind a barrel mere feet away. The woman had one hand stretched out, as if she'd froze mid motion when the sound forced her still, her stance unbalanced. But how had she reached there, concealing her presence, even her own scent, from Teffa?

Len caught her eye, first with a smile, but then tensed as Teffa drew back her teeth in a silent snarl. The woman pressed her hand against the barrel to maintain balance, unable to move until attention died down. But the dock boards croaked again, so loud both of them winced.

Teffa hissed soundlessly at the woman, her claws dug into the wood as if to tear out its throat. Len was jeopardizing everything! They risked imminent discovery because she was stupid, stubborn, useless human who could not *hunt* and should not *be* here. If she lost Grith because of this human—!

But then there was no time to think. Len flinched in shock as Teffa launched straight at her head. She felt the human's shoulders jerk as she darted across. Who could blame her, when Teffa's paws nearly brushed the scratches on her face? With the swiftness and cruelty of a hunter, Teffa bunched her legs, sprang from Len's back—.

And raked her claws across the eyes of the man who'd struck her child, who'd tried to flank Len on quiet steps. The sound he made as she gouged flesh was delicious, pain and fear and a prey's pitiful cry stifled by her fur, and she was lost in that moment of feral, triumphant hate.

Sudden, sharp motion, her quarry slammed to ground. A rush of air warned Teffa to roll bare seconds before Len's fist drove into the man's midsection. His half-uttered cry splintered, the moan of air torn from his lungs making Teffa's blood sing. But even she was surprised when Len's fingers tightened and a sharp crack of magic split the air, so fast Teffa barely registered it. The man's body went rigid, eyes wide open, before slumping silent, his pulse slow and senseless.

Despite herself, Teffa was impressed. The dampener concealed Len's spell, so even within inches Teffa could barely feel it. Stealth and efficiency. Perhaps she had misjudged Len's ability as a hunter.

Len's eyes were sharp again, setting Teffa's fur tingling. Len inclined her head. Teffa twitched her whiskers. That had been too loud, even brief as it was. They had to act quickly.

Teffa led the way, able to slither through narrower paths. Through the shed door she could hear muffled voices, and taste the scents of humans. Her sense of smell led her to a small gap, barely more than a rat hole, in the back wall. Teffa flattened herself by the hole, testing it with her whiskers. It would be a tight fit, but she was thin. She would make it.

Len knew better than to touch her now, but Teffa heard the human's hand brace on the ground by her back feet. The woman's stance was tense as she strained to hear.

Teffa's ears were better. Tok, tok, tok. The clunk of wood on wood kept time, rhythmic. Walking stick, pacing. "And I'm to take your word he's the genuine article?"

"I told you, when we caught him he had whiskers and a tail. If that's not a shifter, I don't know what is. That tracker's from a reliable source. But fine, I'll prove it. Shift, rat."

She recognized that voice. She'd been blind with fire when he'd kicked her, when he'd tossed her towards the blaze, but she recognized the sharp edges of his words. The tapping ceased, replaced by a sudden spike of a sharp, acrid scent. It had been so constant before she hadn't noticed. Fear.

"Shift!"

Not just fear. Terror.

"Fine. The hard way, then."

Skin scrabbled on dirt, a thrashing sound of cornered prey. Rapid, panicked breaths. A sudden dread gripped Teffa's gut, even though her nose and her ears still promised her Grith could not be near.

Then, in a stranger's voice, too low and too dull-toothed, sharp and desperate and filled with tears — she could recognize the sound of human tears — "M-m-*Mimaaaa!*"

Teffa burst inside before she could think, before she could panic because that was not her son's voice, not even speaking *cat!* She heard a gasp, "Taleffa!" behind her, bruised her shoulders pushing through, but she did not care, only heard the blood pounding in her ears and Grith calling for his mother.

Four men whirled, shocked by the spitting cat in their midst. The walking-stick man stood near the far wall, whilst a dark-eyed man who smelled dry with ash crouched in the corner, looming a bundle of brown cloth. A dimly glowing crystal in his fist cast harsh light on the face of —.

Not Grith. A boy. A human boy. Thin and small, barely a child. Sweat plastered down his hair, fear rolled off him in waves, and a dark bruise blackened one cheek. A rough blanket slipped off him, bare skin pale like bone beneath. Cords trussed his wrist, the skin red and chafed.

Everything in Teffa stopped, panicked. That…that wasn't Grith. That wasn't her son. Where was her son!?

"It's just a cat! Sir, please, ignore her. You all, get rid of her!" He glared at Teffa as he dragged the boy by the hair. The child flinched and gasped as the glowing stone touched his skin, his pupils contracting to invisible pinpricks in terrified green eyes.

Confusion, panic, rage slowed her reflexes, and a sudden blow slammed her down, the child's whimper ringing in her ears. She'd lost track of the others.

"Kill the fleabag."

"I wouldn't do that." Orange lightening snapped in

the doorway, its tiny thunder crack splitting the air. A body slumped. Len. Teffa could smell her magic in the air, though she could not see her. Her concealment talents were indeed greater than she'd thought.

The distraction was all Teffa needed to drive her teeth through cloth to flesh. Her attacker squawked and flailed, inadvertently boosting Teffa in the desired direction. She barely landed for a second, hearing Len attack the man behind her. Teffa had other priorities.

The dark-eyed man swung a hand in defense, but Teffa was faster, furious. Her teeth found the pad between thumb and palm, tearing straight through his glove. Never had blood tasted sweeter. With a sharp oath, he reflexively slammed her and his arm against the wall, but the damage was done, he was bleeding, it was enough. He'd let go of the boy.

"Don't move."

Teffa landed on her feet, and added the gleam of her teeth to the threat of Len's blade. The woman held her anchor-stone in her left hand; the orange glow seeming to swallow the stranger's blue, sizzling and ready to snap.

He narrowed his eyes, but Teffa could read the flicker of desperation there. Teffa licked the blood from her teeth. He was no hunter. Coward. Slowly, he raised both hands.

Baring her teeth, Len snatched the crystal from him. "I

will return this to its rightful owner." Knife close and ready, she dragged the man by the scruff, forcing him away from child and cat. As she bound his hands, she barked, "Stay still, stranger. You aren't leaving, either. I'll knock you out if I have to; you'll get what you deserve. Along with this kidnapper."

The walking stick man had not moved throughout the attack, only watched bemusedly. He smiled without warmth. "I've done no wrong, lady mage."

"You came to buy a shapeshifter from known assailants. That is enough."

"Have you any proof?" He leaned on his cane. "What if I were seeking to keep him from cruel hands through taking him in my own? As you do now?"

Teffa was not listening. All her attention remained riveted on the human boy still cowering in the corner. He never took his eyes off her.

The boy trembled from head to toe, fingers so clumsy he couldn't seem to hold the blanket still falling from him. His hair was red, Teffa realized dimly. The orange light turned its edges gold in the dark. Tears, human salty tears of shock and fear, still trailed down his cheeks, across the livid bruise puffing his lip, dribbling into his mouth. "Mim-m-ma."

Something in her recoiled violently. No. *No.* This was not her son. This human boy could not be—! Her son was a kitten! A red kitten! With green eyes, and crooked whiskers and who wanted so badly to be a *cat*.

His face crumpled as he hugged thin arms across his chest, nails raking red streaks on hairless skin. As if he were trying to gouge stripes like hers. He buried his face in his arms and sobbed. "Mima, I'm s-sorry!"

She'd seen his eyes change when that man hurt him, pupils forced to slits. She saw it again now, as he gritted his teeth and *tried* to change. Exhaustion turned his skin as ashen as her fur. He sagged against the wall, curled in on himself, furless and freezing and shaking. Ashamed to look at her.

Teffa's heart wrenched. Just like her kitten when he could eat no more. When he could not grow faster. When he could not be a cat.

Her son.

Grith squeaked as she threw herself on him, wriggling into his arms, burying his tears in her fur, licking his face, his hair, the bruise on his cheek that filled her with rage. Grith! Her baby! She buried her nose in the crook of his neck and inhaled, to make this new scent his too, to make this new Grith hers, too.

Because Grith was red-haired and he *tried*, and he was afraid but wanted to hope. And he knew he frightened her and he was so, so sorry.

For a moment Grith sat motionless, every muscle locked. And if Teffa could weep, she would have then, on hearing his choked cry as he finally clung to her, frightened, exhausted beyond endurance, shaking so badly he couldn't hook his fingers into her fur. How long had he feared her knowing? How long had he tried to hide from her, tried so hard to be the perfect kitten, fearing this day?

She purred, she purred and wiped the tears from his face onto hers, tickled where his whiskers would have been with hers.

"Sorry...." He whispered it, but she brushed the words from his lips, because she could not speak human, only cat, but that word was hers, not his.

It would be all right, she promised. She would keep him safe, she promised. Nothing to fear.

The humans had reached a stalemate, judging by the silence. When Teffa regained composure, Len was watching her, those scratches tilted in a smile. Giving the would-be buyer a threatening look, the woman left her trussed quarry and took a careful step towards Grith. "Those knots look like they hurt, little one. Here, let me—."

A sizzle of energy choked the air, they both felt it. By the quiet buyer, the bound man smiled grimly, clenching his fist around something. "You are not taking me to trial." Harsh red light bloomed like jagged thorns from his hand, where he'd scratched lines into a patch of sand.

"Fool!" The walking stick man jerked back. "You don't

know how to—!"

"Taleffa!"

Cats were hunters, sensed more clearly than humans. Teffa was already springing forward to shield her child. Yet the crackling lance of power was too wild, too unwieldy, with no framework to guide the burst along. Grith, sensing too, froze in terror, and there was no time—!

Instinct warned her, and Teffa snapped out her claws. Just in time to seize Len's shoulder, the woman appearing as if from nowhere, Grith suddenly clutched tight in her arms. Energy behind, wooden walls ahead, nowhere to go. Len charged anyway. The planks shrieked as they broke through, falling, and Teffa only had one moment to panic before all three crashed into the river.

* * *

Grith was so exhausted he nearly fallen asleep in Len's arms as she carried him from the water. Teffa, spitting, wet and gasping, hovered as Len slit the cords hobbling him, baring stark red lines across his bony, furless wrists. Those were bandaged now, the bruise on his cheek gently washed, and he slept bundled in blankets on Len's bed at the inn.

Teffa lay on the pillow beside him, listening to the new cadence of his breathing, his stronger heartbeat in this far-bigger body. Still that same little sigh, though.

THE HUNTER'S BOY

Len walked softly into the room, a wet cloth pressed on her neck where Teffa's panicked clinging had nicked her. She hadn't seemed to mind those scratches any more than the others. With great gentleness, she tucked the blanket more closely about the boy.

Len's hands clasped gravely after she sat down beside Teffa, setting a bundle of cloth on the side table. At Teffa's glance, she explained, "Innkeeper got them. He can wear them when he wakes." She kept her voice low to let Grith sleep undisturbed, but her tone was solemn. "That man will only be the first. Shapeshifters are valuable."

Teffa shivered, and sat up to avoid disturbing Grith. The quick-thinking man with his griffin-cane had shielded the dockyard from the kidnapper's magical folly, and saved the lives of the unconscious men Len defeated. His hastily thrown spell had preserved the dock, the ferry, and even the culprit, to face justice for his crimes. The townspeople, understandably, felt gratitude and goodwill towards him now. Len had stayed long enough to explain her part, and ensure he did not lie too blatantly, before taking Grith away as quickly possible. But, perched on the woman's shoulder, Teffa had seen the unruffled coolness on the griffin-man's face as they departed, and she felt in her core Len's truthfulness.

He would not be the last, and this was by no means his only attempt.

Teffa waited now, because they'd silently agreed when she'd allowed Len to carry her son here that the woman owed her some answers.

Len held up the bluish crystal she had taken from the criminals. "They stole this, and the blast spell that backfired, from a good friend." The stone was quiet now, innocuous, but Teffa pulled back her whiskers distrustfully, remembering how it made her son flinch and forced his eyes to change form. "A shapeshifter, like your son."

Teffa looked at her sharply.

Len's face hardened, in a way Teffa had never seen, her dull teeth clicking together as if to bite. "In his hands, this helps control the transformations. But it can also be used to track shifters. Or force them to shift. Those men hurt my friend, stole it. I came to take it back. But I didn't expect to sense your son in the quarry."

She'd come after him, then, not as a hunter, but as a concerned ally, recognizing her friend's traits in another. Had it really been so clear to Len that Grith was hiding, when Teffa had not known? Teffa regretted those ridged marks on Len's face now, especially where she had gone for her eyes.

Len sighed, slowly cracking the knuckles on her left hand. "Grith will be too drained to shift again for a few days. I don't think he's changed in years...."

He hadn't. Teffa knew. He'd wanted to keep his mother,

keep his home. So he'd stayed a cat.

The future loomed ahead in cold vastness, everything she'd planned fluttering frayed in the wind. Grith was…was a boy. Her son was a boy. He would not be grown in a year. He would grow slowly, carefully.

He could be a cat, part of her argued. He could change into a cat.

But he could not stay one. The thought of spending another three years with him afraid to use his hands, just because she did not have them, made her spine curl. No. It made something drop in the pit of her stomach. She wanted her kitten back. She did. But she had to somehow realize he was sleeping right beside her.

Len rubbed her anchor-stone between her fingers, fidgeting with its cord. "He's young yet. He needs to learn how to shift, so he can choose what form he wants to take. To be a cat, or a boy, or anything else."

She was right. Grith was…both. Her kit was a boy, too. For the first time, Teffa felt a slight stir of wonder, of pride, at that.

"Would you…If you'd like, Taleffa, I could take you both to meet my friend. He could train your son." Expecting a hiss, Len raised a hand and hurried on. "You're doing your best, but I know you're hungry. Come with me. I can't promise it'll be easy. I travel hard, always have. But Grith will be safer with both of us. You'll never have to go hungry again, either of you."

Hunter's eyes did not lie. When they were hunting, using, lying, their edges were like claws, like blades, enough for another hunter to feel, to set their spirit rearing back in threat. Len did not blink, and Teffa saw her sincerity. Her genuine desire to help hung in the air between them.

It...it made sense.

"If anyone asks, you're my spell-companion." The anchor flickered in the firelight, as if hearing its purpose mentioned. Len pressed it against her wrist with two fingers. "You don't have to be. We'll just tell them you are."

Teffa listened, and felt her son breathe against her. Part of her still recoiled from the thought of leaving, of following this new path, of her kitten as boy and human and changing, and of this woman meaning to help. It was all...all so strange, so wrong, so different.

So perfectly what her son needed.

Len's hand bent as Teffa bumped her head against the fingers, and Teffa felt them curl with the woman's smile as she left purrs across tan skin. A moment's consideration, and Teffa let the anchor-stone brush her fur. The little, warm flutter of power, twined branches and clasped claws, was still there, glad and welcoming. The stone remembered her.

Teffa paused, letting Len's aura prickle her fur. It tingled in her whiskers, pleasant, friendly. Perhaps, she thought, not now, but someday, she wouldn't mind bearing that stone, and twining spells again.

She curled next to her son that night, and did not have to worry about rats or hawks or the human snoring softly in the chair by her side.

* * *

A week later, a woman in a travel cloak crouched under the trees by the inn, holding a small, thin boy's hand as he stared at the passing wagons on the road.

Grith trembled faintly, reaching up to bury his fingers in the thick fur of the tabby cat perched on his shoulder. Teffa rubbed her cheek against his, twining her tail around his wrist. The bruises had started to fade now, and he said they didn't hurt.

"We can stop any time," Len promised softly. "If you're tired or scared, just tug my hand twice, ok? We'll leave the road, you can change, and I'll carry you both. Do you want to stop now?"

Grith swallowed, moving his lips, but made no sound. Teffa felt his shoulders twitch, trying to pull back ears that did not move. He shook his head, and tried again. "N-no." His fingers curled into Teffa's fur.

He was brave. He'd always been brave, always trying

even when he knew he would disappoint. Teffa purred a low, constant hum in his ear, and glowed with pride.

Len smiled. "All right." She stood slowly, helping Grith keep a firm grip on her hand. "Let's go, then." She took a step.

Grith let drew a long, slow breath, and Teffa rubbed her whiskers against his hand. You can do this. We can do this. With a quick, firm stride, like that of a hunter choosing a trail, Grith stepped onto the road.

GRIT

BY STEVEN DONAHUE

The banquet hall in the Nordic kingdom of Barlon was crammed with joyful villagers who laughed, sang and danced as they accepted their host's hospitality. Four long, rectangular tables were filled with cooked meats, baked breads, fresh cheeses and potent wines. Music poured out from the nimble hands of the kingdom's best musicians. The revelers heartily feasted on the offerings while they waited for their benefactor to arrive.

Prince Kreg strode into the room with his wife, Lorna, by his side. The crowd parted and quieted as the young, royal couple greeted the townsfolk. Prince Tran followed a few steps behind his older brother. On his arm was a beautiful young woman whose name escaped Tran. The music died down as everyone focused on the regal family.

"We want to thank you all for coming this evening," said Kreg. The crowd cheered. Kreg smiled and gently placed a hand on Lorna's right shoulder. "Today is my lovely wife's birthday, and we are glad to share this wonderful occasion with all of you." The villagers cheered again. Kreg picked up two wine glasses from a nearby table. He handed one to Lorna and he raised his own toward the crowd. "To Lorna." Then he gazed at her. "Happy birthday my dear."

They drank as well-wishes were shouted. Kreg kissed his wife and led her to the head of the main table. Servants brought them plates of food and offered their blessings to the princess. Kreg and Lorna smiled and thanked each of them. Tran sat on his brother's left side and began to eat with less graciousness toward the workers. His date sat beside him. Kreg was used to his brother's arrogance, and he focused instead on the festivities. As he ate, he noticed Grit lying on the floor near him with its ears up.

The elder prince reached down and patted the top of the dog's head. The canine was a shepherd with thick, white fur. A square patch of black fur grew under the dog's right eye. "You behave tonight and I'll see to it that you get some roasted beef later." The dog stared up at him before gazing at the food on the master's plate. "Don't even think about it."

Tran cleared his throat. "Honestly, Kreg, you speak to the beast as if it can understand you." His lips curled into a half-smile as his date laughed beside him. He glared at the woman, who immediately fell silent. "If our crops and cattle weren't yielding so well, we'd be forced to eat the brute."

Lorna gasped. "What a horrible thing to say, Tran!" She gently ran a hand over Grit's smooth coat. "We could never do something so vile. Grit is practically family."

The dog looked at her as its tongue rolled out the ride side of its mouth.

"Don't listen to him, boy," she softly said.

The dog trotted around the table until it sat down by Tran. Its tongue shook.

"He seems to like you," said Kreg.

Tran sighed and drank some wine. Kreg kept close watch on Grit. He noticed that Grit was staring at Tran's plate and that the plate was inching toward the edge of the table, though no visible force appeared to be moving it. No one else at the table seemed aware of the phenomenon.

"It's such a lovely evening," said Lorna. She rested a hand on her husband's arm. "Thank you for arranging all of this." She kissed his cheek and sat back in her chair. "It's too bad your father couldn't be here."

"The king has not returned yet," said Kreg, still watching the dog and the slowly-moving plate. "He did send a wire with his regards."

"How are the negotiations going?" asked Tran.

"Quite well," replied Kreg. "He is hoping for a peaceful resolution with the Magati Kingdom. I don't think they want a war any more than we do." He ate a forkful of food. "Our father is a skilled mediator. He'll find a solution that suits us all."

Suddenly Tran's plate toppled over, and its contents spilled onto the floor. Grit dashed forward, gulping down the meat, cheese and bread. Tran sprang to his feet. His face was crimson. "How the Hell did that happen?"

Kreg and Lorna held back their laughter. Tran's date tried her best to do the same. Two servants rushed over to attend to the younger prince. Grit finished eating and hustled back over toward its master. Kreg shook his head at the dog. He leaned down and whispered, "You just couldn't control yourself."

The dog brushed against Kreg's right shin before looking up at the prince with attentive brown eyes.

The servants quickly put together another plate for Tran and placed it on the table in front of him. He paid closer attention to his food as he gobbled it down. Grit lay at Kreg's feet and closed its eyes. Two violinists approached the royal couple and played a ballad for the princess. Then a procession of villagers visited the main table and paid their respects with humble presents.

The festivities concluded an hour late with a reception

line at the banquet room exit. Kreg and Lorna thanked each visitor for attending, while Grit rolled on its back, waiting for the chance to drift off to sleep. The dog's eyes popped back open as the palace door closed with a thud. Kreg approached the canine. "C'mon boy, it's time for bed."

Lorna walked beside her husband as Kreg guided the dog to its fluffy bed, which was pressed against a wall outside of the couple's bedroom. The dog obediently curled up on the bed and sighed. Lorna kissed Kreg on the cheek and continued on into their room. Kreg waited a moment before speaking to the dog. He leaned down and gently touched Grit's head. "One day someone is going to catch you, my friend," he said. "I don't think they would be as understanding as I am about your gift. Please be careful." Grit sighed again. Kreg patted the animal's head and moved on toward his waiting wife.

The prince found her leaning against a bureau, grimacing. He rushed over to her. "What is it, my dear?" he asked. He slipped an arm around her waist to steady her. She slowly turned to face him with her right hand pressed against her abdomen. She let out a strained breath. Kreg eased her over to the bed to sit down.

"I don't know what's wrong with me," she said, gritting her teeth. She took a deep breath and slowly let it out. "Maybe it was something I ate. I've had this pain in my side for some time now." She squeezed her husband's right hand. "I kept hoping it would pass, but it isn't going away."

Kreg rose quickly. "I'll get Mag right away," he said. "She'll know what to do."

Lorna nodded and Kreg raced out of the room, startling Grit as he rushed past. The dog instinctively followed Kreg. The prince dashed toward the nurse's room and pounded on her door.

Mag opened the door with a startled expression. "What is it, my Lord?" she asked. She was already in her night clothes. She pulled her robe closed tightly against her body. The prince grabbed her hand and told her to hurry to his room.

They found Lorna lying in bed, breathing slowly. Mag immediately went to work. She pressed a palm against the princess's head and checked the woman's cheeks with the back of her hands. She spoke slowly and calmly, asking Lorna what was wrong. Grit stood beside Kreg, as if sensing that something was amiss. When Mag was finished, she led Kreg out to the hallway.

"Well, what is it?" asked the prince. Grit stood close by him.

Mag offered a soothing smile. "It doesn't look serious, my Lord," she said. "She doesn't have a fever and her mind is sharp. I think something she ate didn't agree with her. I'll ask the staff if anyone else reported feeling the same way." She gently patted Kreg's right arm. "She should be fine by morning. I'll check on her then."

The prince let out sigh of relief. "Thank you, Mag," he said. "I'm sorry to have bothered you." The nurse said it was fine and she walked back to her room. Grit settled back into the dog bed. Kreg nodded at him before returning to his room.

He found Lorna fast asleep in their bed. The prince placed a soft kiss on his wife's forehead before putting out the light and easing into bed beside her. He listened to her breathing and said a silent prayer for her. Despite Mag's assurances, Kreg had trouble sleeping. He listened intently to his wife throughout the hours of darkness, but she did not awaken during the night.

The morning came and Kreg tenderly touched his wife's cheek with the back of his hand. He sat up with a start. Her skin was sizzling and she was sweating profusely. He tried to awaken her, but the princess did not open her eyes. Instead she mumbled incoherently as her lips trembled. Kreg sprang from his bed and rushed out of the room.

He banged on Mag's door again, but this time it opened quickly. Mag was fully dressed and her eyes were wide. Before she could speak, the prince took her hand and again pulled her toward his room.

"She is burning up," he said, as the nurse descended upon the patient. Grit slipped into the room, wagging its tail at the excitement.

The prince clenched his fists as he watched the examination. He turned toward the bedroom door as someone else entered. He saw Rog, Mag's sister, carrying fresh towels. Rog gasped at the sight of the sickly princess. Mag glanced at her.

"Get me some wet clothes," she ordered. Rog stood motionless. "Quickly now! The princess is ill."

Rog nodded and rushed out of the room.

"What's wrong with her?" asked Kreg. He inched toward his wife, and the dog stayed near him. Mag didn't answer him. Instead she gently lifted the princess's eyelids for a moment. Rog returned with two wet rags, and she handed them to her sister. Mag put one over the sick woman's forehead. She used the other to dab Lorna's cheeks.

Mag finally rose with a worried expression. She addressed the prince. "My Lord, your wife has a very high fever. She is fighting something off. Her lips are pale and she is struggling to breathe." The prince winced at the news. "She also has a yellow tint to her eyes. Something is affecting her liver. I've seen this condition during the last war." She took a breath. "For her to have all this so quickly, it must be exposure to Wyland Root. It's the only thing that makes sense." She touched the man's arm. "I'm sorry."

"What can we do for her?" he asked. He pressed his lips together and looked over at his wife. Frightened thoughts flooded his mind. *How did this happen? Is she going to die?* He looked back at the nurse, realizing that she hadn't answered him. "What can we do?"

Mag shook her head. "There's nothing we can do for her, my Lord." She paused, speaking softly. "The condition is fatal. She has no more than three days to live."

She tried to walk past Kreg, but he cut in front of her.

"There must be something, Mag," he said. "We can't just sit by and watch her die." He desperately put his hands on her shoulders. "Please, there must be something. Anything." The prince began to shudder. "Can't we contact someone?"

Mag took a deep breath. "I know this is difficult for you. But even if we brought someone else in to examine her, he would say the same thing. I have watched many people die from this. It was used as a weapon by our enemy in our last conflict because it is so effective." She took another pause. "And there is no known cure."

Rog stepped forward. "That's not entirely true," she said. The prince looked at her and asked her what she meant. She nodded before continuing. "There is the Oden Solution," she added. "It could work."

Her sister shot her a stern look. "Rog, this is no time for

fairy tales. The princess is gravely sick and we need to show her and his Lordship our respect." She pointed toward the door. "Go and get some cold water and more wet cloths. We want to make her as comfortable as we can."

Rog started to leave.

"Wait!" shouted Kreg. He moved toward Rog. "What is the Oden Solution?"

Before Rog could respond, Mag answered. "My Lord, it is a child's tale. It tells of a magic elixir said to be able to cure all ills. It is nonsense." She pointed again, and Rog left the room. Mag sat down on the bed beside Lorna.

Kreg sat quickly beside her. "Tell me more about this potion." Mag started to protest, but he cut her off. "I want to know. I'll try anything to save my wife." He slammed the mattress with his right fist. "Now tell me!"

His outburst made Grit bark. The prince quieted the canine with a harsh glance.

The nurse told the prince the tale. "A mother with two sick children sought help from Oden. The god told her to gather four elements to create a cure for her loved ones," she said. She paused and looked at the prince, who told her to continue. "The elements consisted of a rare plant that grows at the mouth of an active volcano, the feathers of a vicious poisonous bird, magical spring water from a cave guarded by a gruesome troll, and the blood of a noble creature."

The prince stared straight ahead as he processed the story.

"It is just a fairytale," she reiterated. "As you can tell, the elements are fanciful at best. None of them are found in the real world." She spoke more softly. "Please, spend what time she has left by her side. It is where you belong."

She rose and moved toward the door. The nurse paused when the prince spoke again. "If I find these fanciful elements, would you be able to blend them into a serum?"

Mag sighed.

"I know. It's just a story. But if I brought them to you, could you do it?"

"If you found them, I would try," replied Mag. "But I don't see the point in wasting time on a fool's errand, my Lord," she added. "Your kingdom needs you here. Your wife needs you here." She folded her hands and let them dangle in front of her. "I will pray for you both."

The prince rose from the side of the bed. "Write me a list of the elements and where the legend says I can find them. Then stay by Lorna's side until I return." He walked past her and stopped at the door. "I'm leaving within the hour. I'll need the list before then."

Prince Kreg saddled up his best horse, a brown steed named Thunder. A leather pack held enough food and water for a three-day journey. The prince also packed a steel sword in a sheath. Tran stood beside him as he made his preparations, while Grit lay on the ground a few feet away from the horse. "I know how upset you are, brother," said the younger prince. "We all are. But do you really think you can save her with magic?"

Kreg sneered at him. "It isn't magic," he said. "I'm relying on science. Maybe these elements together can cure Lorna." He stopped and sighed. "We already have medicines derived from plants and animals. This isn't that different."

"Who are you taking with you on this trip?" asked Tran.

"No one," replied Kreg. Tran's eyes widened. Kreg moved closer to him and lowered his voice. "I don't know who poisoned my wife, so I don't know who I can trust. I have no choice but to go at it alone." He put his hands on his brother's shoulders. "Look after things here while I'm gone."

Tran nodded as Mag slowly approached them. She handed Kreg a folded sheet of paper. "This is my best guess as where to find the elements," she said. Kreg opened the sheet of paper and saw a map with hand-written instructions. "Even if I am right, it won't be easy to get them." She paused and placed a hand on Kreg's right arm. "Please, my Lord, reconsider your actions. It's not too late to change your mind."

"I have no choice," he repeated. Then he climbed onto the saddle and tugged the reins to get the horse to move forward. Grit rose and immediately followed the master. Kreg stopped the horse and addressed the canine. "No, Grit, you stay here."

The dog barked as if arguing with the prince.

Kreg shook his head. "Fine, but you better keep up."

He tugged the reins again, and the horse trotted forward with Grit at its side.

The team rode for more than four hours before the volcano came into sight. It was very close to where Mag had drawn it on the map. Kreg let the horse rest and drink from a stream that ran into a lake. Grit also drank, wagging its tail. The prince washed his face and hands, and sipped the cool water.

The horse suddenly wailed and kicked back onto its hind legs. Kreg rushed over to the animal and saw a razorbor snapping its mouth shut. The monster's sharp teeth just missed the horse's front legs. The creature was 8-feet long, with brown scales over its dark green body and four stumpy legs. Grit stood close to the horse, barking at the intruder.

"Grit, stay back!" shouted Kreg. The prince removed his sword and stabbed at the beast. The razorbor rolled onto its side, evading the blade, before landing on its feet. It then charged at Kreg with its mouth open.

Kreg instinctively raised the sword to defend himself, when the monster stopped in mid-air, as if hitting an invisible wall. The razorbor slammed to the ground, its head bouncing off of the surface. The creature lay still for a moment, and then was pulled back into the water by another unseen force.

The prince looked over at Grit, and the dog was breathing heavily. Kreg immediately realized that his canine companion had just saved his life. He moved toward Grit and rubbed the dog's head. "Thank you my friend. And thank God for your gift."

After the horse calmed down, Kreg remounted the animal and the team continued on their journey. The volcano grew closer and closer, and soon the travelers were only a few hundred yards away from the site. The air grew hot with the stench of sulfur. Kreg rubbed his eyes and tried to see if any plants were growing near the mouth. The trees that lined the road were still, and Kreg thought he heard voices.

Grit started barking as a group of men appeared from behind the trees. They formed a line across the road that forced Kreg to stop his horse. Thunder whinnied and fought against Kreg's grip. The prince patted the horse to calm it. The men on the road were dressed in animal-skin clothing and holding sharp spears. One of them approached Kreg with his spear pointed out.

"Who are you?" asked the man, shaking the spear in his hand. The other men kept still.

"I am Prince Kreg of Barlon," said the royal son. He

glanced at Grit. "Quiet down, boy." Grit stopped barking and moved closer to Thunder. Kreg looked back at the man. "I mean you no harm."

"You are trespassing on Sutan land," replied the man. He jabbed the spear in Kreg's direction. "You must leave. Now."

The man firmly held his ground. Others behind him shouted at the prince.

Kreg smiled. "I did not know this was your territory. I do not wish to intrude, but I need to get to the mouth of that volcano." He pointed to his destination. "It is a matter of life and death. Please let me pass."

The man stared at Kreg and tightened his grip on his spear. "I am Jantuk, leader of the Sutan tribe," he said. "You will turn back or die."

Jantuk tapped the ground with the handle of his weapon.

Kreg sighed and dismounted Thunder. He removed his sword as Jantuk rushed at him. Their weapons clanged as Kreg blocked a thrust by Jantuk. The fighters circled and sparred, while the other men roared at them. Grit barked again, but kept its distance. Thunder moaned but did not run away. Jantuk was quick and skilled with his spear, and it took all of Kreg's skill to fend him off.

The battle lasted several minutes, but neither man could injure the other. Kreg finally had an opening and he knocked the spear from Jantuk's hand. He hit his competitor on the head with the butt of the sword, sending Jantuk to the ground. The other men fell silent when Kreg pointed the tip of his sword at Jantuk's throat.

"I have no wish to kill you, sir," said Kreg, breathing heavily. "I just need to get to that volcano." He pulled back his sword and offered a hand to his opponent. Jantuk clasped the hand and Kreg yanked him to his feet. "Let us be at peace."

Jantuk responded with a nod. "We have no further quarrel with you," he said. "What is it you seek from the volcano?"

The prince explained his dilemma.

The Sutan leader stood motionless for a moment. Then he spoke in a calm voice. "You may pass, but I and three of my men will accompany you to make sure the land is protected."

"Thank you, Jantuk," said Kreg. "You may join us, but it will most certainly be a dangerous trek as we get close to the mouth. I don't want you or your men to get hurt."

"Your concern is admirable," replied Jantuk. "We can take care of ourselves."

Kreg remounted Thunder. The prince and Grit followed Jantuk and three of his men along the road. Kreg then tied Thunder to a tree as they reached the base of the volcano. The men and the dog climbed the steep slope. The ground shook occasionally, and the stench of the sulfur grew more intense. One of the tribesmen grew sick and stopped his ascent. Kreg and Jantuk crept side-by-side up the slope, with Grit and the other men behind them.

Kreg saw the purple plant that he needed for the elixir. It was only four feet from the opening of the volcano. Despite the tremors, there was no lava flowing out. Kreg wiped his forehead and rushed toward the plant. He carefully removed it from the ground and placed it inside a leather pocket on his belt. He nodded at Jantuk and started to climb back down.

One of Jantuk's men passed Kreg and continued to climb up. Kreg saw that the man was heading for a patch of gold rocks that were embedded in the side of the mountain. Jantuk told the man to stop, but the man did not listen. Instead he continued up until he was on the ledge. Then he began to pull some of the rocks out. The ground shook again, and the man suddenly lost his balance. He screamed as he fell into the mouth of the volcano.

Kreg and Jantuk rushed to the man's aid. Grit was fast on their heels. The man managed to grab onto some roots and he dangled over the bubbling lava below. Kreg and Jantuk tried to pull the man out, but he was too far for them to reach. He screamed again as the roots began to break. Kreg watched in horror, knowing he could not help the man. The roots finally broke and the man began to fall.

Just before hitting the pool of lava, the warrior's fall was broken. His body hung in mid-air for a moment before rising out of the volcano. Kreg and Jantuk then grabbed the man's hands and pulled him to safety. As he rested on the ground, coughing, Kreg looked over at Grit. The dog lay on the ground, breathing heavily again. The prince shook his head in relief.

The men descended the mountain and stopped at the base to rest. Jantuk approached Kreg. "I cannot explain what happened up there," he said. He looked at Kreg's face as if expecting an answer. "It is as if the hand of God saved my cousin."

Kreg shrugged. "Maybe it was." Then he shook Jantuk's hand. "Thank you for letting me get that plant. It means the world to me."

"I'm sure it does," said Jantuk. "You still have quite a journey before you. Good luck."

Kreg thanked the other men before untying Thunder and slipping back onto the saddle. Though he was exhausted from the climb, the prince tugged the reins again, and Thunder marched forward. Grit was panting as it strode beside the horse. The prince read the instructions from Mag about where to find the poisonous bird.

The sky darkened, and Kreg set up a camp for the night. He tied Thunder to a tree and started a fire. The prince and his canine companion slept close to the fire, but Kreg could only stay asleep for short periods of time. His concern for his wife's health and his fear of the unfamiliar surroundings kept his mind racing. The morning sun rose quickly, forcing Kreg back onto his tired feet.

He fed the horse and the dog from the provisions he prepared, and then they continued on their way. From Mag's notes, the nest of the poisonous bird was still a few hours away on horseback. He pushed Thunder hard to cover the ground, and Grit had to run to keep up.

The prince soon found the nesting area. It was in the high branches of a thick oak tree. After securing Thunder, Kreg slowly climbed the tree. He spotted the nest and heard hatchlings squawking inside the structure. A northern wind blew through the trees, making it difficult for Kreg to maintain his grip. He inched his way upward, and the squawking grew louder. The prince knew that the birds had sensed his presence. He stopped worrying about stealth and rushed his ascent.

He peeked over the rim of the nest and saw four tiny birds bumping into each other. They were too young to have the necessary feathers, so Kreg left them alone. He decided to wait for the mother bird to return to the nest. Below him, he heard Grit barking. Kreg worried that the dog might scare off the older bird. He waved a hand at Grit to try to quiet the dog, but that only led to more barking. The prince lowered himself on a branch underneath the nest, where he hid in the cover of the thick leaves, and waited.

Kreg's tired body ached as he sat still for more than an hour. Grit had stopped barking and lay down next to Thunder. The prince then saw the adult bird as it flew toward the nest. The black vulture glided toward its destination with something twitching in its mouth. The bird landed, and Kreg saw a brown field mouse drop toward the hatchlings.

The vulture then quickly turned its attention to the intruder. It shrieked and snapped at the prince, as he dodged the bird's beak. Kreg wrapped his legs hard around a branch and fought to snag one of the coveted feathers. He heard Grit barking again. The bird moved from side to side as it pecked at Kreg, making it difficult for him to touch the bird's body. Finally, he backhanded the bird, stunning it for a moment. He quickly ripped two feathers from the beast and ducked below the nest.

The bird recovered and leaped at the thief. Kreg grabbed the bird and pushed it backward, but the angry creature used its wings to maintain its position. The beak nicked his hands and wrists, but the bird wasn't fast enough to bite him and deliver the toxin. In a near panic, Kreg grabbed the bird and smashed it against the tree. It flopped onto a nearby branch before falling to the ground. Winded, Kreg began his decent, when his right foot slipped off of a branch. He reached for another branch, but missed it.

The prince yelled as he fell toward the ground. Just before impact, something broke his fall and he felt his body drift to a soft landing. He rested on the ground for a moment, still breathing hard and trying to understand what had just happened. Then he spotted Grit lying on the grass and breathing heavily. Kreg nodded at his friend and thanked him.

Prince Kreg let his companions rest for a half-hour before moving onward. He tapped his leather belt where he stored the plant and the feathers and realized that he had half of the coveted elements. Kreg looked at Mag's map. The cave was more than a day's ride from their current position. Despite their good start, they would have to move quickly to cover that ground and return home in time to save his beloved Lorna.

Thunder and Grit bravely trotted across the hot, dry land without much noise, but Kreg could see that the animals were getting tired. It had been more than five hours since they left the vulture's nest, so he steered them toward a gathering of trees. It was the first shady spot they had come across in over three hours. He dismounted and gave his companions food and water, while keeping alert for any danger.

They were about to resume their journey when a rattling

sound froze the prince in his tracks. He looked down and saw a serpent slithering toward Thunder. The horse shot back in fear, and Grit barked at the prowler. Kreg kept his eyes on the snake as he removed his sword from its sheath. The serpent stopped and looked at the human. Its tongue flicked in and out of its mouth.

Before Kreg could strike, an eerie red glow emanated from the creature. The snake then transformed into a young woman. Kreg stood frozen in fear. His sword fell to the ground. The woman shook her head, and her long, blond hair waved over her face. "Fear not, my friend," she said with a slight smile. "I will not harm you." She spoke with a noticeable lisp.

"Who are you?" asked Kreg. He stumbled over his words. "What are you?"

Grit stood between his master and the woman, but did not bark.

The woman's smile widened. "I am Durana." She pushed some hair from her face. "Like you, I am on a quest. I wish to break a spell that has imprisoned my betrothed." Her smile faded into a frown. Kreg saw the longing in her eyes.

"How do you know that I am on a journey?" asked Kreg.

Durana pointed toward Thunder. "You have provisions stored on your horse." She looked back at the prince. "And you have the dust of a traveler." Kreg peeked at his clothing.

"Perhaps we could help each other."

Prince Kreg nodded gallantly. "How can I help you, my lady?" he asked. Grit lay down at his feet and relaxed. Kreg noticed the dog's tail wagging. "My friend seems to like you."

The woman kneeled and patted the dog's head. "He is beautiful." Grit sniffed her hands and licked her wrists. Durana stood and faced the prince. "I am lost," she said. "I am trying to find a cave where my Rowen is being held prisoner. The cave is said to have magical waters that can break his spell, but he needs me there to complete the task."

Kreg's eyes widened. "You seek a cave with magical waters?" he asked. Durana nodded. "It is odd that I also seek the same magical water to help save my wife."

The prince slowly picked up his sword and held it tightly. Then he thrust the sword at the woman, resting the tip against her chest. She gasped and raised her hands.

"Please, sir, I mean you no harm," she said, quivering.

Grit barked once before falling silent.

"No harm, you say?" asked Kreg. Durana nodded. The prince kept the sword tip against her. "You just happen to come along the same road at the same time? I don't believe you. Who sent you to stop me?"

He pushed the blade harder against her skin.

Grit barked and the sword was pulled from Kreg's

hands. It fell harmlessly to the ground a few feet away from the prince.

"Grit, no!" shouted Kreg. He rushed toward the weapon, but the sword moved away from him again. Durana lowered her arms but stood in the same place. Grit rushed in front of the sword and let out a low growl.

"Your dog is blessed," said Durana. Kreg nodded. "Not only with power but insight," said the woman. "If you don't trust me, trust him."

Grit moved away from the sword and sat at Kreg's feet. The prince rubbed the dog's head. Kreg retrieved his sword and put it into the sheath. "Forgive me," he said. "Since my wife was poisoned, I don't know who to trust."

"She was poisoned?" asked Durana. Kreg nodded again. "That is why you seek the water. Do you have the other elements?"

Kreg pointed to his leather belt. "I have the plant and the feathers. I need the water and the blood of a noble creature."

Durana pressed her lips together. "The last element is the hardest to find. Are you willing to do whatever it takes to get it?"

"For my wife, I'll do anything."

"You know where the cave is?" asked Durana. The prince said he did. "Let me come with you. You might need me when you get there."

She grasped his right arm and Kreg sensed her desperation.

"Fine, just don't slow me down," he said. He climbed onto Thunder's back. "What other creatures can you turn into?"

"Only the serpent," she said. "That is why it is hard for me to travel. Even in my true form, my legs move slowly." She pointed to her right thigh.

Kreg sighed. "There is only room for me on Thunder." He glanced at the bags on the saddle. "Unless you become the snake again and stay in here." He tapped one of the bags. Durana nodded and transformed back into the serpent. The prince dismounted and carefully picked up the passenger. He eased her into one of the bags and left the top of it open.

The group rode until sunset, and then they set up a camp. Durana helped build a fire. "We need to continue right at sunrise," said Kreg. "My wife is running out of time."

Durana did not argue with him. Grit slept between Kreg and Durana, and was the first to awaken the next morning. As planned, they continued their quest at first light.

Four hours later, they reached the cave marked on Mag's map. There were several openings to the cave, so Kreg and Durana split up to find the magical water. Thunder was tied to a tree before Kreg took a torch from one of the saddlebags and lit it. Grit followed him into the dank cave.

The dog barked at the damp creatures that bumped its paws. Kreg shushed him and carefully stepped through the choking darkness. The duo stumbled through the cave for more than an hour. Then Kreg heard the sound of running water. He followed the sound and hoped that Durana had heard it too.

The sound grew louder, and soon the prince found the stream. He fought the urge to rush to it and bottle up the liquid. Instead he looked around for the legendary guardian. He didn't see anything threatening, so he eased a bottle out of his belt pocket and leaned toward the water.

Something hit Kreg in the back. The bottle fell into the stream but didn't break. He turned with the torch still in his hand and saw a hideous man-beast standing before him. The figure was only four-feet tall, and it had slimy, green skin and broken, yellow teeth. It lunged at him and tried to bite his neck.

Kreg caught the creature with his left hand and threw him against a rock. The troll wailed and hissed at the intruder. Grit barked at the monster but kept its distance. The prince removed his sword and held it in front of him. The troll hissed again and threw stones at Kreg. They hit his arms and legs, so the prince thrust his sword at the troll.

The water guard quickly dodged the weapon and grabbed a large rock. He wound and threw it at Kreg, but

Grit used his powers to redirect the projectile. Kreg thrust his sword again, this time catching the troll's right leg. The creature screamed as yellow blood poured from the wound. Kreg didn't hesitate and moved in for the kill. He lifted his blade and took aim, but stopped when he heard Durana's cry.

The woman rushed over to the injured troll and pulled the creature into her arms. She glared at the prince. "What have you done?" She pressed her hand against the gaping wound. "Give me something to stop the bleeding!"

Kreg removed a cloth from his pocket and handed it to her. "This is the troll that guards the water," he said. "He attacked me."

"He is also my betrothed," said Durana, addressing the wound. Kreg put his sword back in the sheath. She tied the cloth tightly around the troll's leg. "This is Rowen," she said. "He was cursed by a wizard to keep him from his rightful place in our kingdom. That same wizard imprisoned me for three centuries until I was finally able to escape." She held the troll's hand. "I'm here, my darling," she said to the troll. "I'm finally here."

Durana rushed over to the stream. She cupped water in her hands and drank it. Then she returned to the troll. She kissed him passionately and a blue light surrounded them. She broke the kiss and the troll transformed into a young man.

They stood up and hugged each other. Kreg noticed that the leg wound had healed. Durana looked at Rowen and smiled. "We can finally go home," she said. He tried to speak but nothing came out. She gently touched his throat. "Give it time, my dear," she said. She turned to face Kreg. "He was guarding the water until I could drink from it," she said. "He had to make sure nothing happened to the water until I could come and break the spells." She patted Kreg's shoulder. "Take what you need. It isn't guarded anymore."

Kreg watched them leave the cave. Then he found the fallen bottle and filled it with water. "C'mon boy," he said to Grit. "We have just one more thing to get before we go home." The dog followed the prince out of the cave. Kreg untied Thunder and rode toward home. He read Mag's map, which showed a wooded area where noble deer lived.

The team rode swiftly as the third day wore on. Kreg knew he was pushing Thunder and Grit hard, but the fear of losing his wife made him a stern taskmaster. He thought of her lying in bed burning with fever, and he prayed to the gods that he would return in time with the needed elements. Still, there was a nagging voice in the back of his mind that made him wonder if this was indeed a fool's errand.

They finally came upon the wooded area on the map. Kreg slowed the horse down, and Grit matched its new pace.

They trotted softly through the area with the prince keeping a sharp eye out for his prey. It took more than an hour for him to spot the delicate creatures.

Kreg dismounted and quietly tied Thunder to a tree. He moved slowly into position. Through a row a trees, he observed four deer drinking from a small stream. There were two adults, one male and one female, and two fawns. A slight breeze blew across the tiny meadow. He removed his bow and delicately pulled back an arrow. Holding his breath, he lined up his shot.

One of the fawns moved away from the group. It gingerly wandered after a butterfly. Kreg focused on that one and prepared for the kill. The fawn then raised its head and looked in the direction of the prince. The youngster seemed to be staring straight at the hunter. Kreg felt his chest tighten. He blinked his eyes. Shaking his head, he eased the tension on the bow until the arrow fell harmlessly to the ground. The fawn dashed toward its family, startling them. They darted toward the nearest trees and disappeared.

Kreg sat down and leaned against a tall tree. His eyes watered as he dropped his head into his hands. He wept, and his large frame shook. Grit trotted over and sat down beside him. The dog licked the prince's face. Kreg reached out and pulled the canine into his arms. Neither made a sound for several minutes. Finally, the prince rose and untied his horse. He rode dejectedly toward his home, hoping that the elements he did gather would somehow be enough.

The sun was setting behind the hills when Kreg and his team returned home. They were greeted by servants who were performing their nightly chores. Prince Tran then appeared with two guards as Kreg dismounted Thunder. One of the servants took the reins and led the horse toward a stable. Tran approached his brother cautiously. "How was your trip?"

Kreg shook his head. "I wasn't able to get everything." He reached into his belt pockets and removed the plant, the feather, and the bottle of water. "I have been praying that this will be enough." He then addressed another servant. "Please fetch Mag at once."

That servant sprinted toward the castle doors.

The older prince then noticed that Tran and the guards were moving closer to him. Tran suddenly punched Kreg on the chin, causing him to fall to the ground. The guards removed their swords and held them by their sides. Grit barked at the attackers, but they ignored the dog. Tran kicked his fallen brother in the stomach.

"You fool!" he said, seething. "You couldn't just die out there on that wild-goose chase. No. Not my brother."

He kicked Kreg again.

Kreg coughed and wiped his moist eyes. "You," he said,

spitting blood from his mouth. "You poisoned Lorna."

Tran nodded.

"Why?"

Tran hovered over the fallen prince. "Because I needed to get you out of the way." He laughed. "I knew that her death would crush you. You couldn't live without your precious princess. Then I would step forward and take over the negotiations with the Magati Kingdom from father."

Kreg focused on his brother, while also keeping an eye on the armed guards. He bit his bottom lip and waited for his chance to escape. "You want war, don't you?"

Tran nodded. "Of course. War with them is inevitable. Every year they creep closer and closer to our lands." He placed his hands on his hips. "Father thinks we can negotiate with them. He would give away half the kingdom to keep the peace. I won't let that happen."

Mag suddenly appeared and gasped. "What are you doing?"

The younger prince responded without looking at her. "He has returned with your ingredients. Most of them anyway." Tran laughed. "Pity that they won't make it inside."

He removed his own sword and raised it over his shoulders.

"Wait!" shouted Mag.

This time Tran looked at her.

"He doesn't have them all. There's no need to kill him now, my love."

"My love?" repeated Kreg. He saw her drop her head to her chest. "That's why you didn't want me to find these things."

Mag didn't respond. Kreg glared at Tran.

"Then get it over with, brother," he commanded.

Tran started to swing downward, but Kreg quickly kicked his legs out. Kreg shot to his feet and tackled the assailant. The guards moved to strike him. Grit leaped at one guard, sinking its sharp teeth into the man's arm. The other guard kicked at the dog, forcing Grit to turn its attention to him. The dog attacked the second guard, biting him on his arms and legs. Kreg rolled Tran onto his back and punched him over and over in the face until the younger prince stopped moving. Kreg rose and fought both guards, killing them with Tran's sword. The ruckus caused servants and other guards to emerge from the castle.

When the dust settled, Kreg ordered the arrests of Tran and Mag. They were led to the dungeon, while the bodies of the two dead guards were dragged away. It took some time before Kreg realized that Grit was lying motionless on the ground. He rushed over to the dog and pulled the canine into his arms. Grit was barely breathing. Kreg then saw the stab wounds on the dog's back and legs. "No, no, no!"

Mag's sister, Rog, knelt down beside them. She touched the dog, and blood seeped onto her hands. Oddly, she let the blood drip into a small jar.

"What are you doing?" asked Kreg.

"I'm sorry, my Lord," she said. "But I gathered up the elements that you brought home, and I saw that you didn't have the blood of a noble creature. Now you do."

The worker rushed away from her master and entered the castle.

Kreg held Grit for several minutes. Then it was clear that his companion was gone. He rose and carried the lifeless dog inside the castle. Kreg rested the dog's body in Grit's bed and ordered a servant to make plans for the dog's burial. Then Kreg dashed into his bedroom.

Lorna was still in their bed. Her face was white and her skin was hot. Kreg kissed her cheek. He saw Rog mixing the elements together. The would-be nurse then propped up Lorna's head and opened the princess's mouth. The mixture ran down her throat, causing her to cough. Rog closed the woman's mouth. Then she faced Kreg.

"All we can do now is pray," she said.

Prince Kreg stayed at his wife's bedside throughout the night. Rog frequently brought in wet towels and placed them on Lorna's forehead. As the sun rose in the morning, Lorna's fever finally broke. Kreg was holding her hand when her eyes fluttered open.

"My darling!" said Kreg, kissing her cheek. "You're finally well."

He kissed her again.

She sat up slowly in her bed. "What happened?" she asked. She rubbed her eyes. "My head hurts so much."

Rog gently pressed a hand against the woman's cheek and smiled.

"Have I been ill?" asked Lorna.

Kreg nodded and told her what had happened since the dinner party. Her expression changed from shock to horror as he finished his tale. Then she leaned on her husband's shoulder and wrapped her arms around him. "I'm so sorry," she said. "I know how much Grit meant to you." Then she shook her head. "I can't believe Tran would do this."

"He will pay for his crimes," said Kreg.

"We shall have a proper service for Grit," said Lorna. "He deserves a hero's funeral."

Kreg nodded again. "And that is what he shall have." He patted her hands. "But first, you need to rest. I will check on you later."

He kissed her and slowly left the bedroom.

When Kreg entered the hallway, he noticed that someone had respectfully placed a sheet over Grit's body. He lifted the sheet. Tears filled his eyes again. He gently touched the top of the dog's head. "I guess there wasn't time for you to use your gift. I wish there had been." He took a deep breath. "You are a hero, my friend," he said. "And I will never forget you."

The prince slowly replaced the sheet over the dog's body and wept.

HILL 142
BY JASON CORDOVA

"War does not determine who is right—only who is left."
— Bertrand Russell

The wood was death, waiting to reap.

The air around the forest was silent and heavy as war finally reached Belleau Wood. Machine gun nests were littered throughout the once-tranquil hunting ground. Gas and explosives nestled alongside bird's nests. Wire was strung throughout the underbrush while land mines, containing both gas and explosives, lay in strategic places within.

The small patrol had barely penetrated the outer

foliage of Belleau Wood when the hackles in the back of the Frenchman's neck became prickly. The point man of the patrol, he looked at his fellow soldiers and waved a hand, his eyes peering into the darkness. Little was known about what lay deeper inside the forest, and their American commander needed intelligence. But, even he, a local whose family had lived near Belleau Wood for generations, was afraid of the wood.

"What is it?" a voice whispered to his left. Ignorant American, he thought. He searched for the right words before he spoke.

"I feel something."

"That's a heap of help, pal." The American shook his head. "No landmines, no wire?"

"No," the Frenchman was growing more uneasy with each passing second. "It is safe?"

The American, thinking it was a statement rather than a question, turned to the rest of the patrol behind him. "You heard the man. Corporal, go on up. Keep an eye out for mines or wire. Stay low so the Maxims won't hit you. General Harbord needs to know what Fritz has hiding in here before he sends in the main force. Sergeant, watch for nests." He looked at the local. "Frenchy. You can stay here. We'll go the rest of the way and be back within a few hours."

The American soldiers moved past the startled guide

and began to disappear, the long shadows hiding them from sight. The Frenchman shrugged his shoulders and sat down, resting his back against a large tree as he settled in to wait for the return of the Americans.

An hour passed, then two. He wiped his brow. The forest was cool, but a small sliver of fear had embedded itself into his heart. It made him nervous, caused him to sweat. The forest had always been alive with game and birds, but now was deathly still. Death, in one form or another, had descended upon the ancient hunting grounds.

A soft clicking sound echoed through the still night, like nothing the man had heard before. His heart skipped a beat. He peered into the darkness but he could see little. The clicking sound returned and his bowels clenched as a fresh jolt of terror raced through him. He clutched his carbine to his chest, heart hammering. Blood rushed to his ears and he felt a cold spot on the nape of his neck.

Death stalked the wood this night.

A man screamed off in the distance, followed by another, closer cry of pain and alarm. Then silence. The Frenchman stood and raised his carbine. A single gunshot came from deeper inside the wood. He pressed his back against the tree trunk, his hands sweaty.

Out of the corner of his eye he glimpsed something large and white scurry through the underbrush. He cried out and whirled, but he saw nothing. He raised his carbine and aimed it. A soft clicking noise came from the underbrush to his left and he twisted slightly. More clicking. He opened fire.

Something large crashed through the underbrush, white with fine red hair. Atop this monstrosity was a German officer with a surprised look on his face. The beast—the Frenchman vaguely recognized it as a spider of some kind—stumbled to the ground, the abdomen leaking various fluids intermixed with blood. The German struggled to get to his feet. The Frenchman put a bullet into the German officer's head and looked for more spiders.

More clicking erupted from nearby. The scout, terrified now beyond measure as he took another look at the monstrous spider he had killed, ran away from the noise. He stopped after clambering over a fallen tree, his breath coming in short, painful gasps. He took one final look over his shoulder at the dark forest before fleeing, the image of the German cavalrymen atop giant white spiders burned forever into his mind.

* * *

"Look, Captain, I normally would agree with you, but the only survivor of that scouting party said that he saw Germans riding giant spiders," Brigadier General James C. Harbord said as he jabbed a finger at the all-too familiar, kidney-shaped form representing Belleau Wood. The map, which showed everything from the towns surrounding Belleau Wood to "Gob Gully" to the south, was positioned in the center of the table. A few aide-de-camp stood off to the side, silent as they watched the general issue orders. The dim lighting cast long shadows upon the map, and the blackout curtains hid the light from the war-torn outside world. "The only cover we have before we can enter the forest is at the south, and if those German hellspiders are running around down there, then our entire plan is doomed to fail. We need those damned spiders wiped out, and you're the man for the job, even if we only have two 'cats left."

Captain John Thomason peered at the map. He knew what the plan of attack was, had known for six hours since the lone Frenchman had stumbled back to camp, babbling on about giant spiders. It had taken Thomason less than a minute to realize that the dreaded German Höllenspinne Division had finally been moved to the front, and what his next tasking would be. The stories about how quickly and effectively the Höllenspinne had cleared the Eastern Front from all of the special Russian forces had quickly spread, and their legend grew with each telling. Thomason thought that the stories were mildly overblown. It did not make the current mission any easier to accept, however. He looked at the general and frowned.

"Sir, with all due respect," Thomason began, picking his words carefully. "Ghost and King are our last two lions, the last two for at least a year. If we lose them, we have no more for a very long time. Our scouting capabilities, our trench infiltrators, all gone. Plus, we're talking about an entire generation of cats wiped out before passing their traits down. We could seriously damage potential future generations of the cats this way—."

"Captain," General Harbord growled, his voice low. "I don't want to risk losing them either, but we will lose more men if those spiders aren't cleared first. They can direct machinegun nests to where we are attacking, and can report back to their artillery where to hit us hardest, and can hit our men without warning. I'm not risking any more Marines than I have to, and I have to risk your life—and your cat's—to keep the rest of my Marines alive and well."

"I'm sorry, sir," Thomason said, lowering his head. "I did not mean to carry on so."

"Captain," Harbord said, his tone softening. "I truly believe you can do this. We are to do the impossible tomorrow morning, and if we are to do this, those spiders must be gone. You are the man for this job. It's why we started the program in the first place—to do the impossible, to fight the unknown."

"I understand, sir."

"Semper Fidelis, Marine," the general said with a nod of dismissal. Thomason snapped off a salute and wheeled, leaving the general behind as he left the small house.

Outside, the dusk air was cool. June was typically a warm month, though the entire region had suffered through a spot of bad weather the past three days. The rain had been a welcome relief to the residents of Lucy-le-Bocagem the small village where the marines had set up their forward operating base. "Lucy Birdcage", as it was more commonly known by the Americans, had been a fairly hospitable place, though they were within range of the big German artillery guns to the far northeast. The high winds from the previous week's storms had caused the gun to fall silent, though, as well as damaging some of the larger trees within Belleau Wood. That would be beneficial for his purposes, as the undergrowth which had been knocked down during the storms would be soft and pliable, not likely to snap and break. It would allow for Ghost and King, the two American lions left in the battalion, to move quietly through the wood.

"Of course, two thousand pound cats can only be so quiet," he mumbled as he hurried over to the small enclosure where he and Sergeant Jerry Finnegan were camped, slightly isolated from the rest of the Marines. Their fellow Marines, while not exactly fearful of the giant cats, were nonetheless wary of them and kept their distance. This suited Captain

Thomason just fine, since King was what some of the handlers had called "rambunctious" and Finnegan's mount. The plucky man from New York was better matched with King, according to the War Department. Thomason just considered the dark, tawny colored lion a pain in the ass.

Ghost, though....

He thought fondly back to the day when he was first introduced to the lion cub. At a mere ten pounds, the runt of the litter was initially passed over for selection by the Naval Warfare Department before Thomason had taken a liking to the small cat with mismatched eyes. The breeders, pleased that the Navy and Marine Corps wanted all of the litter, told Thomason that the cub was the first that they had ever seen with the lighter coloring. The grown American lion, they explained to him as he picked up the mewling cat, grew to be over a ton in weight and were easy to train—If one began at a young age—and that their coloration helped them blend in to their surroundings. A cat colored such as the runt Thomason was holding, however, would probably be left for dead by the mother in the wild.

He shook off the memories as the large white lion came into view, the mismatched eyes of blue and brown staring intently at him. Thomason knew that Ghost was intelligent, but he was not sure just how smart the cat really was. Sometimes he was nothing more than an extra-large housecat, other times Thomason could mistake him for a born and bred Marine.

"Mission, sir?" Finnegan asked as he came up alongside him. Sergeant Jerry Finnegan was the last remaining lion cavalry NCO from the original platoon, a heady mixture of brashness and experience that Thomason had come to accept and rely upon. Finnegan was much like his own cat: annoying and yet, indispensible.

"The hellspiders are finally here," Thomason acknowledged, using the American term for the German höllenspinne unit. "We knew they'd come eventually. That's why we're down here. Still, I would have loved to have a crack at them at full strength."

"Bully, sir!" Finnegan grinned. "We can lick 'em good, even with only King and Ghost. We'll show the Kaiser just how United States Marines fight!"

"We'll show them soon enough," Thomason said. "We're to clear the wood of the spiders, Maxim gun nests and patrols are secondary objectives. Attack starts at 0300, but we're going in three hours beforehand to start our mission."

"So get some rest then, sir?"

"You read my mind, Sergeant," Thomason nodded. "I'm going to check on Ghost before I take a short nap."

"I've looked over King, sir, and he's in fine shape. That stinger in his paw seems to have healed up nicely."

"Very good. Get some rest, Jerry," Thomason ordered, effectively dismissing the man. Finnegan smiled and saluted.

"Yes sir." Finnegan trotted away as Thomason came closer to the impromptu pens where the lions were normally kept.

Ghost stood and padded over to him, the muscular lion slightly larger than a horse. The paws of his feet were bigger than Thomason's head, and the claws alone made many men shiver in terror. Thomason stopped and crouched down. Ghost followed suit, his haunches raised in the air, the lion ready to pounce. Thomason feinted towards his left before shifting his weight to the right. The cat, not fooled at all, had already sprung.

Thomason had known he wouldn't fool the cat, so he planned accordingly. He let his momentum carry him further right than Ghost had anticipated and he snagged the riding collar that was fitted around Ghost's neck, pulling the cat after him. Surprised, the large cat rolled onto his back, legs splayed open. Thomason grinned and scratched the cat's belly.

"You are such a spoiled little kitty," he told the two thousand pound lion. "Yes you are. Who's a spoiled little kitty?"

Ghost began to purr, a loud, rumbling sound which always caused a few heads to turn. Like the puttering motor of an automobile, the purr of the American lion was something not many had ever heard before. Neither was a horse-sized cat being handled like a household kitten, but Thomason always viewed lions as something akin to a horse — a smarter, faster, deadlier option, but a respected companion and friend nonetheless.

Ghost rolled to his feet and lifted his head, his mouth open as he tasted the air. Thomason scratched behind his ear.

"You look like an ass when you do that. You know that, right? A regular old mule. Do you want to look like an ass? You want to be known as Assface?" he asked the cat as he continued to scratch. He glanced over at the handlers, who were looking on in wry amusement. "Light dinner for both cats tonight. Mission for the boys, and I don't want them tossing up their food in the middle of a tussle."

"Yes sir," they chorused and moved off to procure the necessary foodstuffs to feed the cats. Ghost looked at him as he recognized a word. Thomason smiled.

"Yep, that's right," he told the cat. "We got ourselves a mission. A real mission, not down in the trenches clearing out Fritz. We're going hunting."

Thomason continued on towards one of the ruined buildings near the edge of the village. A collection of tents had been erected in the shade of the ruined building, which he had been told was once a Catholic church. The tents had once been filled with the men of 2nd Marine Special Cavalry, but now they were unused, half-destroyed reminders of the men in his command who would not be making the trip home. Taylor, Williamson, Smith and their cats—all gone. He sighed as an unfamiliar soldier emerged from one of the empty tents.

"Nothing in there, partner," Thomason said as his hand drifted down to where he wore his sidearm. "Move along now."

"Yes sir!" the man replied and scurried away.

"Damn army boys," he grumbled as he pushed aside the flap of his tent. He had learned long ago to not store anything of value in his tent after the "mysterious" disappearance of his whisky flask. His blanket was still there, which surprised him some. He flopped down onto the rough dirt and looked up at the roof of his small tent, which had been haphazardly patched with random swatches of fabric he had scrounged up from other tents. He sighed and closed his eyes.

An all-too familiar noise far away woke him. It was late, and light from the full moon above spilled into his tent. He had slept for a few hours, though it did not feel like it. He yawned and looked towards his feet, where the large form of Ghost lay curled up just outside his tent. Groaning in pain, he sat up. His back popped as he did so.

More artillery rumbled in the far distance, though he

was uncertain who was shooting at who. Or if they were simply shelling an empty no man's land somewhere miles away. Not that it mattered who they were shelling anymore, so long as they were not trying to kill him.

"Ghost," he called out in a soft voice. "You ready, boy?"

The great cat sighed dramatically, stood and stretched out to his full length. Nearby Thomason heard Finnegan wake up King, followed by a full stretch of cursing as Finnegan chastised his cat for marking his territory on the tent guide line. Again. He smiled and looked at Ghost.

"You are a good cat."

He led Ghost to the handlers, who had the specifically designed saddles ready and waiting. Ghost went first and was done in minutes, the great cat knowing exactly what was expected of him and behaving appropriately. The handlers cinched the waist belt and ensured that the neck reins allowed the cat his full mobility before the lead handler nodded to Thomason.

"He's ready, sir."

King was next. The tawny colored cat growled in a low pitch as the handlers struggled to hold him still. The saddle went on surprisingly easy and Thomason thought that all was going well. However, the handlers weren't pleased. One of them, an old ranch hand who had enlisted long before the Great War had broke out, slapped King on his backside.

"Quit holdin' yer breath," he admonished the cat. King exhaled and the handlers cinched the waist belt, ensuring that King would not be able to throw Finnegan easily. Thomason smiled and winked at the handler, who shrugged his shoulders. "Like a troublesome pony, sir. Just gotta know how to work 'em, remind him who's the boss."

"That you do," Thomason agreed. Ghost knelt onto the ground and he climbed on. Ghost rose and waited for Finnegan to mount King. King, though, was being his normally stubborn self, and was circling away from Finnegan, growling the entire time. Ghost turned his head and snarled at King, who meekly replied before crouching down. Finnegan hopped onto King's back, and the great tawny lion rose. Finnegan flashed a toothy grin at Ghost.

"Thanks boy."

"Alright," Thomason said, struggling not to smile. "We have three hours. Let's go."

The pair moved out of the village and turned towards Belleau Wood. Above, the full moon guided them, the bright light allowing them to approach the heavily guarded forest without the use of a box lantern. Still, Thomason knew that they would need to stick to the lesser-used game trails that dotted the area. The Germans would be watching the main paths, and scouts had reported that the south part of the wood had fewer Maxim machinegun nests. That would be their approach as well.

The air was thick and heavy, though a bit cool for early June. Thomason, used to the dry summer heat and bone-chilling winters of north Texas, pulled his collar up to protect his neck. He glanced over to see Finnegan enjoying himself immensely.

"Damn Yankees," he grumbled.

Finnegan smiled. "It's not so bad, sir. Weather's bully, sir."

Thomason shook his head, exasperated. Silence reigned for a few minutes before the New Yorker spoke up again.

"How big you think those spiders are anyways, Captain?" Finnegan asked in a low voice, a faint edge in his tone.

"Dunno. Reckon they'll be almost as big as the cats, though not as heavy," Thomason scratched his chin thoughtfully. "Have to be big enough to carry a man, anyways."

The two fell silent as they approached the near-black woods. The forest was covered in a thick fog, and though the nighttime sky was clear, Thomason knew that deeper inside the wood there would be no moon to see by. He swallowed and, with his knees, moved Ghost into the dark underbrush on the outer fringes of the forest. Finnegan followed a second later on King, the darker lion blending in to the surrounding shadows better than Ghost.

"You better take the lead," Thomason said. "King's better suited for this stuff."

King nudged past Ghost, with Thomason's cat taking offense at the perceived slight. He reached out and swatted the hindquarters of King, who jerked away. Thomason pulled up on the reins a bit.

"None of that, now," he admonished his cat with a soft and gentle tone. "Let him go first and find the bad guys. We'll get to eat them."

Ghost sneezed at him but obeyed. King took the lead and led them deeper into the woods, the leaner cat following the scent markings of game and bypassing the normal human-sized trails. The air grew thicker and the fog heavy as the outside world ceased to exist.

Thomason peered through the fog, trying to watch Finnegan with his eyes as the cats gingerly picked their way through the wood. King disappeared from view many times, giving Thomason the impression that Finnegan was floating though the air. Ghost, his nose better than his rider's eyes, had little problem following King.

"Where is everybody?" Thomason growled. The wood was supposed to be crawling with hellspiders, but the only thing he could see was a few trees. "This stuff is unnatural."

Ghost suddenly stopped. Thomason brought up his

carbine and looked around, but spotted no sign of whatever had caused his cat to quit following King. Ghost took two steps back and scratched the ground. Thomason smiled and hopped down from Ghost's back.

"Good boy," Thomason muttered and brought out a pair of clippers from his saddlebag. Kneeling, he carefully cut the razor wire. The taut wire sprung back into the underbrush, clearing the path. He stood up and looked at Ghost. "Hey, you were supposed to be following King. Where'd they go?"

Ghost stared at him. Thomason frowned. Ghost was obedient and well-trained; surely something had drawn him away from King. He approached the cat and lifted his chin.

"What's so interesting that you'd quit following King?" he whispered. No answer was forthcoming. Thomason shook his head and climbed back atop the cat. He couldn't see hide nor hair of either Finnegan or his mount. "Damn. Now where'd they go?"

A lion's roar from deeper into the wood answered his question. Ghost's ears pricked up at the sound. Thomason kneed him forward. Through the thick underbrush they ran, guided by the occasional roar from King.

Thomason burst into a small clearing and saw the lean tawny being dragged down by a cluster of horse-sized spiders, their white carapaces gleaming brightly in the pale moonlight. Their riders, seated just in front of the massive abdomen of the spiders, were jabbing at the fallen King with what looked like lances. Thomason quivered in rage as the big cat cried out in pain. A deep, dangerous growl emanated from within Ghost.

The spiders swarmed Finnegan as he struggled to his feet. Of King there was no sign. Thomason felt a sick feeling in his stomach as his eyes met Finnegan's. With a strangled cry the man was dragged down into the underbrush, the massive spiders making short work of him.

"Christ Almighty," Thomason swore under his breath. He dismounted and raised his carbine to his shoulder. "Ghost, go left. Kill." The white cat disappeared across the clearing, heeding his rider's commands. Thomason took careful aim and began to fire at the spider riders.

He took three before the others realized somebody was shooting at them. The five remaining höllenspinne scattered, with one running directly towards him. Surprised, Thomason opened fire again, raking his carbine left and right as the German struggled to dodge the continuous gunfire. Thomason stopped firing as the rider fell from his mount and crashed heavily onto the ground nearby. The spider reared up and began clicking furiously. Thomason raised his gun and pulled the trigger.

Nothing.

Swearing, Thomason cast aside the empty carbine and

fumbled for his revolver. The spider lowered itself to the ground and charged him. In an instant Thomason knew that he would never get the sidearm out of the holster in time. He was dead.

Ghost appeared from the thick fog, the white cat leaping through the air. The spider never saw the big cat's arrival and didn't stand a chance as Ghost's entire weight came crashing down upon its back.

The spider made a satisfying crunch beneath Ghost's paws, the heavy lion easily crushing the arachnid. Abdomen ruptured, the spider lay in a ruined heap, legs splayed out in eight different directions. Thomason looked around for any sign of the rider, the morning fog beginning to lift as the day began to warm. He knew that they were exposed, sitting out in the open, but there were only a few of the spiders left. He needed to know where Fritz was hiding.

He spotted the still form of the German hellspider rider lying crumpled next to a bush, clutching his stomach. He could see the man's blood mixing in with the earth and knew that he was not long for this world. He glanced quickly around.

"Still," he commanded, and the lion crouched low to the ground, flattening himself as low as he could. He knelt down and crawled to where the cavalry rider lay. He pulled his revolver out of the holster and prodded the German with it.

The German groaned and rolled over slowly. Blood leaked and gurgled from a messy chest wound, the steady flow telling Thomason everything he needed to know. He shook his head.

"Mein schmerz zu beenden. Bitte?" the German hissed as he closed his eyes. He turned his head away. Thomason, whose command of German was spotty on the best of days, shook his head.

"I don't understand," Thomason said. He looked around but could not see any of the other hellspiders. "You speak English?"

"Pliss," the German whispered, his face contorting into a grimace as a fresh wave of pain hit him. "Pliss keel."

Thomason finally understood. He nodded once in agreement and patted the German's arm. He whispered the Lord's Prayer softly under his breath as the German grasped his hand. Surprised, Thomason accepted the momentary camaraderie from the dying man. He cocked the hammer back on his revolver and pressed it against the temple of his enemy, right above his jaw. He pulled the trigger. The shot echoed loudly. The hand clutching his fell limp.

He stood up and looked around—a tranquil scene, with wildflowers and grass growing high on the outskirts of the dark and forbidding forest. Overhead the sky was beginning to clear. It was a perfect day, one that he would have loved while sitting on the steps of his family's house on the prairies of Texas, sipping sweet tea and watching Ghost try to catch prairie dogs.

He knew King was dead, the venomous poison from the spiders making short work of the leaner lion. Finnegan had been torn to pieces, a small part of his brain recognized that the lump of clothing and blood had once been a man. He pushed it all aside, though, and tried to remember what he was supposed to do. Duty. That was all that was left for them.

He did not know what the German soldier really thought of what they were doing, but he guessed that all soldiers were the same. King and Finnegan, dead. The other dozen who had come before them. The Germans, the Austrians, the Brits and French. They all did their duty. They were loyal to their country. They obeyed orders. He looked back at Ghost, who was watching him with his mismatched eyes. Thomason motioned for the cat to come.

"What's our duty, boy?" he whispered into the cat's ear as the great lion head butted him, a soft purr beginning to grow in his belly. Thomason smiled sadly and scratched Ghost's ear. "Let's finish this and go home. We have a duty, too."

As he grabbed for the pommel of Ghost's saddle two more Höllenspinne burst into view, their guns firing sporadically as they aimed at him. Ghost dashed off to the right while Thomason rolled left, his sidearm up and tracking the lead spider before he had time to think. Two quick shots dropped the rider, and four more rounds caused the spider to stagger and fall.

The second rider fired off a quick burst from his carbine at Thomason, the rounds chewing up the foliage next to him. Before he could take better aim, though, Ghost's massive bulk erupted from a cloister of trees nearby. The German managed to turn and fire off a single shot before Ghost's jaws clamped down upon his exposed throat. The German's screams were abruptly cut off. Raising his bloody muzzle, Ghost swiped at the rider-less spider, who clicked loudly and started to skitter away. The lion leapt through the air and landed atop the spider, crushing it. Ghost lowered his head, sniffed, and turned back towards Thomason. He kicked dirt onto the ruined spider, then trotted over. Thomason, adrenaline pumping through his veins, smiled.

"Oorah," he growled and patted Ghost's bloody head. "Should've named you hellcat." He hopped up onto Ghost and flinched, his left leg sore. The two began to move into the dark undergrowth of Belleau Wood, hunting for the last few hellspiders which lingered. His hand brushed his trousers and came away wet. Annoyed, he lifted his hand to inspect it. His eyes widened as he saw a large streak of blood on his palm.

The pain struck; an icy, burning, stabbing pain in his hip. Surprised, he looked down and saw blood running down his trousers. He'd been shot; but in the excitement and rush of combat, he hadn't felt it. He could see a small, dark hole that was filled with blood. He kept looking, shocked at how much blood he was losing, and felt his seat shift. He suddenly did not have enough strength to stay upright and he fell, crashing heavily to the ground. He groaned and closed his eyes for a moment as the pain almost caused him to black out. Ghost stopped and looked down at his rider. He stuck his nose against Thomason's exposed neck and pushed slightly, trying to get him back to his feet.

Thomason groaned, a filmy haze of red clouding his vision as his hip throbbed painfully. He couldn't remember being shot, though the past ten minutes had been frantic. He lifted his head and looked around. No Germans were in sight, though with the spider's ability to run in the trees, that meant little to him. He motioned for the cat to come closer.

"C'mon boy, we gotta finish this," Thomason muttered as he used the massive bulk of the cat to pull himself upright. He fought off a sudden wave of dizziness and leaned against Ghost. Carefully he climbed into his saddle and scratched the cat behind his ears. Ghost, like all the other American lions under the University of Texas' breeding program, was trained to assist an injured rider. It was part of the breeding, and also a part of the bonding that came along with raising a lion from birth. Thomason was pleased with his cat. "Good boy, good boy," he murmured, the pain ebbing slightly as he shifted slightly in his saddle. "Only three more spiders, then we can rest boy. Steaks, fish, chicken, whatever you want. Hell, you want a beer? Sounds good to me. Let's just get through this."

Ghost began to move through the heavy thicket. Thomason, still mildly woozy from the blood loss and pain in his hip, peered through the dark forest, searching for any sign of the Kaiser's troops. He could see evidence that they had been there, with trampled bushes and well-used game trails as clear to him as a paved road would be. Still, without the Germans raising a flag and simply announcing their presence, finding more machinegun nests was going to be tricky.

"Well, I'll be hornswoggled," he muttered as he spotted a Maxim nest with a small flag flying next to it. He shook his head in wonder, though he was a bit surprised that any German would announce their presence so boldly. He could see the three German soldiers peering out intently into the wood, looking for any sign of advancing enemy soldiers. Their position was well-defended with clear lines of fire and good cover. Thomason was almost impressed with their preparedness.

Unfortunately for the Germans, they were looking forward, not behind them.

Thomason leaned forward and tapped Ghost twice on his shoulder. The big cat immediately crouched down and Thomason, wincing in pain, slid off of the lion. Ghost waited for his next command.

"Kill," Thomason whispered and pointed towards the nest. Ghost turned his head, spotted the machinegun nest and began to slink around towards the left of the nest. Thomason wondered for a brief instance where he had lost his carbine at before he pulled the weathered revolver from its holster. Moving quietly forward, he approached the German position and waited.

Ghost, away from the nest and protected by a small cluster of trees that had grown into one another, roared loudly. The Germans reacted swiftly, turning their machinegun towards the sound of the lion. They opened fire at random intervals, trying to locate the cat. Ghost, though, was out of sight and already moving away from where he had roared from.

The Germans turning, however, gave Thomason the perfect opportunity to ambush their nest. He raised his sidearm and moved quickly forward, firing his gun rapidly into the backs of the Germans. Two slumped down into the nest, dead, while the third tried to turn the machinegun around. One more shot from his revolver took care of the survivor.

Thomason looked down at the quiet nest. "Well, that was easy."

Time slowed, then stopped as Thomason turned his head at the first sound of the machinegun opening fire on him. No wonder his approach to the nest had been so easy: there was a second one he had missed entirely. His brain screamed at him to move faster, to duck, to hide, to do something. His body could never match the speed at which his mind was moving, though, and felt a punch to his stomach as a round struck home. He stumbled as rounds from the machine gun kicked up the dirt around him. Another struck his ankle and he nearly passed out as he lost feeling in his foot. He fell to the ground and waited. Death would not be long now.

A shadow loomed over him and for an instant he saw Death. It was just as bad as he thought it would be: fear, terror, a little bit of acceptance. He could live with dying in a war, to do what he was ordered. The hill was almost fully cleared of hellspiders and machine gun nests. He had done his duty. He looked into Death's mismatched eyes. He blinked and rubbed his grit-covered face. Ghost stood there, defiant. Had he been hallucinating?

"Run..." There was no need for Ghost to die too.

The big lion roared loudly as rounds tore into his

body, Ghost's massive bulk protecting Thomason from the machinegun. The cat staggered as rounds continued to pour into him, the German Maxim merciless. Thomason cried out as he watched the cat fall, blonde-white hair stained red with blood.

He grabbed a grenade from his belt and, with a painful grunt, heaved the small explosive towards the machinegun nest. He reached for another, pulled the pin, and hurled. And another. And another.

Loud, concussive explosions filled his ears. The machine gun fell quiet. He blinked. Nothing stirred in the wood.

"Ghost...?" he whispered, his throat surprisingly tight. He reached up and yanked his collar open. He couldn't breathe well for some reason. He looked over at the big lion. He tried again. "Ghost. Come."

The cat gave a pathetic, painful response. Ghost moved slightly and turned his head to look at Thomason.

"Come on, boy."

The cat dragged himself closer, leaving a dark trail of blood which was mixing in with the dark colored earth. Thomason did not want to see the grievous wounds that were hampering Ghost, but he knew he had to inspect the cat. When Ghost was close enough, Thomason gently put his hand on the back of Ghost's neck. The cat bowed his head. Thomason began to look over Ghost and stopped almost as soon as he began.

The machinegun had shredded the poor cat. Bloody holes raked up and down Ghost's side and chest, while flaps of fur hung bloody and loose. Thomason suddenly realized that his cat had saved his life, but at the cost of its own. He knew that even the toughest lion could not survive the damage that Ghost had taken. He checked for more damage but realized that it was futile. There was too much blood.

He saw them before he heard them. The last two Höllenspinne had come out of the forest, the men atop their monstrous spiders. Their guns were aimed in his direction but not directly at him. They were, Thomason realized, far more afraid of Ghost. The spiders chittered loudly but stayed back, keeping a good distance between the cat and themselves.

Ghost tried to move, to protect Thomason from the oncoming menace. He was too badly wounded, though, and could only feebly snarl at the spiders. Thomason had to do something, before the spiders killed them both. He looked around for his firearm but couldn't see it anywhere nearby. The spiders moved closer and he began to grow desperate.

He pulled the cat closer, trying to shield it with his body. The cat was too big, though and he could not protect all of Ghost from the advancing Germans. He struggled with Ghost before pulling out his Bowie knife. It was a pitiful weapon against the spider-riders and their guns, but it was the only thing he had left. He looked at them in defiance as he bared the blade before him.

"Come get some, you Kraut sons of bitches!" he screamed, his breaths coming in ragged gasps. "I'll kill every last one of you if you touch my cat!"

The Germans brought their spiders to a halt, their carbines pointed away from Thomason and Ghost. They looked at one another before looking back at the badly wounded lion and its rider. They leaned close to one another and began to whisper intently.

"It's okay, boy," Thomason told Ghost as he stroked the large cat's furry head. He pulled the cat tighter against him, feeling the giant cat's fluttering heartbeat against his chest. He was almost too heavy, but Thomason didn't care. Ghost mewled in pain as he struggled to crawl onto Thomson's lap, just as he used to do as a small kitten years before. Thomason scratched Ghost's ears as the cat managed to get his neck and part of a shoulder onto Thomason's lap. "Shush. I'm here. It's okay, boy. It'll be okay. I promise. It's okay."

The Germans looked back at the two on the ground before wheeling their mounts around, the spiders making loud noises as they began to skitter away. Thomason stared at their retreating forms until they disappeared into the night. He blinked back more tears. He was not certain why they decided to leave the two of them alone, but he could hope that even the greatest war could not strip man of his honor.

He coughed and felt his gut wound leaking, his blood mixing with Ghost's. It didn't matter. Thomason closed his eyes and leaned his head against the tree, pain and weariness nearly overwhelming. The desire to just close his eyes and rest, to give up, was overwhelming. It was a comfortable rest which awaited him, if only he would fall asleep. Just a short rest was all he needed.

He forced his eyes open. He would not succumb. Not yet, not like this. He owed the great cat that much. After deliberately taking the bullets from the heavy Maxim gun that was meant for him, he owed Ghost so much more. He watched the rhythmic rising and falling of Ghost's side as the lion breathed, the small cloud of dirt which rose every time he exhaled. His own pain temporarily forgotten, Thomason tried to ease the suffering of his best friend. He scratched the cat's ears and felt the telltale rumbling of Ghost's familiar purr. He smiled softly as the purring grew louder, defiant, until it faded to a quiet buzz, then was silenced forever.

Ghost breathed out one final time, a heavy exhale, stubborn to the end. Thomason felt the great beast let go finally, relaxing, peaceful at last.

He continued to scratch his ears long after the noble creature's body began to go cold, holding his best friend close as the Great War raged on.

DOOK

BY HERIKA R. RAYMER

She had no other way.

Amber Perkins reminded herself of this fact as she entered Milan, Tennessee. She went over the details of the plan in her mind again, making sure that she had covered every possible angle and conveniently distracted herself from the prominent cemetery she passed on Ellington and First. Driving through downtown Milan, she idly noticed how it had built up. Then again, it had been several years since she moved out.

Still, after seeing the pawn shop, she silently thanked her good judgment at keeping friends in her old home town. Otherwise, she never would have known her good-for-nothing half-brother was trying to sell her inheritance. More specifically, he was trying to pawn the vintage brooches her grandmother had left her. They were still hers by law, and if he tried to sell them there were too many relatives and mutual friends who would notice.

Muttering a few choice names for Barry, she saw the impressive wooden wishing well next to Woodridge and turned right. It did not take her long after that to find his house, and still she wondered if there was not something else she could do. It just felt like she was sinking to his level somehow. She liked to deal with people directly. Yet he refused to talk to her on the phone, did not return her messages or emails, only reluctantly talked to a lawyer (most likely because he knew full well she could not afford to keep one long), and was being very careful with whom he talked to among family and friends when it came to her. He knew her radar was up, and he was trying to stay off of it.

As if he could, given that he still had her property.

His track record with family was not the best. He had moved in with their parents when he lost his job and ended up 'borrowing' a couple thousand dollars' worth of items that never were seen again. It was when the cops arrested him on drug charges for the third time that her parents finally realized they could not help him.

And she had trusted him with something so very precious, believing he had changed after being in rehab.

Sighing, she pulled up the driveway and put it in

park. The engine was still running, cooling the inside of her vehicle, as she reached into the backseat and opened the cage door. Driving many hours with two energetic ferrets was never wise unless one was prepared. There were even little hammocks in there for them to sleep in when they got tired. The whole back seat right now was one large ferret cage. On cue, two furry bodies hopped out and crawled to the passenger seat, where they ran around one another for a moment and then sat down to look at her.

"Okay Sitka and Gizmo," she said as she gently picked up the two ferrets. "Time to help Mama. Ready to play?"

They wagged their tails as they began to cluck excitedly, indicating their delight at the upcoming game.

She really wished that she had another way of getting the vintage brooches that her grandmother had left her, but with the way dipstick was acting, this was her final option. A friend had recommended she call the police on him, but she knew he had friends in the department who would alert him and give him time to hide the brooches. It had happened when she and her Dad had visited. She knew he had them, but when her father asked where they were, he claimed not to know. Looking through the house with his permission had turned up nothing.

Amber knew he still had the brooches, because it was not too long thereafter that he had tried to pawn them.

She shushed them to let them know that they needed to be quiet.

They leaned forward to lick her nose and then turned to her oversized handbag. She carefully placed them inside and zipped it closed enough to allow them to exit when needed. Given what she knew of her half-brother's patterns when he was in high school, she guessed that the moment he saw her car in the drive he hid the antique brooches between his mattress and the box spring. Rather obvious, but it was where he used to hide items when he was younger. She was just glad now that she never let on that she knew. It was also the blueprint she used to train Sitka and Gizmo.

Exiting the car after turning it off, she carefully balanced the handbag over her shoulder and made her way to the front door. The cool from the car's air conditioner evaporated off her arms in the June heat. Her hand had just lifted to knock when it opened. Barry stood there in shorts and a t-shirt, looking at her with open contempt.

"What are you doing here?" he growled.

"To try and appeal to your good side," she answered. *Providing you have one,* she added silently.

"I already told you and Dad, I don't have them."

"You gave me an empty box, Barry."

"Then it's the broker's fault," he pointed out testily. "Not mine. They must have gotten lost in the estate sale."

Amber's jaw clenched as she silently counted to ten. They shared a paternal grandmother, and it was at her death that they had been given certain items in her Last Will. The rest had been at the mercy of the state. It was her bad luck that she was out on a job when the broker said they needed to claim their inheritance; it was further her bad judgment to believe that her half-brother could be trusted to get her part of the items and turn everything over. She was not going to let him get away with it.

She reached up to wipe away some sweat from her brow. "Could you at least let me come in out of the heat?"

His mouth twisted as he thought about it, but he begrudgingly unlocked the door and let her in. In the shade of his house, she was a bit cooler. The distant clatter of his old air conditioning unit told her it was on, but it was losing to the Mid South heat. She would feel bad for him if he wasn't such a pain.

"Bathroom?" she asked.

Barry jerked a thumb behind him.

Not expecting him to offer her a soothing drink, she made her way through the front room where the television and couch was, turned down the small hall which connected the front room to the kitchen on the left to the bedrooms on the right, and went to the single bathroom. Thanks to how the house was laid out, both bedrooms were close to the bathroom. The master bedroom, meaning his room, was right next to the bathroom. Perfect.

Once in the bathroom, she partially closed the door and set her purse down. Turning on the water to cover any sound, she helped her ferrets out. She let them drink from the basin and then set them down. After washing her face, she leaned down to pick up the purse.

"Find the pouch," she told them. Then she made a shushing sound, letting them know the game had started and they had to keep quiet until done.

Sitka and Gizmo stood on their hind legs and hopped a bit. Their little heads turned quickly as they tried to take in their new surroundings. The beginning sounds of clucks, but she shushed them again. They quickly wandered around the bathroom, sniffing and inspecting. To redirect their attention, she said it again.

"Find the pouch."

Immediately the two ferrets dashed for the door and waited. To cover their exit to the bedroom, she opened the door and went into the front room. She really did not think there was a danger of her half-brother noticing, the guy was notoriously arrogant.

Just as she thought, he had deposited himself in a large recliner and was waiting for her. Knowing he would not invite her to sit, she just crossed the room and eased herself down onto the couch. He looked at her sidelong and took another long drink. He obviously wanted to let her know that she was not welcome and he was not going to get her a drink.

Ignoring the slight, she just reached into her handbag and pulled out a bottled water. Uncapping it, she took a long drink. She would need it for the excuse to get to the bathroom later. When she recapped the drink, she saw two furry bodies darting around the corner into the master bedroom.

Now to mentally time it.

Right now the ferrets were in the bedroom looking around, getting familiar with the strange surroundings. She just hoped they did not make too much noise. Or worse, get distracted from the game.

"Why don't you just admit you have me wrong?" Barry asked.

Amber looked at him. "I would like to, but you are not known for your honesty."

"Again with that," he groused. "I went to rehab. I'm clean."

"I believe that you are clean," she said with a shrug. "But after so long of being burned by you, trust is harder to come by."

He snorted and took another drink.

If Sitka and Gizmo were following the plan, right now

they would have determined where the bed was and were trying to figure out how to get between the mattress and the box spring. This had been fun to watch at home. She had started by taking their favorite toys and hiding them in obvious spots, and watched as they climbed onto couches and up bookshelves. When she placed a toy on the kitchen countertop, Sitka amazed her by opening the small doors under the junk drawer, using the jars there as stairs, pushing the drawer until it was slightly open, squeezing in the drawer from the back where there was space, and moving aside the junk until she crawled out of the drawer and onto the counter to get her toy.

Gizmo was just as crafty. When Amber had advanced their hide-and-seek game to where she was hiding their toys in places, she put his toy in the couch cushions. It had taken him a while to find it, but when he did he pushed at the pillows and tried to pull the couch cushions apart. They were too heavy to move. It was when he took the remote control and managed to dig the toy out that she rewarded him with treats. Encouraging this type of behavior was a bad idea, she knew. However, so long as she presented it as a game and played it with them, she hoped they would not want to do it on their own.

"What I don't get is why you think I would want to keep those brooches," Barry was saying, drawing her back to the present. "What would I need with women's jewelry?"

She rubbed the back of her neck. "I don't know. Maybe you have a girl you want to impress."

"With that old junk?" he asked incredulously.

Amber gave him a hard look. "Some girls like class."

He laughed and shook his head.

Sitka and Gizmo should have figured out which piece of furniture was the mattress and spring box by now. She just hoped that he had not had time to stuff the brooches too far back. She was taking a big chance in guessing he had put them in a pouch or bag or something like that. After all, it was what she had used in the 'game' with the ferrets.

First she had hidden their toy in a small bag to get them used to the idea of finding their toy inside something. It was amusing to see how the ferrets puzzled over the bag opening, closing it and opening it with their little paws and poking their noses in. They clucked and wagged their tails and often forgot their toys in the new adventure of seeing what they could fit in the bag. Little items disappeared from around the house. Rings, earrings, beads, decorative figurines (sometimes broken to fit), and other small items would be stuffed into the bag. She would see them later, playing with the items.

Sitka liked shiny items while Gizmo liked the ones that made noise. The little female would pull rings out and look at them, sometimes even try to wear it. Gizmo was different. He would run with the pouch and then pull out his items and shake them and wait for noise. Amber sometimes got little kids' meal toys for Gizmo to play with and was not surprised when she found them in the pouch. The pouch was fast becoming their favorite item.

So, when she started taking it from their cage and putting it between the mattress and box spring, she just waited to see when they would figure out where it was hidden.

"You women make no sense," her half-brother was saying. "Putting so much in little trinkets like that."

She sighed and took another drink of her bottled water. "I don't expect you to understand. Most things are just for you to sell."

He glared at her. "You buy and sell things. That is what they are for."

"Not all things."

"Women," he muttered sullenly.

"Barry," she said softly, trying one last time to reason with him. "They mean a lot to me. They are all I have left of Gran. Please, just..."

"For the last time," he said tersely, "I don't have them!"

The siblings glared at each other.

In her mind, she was seeing the shock on his face when he checked his safe spot and discovered they were gone.

Dook

Once the ferrets had figured out that their pouch was in between the mattress and the box spring each time it disappeared during the game 'find the pouch', they would always make a bee-line for the bedroom and search the bed. They would stand on their hind legs and push their forearms between the creases, like little kids. They would also use their noses. At first they would search the same side of the bed, and then fight over it when they found it. More than once she had to break up a wrestling match where they began barking and getting a little too rough. She managed to find a way to distract one or the other, but eventually they managed to find a solution themselves.

Sitka and Gizmo learned she never hid the pouch in the same place, so they began to split up and search different areas of the bed. Whichever one of them found the pouch would dook, a ferret form of laughter, loudly and dance for joy before running off with their prize. Since stealth was part of her plan, she had to break their habit by waiting until the ferrets no longer gloated over their find before moving on to name the game 'find the pouch'.

Now whenever the pouch disappeared and she said 'find the pouch', they went to a nearby bed to look. She had tried it at a friend's house, amusing them with the show. She had even tried it at her Dad's house. Each time when she said 'find the pouch', the ferrets would run until they found a bedroom and then search the mattress.

So if they had not found the pouch yet, the little minions were most likely on either side of Barry's bed, up on their hind legs, pushing into the folds between the mattress and the box spring—looking for the coveted pouch. Amber was glad she would not have to worry about any dooking, though she would not be surprised if whichever one found it decided to dance in front of the other to gloat. Just for a bit. She only prayed there was no gloating bark from the winner.

"Is that all you are here about," he asked icily.

"Mostly," she admitted. "Though it never hurts to check on you and see how you are doing. We are siblings."

He grumbled. "Only because my mother married your father."

"That is usually how it happens."

If looks could kill, she would be really hurt.

There was a darting motion around the corner. Thinking she knew what it meant, Amber stood and placed the water in her bag. "Alright, if you won't be reasonable I guess there is nothing more I can say."

He snorted.

"Give me a minute and I'll be gone," and with that she returned to the bathroom.

Her timing was perfect.

As she walked in, she saw the ferrets beginning to

wrestle over a pouch. She turned on the fan, just to be sure Barry could not hear her. Closing the door, she knelt down while reaching into her bag. By the time she crouched down, Gizmo had gotten the pouch from Sitka. He celebrated his victory by dancing. He stood up, tail upright, and waved his upper half back and forth while hopping up and down. He opened his mouth to start dooking, but Amber beat him to it. Pulling out some treats, she distracted them with the nibbles and took the pouch. Seeing Sitka take the treats first, Gizmo dropped the bag and rushed forward for his share. She readily handed it over. The ferrets began to chew happily.

Opening the pouch, she could see the brooches inside. Taking time to empty the contents onto her hand, her eyes welled up as the precious jeweled pins spilled onto her palms. They were all there, thank goodness. Putting them back in the pouch, she quickly put it in the handbag.

Seeing where their new toy disappeared to, the ferrets needed no encouragement to crawl back into the bag. After everyone was secure, she straightened, washed her hands, and opened the door. It was no surprise to her that Barry had not moved from his spot.

Will not even get up to see me off. She bristled.

"Goodbye," she said.

He just lazily waved a hand.

Sparing him a scathing look, she turned and stormed

out the door. It was what he expected, so she had to act the part. She did not turn around when she got to her car, just got in the car and drove off.

Amber waited until she was out of the neighborhood and turned into the first safe place she could. She opened the handbag and put her ferrets back in the cage in the back seat. They happily drank from their water bottles and began playing with the toys and mini-wheel in there. After a while, she could hear them dooking. Sure that they were sufficiently amused, she turned again to her bag and pulled out the pouch.

She clutched it for a moment, still not believing she finally had them. Opening the pouch, she gingerly took out each brooch again. Gram's voice filled her mind as she recalled the tales behind each one. She relived the cherished memory of her grandmother telling her those stories as she touched their multi-faceted surfaces.

Swallowing thickly, she reluctantly put them back in the pouch, put the pouch in her lap, and merged back onto the road.

It was a long drive back to Memphis.

BROTHERS
BY ESSEL PRATT

Pausing before a rusty, yet ornate, wrought iron gateway, an aged wolf named Jakel reminisces as he stares at the once beautiful symbols adorning the scrollwork. A rough breeze rocks the unfastened entry as it screeches upon non-oiled hinges. Each squall uplifts loose dust from the forgotten entrance, exciting the specks as they travel along the windy waves. Decaying leaves retreat to dark corners, revealing an unkempt path into the hushed cemetery. The aged wolf sighs deeply as he strains to stand upon his tired legs, his old bones crackling as he does so, before entering the forgotten graveyard.

Many memories dwell inside, good and bad. Out of respect, he bows his head while passing through the entryway. Embarrassed of his appearance, he tries to remember the glory days when his fur wasn't matted and his vigor was rivaled only by the most courageous hero.

Within the gates, overgrown brush and disobedient weeds conquer the once pristine necropolis. Ground level markers are all but lost within the underbrush and most of the aged headstones have deteriorated under the onslaught of harsh weather and layers of moss. A once magnificent mausoleum now hides in disgrace behind crumbling stone and invasive cat's claw vines.

This is the resting place of heroes. All gave their lives in battle. Some did so with a goal to conquer an evil force, yet others wandered here by chance. Whether intended or not, everyone that slumbers here has perished while battling an evil being and has died with a heroes honor.

As the lone wolf traverses the unkempt pathways he lowers his head in respect for all the good men, as well as the few women and children, that adorn the soil of this sacred land. Tufts of his matted fur catch on the thorny bushes lining the path, scratching at the dry skin underneath. Drips of blood escape his lacerations, dropping to the ground in honor of the fallen. He pays no mind to the wounds as he keeps his pace.

Somewhere, amidst the bramble, his beloved master rests at peace in the shadow of a beautifully sculpted headstone. Once a breathtaking bronze, an emerald patina now adorns the towering obelisk. The tip can be seen protruding beyond the formerly flowering mound at the center of the graveyard. Keeping it in sight, Jakel continues his pace onward.

Each step sends pain shooting through him as he remembers back to the time his muscles were agile, and his bones were strong. He thinks back to when his master, no... best friend, Manfred, and he traveled the lands searching out evil and hate. Their bond was strong enough to consider each other as brothers, and they had pledged an oath to one another with a vow to overcome evil and restore the land to peace and prosperity.

Jakel's thoughts drift to the days they battled alongside one another. Together, they were a force to be reckoned with. Kingdoms were liberated from trolls and witches, towns were rid of soul stealing vampires, and forests were weeded of nefarious fairies and sprites. No evil was too frightening, and no adversary was out of reach. They fought it all, no matter the cost as long as the world became a better place.

As he approaches Manfred's grave, his mind traces his body, recalling the story behind each scar. Most had happy endings, some were the result of goofing around, and even more were the result of fierce battles while having fun at the enemies' expense. But one, a missing portion from his ear, is the most memorable of them all. That long ago healed wound reminds him of the day the apocalypse ended and the magic died.

The day he lost his best friend and brother.

* * *

Blue and pink clouds intertwined amongst the still night sky. From time to time, a sliver of the moon's light darted through the thick canopy as if to announce its presence. Despite the overcast, their surroundings radiated an eerie glow.

Their Journey led them from a less than traveled path within a healthy forest out to a dusty trail, lined with decaying cars and a multitude of discarded electronic devices. Not since the days before the great apocalypse have so many machines been gathered in one place.

The collection possessed their attention as they grabbed items that were unfamiliar to them, guessing as to their past purpose. Manfred found an old keyboard mouse and pretended to slay a beast with its whipping cord. Jakel laughed as the tip cracked in the midst of the stagnant air. In uncertain times as these, where maleficent beings thrived on magic and the weak, laughing kept their insanity at manageable levels.

They could not help but to laugh at humanity's dependence on these fragile machines and how one massive explosion destroyed all that their ancestors had tried to accomplish with them. They pondered how the humans coped once the dust had settled, as the land renewed itself over time, ushering forth a new age as the devolution caused by these rotting machines was finally unhindered. How they managed to adjust as magic returned to, and gained control of, the land as the people healed, forcing them to rely less on their mechanical crutches. Most of all they wondered about the interaction between man and beast, as they became vocal equals in the world, and how they learned to rely on one another as something other than just pet and master.

Throughout the discussion, they continued down the decrepit path unaware of their destination. Their loud voices and guffawing laughs echoed amongst the silence of the landfill. It wasn't until a sudden drop in temperature bit at their skin that they became much more aware of their surroundings.

They had reached the end of the trail. Before them spanned a field of gray grasses dotted with a few large boulders. The concentration of magic within this area was astronomical. They could feel the power surge through their pores as though a million beating drums silently pounded simultaneously all around them. It was uncomfortable, yet mesmerizing.

Jakel cautioned Manfred to take it slow. His sensitive nose smelled an evil that they had not yet faced, and he worried that his human brother would carelessly jump into action. The time for play was over.

Their feet crushed the dying grasses underneath each step, crunching sounds echoed around them. Each stride took them deeper into the coldness. Jakel kept close to Manfred using his fur to warm his friend's flesh.

About 200 paces in, the cold dispersed. The pair stopped and surveyed their surroundings. Set into the ground upon a small heap before them was a circular stone embellished with what appeared to be a cryptic seal. The drumming pulsations around them seemed to originate from within. Jakel placed his left paw upon the stone. Searing pain bit through his flesh as the cold frostbit his exposed pad. He let out a yelp and then licked his paw until it had warmed. While doing so, he looked up at Manfred and noticed fear in his eyes. Jakel had never seen such an expression garnish his usually carefree face.

Both warriors took a few steps away from the seal, fearing the evil inside would draw them inward. As they retreated, an aqua blue light radiated from the spot. Within the glow, the figure of an old man materialized. He stood there, staring at the heroes without moving a single muscle, as though frozen in place. His body sourced the entirety of magic in this substantial area around them. Their bodies shivered, not from the cold, but fear.

With caution, they retreated behind a nearby boulder

to monitor the demonic wizard before them. As they moved, his eyes followed. Manfred looked down at Jakel and stroked his silky fur as though to tell him it would be okay. Jakel looked up at Manfred and whispered, "This is it."

Both of their hearts pounded as they waited for the magician to make the first move.

As he stood there, the magician's aura rapidly radiated with various shades of iridescent blue waves. Their motions becoming more chaotic as every moment passed, eventually the aura consumed him within their pulsating swarms. A slight buzzing sound could be heard just before the aura exploded through the field, obliterating the grasses and crumbling the boulders.

Covered in rock dust, Jakel and Manfred were protected from the blast by the boulder they hid behind. With their unobstructed view, the wizard was in plain site before them. They had no plan of attack and nowhere to go. Manfred looked down at his wolf breed brother, grasping his sheathed blade by the hilt. He darted towards their nemesis. Attempting to delay his friend's approach, Jakel bit at his pant leg, tearing a hole in the fabric.

He watched as Manfred lunged, only to be stopped in his tracks by an invisible wall. The impact knocked him hard to the ground, immobilizing him. Before Jakel could jump into action, the wizard spoke, "You dare attempt to challenge me, Asatru?"

He waved his hands in a figure eight pattern, sending Manfred soaring through the air and slamming backwards into Jakel.

Both had heard the name Asatru in their travels. He was the Lord of Magic. All magic in the land originated from his existence as a result of its slow seepage from his crypt. Jakel's paw on the stone must have disrupted the frozen seal, releasing him from the tomb. They had no choice but to defeat him. This is what they had journeyed for all their lives.

Before lunging head first into the fire, Manfred waited patiently for Asatru to make the next move. Jakel stood by his side, ready to cover him when needed. Both feared their death, but feared the darkness that would overcome the world if they failed even more.

The pair, unsure of their adversary's strength, waited for him to react. Asatru peered at the heroes, annoyed at their presence and decided to end the confrontation quickly. He raised his arms high above his head. Blue bolts of energy jumped from his elongated fingers, concentrating in the empty space between. It took a few moments for the power to focus into an intense ball of power. The light within flickered just before the magician threw it towards the heroes. Instinctively they jumped away from the blast.

Each lay opposite the impact, and jumped quickly to

their feet. A quick glance let the other know that they were okay. The sheer power he had summoned enlightened them to the severity of the situation. They knew that they would need to act fast if they were to have a chance. Both focused their attention back on the evil before them.

Jakel jumped to action before Asatru could summon another blast. He ran full speed and lunged at the wizard, causing him to stumble backwards in an attempt to regain his footing. Manfred was close behind. His blade stuck in the sheath, so he also lunged at Asatru, this time knocking him to the ground.

With the wizard lying helpless, the heroes reacted quickly. Manfred finally unsheathed his sword and pounced upon Asatru's chest. He raised his blade high into the air, expecting to plunge it deep into his heart. The magician reacted by raising his arm to summon another blast upon Manfred. Jakel plunged his teeth deep into Asatru's flesh, causing the focusing energy to explode outward.

Both heroes were thrust away from Asatru as the force of the blast dispersed into the air, unfocused. Their bodies rolled atop the ground until they came to rest. Dazed, they struggled to regain their footing. As their composure returned, Asatru once again summoned another concentrated ball of energy above his head. With nowhere to hide, and exhaustion creeping up on them, they had to act fast.

Knowing it would take a few moments for the power to reach its full potential, Manfred jumped into action. He sprinted forward, sword drawn, and lunged at the magician once again. His blade sliced deep into Asatru's right arm, spilling frigid blue blood from his veins. The electrical summon nullified as Asatru grabbed at his injured arm. Blood poured from the gash, as it splashed to the ground and formed an icy puddle. As the ice enveloped them, Manfred felt the chill infiltrate his shoes and slowly consume his flesh from his toes upward.

Jakel was quick to aid his friend. He ran to Manfred's side, back feet propelling him through the air, aiming to knock his brother free from the wizard's grip. Mid-jump, Asatru grabbed Jakel by the ear. Without loosening his grip he flung Jakel to the side. The force was so strong, and the grip so tight, that a large chunk of his ear remained in the wizard's hand. A loud yelp escaped Jakel's lips as his ribcage shattered upon impact.

Manfred heard the pain escape his friend and did the only thing he could. With the ice quickly solidifying his body, he used his still malleable arm and plunged his sword deep into Asatru's heart. The impact erupted into a flash freeze that consumed them both. Jakel could only watch as his lifelong friend became one with the evil wizard atop the mound that once held Asatru within his crypt.

BROTHERS

His body battered and broken, he stood despite the pain. The stabbing sting of his ribs forced him to approach the mound slowly. He noticed a drastic change in temperature as the once horrifying clouds dispersed and allowed the fresh morning sun's rays to spread warmth over the land. The fresh heat was quickly melting the icy prison that held the two together. As it did so, Asatru's body was returning to its pure magical form, swirling beautifully above their heads as his black heart fell to the ground and quickly decayed into dust. Manfred's icy flesh also melted, leaving only his stripped bones to fall into a pile at the bottom of the mound.

As he approached the mound, Jakel smelled the beautiful aroma of flowers. He clawed his way to the top and found that the melting ice had ushered forth a bed of daffodils where the seal once stood guard.

Atop the mound, he stared down at Manfred's skeletal remains. Tears gathered in the corners of his eyes. Although victorious, the loss of his friend was crushing. He could think of nothing else but to give Manfred a proper burial. He surveyed the area and noticed a spot on which the sun's rays shined extra bright. It would be a perfect resting place, he thought.

His tattered body hindered the process of digging the hole where his friend's body would remain at rest for all eternity, nevertheless he remained persistent. It took a couple of days until he was satisfied with the depth. Each day, the swirling magical swarm above him seemed to dim just a little.

Once the hole was adequate, Jakel grabbed Manfred's bones within his jaws and one by one dropped them into the grave. His heart felt like it was ripped apart with each fragment he moved. He left the skull for last, rolling it with his nose to its final resting place. As it balanced, shaking on the edge before joining the rest of the body, Jakel pursed his wolf lips and gently placed a kiss on Manfred's skull. Tears spilled from his eyes the entire time he replaced the dirt back into the hole.

With the grave filled, and no more tears left to cry, Jakel rested on top of the fresh burial plot. Exhausted he closed his eyes and slept for three days straight.

While sleeping, he dreamed that the magical aura above burst into action. A small form broke off from the mass and shot directly into the head portion of Manfred's plot. From the ground, a magnificent obelisk grave marker emerged. Engraved upon its base was the story of how Manfred and his wolf companion saved the world from the evil incarnation of magic.

With Manfred's grave properly marked, a large mass of the magic shot into the surrounding soil, where many more warriors had fallen while attempting to overcome the demonic magical being's advances. Their markers may not have been as fantastic as Manfred's, but each told the story of the warrior resting beneath. When only a sliver of magic danced above him, Jakel woke from his slumber.

His eyes still foggy with sleep, Jakel looked around at the new monuments that had erected during his slumber. The marker towering above put his mind at peace. He knew his friend was resting serenely amongst the other warriors that surrounded him. Jakel was proud of his brother for the sacrifice he had so selfishly offered, but still heartbroken that he had lost his only friend.

He heard a rumbling and jumped to his feet. Forgetting about the broken ribs he forced back a yelp as he cringed in pain. The remaining magic worked itself into frenzy. A single droplet of the iridescent aura fell from the sky onto his face. Warmth rushed through his body as the aching ceased, and his wounds healed. He bowed his head to the power that bestowed health upon him, just as the remaining aura gathered upon an empty plot of earth.

From that spot, a magnificent mausoleum manifested from the soil. Carved into the plaque above the doorway were the words, "To the souls forgotten and lost in battle".

With the erection of the bodiless crypt, the magic had vanished. Not just the magic within this beautiful cemetery, but all magic in the world.

Feeling empty, Jakel kneeled on his front paws to whisper, "I love you brother", but no words escaped, only a soft howl.

The magic had also left his body. Without speech, he would not be able to share his tale with the world; instead, he was just simple wolf without a master. Not knowing what was left for him, he walked towards the ornate wrought iron entry in search of his next mission. As he did so, a splinter of Manfred's sword shined in the sunlight. He picked it up with his teeth, where he carried it against his gums in memory of his best friend.

* * *

Many years have passed since he has been here. Although the marker has tarnished and the unkempt land has overgrown, it still feels like only yesterday he fought here by his human brother's side. The pain in his heart never fully resided, yet being here now makes it less raw.

For a long time he has wandered aimlessly, searching the world for even the slightest hint of magic in hopes of destroying it, so others will not have to suffer the same fate as his brother. His travels have taken him to distant lands where he had found only sleight of hand and optical illusions. Despite the unmapped courses, somehow his journeys have brought him back here.

BROTHERS

And he couldn't be happier to be reunited.

Slowly he wipes the leaves and debris from atop the grave, revealing the compacted dirt floor below. The grass had long ago died off. Poking from the dirt, he notices a sparkle. Digging a shallow hole with his paws, he finds another sliver of Manfred's sword. Reuniting it with the first shard that he has carried around for so long, he places it into his mouth. Hoping to find more, he digs deeper into the earth until fatigue overwhelms him. The hole is now rather deep. Being this close to Manfred comforts him, so he closes his eyes and twists his body into a comfortable position. His wounds have stopped bleeding, and his muscles are relaxed. The pain he had felt has diminished to nothingness as his last breath exhales from his lungs.

* * *

From within the mausoleum a tiny spec of light floats towards his body. It circles a few times and whips up a brisk wind. The last remaining speck of magic ascends into his body, softening his matted fur back to its youthful appearance. For a moment his body radiates as it did in his prime, while the winds push the loose dirt back into the hole and bury him with his brother. Finally reunited, both brothers can rest in peace.

EZRA'S GIRL
BY LISA HAWKRIDGE

The mid-morning sun is beating down on the deck, and the day is warm. There's enough of a breeze to push the ship along, but unless Captain Hamreth makes Nimra set her wind spell on the sails, you aren't getting anywhere in a hurry. This suits you just fine, because you've got a sunny spot to bask in, and since your semi-beloved human companion Elena had last watch last night, she's sleeping, and you don't need to be coiled around her neck. She's a good source of heat, but on a day like today, the sun is nicer.

You watch disinterestedly as the crew members hurry about, trying not to be stuck doing nothing. There are ten warm bodies on the deck, eight humans, one with the tell-tale wings of a winged-man, or winged-woman if you want to be specific, because you know it to be Leila, given that her two brothers stood watch with Elena last night, and Casivic, a small fuzzy pain-in-the-ass you've been ordered not to kill, because she's the companion of one of the crew-members. You can hear the rats scurrying under the deck, as always, but you just ate one and are full for now. Other than the slight tinges that always surround Nimra and Timor, there aren't any magical signatures. In short, it's business as usual.

Things change when seven-fingered Sven, who's perched on the top-mast of the main sail on look-out, calls down, "There's a ship coming!"

You stick your head up, and everybody around you tenses, and you see the magic build around Nimra's hands as she gets ready, in case it's an empire ship and you have to flee at a moment's notice. Calvin, who's in charge if the Captain's not on deck, calls up to Sven, "Well?"

"Hang on a second," Sven calls back. "I'm trying to see."

There is a very tense pause as everyone waits with baited breath. Korik pulls her knife. Hared, Nimra's younger son, clings to the back of her legs. Finally, Sven calls down, "It's a Ghisic ex-Navy. We're good."

Everyone lets out a sigh of relief. Nimra lets out a puff of air to release the magic she'd generated, Hared let's go of her legs, and Korik puts her knife away. You settle back down and don't bother going to wake Elena up, instead letting the sun keep you warm, and going back to watching the crew with half lidded eyes. Casavic tries to ruin your peace by coming over and chirping at you. You hiss at her and she bats you with her front paws. Since you have no paws to bat her back, you smack her with your tail. What might have turned into a fight gets interrupted when Casavic's master gives her a whistle, and she trots off with an important air and you go back to your basking.

A few hours later, the Ghisic ex-Navy ship comes into view of those on the main deck, and everybody flocks over to the starboard railing to stare at it. You slither your way over and climb up onto the railing to get a glimpse of it because you can't see over the heads of all the humans. You were sure you were just going to dismiss it after one look, just to be on the safe side. Instead, what you see makes you stare. The entire hull of the other ship is glowing and pulsating with magic, which is far from normal. You're the only one who can see it, but Nimra can sense it, as all the gifted can; you can tell by the way she frowns and stares. You decide that the best course of action is to go and wake Elena up, and you slither down to the deck, back past all the humans, and make your way over to the stairs that lead below decks.

The stairs are always hard on your body, because you have to drop down onto each one from the one above, but you thump your way down. The main crew cabin where Elena has her hammock it just past the bottom, with a door on the right side. Elena's hammock is the middle hammock on the right side of the room, and she's sprawled out across it, one leg dangling over the edge. You see that as your chance and raise your head and upper body up so you can coil around her ankle and pull your tail up after you.

She feels your presence, but isn't quite awake yet, and she swings her leg back up onto the hammock, and you cling tightly to keep yourself from falling off. When her legs stop moving, you uncoil yourself and slither up her body to her chest, then lean forward and hiss quietly in her ear. She reaches up, still half-asleep and goes to shove you away. You rear up and slam your jaw down on her hand, and she sits up, causing you to slide down into her lap. She rubs her hand and yawns. "Alright, I'm up. What's going on?"

Sometimes you wish you could speak a human language or two, so that you could explain things to Elena, and you wouldn't have to resort to a combination of emphatic gestures and nodding and shaking your head, which was the second thing you learned when you moved in with Elena. Since that's just wishful thinking, you coil around her neck and reach your head and your upper body out. Then you tighten around her, not so much that she chokes, but enough that she can feel it, and pull your head in the direction on the door.

She's silent for a moment, and you try to be patient because you know she'll get it eventually. She always does.

When she finally says, "Something's happening up on deck, isn't it?", you nod your head. She yawns and says, "Alright, let's go."

You drape yourself around her neck, because there's no sun down here, and she is very warm, which is part of the reason you didn't just slither away when you met her.

You have to give the woman credit for being smart. As soon as she gets up on deck, she notices Calvin staring out at the Ghisic ship and makes her way over to him to ask what's up, because he rarely just gazes out at the sea, that being the Captain's department. She stands next to him, looks out, sees what he's looking at and asks, "What's the deal with that ship?"

You make your way down her neck and wrap yourself around her wrist, since there's no reason to be around her neck for warmth when the sun is beating down, and communicating is easier when you're down here because you can be more fully in each other's lines-of-sight. Calvin looks at you for a minute then says, "Good morning to you, too. The ship is Ghisic Ex-navy. Sven spotted it almost three hours ago. We're almost near enough to talk to them."

Elena purses her lips. "Is there anything special about this particular ship?"

Calvin looks at her and raises one eyebrow, "Other than the fact that it's a Ghisic ship?"

Although most ships you attack eventually, one way or another, Ghisic ships you never attack, because of solidarity and water purifiers.

Elena sighs. "Never mind." She turns around and makes her way over to the main mast, then settles down on the deck, her back against the mast, and holds her arm with you still wrapped around it out in front of her, so you two can face each other. She looks at you. "Alright, so Calvin thinks the ship is just a ship. Is that true?"

You shake your head. Elena bites her lip. "Alright, what's the deal with the ship?"

You jerk your head toward Nimra who is fixing an extra sail because Timor is below deck, using his gift of healing to patch up Korik, creating a magical signature you can see from up here though you know Elena can't. Nimra is the closest magic user. Elena glances in that direction, then looks back at you and asks, "Is it the ship Nimra was born on?"

You shake your head again, and she glances back at Nimra. "It doesn't have anything to do with Nimra specifically, does it?" She looks back at you.

You shake your head again, confident that's she's almost got it. "Someone on the other ship is using a Gift, aren't they?"

You nod your head, because that's all humans understand of magic, and it's true anyway. Elena smiles.

"Alright, I finally got it."

You twist yourself around, and make your way onto her hand, then start twisting your way down until you're dangling from her finger by just the tip of your tail. She gets the idea and lowers her arm down so you can get onto the ground and find your sunny spot again. You settle in, and she sits down next to you and yawns. Just then a yell comes from the other side of the deck, "We've got a hole!"

Calvin turns to the two of you and says, "Since you're up, make yourself useful and get the patch kit."

Elena stands up and glares down at you, then looks up at the first mate and says, "Yes, sir." She holds out her hand to you, and you move away, just an inch, because you have no intention of being involved in the slapdash repair efforts. She rolls her eyes and says, "Fine, be that way. I'll come get you when the Ghisic ship gets to ours."

True to her word, no sooner do you hear the thump of a gangplank being thrown over then secured between the two ships than Elena scoops you up and slings you over her shoulders, where you squirm your way under her shirt to be right up against her improbably warm skin. She makes her way over to the gangplank where the entire crew, including Arden and Hymore, who have finally woken up, and the Captain, making one of his rare appearances on deck, is gathered. You poke your head out from Elena's shirt to get a good view of the proceedings.

There are three people standing by the edge of the gangplank on the deck of the other ship: The captain, still wearing an old war uniform, an older man, who is probably his first mate, and a young woman, who is radiating a gifted signature. After the captains exchange the traditional greetings, the Captain of the Ghisic ship climbs up onto the gangplank. Making the crossing between two ships is a dangerous venture even on a balmy day like today, but the Ghisic captain is calm and collected and makes keeping his balance look effortless.

Captain Hamreth steps forward and says, "Welcome aboard Vvylantif ViStestnesh, I am Captain Hamreth. Would you like to refresh yourself first, or will we get straight to business?"

The Ghisic Captain glances back at his first mate then says, "I think we can get right to business. I am Captain Yorick. You want water, yes?"

Captain Hamreth nods. "We would like to top off our supplies, yes." He always says that, whenever you encounter a Ghisic ex-navy ship. Water is life and everyone knows it, and the Ghisic ships can literally create drinkable water from the illness inducing lake water. "We have some very nice melons we took from an Empire ship a while back…"

Captain Yorick holds up his hand and Captain Hamreth

trails off. The Ghisic captain glances back at his own ship. "It is not unheard of for ships to trade crew members, provided the peoples in question agree, no?"

Captain Hamreth glances around at his assembled crew, took a deep breath in and said, "It is not unheard of. What kind of person do you need?"

The other captain purses his lips and says, "I would talk to you alone."

Captain Hamreth shakes his head. "I won't make back room deals with my crew's lives."

The Captain Yorick nods. "Very well. I have found... something," he glances back at his own ship, "that will help the war effort very much, and we need someone to smuggle h—it across the border and the troops there. Someone who grew up in the empire and knows its ways, but is not a wanted criminal there. Is there any such member of your crew?"

Captain Hamreth, as is his habit, begins to think out loud. "Let's see, Leila is technically an escaped slave, although she was too young to remember escaping. Arden and Haymore have never been to the empire, for good reason. Calvin I need aboard, and his face is still on wanted posters in a few small towns anyway. Nimra is Ghisic, came aboard in a deal much like this one, as are Hared and Aaron, who've probably never set foot on land in their lives. Sven has a rap sheet as long as my arm. Korik has murdered a few people, and Timor's been pinched for stealing, and they're both Tanicef ViRraez like me, so they'd be considered outsiders on land. That leaves… Elena."

The other captain says, "Very well. If Elena comes aboard my ship, and takes this mission on, you will not only have all your water barrels filled but have five more on top. I will start bringing it over when she is aboard my ship."

Captain Hamreth bites his lip and looks at Elena. She swallows then steps forward and says, "I'll go." Then, she spins around and everybody stares at her as she raises her arm and holds out her hand to you. When you've wrapped yourself around her wrist, she brings her arm up so that the two of you are face to face and asks, "Well, will you come with me?"

You nod and start twisting up her arm, and she raises her arm to her neck so you can reach out and wrap yourself around it. The she lowers her arm to her side and heads to the gangplank. You shift your weight as she climbs up so it's centered and won't throw off her balance.

Just as Elena's about to start her crossing, Leila calls out, "Wait, what about your stuff?"

You're pretty sure Elena fell asleep with her Canteen and her flask on her person last night, and given that she never takes off her money pouch or her bracelet, you wonder just what Leila thinks Elena has back in the sleeping quarters that's so important.

Elena shrugs. "There's nothing important I don't have on me right now. Keep it safe for me, or cut wing wholes and wear my clothes for yourself. I'll see how they look when I get back." She hesitates for a moment then asks Captain Yorick, "When whatever it is is across the border, can I come back to the Vvylanif?"

Captain Yorik shrugged. "We run into them again, I will not stop you."

You know that the chances of that are slim to none; you still haven't run into the ship Nimra was on in the half a year she's been aboard, but Elena smiles and says, "Well, I'll see you all when the wind blows us back together."

Korik snorts. "Yeah, if you don't get stabbed by the soldiers at the border."

Timor frowns and puts his hand on Korik's shoulder. "Don't say that."

Elena just forces a smile. "I'll be fine."

And with that, she sets out across the gangplank slowly, one foot in front of the other. Captain Yorik gives some kind of signal to his first mate on the other ship, who sets off, then says something to the assembled crew, which you can't quite hear because you're already three quarters of the way across the gangplank. He starts after you, and a minute later, Elena hops down onto the deck of the Ghisic ship.

The young gifted woman, who has been watching the whole exchange on the other side, looks down at the ground and says, "Are you the one who's going to get me safely to Ghis?"

Elena looks at the woman, cocks her head to one side, frowns, and says, "Wait, I have to smuggle you across the border?"

Just then the Captain of this ship hops off the gangplank and lands neatly on the deck. "I would have told you before, but I didn't want the whole crew knowing."

The young woman turns, blushes, and says, "My name is Bernadine."

Captain Yorick claps her on the shoulder and says, "Bernadine will be the salvation of the Ghisic cause."

You think that sounds a little far-fetched, but you aren't one to talk about the war, because you didn't know it existed until Elena's brother Nathan joined the army and the family argued about it for days. Elena opens her mouth, like maybe she's going to say something, but before she can, the first mate comes back, leading ten crew members who are carrying five barrels of water between them. He says something to the captain in Ghisic, and the captain responds in kind, then turns to Bernadine and switches back to your language. "Take our new crewmate down and find her a bunk yes?"

Bernadine reaches out and takes Elena's hand and pulls her toward the center of the deck. You poke your head out from under Elena's shirt to get a better look at things. There are at least four gifted people aboard this ship, Bernadine having the strongest signature by far, and you can see that there are at least two or three dozen warm bodies, none of them winged-men, but some of them children. Bernadine turns around, and she lets out a high pitched scream, and you and Elena both start looking frantically, trying to see what had frightened her so much. Finally, she manages to squeak out, "Ee...Eeshka" which from sitting in on Elena's lessons with Nimra, means snake, and you duck back into Elena's shirt when you realize she's screaming at you.

Elena realizes it a split second later, and says, in her best attempt at Ghisic, "He's Harmless." She grabs your head, and you let her pull you out into the light. Bernadine swallows nervously but reaches out and lays a hand on your head. It's actually uncomfortable, but you know she's skittish, so you don't move. Elena smiles. "See?"

Bernadine takes her hand off your head and tells Elena, "Your accent was terrible."

The corner of Elena's mouth twitches up, and she says, "Why don't you help me?"

Over the next few days, Elena spends her time sitting with Bernadine in the latter's cabin, practicing her Ghisic, and coaching Bernadine on speaking your language. You catch rats in the hold and try to sunbathe on deck, but the crew doesn't like you. When one of them throws a knife at you, you hastily retreat below deck and spend the rest of the time firmly attached to Elena. The two of you end up meeting Horatio, Bernadine's brother, who is over protective of her, because he raised her since her parents died when she was two. You end up getting much better at understanding Ghisic, and find that the crew is insulting you and Elena behind your backs, which you don't begrudge them.

Elena, Bernadine, and you, hiding up Elena's skirt, are dropped somewhere on the coast in a small inlet almost directly between the Arad and Drestim rivers, fed by an offshoot of the Arad. Captain Yorick puts her hand on Elena's shoulder and asks, "How long will this take?"

Elena shrugs. "Just about a week, tops."

The Captain nods. "I will come back for you in ten days time, here at this place. Have her safely across the border, and be back, or else."

Horatio doesn't say anything, but from the way Elena's shaking, you can tell he's getting his point across. The two of them turn tails and head back to the ship. You slither up Elena's leg and then between her legs and up her torso, which is always awkward, then poke your head out her neck line. It is very dark, although that doesn't pose a problem for you, and you recognize the inlet that you set sail from last time you were on land.

Elena is coming to the same conclusion and has bent down to examine the stream. She stands up and says, "Alright, let's head for Final Gate. It's this way."

Bernadine follows and says, "Wait, hold on. We're leaving now?"

Elena nods. "Yeah, if we hurry, we can make it to the city before daybreak. From there, we can find a smuggler." She pauses for a moment and looks at you. "This is the same place where we got on the Vvylanif?"

You nod once.

"Why can't we have light?" Bernadine whines, and you hear Elena sigh.

"It's not like we have a lantern. Besides, I know where I'm going." You really hope she does, although she seems to be on the right track because you recognize this semi-forgotten trail as well. You can feel Elena's heart pounding, and can hear Bernadine whimpering ever-so-slightly. You want to tell them that it's okay, and that all the heat signatures you can see are stationary.

They tramp along in relative silence for a while, with neither of them saying anything. Finally Bernadine says, "Where are we going again?"

You're sure Elena rolls her eyes. "I told you we're going

to the empire city of Final Gate. We can head out for the border from there. There are people, like my b…well there are people who know how to get across the border without getting caught."

Bernadine frowns. "What do they do if they catch you?"

Bernadine stops, listens for a moment, then says, "Well, they'll either perform perversions with our corpus, or maybe just kill us, depending on their mood."

Bernadine doesn't say anything for the whole rest of the trip.

True to Elena's words, you make it to the outskirts of the city just as the sun begins peeking over the horizon. She turns to Bernadine. "Here we are. Listen, if we meet any Enforcement Officers, let me tell them you're my mute cousin and don't speak. They'll know you're Ghisic the minute you open your mouth."

Bernadine looks hurt. "Is my accent really that bad?"

Elena shrugs. "No, but it is noticeable, and suspicious."

The outskirts of the city are mostly slums, which even at this hour are alive, as old women slip out of their homes to gossip and fetch water, while drunkards wind their way home, and children feed chickens crammed in the narrow gaps between the houses and get pecked collecting eggs. Elena and Bernadine make their way carefully along, trying not to step in the refuse lining the streets. A young man tries to pick Elena's pocket, but you snap at him and he leaves you alone, and you would laugh, if you had the vocal chords for it.

When the three of you get to the main gate, it's already open, letting people in for the market just inside the walls. Elena slings her arm around Bernadine's shoulder and says in a low voice, "Remember, mute cousin."

There's an Enforcement Officer, at the gate, and when he sees you don't have anything to sell, and have a snake in your party, he stops you and says, "Halt. State your name and purpose."

Elena smiles. "I'm Elena, and this is my cousin Amara. We came to the city to see our aunt Edna." He waves the three of you through, muttering about southerners under his breath.

The market is not quite crowded yet, as most of the people there are vendors setting up their wares. Elena pulls Bernadine along, weaving her way through the stalls, vendors and early customers. "My aunt lives just past the market plaza. Once we make it through here we can go see her, and she might just be willing to get us a little breakfast."

You've been to Elena's aunt's house before, just before you set off sailing, and when you and Elena were still living at home, she and her son Aaron would come every year for the Flood-Tide festival. You are partly looking forward to this and partly dreading it. Aunt Edna lives in one of the small stone houses just past the market square that she inherited from her late husband.

As Elena leads Bernadine up the steps to Aunt Edna's door, Bernadine frowns and says, "I thought you were supposed to be smuggling me across the border. What are we doing here?"

Elena rolls her eyes. "You can't cross on an empty stomach. Besides, the border is barely two days away, and we'll be killed if we don't take the time to find a guide first. And it just so happens that some of the best guides live here." Bernadine still doesn't look quite convinced, but Elena's already knocking at the door.

The woman who opens the door is surprisingly short and skinny, with dark brown hair and a white apron. She takes one look at Elena and throws her arms around her. "Oh I haven't seen you in forever, darling. Do come in. Oh, Ezra, you're such a cute snake, aren't you. Who's your little friend?"

Elena kisses her aunt's cheek and says, "This is Bernadine, and she needs to get back to Ghis where her brother Horatio is waiting for her. I was hoping…"

Edna releases Elena and says, "Oh you poor thing, come inside. My son Aaron and my nephew Ian are the best at getting things across the border. I'm sure they can help you.

But come have some breakfast." She turns then to lead them inside, then turns back around and pats your head saying, "And I've got a cookie for you."

You lean forward eagerly at the thought.

Bernadine cocks her head to the side and says, "Cookie?"

Elena nods, "Yep, that's Ezra's dirty little secret. He'll do practically anything for a cookie."

You would be annoyed, but she's right. Those things are good, and you haven't had one since you set sail a year and a half ago.

Bernadine frowns. "What is a cookie though?"

Elena looks at her like she's crazy. "A small sweet kind of bread-like except not as chewy…confection?"

Bernadine shrugs. "Never heard of them."

Elena sighs. "Well, my Aunt Edna makes the best baleberry cookies ever, so you're off to a good start." Elena can actually make better ones, but you can't tell her that.

You emerge from the hallway Aunt Edna's been leading you down into the kitchen where Elena's brother Ian and her cousin Aaron are sitting at the table. Ian stands up. Elena runs to hug him. While she's got her arms around him, you wind your way down her torso until you're level with the table and make your way onto it. Aaron moves his glass to clear your path as you slither across the table, and Aunt Edna holds up a cookie and you unhinge your jaw to swallow the thing. She smiles and pats you and says, "Who's a good little snake? You are, yes you are."

Which is incredibly annoying, but you put up with it.

Elena takes her place next to Ian, who sits back down. Edna pulls out a chair next to Aaron and gestures for Bernadine to sit in it before offering her a cookie. Ian looks at his sister and asks her, "So why did you leave?"

She scowls. "I left because you and Nathan left first! There was nobody left, so I set off to find people. Why did you leave?"

Ian frowns, "I couldn't look dad in the eyes, not after what happened. Besides, I went home for Flood-Tide, and you didn't."

Elena looks away. "We were stuck just past Victory Post without wind."

Bernadine finishes her cookie. "That was really good." She turns to Aunt Edna. "Thank you, ma'am."

Aunt Edna smiles. "Of course, dear. Now you should all have some real food." She brings two more plates to the table, each with sausages and a biscuit covered in Gravy. She puts her hand on Bernadine's shoulder and turns to the boys, "Now when you're done with breakfast, you're going to set off, and you're going to get this little girl back to her brother."

Aaron and Ian look at each other. It's Aaron who speaks first. "Alright. We have a load of...stuff we were going to take anyway. We'll make sure she gets there. After breakfast, of course."

His mother kisses him on the head. "Of course."

Having decided that you aren't getting anymore cookies, you slither over to Elena's plate, and she doesn't complain when you lick some of the gravy up. Real meals are something you miss about living on land. When you've had enough, you languidly wind your way up Elena's arm to settle around her neck and soak up her body heat.

Ian turns to Elena and says, "So you brought Ezra with you when you left."

Elena shook her head. "He came with me of his own free will."

You sometimes wonder why you did it, especially since her father would have been good to you, and then you wouldn't have been dragged from one end of the lake to another.

The five of you—you, Elena, Bernadine, Aaron and Ian—set out after breakfast, with a large box that they were going to bring across anyway, and a bag full of baleberry cookies from Aunt Edna. You don't get stopped at the gate. By this point the market is in full swing and there is a constant stream of people in and out. The slums are kind of seedy, but nobody bothers a group as big as five. You see the man who tried to pickpocket Elena earlier and hiss at him. He shrinks back.

Once you're beyond the city Aaron starts heading down a small forest path. Ian follows, carrying the chest, and the rest of you follow after. This seems to be some sort of queue for the humans to start talking. First was Bernadine. "Why did you lie to your aunt about me?"

Both Ian and Aaron glance back at them and frown. Elena sighs. "My aunt hates the war, or what's left of it. Her husband died in the war, defending from an attack. She only wants peace, but the Empire's not going to stop until Ghis is conquered and Ghis won't let that happen. She does her best to keep both sides out of harm's way, powerless as she is, which is why I'm guessing you didn't tell her you were smuggling weapons in that chest."

Aaron glances back at Ian and the two share a look. Finally Ian says, "Alright, you got us there. So what's the truth?"

Elena sighs. "The truth is, I was living on a pirate ship, the Vvylantif ViStestnesh, whose captain is a River Boy. But anyway, we wanted to trade with one of the ships that used to be in the Ghisic Navy, before the Empire conquered the land where Final Gate is now and cut them off from the mainland, and..."

"We still are the Ghisic Navy," Bernadine interjects, then blushes when everyone looks at her. "I only meant..."

Elena nods. "I know what you meant. Anyway, we wanted to trade with this ship —."

"Since when do pirates trade?" Ian asks.

"Would you stop interrupting me?" Elena snaps, her temperature going up a few degrees before dropping back when she takes a deep breath and lets it out. "I was getting to that. Ghisic ships have some sort of water purification system built in that makes lake water drinkable."

Aaron frowns. "They can do that?"

Bernadine nods. "Yeah, we developed the purification system before the war."

"Anyway," Elena continues, "We wanted to trade water, and Captain Yorick said he'd top off all our barrels and give us five more if I agreed to undertake the mission of getting her across the border. And I agreed. He said he'd come back to our drop point in ten days, and I can meet him there, and go back to the Vvylantif when they run into each other again."

Aaron frowns. "That seems highly unlikely."

Ian looks at her. "Why'd you do it?"

Elena sighs. "I...I did it because I owe Captain Hamreth everything, because I didn't want little Hared to have to go without water, because Nimra taught me how to speak Ghisic, because...because when you're out on the lake, you have to be able to rely on your crew, and I didn't want them to not be able to rely on me." Her heart beat goes up and her breath gets shaky. Ian seems at a loss for words.

To offer a distraction Aaron turns to Bernadine and asks her, "What's so important about getting you over the border?"

Bernadine blushes. "We'll I'm gifted, and Captain Yorick thinks my gift could be useful."

Ian purses his lips. "Show us."

Bernadine reaches down and picks up a pebble. Seeing a bird in the sky, she sends the rock toward it, by using her gift, and it's so powerful, you lean back a few inches in surprise. The bird, which was so far up it was just a spec, comes crashing to the ground, the rock having gone straight through his heart.

Ian blinks, "Impressive."

Aaron looks around. "Sure. Anyway, we're getting near the place where the patrols occasionally come, so be quiet."

You walk along silently for a few hours, until you start to see distinctly human-shaped heat signatures coming toward the trees. You nudge Elena on the jaw, until she whispers, "What is it?"

You sweep your head around, indicating the surrounding woods. It's a long shot, but you need her to get it, before it's too late. She suddenly pales and her heartbeat gets faster. "We're surrounded?"

You nod your head solemnly.

Elena carefully makes her way closer to Ian and bends forward to whisper in his ear, informing him of the situation. Bernadine sees this and quickly moves forward to talk to Aaron, probably to ask what their deal was, but you can't hear them because you are around Elena's neck. The ambush is getting closer and closer slowly, until they suddenly attack.

You see out of the corner of your eye that Aaron charges his way through the soldiers and Bernadine shoots one of them, but you have other things to worry about like the fact that one of the soldiers attacks Elena, who is unarmed. She manages to dodge his weapon and land a solid punch that sends him reeling a bit, but then there's another soldier coming at her from a different angle and without thinking you launch yourself off her neck and onto his and tighten yourself around him, cutting off his air until he passes out. You almost keep squeezing to kill him, but just before he loses consciousness, he mutters the name "Alyssa," and you suddenly wonder if this Alyssa is waiting in some small town like the one Elena grew up in, wishing he would hurry up and get home and being afraid of him dying, and suddenly you can't be the thing that takes him away from her.

You release and leave him lying on the ground. Elena has jumped on the back of a soldier, who Aaron and Bernadine have just escaped from, and judging by the way he's got his hands, she probably kneed him strategically as well. Ian is backed up against a tree, trying to fight off three soldiers with his knife. You know he's good at fighting, so you leave him to it and slither forward to trip the soldier who is trying to bash Elena against a tree—and has gotten her to take a pretty nasty stab wound from a low branch but hasn't gotten her to let go. He falls flat on his face, but by the time you wriggle out from under his legs and Elena manages to sit up, given that she's bleeding pretty badly and the adrenaline is starting to wear off, you're surrounded by a tight ring of five soldiers pointing swords at you. Elena surrenders, and one of them steps on you. Meanwhile, the three other soldiers have managed to keep hold of Ian, who is writhing and yelling. Suddenly, you can tell that something has caught Ian's eye, and you can see Aaron and Bernadine standing, semi-concealed, probably barely within human sight range. Ian looks back the way you had been coming and says, "And there they go, off to tell Aunt Edna what happened."

The leader of the unit dispatches two of the men guarding you to go look for them in that direction, while Aaron and Bernadine slip away in the other direction unnoticed. Meanwhile, Ian is set down, with a sword pressed to his throat to keep him from trying anything, and he and his sister are made to march down to where the battalion has set up camp, while one of them ties a rope around you and drags you along behind. Other soldiers not on patrol watch as your procession enters the camp, calling out to their friends in the unit that captured you, who call back. One young man just stares though, fists clenched and horrified, and when you're dragged close enough to get a good look at him, you realize with a start that the young man is Elena's older brother Nathan.

Elena is bleeding pretty badly, and the soldiers knocked Ian unconscious during their trip back after he attempted to break free, so they're both brought to the medical tent, along with the man you knocked unconscious and the man Bernadine hit, who are both carried by their comrades, and the men who were injured in the knife fight, who walk under their own power. After a brief argument, they decide to drag you in there as well, and when Ian and Elena are tied to cots in the infirmary, they tie you to the end of Elena's bed. They then search both their bodies and take all of Ian's weapons, but leave everything else they were carrying, including, to your surprise, the money in Elena's neck pouch. The area of the tent you are in is partitioned off, and you watch nervously as the doctor begins trying to patch up Elena's wound.

When the doctor leaves, Ian opens his eyes and says, "Hey, Ezra." You try to move toward him, but your ropes are too tight. "Damn, they tied you up too."

He pulls as hard as he can against his ropes, but he

makes no headway, and eventually collapses back down and sighs in frustration. Elena opens her eyes a crack and says, "Calm down. They haven't killed us yet."

The partition curtain moves and Nathan enters. "That might change. You're going to stand trial for treason. They've had a rash of smuggling recently and want to make an example out of you."

Ian looks at Nathan, "Hey, listen, I know we don't always agree—."

Nathan snorts. "That's an understatement."

Ian scowls. "Look, did you come just to gloat?"

Nathan rubs his chin and sits down on the edge of Elena's bed. "I can bust one of you out. But not the other."

Elena points at Ian and says, "Him."

Ian points at Elena and says, "Her."

They look at each other. Finally, Elena says, "Look, I'm injured. You'll have a better chance of making it."

Nathan purses his lips and says, "Much as I hate to admit it, she's right. We have to hurry." He pulls a knife and cuts Ian's wrists loose. While he's working on the feet, Ian looks at you and says, "What about Ezra?"

Nathan gets done with Ian's ropes and stands up. "I'll cut him loose, and he can follow you or stay with her as he chooses." He begins to rummage through his back and finds the baleberry cookies Aunt Enda packed. He offers one to

Nathan and hands one to you.

Suddenly you feel guilty going free while Elena is tied up and being tried for treason, but you know staying here won't do her a lick of good anyway. You make your choice before Nathan even finishes cutting your rope.

There is one last thing you can do for her though.

While Ian and Nathan look on in amazement, you slither over and gently place the cookie in her mouth. Cookies are good, but she deserves one. You leave her and drop to the floor, and make your way up Ian's leg while Nathan is pushing the two of you out, telling you to hurry before you miss your window of opportunity.

However much you may care for Elena, you are a practical snake.

LOOK WHAT THE CAT DRAGGED IN

BY S.H. RODDEY

I. Delilah

A human foot.

That little black and white menace most people called a cat was always bringing me living-impaired presents, but this one was going way too far. It was bad enough to step out the back door and find him sitting there with parts of mice or birds clutched in his little iron jaws, but this? No freaking way. The sight of it made me want to vomit.

"Miko! I can't believe you would bring that thing into the house!"

"I found it, Delilah," he said, his tail twitching in that annoying way cats have. "You know I always share my discoveries with you."

I sighed. Miko really did mean well by bringing it to me. I knew because, just like this time, he always told me.

Yes, my cat talks. No, I'm not delusional. He speaks English, Spanish, and Russian. I don't know why, but he does. To hear him tell it, all cats have a proclivity to speech. Most just choose not to exercise it because they will not condescend to speak to humans. Typical cats, I suppose.

"Really, Miko, thank you. But your sharing isn't necessary."

"I am afraid it is, Delilah. I found this in the back yard. There are other parts too. Same human." He sniffed at the foot and his furry lip turned up into a snarl. Even Miko looked a little ill. "Dead about three days by the smell of him."

"That's really gross," I said.

"I agree," he replied, annoyed. "So why don't you contact the authorities and have them remove it from my yard?"

I snorted. *His yard*... no matter that I was the one paying the mortgage and taxes on it. This particular cat was of the most annoying breed: Linguistically Capable. Whoever first said cats have staff instead of owners must have had a talker too.

"Only if you promise to just be a normal cat while they're here."

Miko lay down and licked his paws — totally disinterested

in me, the police, or the foot he'd dragged in—and laid on my clean kitchen floor. "Fine."

Ugh...annoying creature. So I once again followed his wishes—because that's obviously what feline staff does—picked up the telephone, put on my most panic-stricken voice, and dialed 911.

"911, what's your emergency?" the operator's drone suggested boredom and complete disinterest. I'd hate to see how they reacted to a real emergency. I started gulping for air.

"My...my cat just brought a foot into my house!" I broke down sobbing. Miko shook his head and turned away from me. The little snot went to sleep, as disinterested as the operator. No, I wasn't really that distraught, but I thought a little melodrama would only help get them here faster.

"Ma'am," the operator snapped, "if this is a joke—."

"A HUMAN FOOT!" I shrieked.

Silence. That did the trick. Miko's tail twitched in annoyance. He looked up at me with the feline equivalent of a scowl.

"I'll connect you. One moment," she replied blankly. Miko snorted and rested his head on his paws.

"I keep telling you humans are stupid creatures." He sighed. I laid my hand over the mouthpiece and pulled the phone away from my face.

"I am a human, and you choose to associate with me. What does that say about you, furball?" I retorted as the phone clicked to a new line. The cat muttered something unintelligible.

"Captain Grieves," the man on the other end said. "How may I help you?"

"My cat just came inside with a human foot," I replied, staring at the culprit with a sour look on my face. Again, I got silence as a response.

"Ma'am —."

"Delilah," I said.

"Delilah," he echoed, "do you know where the cat found this foot?"

"In the back yard, I think." Miko nodded once even though he appeared to be asleep. "He was only outside a few minutes when he came back with it. Last time I looked out the window, he was digging around in the flower beds near the fence." Another moment of silence, and the Captain cleared his throat. Under the buzz of the quiet line I heard his pen scratching on paper.

"What road does this yard front?" he asked as the beginning of his quiz on the specifics of my yard.

"Poplar Avenue. My back fence is about ten feet from the road and there are trees between them."

"So that puts your house on…"

Look What the Cat Dragged In

"Crabtree Drive." I gave him my address, and he said he would be there in fifteen minutes.

Like clockwork.

As I ran to answer the door, I shot a dark glance at Miko. "Remember…a normal cat," I reminded him.

He hissed in my general direction then went back to ignoring me.

On the other side of the door was a very large, very dark-skinned man. He towered over me in an impressive way — but at 5′2″ that doesn't take much. Regardless, he absolutely filled my doorway and his dark, serious eyes were frightening from my vantage point.

"Miss Cipriati?"

"Yes, sir."

"You called about *something* your cat brought in?" The way he said the word "something" made my skin want to crawl. He almost looked like he would be sick. I knew the feeling all too well.

I shuddered the thought away and nodded. "It's…in the kitchen."

I led him through the house, shooting one final look at the cat before pointing to the dirt-caked appendage. Captain Grieves took one look at it, coughed indelicately, and backed into the living room. He pulled a cell phone from his pocket and held a quick, quiet conversation with the person on the other end.

Twenty minutes later, my house was full of cops and forensic specialists. It was like *CSI: Miami* come to life—just without the witty detective and hot sidekick. I was shoved out into the front room away from the foot, the windows, and all of the hullaballoo. Two different officers questioned me relentlessly, almost like they were trying to trick me into saying I'd cut the person up and planted it back there. Through the crack in the door I spotted Miko, who still lay on the washing machine, ignoring everyone as only cats do.

In the four hours they were there the specialists found most of the body, in pieces, scattered across the fence line of my back yard under my pretty new flowerbeds. They bagged it, took my statement, scratched Miko's ears, and left.

Two days later, Captain Grieves showed up with a warrant for my arrest.

II. Miko

When the men in blue came and took my woman, I knew I was her only hope. Humans by nature are very stupid creatures, and it was obvious from the start that they simply looked to point those meaty digits they called fingers at the most convenient target.

Look What the Cat Dragged In

Delilah did not murder the man outside—of that I was certain. Her scent scarcely lingered on the roots of the flowers she had planted a week ago, but the scent in the earth was one I'd never smelled. After the bumbling humans vacated my home, I went back to the flower beds in search of the scent. Thanks to the tromping boots and lack of respect on behalf of those foolish investigators, I discovered I was left only with memory scent. So, I hopped the fence, picked up the trail of a vaguely familiar odor, and followed it as far as I could, which was not far. The smell of human machines and their horrid byproducts drowned the scent too well.

Delilah had a horrible habit of watching true crime and police shows. Some of the things of which they spoke were true—in that the murderer always returned to the scene of the crime, and there was always evidence. The only problem with that second scenario was that small-town law enforcement authorities were never very good at finding evidence. No, they're much too busy sitting in the diner stuffing their faces and gossiping to be of useful service.

I sat on the windowsill above the sink and watched the fence. It was not a hard chore—I quite enjoyed the stillness and silence. I would have appreciated Delilah's affection, but I have no intention of admitting that to her.

In the three days after they took her, I noticed a tall, red-haired human male walking by between the trees. He was the freckled kind, with an asymmetrical face and eyes that were beady and much too small for the head he possessed. Every time this man passed the fence, he stopped to contemplate the police tape as one of my kind often contemplates its dinner.

After his departure, I went to the fence and checked his scent. It matched.

With no human and no hope of helping said human from the kitchen, I followed the fresh scent across the road and over six blocks. At the end of the trail I found the human's habitat.

It was filthy. Old food containers littered the floor. Dirty clothing hung from nearly every surface, and the entire domicile stank of a dead skunk. Immediately, I knew this was the murdering human. My human was clear—almost. Another thing Delilah's shows taught me was that all humans involved had to be aware of the facts. I could easily tell them… but the blasted girl made me promise to be a "normal cat." And cats, once giving their word, never break a promise.

Stupid human.

If only she and her fellow bipedal fools knew the true capabilities of our kind they would be astounded, quite possibly to literal death. Human hearts were very fragile things, after all.

I was, in fact, a normal cat. I just chose not to hide my talents from my woman. She took care of me as only a nurturing woman could, and despite her annoying habits she loved me. I also cared for her more deeply than any cat would like to admit. Nonetheless, that "normal cat" hurdle did not stop me. I am, after all, a feline. And we felines are very resourceful.

The murdering human left a window open, and I used it to my advantage. I went inside. The smell of decaying garbage was overwhelming. It was obvious that this creature never cleaned. The smell of rot clung to everything in here.

The body was disassembled here. I could still smell the blood and bone. With such an acute olfactory sense I had no choice but to smell the dead man's bodily fluids and the acrid scent of death. I had to find something that belonged to the dead man. Identification. A license, maybe. I was in luck. The clothes still lay on the bathroom floor. And in the pocket, a wallet that smelled faintly of the dead man. I picked it up, exited unseen through the window, and went back to my home. I had to get to Delilah, but had no idea how to find her.

III. Delilah

"I already told you I don't know who the man is or where his body came from!" I rubbed my tired eyes and shifted in the hard chair. I'd already been in the interrogation room nine hours when the peon they'd sent in to play bad cop finally gave up and left. My legs were stiff and my back ached. Since I'd been in the chair, I'd been given two warm bottles of water and half a ham sandwich. I was exhausted and hungry, and I may or may not have been willing to do illegal things to get a soda. When Captain Grieves finally came in to talk to me, I was ready to curl up in the corner and cry.

"Are you hungry, Delilah?" he asked, and for the first time since being brought to this hellhole I felt like someone might actually care about my wellbeing.

"Yes. And I'm thirsty. And tired." The tears started to well up in the corners of my eyes, and I didn't care. I was too worn out to stop them. "I don't know anything, and I want to go home. I miss my cat."

"Come on," he said, and held the door open with his foot. "I'll take you to get something to eat." I didn't believe him. At this point I didn't trust anyone or believe anything. I'd been abused badly enough already. When I didn't move, his thick eyebrows knitted above his nose and he frowned. "For the record, I don't think you had anything to do with it. But my hands are tied."

"How convenient," I snorted. "Since you're being so kind as to feed me, will you at least send someone over to my house to feed Miko? He's probably starving."

Look What the Cat Dragged In

IV. Miko

I watched for two days, and finally one of the men in blue happened by. Needing to get to him, I circled to the front of the house and went after him, meowing. At first I thought he would be the type that would kick at me and tell me to "shoo," but I was wrong. To my surprise he came into the yard and pulled Delilah's keys from his pocket. I have never been happier.

"Hey, kitty," he said when he noticed me. Holding out his hand as he squatted was a welcome sight, and I bumped my head against his fingers gratefully. "You hungry?" I meowed again—a deplorable thing, but expected of cats by humans.

Again, fools.

I'd love to bite my ancestors for that one. Why they decided thousands of years ago that we should resort to such guttural sounds, I will never know. The whole concept disgusts me. The Egyptians had no problem with our ability to speak—they revered us as Gods for it. Why should modern humans be so bothered by it? Because our ancestors felt the need to make us not appear to be the smartest creatures on the planet, we as an entire species are left to communicate through a series of sounds humans consider "cute". It is truly amazing how so small a creature can turn so large a person into a drooling puddle with only a purr and a head bump.

At least this way the humans are at our beck and call, and that part I quite enjoy.

No matter.

I allowed the human to scratch my ears and I forced myself to purr as he rose and started toward the front door.

"Let's get you fed," he said. I followed along, because to be perfectly honest I was tired of catching my own dinner. The mess in the cans Delilah occasionally bought was much preferable to raw field mouse. I led him to the shelf, suggesting its location with my head against the handle, and meowed in approval when he popped the lid on the can. Then I allowed him to scratch my ears and turn away while I ate the contents of my bowl. When I heard the front door close, I remembered why I was so happy to see him.

I retrieved the dead man's wallet from its hiding place and ran through the small door. Before he made it to the sidewalk I was at his feet, once again meowing for his attention.

"Whatcha got there?" he asked. I pushed it toward him with my nose and he took the hint. "What is it, fella?" When he opened it, the color rushed from his face and he screamed for his partner, who was waiting in the car. "Where did you get this?" he asked me, then shook his head and answered himself with, "You're a cat. How can you tell me?"

Look What the Cat Dragged In

Oh, but I could. Even though I was not allowed. Call it a misguided sense of duty to my human…or self-preservation. Either works.

Another human appeared from the blue and white car and he, too, looked at me with the most overwhelming expression of surprise. They were already frightened, so I couldn't speak to them. At least I had their attention now. It was time to put on a show and hope for the best. I decided that it was best to follow Delilah's wish, so as loudly as possible I began to chatter and howl. Then, I circled their legs, started toward the murderer's home, and repeated.

"I think he wants us to follow him," the second one said. So I kicked up the howling to mark my approval and went toward the house, pausing to look back at them every few paces.

"That's crazy. He's a cat and he probably wants food."

"No," the second human said. "He's trying to tell us something."

"How can you tell?"

"Look at how he looks at you." Great! One of them had some sense!

"This is nuts."

"He had the wallet. Maybe he knows something about the murder." Good little human. Now if only they would stop talking and follow me. Finally, the dumber of the two, the ear-scratcher, shrugged.

"What could it hurt?" he said and rose to both feet. "Come on." So they were both coming. It was probably a wise choice. One wasn't too bright. The other was likely a coward, but so long as Tweedle-Dee and Tweedle-Dumbass were together, I was certain they could puzzle it out and do the right thing.

I rounded the corner and crossed the street, and the smell of decay wafted from the very bricks of the house. I stopped, wound myself through their legs, and shot toward the house; more specifically, to the open window. My companions watched the scene from the sidewalk, presumably because they did not have a warrant or just cause.

Alright, I admit it. Detective Horatio Caine fascinates me. I watch *CSI: Miami* with Delilah and greatly enjoy it.

The window was open. Lucky me. So I slipped through, padded carefully over the increasing piles of garbage, and found the dead man's clothes. As I turned them over and over again, I searched for something to alert these men to the presence of the dead man's things. The orange tee-shirt, I found, had a small badge, much like the one Delilah wore for her profession. The name on it said "Henry".

Ah...the curse of opposable thumbs. Or more precisely, not having any. I had no way to remove the item I wished to pilfer, so I was forced to drag the whole shirt with me, much to the detriment of my stealth. Naturally, it hung on every item I passed, causing enough commotion that the red-haired slob came to investigate. And of course, he found me…halfway to the window with the dead man's shirt in my mouth.

He ran at me, shouting furiously and swinging a chunky fist. He stumbled once but quickly regained his footing and came after me a second time.

I closed my teeth tightly around the badge and shot forward only to have the fabric catch on yet another obstacle. The dirty, little man was fast, and his fingers locked around the shirt as I leapt for the window. It tore under my teeth and I fell short several inches.

Claws — my saving grace that day.

I latched onto the wood, yanked myself up, and slipped out the window just as he slammed it, narrowly missing my tail. At least I had the badge. And my luck held as I ran back to the waiting officers and dropped the nametag in the outstretched hand. A bit of orange fabric still clung to the pin-back.

The ear-scratcher uttered a few obscenities as he looked at it. Then, his partner was on the radio asking for a directive.

"You think he'll let us take him to the station?" he asked. The other shrugged.

"Dunno."

The station — it was my best hope of finding Delilah. I let

out a long, and hopefully approving, meow, and sat at their feet with my tail curled around my paws. They glanced at each other, had a short conversation in which I had absolutely no interest, then glanced back at me.

"Should we pick him up?" the ear-scratcher asked.

"I don't know..." the other said, sounding quite apprehensive.

"Oh, for the love of Pete..." and the man with the magic fingers swept me up into his arms. I adjusted my weight across his arm and suppressed a disgusted shudder as I began to purr—disgusted by the purr, not the fact that he was willing to carry me. I much prefer to be carried—it beats getting sand in my claws.

He very gingerly laid me in the back seat of the cruiser and took me with them back "to the station." Inside the station, they told anyone who would listen about my ability to show them "new evidence." I ignored the praise in favor of searching out Delilah. It wasn't hard to slip away unnoticed from the humans because I am nowhere near as clumsy, and I can move silently across nearly any terrain. The need to leave was strong because my human was somewhere in the building. I could smell her.

This was one thing about small-town America that I appreciated: the holding cells were attached to the police station. It made finding her just that much easier. So, up the stairs I went, slipping easily past the guard who took no notice of me, following her week-old scent to the cage where she stared miserably out of the barred windows. Once again swallowing my pride, I meowed.

"Miko?" she asked, turning. I noticed she'd been crying heavily. I meowed again. "How on Earth did you get in here?"

Smelling no one else close enough to hear, I jumped into her lap and spoke quietly. "The men in blue brought me. Delilah, I found him."

"Him?" she asked. I waited patiently as realization dawned on her. She was an exceptionally bright human. "How?"

"I saw him..." I told her of my findings and the adventure leading up to this very moment. A small hope flickered in her eyes. "So you see," I growled as the story wound down, "binding me to the 'normal cat' bit has made this infinitely harder than it needs to be. Speaking freely would make this much easier."

"Or they'd shoot you on sight."

"For you, Delilah, that is a chance I am willing to take." And I meant every word of it. She hugged me tightly to her, her tears soaking into the fur of my neck. "But I should get back now," I told her, regretting the look of sorrow on her face. At least I was able to provide her this small bit of comfort. "They will wonder where I am."

"Thank you, Miko," she whispered. Delilah kissed my nose, scratched my ears and very reluctantly put me down. I glanced back at her saddened face one last time before slipping through the bars and back downstairs.

They hadn't missed me yet. The two officers were discussing the paperwork for a warrant when I returned. Captain Greaves—the man that had arrested my woman—was the first to see me.

"That's the cat?" he asked.

One of my new friends nodded. "That's her cat."

The Captain looked at me, confused. Even though he was only doing his job, I was predisposed to not liking him. Doubly so after the sneer he reserved just for me. "How would he know?"

"Maybe because he could smell it?"

Ha. Leave it to a complete fool to be right on the nose. Pardon the pun.

"Gentlemen," the Captain said sternly, rising from his seat, "you do realize I can't issue a search warrant on the grounds that a cat brought you a wallet and a nametag, correct?"

The two officers slumped in their seats. The more I listened, the more I feared I would have to break my promise to Delilah. I had no other way to explain what I had seen, heard, and smelled. My officers put up a good fight, but in the end the Captain returned to his office without giving that much needed warrant. I followed him.

"Hi, Miko," he said as he noticed me. The contemptuous look was gone, replaced by an informed sadness. He remembered my name, which was fairly impressive. "Listen," he continued, and dropped his hand to his side. "I'm sorry I had to take her." I bumped my head against his fingers in a gesture of goodwill. Those large hands of his made great ear-scratchers, I quickly learned. "If I'd had any other way…" he sighed. I leapt to his desk and sat down. He leaned forward and looked me straight in the face. "I wish you could just tell me what you know. It would make my job so much easier."

It was time. I had no other option. "Since you asked so nicely."

The large man stared at me, slack-jawed. The muscles in his face worked his mouth several times, reminding me of that blasted goldfish Delilah used to have. Somehow I had the feeling he would not taste as good as the goldfish did.

"You…spoke?"

"Yes," I sighed. "Delilah made me promise not to, but I fear there is no other way."

"I'm going insane," he said as if he'd not heard me. He rocked back in his chair and stared at the ceiling blankly.

"I am afraid not." Slowly, his eyes refocused on me.

"That I speak is unimportant. It is what I have to say to which you should pay close attention, Captain." He stood and closed the door to his office silently, then returned to his seat.

"Go on," he whispered. There, in his eyes, I could see the incredulity. He could not believe he was speaking to a cat. I had often told Delilah that human eyes always betrayed emotion. Just beyond them lurked that soul-deep connection that spoke volumes to those patient enough to pay attention. This man, while incredulous, was also hopeful.

"The red-haired man…his scent was on the body. He returns to my yard every day to see what he has done…." For the second time I recounted the events leading to this very position, "So you see, my woman is innocent."

Captain Greaves scrubbed his hands down his face and grunted. I was happy at that moment to be a cat, silly speech-stigma notwithstanding. At least we were able to wrap our heads around strange situations, such as other species' abilities to speak.

"I wish it were so simple," he groaned finally. "But I can't simply issue a warrant on the testimony of a cat," he eyed me warily, "speaking or not."

How humans came to inherit the Earth as the dominant species, I will never know. I briefly considered telling this man why I thought so, but settled instead for giving him an easy answer.

"Consider it an anonymous tip, which gives you just cause." His face lit up, then he looked at me suspiciously again.

"How do you know all of this?"

My tail twitched in annoyance. He was wasting valuable time. "Delilah watches CSI a lot."

"I see." He and I considered each other for a long moment. There was still apprehension growing in his eyes — as if he would simply consider himself a madman once I was out of sight. Then, he spoke the most unexpected words possible. "Delilah is very lucky to have you in her life."

Speaking of …

"Might we speak to her?" I asked.

"Unfortunately, procedure dictates quite a bit of paperwork. Let me file the warrant, then I'll have her transferred."

"May I sit with her until then?"

He tossed the idea around the caverns of his mind. "I don't see why not," he said finally. "I will see you to her."

With no pretense of "normal cat" sounds, he picked me up and carried me upstairs. Delilah was ecstatic to see us both. As I slipped through the bars and into her waiting arms, she sighed.

"You have an extraordinary cat, Miss Cipriati," Captain Greaves said.

Delilah groaned and glared at me. "What did you do?"

"Only what was necessary," I replied, feigning disinterest.

"Let us just say I received a well-informed anonymous tip that, if is as it should be, will secure your freedom." His smile was warm and hopeful, and I could see the relief in Delilah's eyes. Again, if only humans could see their eyes the way we do....

"I will return as soon as possible," the Captain said, speaking to me. "Keep her safe, Miko."

I nodded and went to sleep in my woman's lap, tired of the human emotional battle.

* * *

When Captain Greaves returned, he carried keys and release papers. Whether it was in her best interest or not, Delilah was able to look into the face of the man that had so wrongfully put her here. He was being brought in as she was leaving. He glared at me, and somehow he knew his potentially long-term incarceration was my fault.

But I didn't care. My woman was free, and we were on the way out...until the Captain diverted us into his office. He took a seat behind his desk, looking conflicted.

"First," he said nervously, and drew in a deep breath, "I wish to extend my sincerest apologize for the mix-up.

Look What the Cat Dragged In

Unfortunately, these things happen from time to time."

Delilah, gracious as always, raised a hand to stop him. "Accepted, Captain. I understand you were only doing your job."

Relief flooded his features, but he was still on edge. Apparently the best was yet to come.

"I have a proposition for the two of you." Meaning me. "This extraordinary cat has talents that could be used for the greater good."

I flattened my ears and narrowed my eyes at him. "Are you asking me to be a contracted anonymous tip, Captain?"

He smirked, obviously liking my phrasing.

"Why, I suppose so. With your nose, knowledge of police workings, and the ability to speak, you could be a great asset to us, Miko. Paid, obviously, through Delilah as a 'special services' consultant."

At Delilah's urging, I accepted the offer. Then, as we left, I turned back and looked up at Captain Greaves. My next words, I'm certain, changed his life. "Yes, my intelligence and olfactory senses are unparalleled, but you should know, Captain, that all cats can speak. Most just choose not to."

I walked out the door, Delilah giggling happily behind me.

THE WOLF SENTINEL
BY STEVEN S. LONG

Another Gold-Red Leaf Time arrived, and the Swift Grey Lord of the Forest didn't know if he would live to see the Green Blossoming again. He'd lived by himself for nearly two passings of the seasons, ever since Sharp Fangs Scarlet turned on him, defeated him in fair combat, and took his place as leader of the Great Pack of the Northern Forests. Scarletfang had driven him away then, as was the ancient custom. He'd fled into the forest to a life of solitude, a fallen king in exile unto death. Age was creeping up on him, slowly but inexorably; his eyes were less keen now than two winters ago, his jaws less strong. Soon, all too soon, catching his food would become impossible; he'd have to eat carrion and whatever else he could find until starvation or some stronger predator took him at last.

Such was the way of things, and he did not question it — not until the day the thunderclap frightened him and he felt a Call thrilling along his nerves that he couldn't turn away from.

He saw the lightning bolt, blue-white and crackling with power, strike out of the sunny, blue sky at the two-legs' road far below him. Then he smelled the wisps of smoke rising from where it struck. It all felt unnatural — and smoke meant fire, the only thing he truly feared. Instinct said he should run away until his tongue lolled out and he had to rest, but the Call stopped him. He could neither understand nor explain it, but something told him he *had* to go down to the road and learn what had happened. A feeling as strong as the urge to mate in late winter filled him, an irresistible drive in his soul and blood. He started down the hill.

He went warily, using all the stealth his kind possessed. He blended in with the rocks, trees, and ground like no two-legs ever could. As he approached the road he became more cautious still, for wherever two-legs went, danger usually followed. His nose picked up no scent of living thing, though, only a sharp, burning stench.

At last he came to the edge of the forest and stopped. Crouching next to a rock that matched his own dark grey color, he looked and listened, alert for threats despite the feeling that urged him onward. Sensing nothing, he moved forward, head low to the ground, body tensed to flee.

He had seen death among the two-legs before, when they fought one another with their large metal claws. But this was nothing like that. Bodies of two-legs and horses were strewn around the road in a wide, rough circle. Lightning had struck each of them down; their burned, smoking flesh showed him that clearly enough. Here and there tiny flames still flickered on clothing or hair; he gave these a wide berth.

The smell of cooked meat tantalized him, but he didn't stop to feed; a stronger compulsion drew him on. In the center of the circle of bodies he found a two-legs who still lived. He lay face down on the road. A cloak covered most of him. His left arm stretched out to the side, its hand clutching a long stick of polished black wood. He showed no sign of lightning-strike, but he lay there as still as the others.

Without knowing what gave him the idea, Greylord began licking the living one's pale face. He kept at it until the two-legs stirred. The two-legs groaned and lay there for a moment, then tried to get up. He hissed in pain and fell back to the ground. Slowly he rolled over on his back, favoring his left leg. Exhaustion showed on his face.

As he sat up he noticed Greylord. "It worked," he said thankfully, as if he knew a wolf could understand his speech. "I wasn't sure I sent the Call before I collapsed."

He moved his left leg some more, wincing in pain if he

shifted it more than a paw's width. His expression became grim.

At last he looked into Greylord's eyes. "I need your help, forest brother. When these bandits ambushed me I had to expend nearly all my power to call down lightning to destroy them; I had no time for anything easier or more subtle. It will be some time before I have the stamina to cast more spells of any strength.

"With the last of my power I sent the Call. It brought you here, but that is all it can do. I cannot compel you, for it does not lie within my power to affect the mind of a beast in that way—and even if it did I would not force you to serve me against your will. But my life is in danger, and without your help I may not survive. Will you help me?"

His words puzzled Greylord. A two-legs asking him for help? Such a thing had never happened before in all the sagas of the Great Pack. No wolf had ever howled a tale of a two-legs who did anything but hunt and kill. Some of the oldest songs spoke of two-legs who lured wolves away from the forest, who tamed and weakened them and sometimes made them the enemies of their ancient cousins, but this was a different matter. None of the laws of his people spoke to this. He could rely only on his own wisdom to guide him.

He sniffed again. Through the smells of fire and smoke he scented no treachery on the two-legs, no odor of fear. Few of his kind could sit so close to one of the Great Pack, even an old one like him, and feel no fear. He admitted it to himself reluctantly, but there was a...nobility to this two-legs that most of them did not possess. His words were true, his heart pure, his need genuine. He had a wolf spirit.

Did he want to help the two-legs, though? Mind and instinct told him to leave the two-legs to his fate, to run back into the hills and hide until the two-legs fought his own battle, lived or died, and left the forest. But the two-legs was weak and hurt, like a pup. He remembered the days when the pups were his, and he protected them from every danger in the forest. It felt good, protecting the pack. Maybe the Great Hunter had sent this two-legs to become his new pack.

He sat back on his haunches and barked a reply, bold and strong.

Relief flooded the two-legs's face. "Thank you, noble one. Your kindness brings me hope. I am Vorgath of the Hrusari, and you have my gratitude."

This was a properly respectful response. Greylord bobbed his head in acknowledgment.

"I have to get away from here, in case these bandits have frie...packmates," Vorgath said. "That means I have to walk, and right now I can't. When they shot my horse out from under me I landed badly on my left leg. My ankle's sprained, maybe even broken.

"I never studied the healing arts, but I know I have to make a splint so I can stand up and use a crutch. Can you bring me a sturdy branch, one that's straight, not too old, and a little thicker than this?" He held up his thumb to show the thickness he meant.

Greylord bobbed his head again and loped off into the woods. He didn't think about pieces of trees much, so it took him a little while to find a branch he believed would suit Vorgath's needs. Grasping one end of it with his strong jaws, he dragged it back to the road and dropped it next to the two-legs.

Vorgath looked it over carefully and tested its sturdiness with his hands. "Just what I needed," he said to Greylord by way of thanks. Then he drew the long metal claw he wore at his left side and started cutting at the wood. He worked on the branch until he weakened it enough to break it over his right knee into two equal-sized lengths. Then he trimmed the ends to remove the sharp edges and points. "Never thought I'd use a Runeblade to chop wood," he muttered.

When he finished with the branch, he took off his cloak and used the metal claw to slice strips from it. Then he put the two pieces of wood on either side of his left leg and tied them tightly into place with the cloth strips. By the time he ran out of strips his ankle was wrapped so firmly Greylord didn't think it would move at all.

"All right, let's see if this works," he said. Using his polished black stick as a crude crutch, Vorgath got to his knees and then, shakily, to his feet. Sweat was pouring down his face by the time he stood upright, and he winced every time he put even the slightest weight on his left foot, but he seemed satisfied.

"The sooner I'm gone from here, the better, but I can't go far on this foot. I need a safe place to hide, not too far away. Is there a cave near here? A hollow tree?"

Greylord thought for a moment then headed west. Vorgath followed, but he could barely take two steps without having to rest, leaning on his polished black stick with his left foot up in the air like a crane. It took nearly two hours to reach the place Greylord knew of.

It was a small hollow, barely more than a dip in the forest floor, with some moss-covered rocks along one side. Many winters ago, before Greylord had even been whelped, the wind had blown over an enormous old oak, and as it fell across one end of the hollow it knocked over another tree. Where the trunks crossed dirt and forest litter collected, and as the seasons passed it became like a small, shallow cave. It was barely big enough to shelter the two-legs from the rain, but it would do.

Vorgath sat down under the log with a grateful sigh, putting his left leg straight out in front of him on the ground.

"I'm going to sleep now," he said, his eyes already closed. "Will you be here when I wake up?"

Greylord barked in the affirmative then lay down a short distance from Vorgath. But his yellow eyes didn't close; he remained awake and alert, standing guard over his two-legged pup.

* * *

Vorgath awoke as twilight descended on the forest. He didn't look nearly as tired, but from the way he moved his left leg it had gone stiff. He moved it around a little, careful not to hit his foot against the ground.

"I lost all my supplies when the bandits attacked me — my food, my water," he said. "Could you catch me something to eat and bring it here?"

Greylord felt hungry himself, so he barked softly and headed off deeper into the forest. His hunting skills, learned from his father Strongjaw, were second to none, though he was too old and weak to have any hope of bringing down a deer. He went to the forest lake to look for ducks.

The Great Hunter favored him; he caught a duck quickly. After he'd eaten most of it he killed another that carelessly came too close to him. He carried it back to the two-legs.

Vorgath smiled when he saw the duck. "Almost a gourmet feast!" he said when Greylord laid it down beside him. While he'd been out hunting, Vorgath had scraped together a small pile of sticks and dried leaves and cleared the ground around it. Now he set to work plucking and preparing the duck, laying the pieces on what was left of his cloak so they wouldn't get dirty. It looked like a lot of unnecessary work to Greylord.

"I need to light a fire now, to roast the duck," he said at last. "Is that all right?"

Fire! Greylord scrambled back to the edge of the hollow, then stood there watching. He had promised this two-legs his help, so he wouldn't leave, but he had no desire to get any nearer to fire than he had to.

"Thank you," Vorgath said. "I think I have enough stamina now to try a minor spell." He held his right hand over the pile of sticks and leaves, and Greylord saw for the first time a dark metal ring on one finger. Then Vorgath spoke a Word, one Greylord couldn't understand at all, and a spark jumped from the ring to the leaves! They started to burn. Vorgath fed more sticks into the pile until he had a steady fire, then put the duck over it to roast. It smelled delicious. Despite his fear of fire Greylord couldn't help creeping a bit closer as he salivated, hoping to find a way to snatch a bite.

Vorgath laughed. "Here," he said, tossing the wolf a wing when the bird was done. Greylord devoured it in a few quick bites and looked up for more, but Vorgath had his own appetite to satisfy.

What he didn't have was water. "Did you get the duck near here, forest brother? Could I walk there?" Greylord barked no—a two-legs reduced to a one-legs couldn't make it to the lake before morning.

The weather came to Vorgath's rescue. A storm woke him up around midnight. He held out cupped hands to catch the rain and greedily drank handful after handful. By the time the storm passed he'd slaked his thirst—but Greylord knew his pup couldn't rely on rain every day.

* * *

The next morning the look of fatigue had left Vorgath's face, and he could move around more easily than the day before. Several times he stood up and hobbled around the hollow using his polished black stick. He still moved slowly, but he didn't have to stop every step or two and didn't wince so intensely when he accidentally put a little extra weight on his left foot.

"It's only sprained," he said. "Maybe in a day or two I can start walking out of here. Once I get back to Helgenford I can buy a horse and ride to Odellia. If I don't take word of Lord Elgard's treachery to the King, the western half of Thurstan's kingdom will be up in arms against him before he even knows it. I'm only a warlock; I lack the Wizardry to send Thurstan a message over such distances even if I had the strength to cast the spell." Greylord didn't understand most of what Vorgath said, but he could tell it bothered him.

Around noon he decided to go hunting; sitting in the hollow with the two-legs all day held little appeal. But it was a poor time of day for such things; all he caught was a single mouse. He'd have better luck in the evening.

He returned to the hollow just in time to hear more two-legs approaching. Vorgath had heard it too; he squeezed himself as far back beneath the sheltering logs as he could, hoping to pass unseen. Greylord crouched beside the rocks next to the hollow and waited.

"Haw!" he heard a rough voice say. "A blind kid could follow this trail."

"Quiet!" a second voice said. "He could be anywhere; you want him to know we're after him? You saw what he did back there."

The sounds of their approach came closer, and closer, and at last they came over the hill in front of the hollow. One was short and scar-faced; the other taller and crafty-looking. They wore simple, weather-stained clothes. Each of them carried something Greylord recognized: a bow held at the ready, arrow nocked to string but not pulled back. Their harsh looks and scars told of a life spent in deadly pursuits. Greylord could smell their sour odor even from across the hollow.

They saw the remains of Vorgath's campfire—and then Vorgath himself. Both of them drew back their bows. "Slow and steady, wizard," the tall one said as they carefully advanced into the hollow. "We can't miss, this close up. Even you can't stop an arrow. Keep your mouth shut, stand up, and raise your hands."

Vorgath began to comply, but then with a blood-chilling snarl Greylord launched himself at Scar-Face. Before the two-legs could bring his bow to bear a hundred pounds of snarling wolf slammed into him and locked its jaws around his throat. He fired his arrow wildly into the air and let out a gurgling scream.

The tall two-legs turned and aimed his arrow at Greylord. Vorgath threw a stone, hitting the archer's wrist and spoiling his shot. The arrow thudded into the ground a tail's-length away from Greylord. The wolf leaped on him, and before he could draw one of his metal claws sharp lupine fangs had torn his throat out too. After a few moments Greylord backed off, his muzzle red with blood.

Vorgath limped forward. "That was well done, my friend," he said. "You saved my life—again."

Greylord barked his appreciation of the pup's respect.

Vorgath found a waterskin and pouch of food on each body and quickly drained one of the skins dry. After he'd satisfied his thirst, he bent over to examine Scar-Face more closely. His face turned serious. "I know him. He's one of Lord Elgard's huntsmen; I saw him when I stayed at Elgard Castle. That traitorous snake must have sent him and his friend to find my trail."

Vorgath's expression became grimmer. "Gods of Hrusár! I've been a fool. Those weren't bandits who attacked me yesterday. Elgard sent word to his allies, and they set up an ambush. I should have known. I should have ridden quicker. Now I'm stuck here with a bad ankle!"

Greylord wasn't sure he understood. Another pack planned to attack Vorgath's pack, and he wanted to warn them? That seemed like it. No wonder he was angry.

"Wait a minute," Vorgath said, whatever that meant. "These two didn't walk all the way here from Elgard. They must have horses! Probably left them back at the road, or just off it. I can't ride fast like this, but I can still ride. Let's go look." He began hobbling back to the road as fast as he could; Greylord walked beside him.

It didn't take long to find the horses. Elgard's scouts had tied them to trees just off the road, far enough away from the rotting corpses that the smell wouldn't spook them. "You'd better stay back," Vorgath said to him. "A wolf like you will terrify them." Greylord sat down and watched.

Vorgath examined both horses, then limped back to

where Greylord waited. "They're in good shape, not too tired. It won't be an easy ride, but I can leave now. Goodbye, forest brother. I cannot repay the great debt I owe you now, but if I ever can, you have the word of Vorgath the warlock that I will." He bowed, and it looked to Greylord as if he wanted to touch him in some way but knew the noble wolf wouldn't permit such a liberty. Vorgath turned, hobbled back to the horses, carefully mounted one, and began to ride east down the road.

Greylord looked on mournfully. His new pup was leaving; once more he was without a pack. But the pup hadn't left the forest yet! He stood up and loped along through the woods beside the road, keeping a careful eye on Vorgath from the shelter of the trees.

The two-legs rode for over an hour, making the best speed he could with his injured ankle and tired body. He ate from one of the food pouches, drank from the waterskin that still held water. He stopped once to refill both waterskins at a small roadside waterfall.

Then Greylord heard the sound of galloping horses approaching from the west. Vorgath heard them too; he urged his horse to greater speed, but didn't dare reach a full gallop without being able to use his injured left foot in the stirrup. Greylord ran to keep up.

Soon three men appeared on the road behind Vorgath,

riding hard. One shot an arrow at him, but it went so far off the mark that he put his bow away and concentrated on keeping his mount running at top speed.

Seeing which way the wind blew, Vorgath pulled his horse up and turned to face his pursuers. They slowed as they got closer; the one with the bow drew it, nocked an arrow, and aimed at Vorgath; the other two drew their long metal claws as they fanned out to form a loose semi-circle around him. Greylord crept quietly to the edge of the road and hid in a thicket downwind from the horses. His two-legged pup needed some help still.

"So Lord Elgard sent more of you," Vorgath said. "Didn't you see what I did to the last group of butchers he put on my trail? Leave now and return to his castle, and I'll spare your lives." His eyes almost seemed to glow with the intensity of his gaze.

This took the three men aback for a moment, but then the biggest one let out a bark of laughter and pointed his long metal claw directly at Vorgath's throat. "You're all talk, sorcerer. If you could kill us you'd have done it by now. Drop that stick of yours and raise your hands, or we'll cut you down right here and spare Lord Elgard the trouble."

Greylord lunged. He came from behind and attacked the archer's horse from beneath, ripping out its guts with his sharp fangs. The horse screamed and reared; the archer flew out of the saddle, firing his arrow high into the trees, and hit the ground hard. The other horses, scenting the wolf, snorted and reared; their riders fought to keep them under control and stay in the saddle.

With lightning speed Vorgath drew his own short, slender metal claw and struck. The tip of it slashed through the throat of the two-legs who'd spoken to him, leaving his head half detached from his neck. As that two-legs began to fall from the saddle, Vorgath spun his horse to the left, wincing in agony as he put pressure on his left foot, and blocked a blow from the other two-legs's axe. The force of the attack knocked him sideways in the saddle.

Greylord leaped up and bit down hard on the attacker's leg, tasting his hot blood. The two-legs snarled in pain, raised his axe, and brought it down on Greylord's back. He let go his grip and fell to the ground.

"No!" Vorgath shouted, recovering his balance a second too late. He thrust, plunging the point of his metal claw through the two-legs's chest and into his heart. He whipped it out again, and with a gasping groan the two-legs plunged from the saddle. His horse bolted, trying to catch up with the other one that was already long gone.

Vorgath dismounted as quickly as his balky horse and injured ankle would let him, then knelt clumsily on the ground by Greylord's side. Gently he stroked the wolf's fur.

"I'm so sorry, forest brother," he said, his voice hard with sorrow. "I couldn't attack fast enough to stop him. Once again you've saved my life. But I wish it wasn't at the cost of your own."

Greylord whined a little, feeling his own blood running down his side, but his heart was glad. The two-legged pup was safe; the pack continued. And that was what mattered. He closed his yellow eyes for the last time.

MEMORANDUM
BY LAURA ANNE EWALD

TO: Mr. Hyde Watum

FROM: Aela Jeun

DATE: Comdate 08/14/269

CASE: Commonwealth v. Galactic Sociological Research Institute

OFFICE FILE NUMBERA: 865-4

DOCKET NUMBER: COM. 9-357-1801

RE: Printed evidence and declaration of Doctor Mroweo I Isstu in support of negligence charges against the Galactic Sociological Research Institute (GSRI) and in support of the innocence of Doctor Reni Lira regarding counterclaims as filed by the GSRI.

The following is a translation of a work published in a collection of children's stories on the world designated

YS*872-3 in the indigenous language English by Robert Michael Brown, fifty-three years (local) after the ill-fated landing of the GSRI's survey team of Doctors Reni Lira and Mroweo Hsstu:

LOCAL RESIDENT ACCOUNT: "The Witch"

That was the summer we had a witch come to live in our town. Oh, I guess she wasn't really a witch — Granny always said real ones are only in fairy tales and ghost stories — but it's hard to know for sure.

Our gang was all set for the summer's first scoutin' trip. We were all real excited. The high valley was too far to go in winter, and even in spring it was still snowed in. So it was just understood that nobody went up there until after school was out. We'd started early and made it to the head of the valley before even Henry was wantin' lunch. We'd moved real quiet — you always have to move real quiet 'cause of Injuns and bears and all — and it was sure a good thing, too, 'cause we'd just come to the edge of the woods when we saw her.

She was down on the flat. It was flooded with the spring run-off, but she was down there anyhow, with her skirt hiked up and tucked in her belt at the front. She was barefoot, though it was kind of hard to tell 'cause of the mud all over her legs and feet. She was all stooped over, diggin' stuff out of the marshy ground and puttin' it in a big round basket. A black hood hid her face, and when the breeze died down, so the trees stopped whisperin', you could hear her singin' in a weird kind of way that made the hair stand up on the back of our necks.

Keepin' an eye on her, we skirted the open valley floor and came around to find we'd had reason to be worried. That old woman didn't just happen to be in our valley on that day—she'd come to stay! There was an old trappers' cabin in the back of the valley that we'd used for four summers runnin', spendin' the night in it when we came up. Well, that old lady had moved in, and from the look of things, she wasn't plannin' on leavin' anytime soon. It's not that she had a bunch of stuff—just a carpet bag, a blanket, and a couple of pots—but the place was clean! I mean everything looked like she'd been scrubbin' it for weeks. There wasn't a speck of dust anywhere. Outside, the porch'd been swept and the yard raked, and there were some new shingles on the roof. Inside, the floor was washed and the fireplace scrubbed right down to the stone. You could even see through the windows. Nobody does that kind of cleanin' if they're not plannin' to stay.

Well, we'd been lookin' around some when all of a

sudden we felt like somebody was watchin' us, and then we heard this real scary kind of growl. We looked up into the rafters and saw the biggest, meanest ginger cat you ever saw. It started snarlin' and spittin' somethin' fierce, yellow hair standin' out all over, and we scrammed out of there faster than I can tell.

We only went back to the valley a few more times that summer. She was always there, routin' around in the ground for stuff or fixin' things around the cabin, hidden in that black cloak and singin' all the time. That great big cat was always around, too, and though the witch never once looked our way, that ol' cat never took his eyes off us.

Later on, I met up with Reverend Young at the fishin' hole, and I asked him 'bout her. You could ask Reverend Young things 'cause that's the kind of man he was. Some of our folks didn't like him much, but we figured it was only 'cause he wasn't old and wrinkled like Reverend Grissom, and he wasn't safely married. All of us in the gang liked him 'cause he did fun things like fishin' and swimmin'. Anyway, when I asked him 'bout the old witch, he looked at me kind of funny and asked me why I thought she was a witch. I said how else could she've gotten up to the valley in the first place so early in the year, let alone lived up there all by herself? And why did she spend all that time diggin' for stuff, and what about that cat? He said he didn't know about all that, but he'd been up to see her several times, and as far as he knew, she was just a harmless woman who didn't have any place else to go.

Well, that stopped me short, I can tell you. Here we were, all scared of her, and Reverend Young'd been talkin' to her all this time. He told me he'd been tryin' to get her to move into town, or down to the city, before the winter snows. I asked him if he'd been able to talk her into leavin', but he said he didn't think so.

It was about that time people started gettin' sick. At first it was just the little kids and the old folks. Then anybody'd get it. Doc Trimble was kept runnin' all over the place. My family was lucky — my big sister got some fever but nothin' like what other people had. It was real scary, and nothin' Doc nor anybody else did seemed to help. People started talkin' then, whisperin' and sneakin' looks up the valley, and they'd all be talkin' 'bout the same thing: the witch.

Now, I started feelin' kind of bad when that happened. Us kids'd called her a witch just 'cause she scared us and was livin' in our valley. But now the grownups were callin' her that and actin' like they really believed it. That was scary. Reverend Grissom and Reverend Young preached against talk about witches and magic and such, but nobody seemed to listen.

Then the Widow Craig died of the sickness, and old

Harry Martin, too. And the Landson's youngest girl looked to be real close. I was just comin' onto Main Street one evenin' after finishin' up some chores for Doc, when this whole mob of people started gatherin'. Mr. Landson was leadin' 'em, and they had clubs and shotguns, and Mr. Cleary had his dogs. Their horses were saddled and somebody was handin' out torches on account of it was gettin' dark. I didn't know what to do, so when they rode out, I high-tailed it over to Reverend Young's place.

The Reverend hardly had his eyes open when I got there, but as soon as he heard the news, he woke up sure enough. His face went stark white, and he didn't say a thing—just grabbed his coat and ran to saddle his horse. I took off home to get our mule. I didn't know what was goin' to happen, but I didn't want to miss any of it.

When I got up there, it was really a sight to see: all those scared and angry men with their faces glowin' in the torchlight, and the Reverend standin' on the porch of that old cabin starin' 'em down. Mr. Landson was yellin' 'bout how there'd been no witches in these parts for close to seventy years, but he was willin' to get rid of this one the same way his pa'd told him they'd got rid of the last one. Some of the others were lookin' to throw their torches onto the roof of the cabin and let the fire take care of her. Reverend Young looked scared, but I gotta say he was the bravest man I ever saw, the way he was standin' there blockin' the door.

The mob got tired of waitin', though, and finally Mr. Landson and big Mr. Bower got off their horses and moved to shove Reverend Young aside. He tried to fight 'em, but Mr. Bower shoved the Reverend aside and smashed in the door. He hurt himself, too, on account of the door not bein' latched—it just opened, and big Mr. Bower went flyin' through!

But nobody was in the cabin. There was a fire burnin' in the hearth, and fresh-baked bread sittin' on the table, and the lamp was lit, but the witch was gone. Mr. Cleary got his dogs workin', but they couldn't find a trace of her. It was well into mornin' before they finally gave up lookin' and fired the cabin. I guess they figured they'd scared her off, and she wouldn't come back, if the cabin was burned down. As the mob headed for home, I found Reverend Young sittin' on a log across from the smokin' pile. He was tired like I'd never seen before, but he sent me home without him. I don't think he got back down 'til real late the next day.

Right after that, summer started to cool off into fall, and people started gettin' better again. Doc said it was on account of the weather and the sickness just passin'. Reverend Grissom said it was 'cause the whole town had worked and prayed together. Most people thought it was 'cause the witch was gone.

About the time school was startin' again, Reverend Young went away to the city for awhile. When he got back, he had a real surprise. He'd found himself a wife. Now, she was tiny and really pretty. She talked real pretty, too. Reverend Young said she talked that way 'cause she was from a long, long way away. I was real happy for him, 'specially when I found out she liked to do fun things, too. She even went fishin' sometimes.

But I got to tell you, there was somethin' 'bout Mrs. Young that hit me from the start. I knew I couldn't have met her before, but there was just somethin' 'bout her that made me think I'd seen her someplace.

It was almost Christmas before I finally figured it out. I was over at their place splittin' some wood for 'em, on account of the Reverend bein' so busy, when I heard Mrs. Young singin' from inside the house. She was singin' carols this time, but there was no mistakin' that voice. And when I looked up, there it was, sittin' in the parsonage window: the biggest, meanest ginger cat you ever saw.

DECLARATION OF DR. MROWEO HSSTU:

I must say I nearly laughed like a human when Dr. Lira brought this story to my attention, for I will never forget the look on the face of that yearling — your pardon — that human youth, when he saw me sitting in the window. Humor aside, however, I am happy to testify that the preceding is indeed an accurate, if limited, account of what happened to my partner, Dr. Reni Lira, and myself some sixty years ago. The fact that it is limited should lay to rest any discussion about the interference our presence might have represented. Even beyond the fact that this story is told through the eyes of a child (as it was remembered by an middle-aged man), I would also like to point out that with only one exception, this is the *only* version *anyone* from that planet *could* tell. Let me explain.

Concerned with the possibility of cultural or technical interference, Dr. Lira and I have kept a close watch on those who would have seen us, before we entered Mr. Brown's village as welcome members of the Reverend Young's family. There were a total of seven members in Mr. Brown's "gang." With the exception of Reverend Young, they were the only ones to see us, before we could come under our permanent cover.

Of the seven youths, only two are still living. The first died only two years after this incident in some kind of accident. The second was killed in what is known there as the First World War. The third, who survived that vicious conflict, was later killed in what is known as the Second

World War. Numbers four and five died of natural causes, one of heart failure and the other of lung cancer. Both were apparently habitual smokers of a certain vegetation grown on YS*872-3 for that purpose—a rather nauseating habit of which the only redeeming factor seems to be a voluntary contribution to the control of population growth. (More on that in my journals.)

Of the two remaining individuals, Mr. Brown has spent his entire life entertaining children with his stories, books, and plays, and the other, a Mr. Cleary, Jr., still raises hunting dogs in that still-primitive village in the mountains. This story, published twenty-six years ago locally, is the only indication any of the original seven ever remembered that summer of "the witch."

The exception, as I said before, was the Reverend Young. In our defense, I must emphasize that he was a clergyman of the local religion, and, therefore, even if he had not taken us into his care, his vocation would have ensured his confidentiality. Be that as it may, I can assure you he came to have far more important reasons for our security. Let me explain by going back to the beginning with my own perspective on what happened when Dr. Lira and I found ourselves inadvertently dumped on this primitive world by the less than thorough Galactic Sociological Research Institute.

Memorandum

Dr. Lira was, at that time, a highly competent shuttle pilot, which is why we were not accompanied to the surface of YS*872-3. (If you will permit me, for the remainder of this testimony I will refer to the planet designated YS*872-3 by its local name, Earth.) Looking back on it, we both realized it would have been far better to have utilized the Research Institute's shuttle corps as it would have saved us a lot of trouble.

Earth had actually been surveyed from space less than a half-century before. Projected to have been nearing the era of space-age technology by this time, my partner and I were sent to set up the first ground-side survey base in preparation for a future first contact. As is normally the case, our shuttle carrier came in above the plane of the orbital ecliptic and took up a protected position behind a neighboring planet lest any local technology record our approach. Dr. Lira and I then set out in our shuttle which was to act as both transportation and a ground lab.

Proof of the following is found in the fact that today, almost sixty years after the start of our mission, the people of Earth are only just beginning to send human beings into orbit. When we were left off for our survey, they were still *fifty years from the first artificial satellites!* We should not have been there in the first place, a fact which Dr. Lira and I realized upon approaching within scanner range of the planet. Our response was immediate: a swift reversal of our course in order to rendezvous with our carrier ship. However, as you now know, the *SS Tri Fates* had already made the jump to light speed! She had, for all intents and purposes, abandoned us to our fate *without first receiving confirmation that we were safely down!* Time is credits, as they say. Dr. Lira and I were victims of the GSRI's warped priorities. We were left to fend for ourselves, to make the best of an extremely difficult situation. Earth contained the only breathable atmosphere in the YS*872 system. We had no choice but to make a landing and proceed as well as possible under the circumstances. The only thing I will admit we should have done differently is our choice of piloting the shuttle ourselves. If we had utilized one of the *SS Tri Fate's* pilots, they would have been forced to wait long enough to recover their pilot and secondary shuttle, and, therefore, we could have returned with them.

Suffice it to say that we were stuck. Not having any alternatives, we landed as originally planned in the mountainous country of the northeastern region of the continent we now know as North America. We chose a high valley that, while still surrounded by snow at the time, seemed to afford the seclusion we would need until we had decided exactly what to do.

I must say here that my partner, Dr. Lira, was marvelous through all of this. She was, after all, in the greatest danger of discovery. My own cover was not affected all that much. In spite of my relatively large size, I could easily pass myself off as a member of the species *Felis catus*, an intelligent, though non-sentient, species which had been domesticated by Earth humans throughout their history. Dr. Lira, however, would have a much more difficult time making her way unobtrusively through this world which could only be described as primitive.

The word "primitive," I realize, can cover anything from prehistoric society through rudimentary computers. Let me give you an idea of the most advanced technology with which we were faced on Earth. The internal combustion engine had been invented by this time, but its use, particularly in the rural area where we landed, was extremely limited. The village physician owned one of these "automobiles," as did the veterinarian who lived the next valley over and the circuit judge who came through once a month. Everyone else relied upon beasts of burden for both transportation and agriculture. The only major land transportation at this time was the "railroad," a train of cars which was pulled along metal rails by a steam-powered engine. The first powered aircraft had gotten off the ground, but the invention was not yet a practical reality. Some of the village had electricity, though many of the outlying homes did not, and buildings were still heated primarily by burning fossil fuels or wood.

The radio had been invented, but no one had one, and there was not yet anything broadcast widely to listen to even if they did. The first rudimentary computer was not to be invented for almost another forty years.

This, then, is the world in which we found ourselves. We learned later that our immediate environment was considered somewhat primitive even by contemporary standards elsewhere, but at the time we were only just getting our whiskers wet.

We had landed at night, local time. When scanners showed no signs of tracking technology, Dr. Lira made a couple of low flights over communities so we might get some idea of costume, transportation, and so forth. The first thing we did upon landing was stabilized the shuttle and setup the cloaking force field. With our security established, we studied the tapes and used the synthesizer to produce clothing and travel items for Dr. Lira's cover. We then left the protection of the shuttle and searched for a place to establish camp. We could not, after all, remain in the shuttle/lab forever. The cloaking force field had a one-hundred-fifty year guarantee, but its life would be considerably diminished, if we used up the shuttle's power supply by simply living there. Abandoned as we were, we couldn't even count on contact or recovery in the standard five-year period. (As it turned out, of course, we did exactly the right thing in light of the fact that we were not contacted for recovery for almost *sixty years!*)

Our first morning out we came upon an old abandoned habitat. We decided it would suit our needs and began the arduous task of preparing the site. I must confess that I was little help to Dr. Lira in this regard; my people are simply not built for such labors, so I am afraid Dr. Lira was the one to do all the repairs. I contributed by making daily trips to the lab for exhaustive study of the tapes of the original orbital surveys and our own brief fly-over. Dr. Lira had already proven to be quite receptive, for a human, to my telepathic "broadcasts," and so while she worked and I studied, we both assimilated all available information on the world in which we found ourselves. I also spent hours roaming further and farther from our secluded site. I soon knew the village quite well. I had even managed to make a contact of sorts with some of the local "cats," as they were called. They tended to be extremely wary of me, due, no doubt, to their limited intelligence, but after a time I managed a grasp of their rudimentary language and found a new source of information. Unfortunately, that information tended to center around such things as where the best food scraps were disposed of, who was available for courting, and which "dogs" had to be avoided. I did, however, manage to learn which business was where, information which might prove useful should my partner and I decide to move into the village. Of the other creatures I met, I found most to be analogous to any other early human society. The "dogs" were sometimes troublesome, but my size and training in self-defense created a situation in which I was rarely called on to face the same beast twice.

Our contact with the natives this first summer was only twofold. The first was the seven-member "gang" of youths of which Mr. Brown had been a part. As it turned out, I was the only one who actually spoke to them. For some reason they seemed to be quite fearful of Dr. Lira and were considerably furtive each time they came to the valley. Dr. Lira, of course, knew they were there, for I would always contact her when I saw them, but we agreed it might be better if the youths believed themselves to remain unobserved by her. I'm afraid the young Mr. Brown was quite correct in his assessment of my welcome that first day. I did raise my voice to him, but I was a bit tired at the time and rather irritated that they had simply walked into our home without so much as a by-your-leave. I might add that we both found it rather amusing that the boys assumed Dr. Lira to be a "stooped over old lady." A being with the life expectancy of one-hundred-twenty-two-point-three years, Dr. Lira was, at that time, only just into her second quarter. She was also, if I may say so, quite beautiful for a human.

Our second contact seemed to appreciate that fact. He was much more open than the youngsters had been, riding across the meadow and up to the habitat. We learned later that he had heard about us by means of rumors some of the youths had been spreading. He introduced himself as the Reverend David Young, by which we were able to determine that he was a member of the clergy of the local religion. He was a very gentle, soft-spoken man, whose main concern was for our safety. The snow we had encountered upon our arrival was nothing compared to what we could expect during the winter months, so David Young did try to talk Dr. Lira into coming down out of the high meadow. Dr. Lira was able to put him off for a time. We hadn't yet decided whether to spend the winter in the shelter of the shuttle or try to make it in society. Either way we needed time to organize our thoughts and study in preparation.

David Young came more and more often as the summer went on. I could not bring myself to suggest that Dr. Lira try to discourage him, for his visits were very important, both as a window into his society and as company for my partner. Humans are, as you know, social creatures, and though I could provide a certain amount of companionship for her, she needed some contact with her own kind.

As it turned out, the decision to leave the high meadow was made for us by a rather frightening sequence of events. The sickness about which Mr. Brown wrote didn't stop at the village — it made its way into our habitat as well. While I was not affected by it, Dr. Lira became quite ill, and, much to my chagrin, I realized that either the Reverend Young or I had brought it to her. The fever came upon her quite suddenly, and she soon found she could not even stand. I frantically searched our medical files and, luckily, found a treatment which finally began to work, however slowly. I will admit that we had, at first, feared it was something we had brought with us, but upon further analysis in the lab, there was no doubt it had been a local bacterium—something which accounted for the fact that Dr. Lira actually suffered far more severely than the local adult population. I am certain that without our medical supplies, Dr. Lira would not have survived.

I can only thank the Creator that my partner's recovery was sufficient for her to leave our habitat on the night the villagers came to do her harm, though she was still very weak. I am also thankful I had somehow felt the need to keep an eye on the village during that time. David Young had told us about the "witch" rumors, and it didn't take a mystic to see what that mob was up to that night.

I barely managed to get Dr. Lira to the safety of our shuttle before the villagers arrived at our habitat. I watched from the branches of a nearby tree as the drama unfolded. The Reverend Young was as protective as Mr. Brown wrote, and I feared for his safety as well. When the mob finally set our habitat on fire, I could only think of Dr. Lira, safely hidden under our cloaking force field. Thank the Creator! The only scent Mr. Cleary's dogs found that night was my own, and it must have carried all of my fury, because they chose not to mention it to their master.

When David Young was left alone at the site, I had a decision to make. I confess here and now that that decision was mine and mine alone. Dr. Lira was in no condition to argue with me about it. Even as I scrambled down the tree I was contacting my partner, telling her to put the med kit into the carpet bag and get away from the shuttle, since I was bringing help. Unfortunately, Dr. Lira was, by that time, quite incapacitated. Even with all the time it took me to get David Young to follow, she was still inside when we arrived. My colleagues will tell me that I could have cared for Dr. Lira in the shuttle until she was well enough to leave, but you must remember that I was rather young then, too. I had been nursing my partner for days, and I knew I was simply not up to giving her the care she needed.

I was not entirely certain Reverend Young would follow when I entered the shuttle. I will never forget his expression when he saw me disappear through the cloak, but he did, indeed, follow me into what to him must have been a terrifyingly alien place. I will also never forget the change in him when he saw Dr. Lira unconscious on the shuttle floor. He showed such care and tenderness as he lifted her onto the couch and covered her still, feverish form with a blanket that I knew I had believed rightly about him.

The exterior monitor showed it was daylight by the time Dr. Lira stirred. I reassured her telepathically until she was aware enough to understand that David Young was with us. She mildly chastised me, but I could see she was extremely relieved to find him there after what had happened the night before.

Much to my own relief, our new friend began to take charge then. He didn't understand very much of what he now saw, but his main concern was for our well-being. (I caught him shaking his head as he eyed me once or twice, obviously as taken with the reality of *me* as he was by the shuttle and cloaking force field.) He insisted we not stay there. Even with the shuttle, there was always the possibility that the villagers would come back looking for us. There was also no way he could come to spend time with us there without arousing suspicion. Dr. Lira and I conferred. I realized how fearful her weakness made her feel, and I assured her that I was certain we could trust this man. She agreed finally and rather tentatively asked him what he thought we should do.

David Young's solution was a practical one. He told us that an aunt who had raised him lived not far away in a city called Boston. He could take us as far as the railroad station, and put us on the train bound for Boston with enough local credits to take us to his aunt's home and a brief letter to that woman explaining our need for a place to stay. Dr. Lira looked doubtful, but David Young assured her that his aunt made a life of taking in strays of various sorts, and as his friends, we would be most welcome.

To say he was quite correct in his assessment of his female relative would be to understate the warm welcome we received at the hands of that wonderful woman. Dr. Lira had been absolutely exhausted by the journey, but when the senior Miss Young opened the door on the white-faced stranger with the huge ginger cat in her arms, she didn't even pause to read her nephew's letter. Dr. Lira was put to bed in short order, and I was left to freely observe. Not wanting to give us away to a second native, I contented myself with purring my gratitude, something which Miss Young seemed to understand perfectly without a telepathic link.

By the end of the week, Dr. Lira had recovered from the fever, thanks to Miss Young's ministrations, though she remained weak for quite some time. At the end of the second week, the Reverend Young arrived. He said that since things were now settled in the village, the Reverend Grissom had encouraged him to take a few weeks to recover, himself, from all that had gone on that summer. Miss Young had been delighted, and I know Dr. Lira was pleased to see him.

By the end of his month there, David Young asked Dr.

Lira to marry him. Even without a telepathic link, which I was never able to establish with the man, I could see he loved her very much. She felt the same way but was torn between her love for him and her responsibilities as a Research Institute surveyor. There was also still the very real possibility that we could be contacted for removal at any time. After much discussion, I told her that I thought she should go ahead and marry the man. If he truly understood her position on his world, and still wanted to make her a part of his life for however long he could, then I believed, and still do, that it would be all right.

And that is the story of how Dr. Reni Lira and I came to live in that small village with the Reverend David Young so that Mr. Brown's story of "The Witch" came to have that particular ending. We continued to live and work there for nearly a decade until the senior Miss Young could no longer live alone. At that time, the Reverend Young requested, and was granted, a transfer to a church in the city of Boston so that we could move in with his elderly aunt. To that place Dr. Lira and I took one portable com-unit and a number of small data scanners. Everything else we left sealed in the shuttle.

As the full extent of our work shows, we were far from idle in the years that have passed since our ill-fated drop-off. When Dr. Lira's husband died in his sleep at the local age of eight-seven, we were still living in the old house in

Memorandum

Boston, and Dr. Lira and I continued our work there until the Commonwealth Space Service vessel, *Explorer*, made contact with us late last year. Our work wore out three separate data scanners, but we have managed to accumulate an astonishingly complete look at one of the most exciting and dynamic periods in the development of any world. It is our hope that YS*872-3 will not be abandoned by the Commonwealth but will continue to be the object of study. Like all sentient races, the human beings inhabiting the planet Earth are often brilliant and, at times, frightfully volatile. I pray they will be one of the races to survive that deadly combination in order to reach out to the galactic community when their time comes.

I have probably gone on long enough, but I felt it extremely important that our story be told in its entirety. I did, of course, leave out a great deal of detail. However, all of it is available to anyone who wishes to confront the results of our almost sixty years of research.

The most important thing for Dr. Lira and me is that the Commonwealth be made aware of the beginning of our adventure, both to ensure it doesn't happen again, and to encourage searches for other survey crews who may still be out there, abandoned as we were. The counterclaims, as filed against us by the Galactic Sociological Research Institute, matter very little in the face of what might be happening at this very moment on some other unsuspecting world. We, ourselves, have no complaints. We were extremely fortunate to live full and happy lives, even as a result of our abandonment on YS*872-3, though we will be the first to admit that our recovery, before the point at which either of us had reached an age when health had become a concern, was certainly welcome. It is also comforting to know that the one-hundred-fifty-year guarantee on the shuttle's cloaking force field will not need to be tested.

In spite of our personal success, however, we continue to be concerned that someone else will not be so fortunate, a situation which could result not only in the loss of talented individual researchers but possibly in the destruction of entire worlds.

I declare that the foregoing is true and complete to the best of my knowledge.

Dated this 8th day of the 14th month of the 269th year of the Commonwealth of Planets.

Dr. Mroweo Hsstu, PhD.

Dr. Mroweo Hsstu, PhD.

THE HAT
BY CINDY KOEPP

C loud snatched the slice of apple from Ingrid and clutched it in one foot. The fruit made a satisfying crunch when Cloud nibbled off the first beak-full. Being a special agent for the king was such a tasty job.

"Snack? Snack?" Ash sidled as close as their cage bars allowed.

Cloud turned her back on the gray parrot. "No."

"Of course, you can have a piece, Ash, but you can't have Cloud's." Ingrid stepped over to Ash's cage to dole out his share. She moved down the line and held a slice through the pionus's bars. "Here you go, Cappie."

Cappie reached out as if sudden movement would cause the food to evaporate. Once his beak clamped down on the fruit, he retreated to his perch faster than a falcon in a stoop.

Cloud paused her munching. "Silly bird."

The last piece of the apple vanished down her throat. She fluffed out all her feathers and shook, billowing white feather dust in all directions.

Ingrid continued around the rectangular room handing out apple slices to all the other birds. Her green dress was a good match for the feathers on Cappie's back, and her blond hair looked like the lutino cockatiel on the other side of the room. She did a good job of blending in with the whole flock.

Once all the birds had their snack, Ingrid served herself a piece of apple, too. Cloud's pet human was such a good little caretaker. The birds always came first.

A light knock on the door preceded Ash mimicking the sound with flawless accuracy. He was so good at that.

Why can't I be that good?

Ingrid turned toward the door. "Come in."

The door opened far enough for Frank and Mick to slip in. Any taller and Frank would have to duck under the door frame, but if he didn't start watching how many snacks he had, he would be as round as he was tall. The top of Mick's head came to Frank's eye-level. Today he had brown hair, but that could change. How one human could have so many different hair colors, face shapes, and voices was beyond Cloud, but he was a nice human. He'd be even better if he brought a snack with him from time to time.

THE HAT

Cappie jumped from his perch to the side of the cage. "Hi, 'Ick! Hi, 'Ick!"

"Hello, Cappie." Mick strode over to the pionus's cage. "How's my favorite pi today?"

Cappie tucked his beak to his chest and fluffed up his head feathers. Like a good human, Mick gave Cappie's head a little preening.

"Here you are." Frank joined Ingrid at the table. "I've been looking for you."

Ingrid rolled her eyes. "It's feeding time. You thought I'd be anywhere except the aviary?"

Silly human. Cloud preened a couple feathers back into place.

"I guess I didn't track the time." Frank set a hat on the table. "We have a mission. Gregory Brown is in the area."

Ingrid sat up straighter. "Oh, no. What's he after this time?"

"Information of some sort." Mick left Cappie and joined the other humans. "Probably about the castle defenses."

"And if he offers enough money, someone will take him up on it," Frank said.

Last time that nasty human had put in his appearance, Cloud had donated one of her white wing feathers, already molted of course, for Mick's disguise. She'd molted since then, so Ingrid's supply of nice, white feathers was full.

Frank tapped the hat on the table. "One of Mick's informants says the feather color will be pink this time."

Cloud hissed and looked at Cappie in the next cage. Some of his feathers were pink, especially on his tail. Then again, white feathers could always be dyed to whatever color they needed.

"So, we're just going to intercept the information again and let Gregory slip away?" Ingrid rolled her eyes. "He'll be back to try again. You—."

Mick held up his hand. "We're going to try to get both the informant and Gregory this time. I'm going to need some of Cappie's tail feathers and your best retriever to get Gregory's hat and prove he has the information hidden there."

"Cappie is the best retriever, all right." Ingrid walked over to the pionus's cage and unlatched the door. "I don't know if he's big enough to pick up a hat, though."

Cappie hopped onto her hand without a fuss while Mick put on the hat and stood on the other side of the room.

Cloud danced from foot to foot. She spread her wings and flipped up her crest. "Go, Cappie! Go, Cappie!"

Mick chuckled. "Not so loud, Cloud. You'll make him nervous."

"It'll be loud enough in the crowd." Frank shook his head. "He'll have to be able to do it in spite of distractions."

Ingrid held Cappie close to her face. "Cappie, hat.

The Hat

Cappie, hat. Hat. Go."

The pionus launched from Ingrid's hand and flapped his bronze and blue wings hard to come up to speed. Cloud continued to chant her encouragement. Cappie had only been with the king's agents a few short months. The fledgling was a smart bird, but he would need all the help he could get. As he neared the target on Mick's head, Cloud added nodding to her grand display. With her cheering for him, how could he miss?

Cappie grabbed Mick's hat in his talons and flapped hard again but lost momentum and height. The pionus squawked at half the volume of a cockatoo, still not bad for such a small, stout bird. Cloud froze as Cappie plummeted and landed hard on the wooden floor.

Cloud lowered her crest and tucked in her wings. "Aww, poor Cappie."

Ash laughed.

"Shut up, Ash!" Cloud shrieked, fluffed up her feathers. "Shut up!"

Ash imitated a door knock then laughed again.

Ingrid rushed over and offered Cappie her hand. "What do you have in this hat?"

"Some coins and paper." Mick retrieved his hat. "We're pretty sure Gregory keeps all that tucked in the hatband."

Cappie scrambled up to Ingrid's shoulder and perched

next to her cheek.

"There's no way." Ingrid preened Cappie's head. "He's just not going to be strong enough."

"Who else is a good retriever?" Frank scanned all the birds. "Ash?"

Ingrid shook her head. "Not if you want the hat and its contents in one piece. He could probably carry the hat, but he wouldn't waste any time chewing on it." She surveyed the birds. "Cloud's the only other one big enough. She's just not much of a retriever."

Of course, not. I'm not a dog, but I can bark like one! Cloud imitated one of the huge dogs that guarded the king.

Ash echoed and added in a few other animal calls.

Show off.

"Well, let's try her." Mick planted the hat back on his head. "If this doesn't work, we'll have to use Ash and get to the hat before he does too much damage."

Ingrid put Cappie back and opened Cloud's cage. "Come on. Step up."

Cloud raised her foot as high as she could before stepping over to Ingrid's hand.

Ingrid held Cloud up close. "Cloud, hat. Cloud—."

"Honk!" Cloud grabbed Ingrid's nose.

"Stop that." Ingrid frowned and pushed Cloud's beak away. "Show time."

THE HAT

Oh. Show time. Not play time? Fine. She shifted her weight from foot to foot and waited for the show command.

"Cloud, hat. Cloud, hat. Hat. Go."

After turning in place to face the right way, Cloud crouched and leapt into the air. She flapped a few times to get speed and circled the room. The air streaming through her feathers felt wonderful.

"Cloud, hat!" Ingrid ordered.

Yes, hat. I know. I need speed!

Circling one last time, she dropped down to hat-height and buzzed past Mick's head, catching the hat in both talons. Elephants weighed less. No wonder poor Cappie had done his best rock impression. Cloud flapped hard, tightened her grip, and made for the nearest safe perch, the table. She dropped the hat, made a tight circle, and landed on top of it. Flaring her crest and nodding, Cloud let loose a screech worthy of an umbrella cockatoo.

"Too loud. Too loud," Ash protested.

She let out another cockatoo shriek.

Ingrid sighed. "It's too heavy for her, too."

Frank sat at the table. "Yes, but if she perches on it like that, I'll bet a big-beaked, shrieking parrot will make most people pause if they want to go for the hat. This could work. We'll just have to get to Cloud before Gregory can." He offered his hand. "Good job, Cloud."

She climbed up on his fingers and tucked her forehead down onto his hand. He rubbed under her crest. He could do that for years, and it wouldn't be too much. She did her best impression of the queen's purring cat.

Ingrid and Mick joined them.

"The exchange is supposed to be at the fair." Frank pointed at Ingrid. "I'll be your manager, and you'll do a bird show with Cloud and whoever else you think could use the practice. I'll be in the crowd to signal you when it's time for Cloud to do her thing."

Cloud stood up straighter. For the sake of the king, she'd do this dog job, but there'd better be a snack in it for her.

* * *

The sun chased away the slight chill in the breeze. Cloud tucked a foot into her feathers and ground her lower beak into her upper one while she waited for her turn. Ingrid ran the other birds through one of the usual routines while a crowd gathered at the foot of the shallow stage and watched. The cockatiels chased each other around in an aerial game of tag orchestrated by minute hand gestures from Ingrid. Cloud kept her teeny cousins in the edge of her vision while scanning the crowd. Her higher perch gave her an excellent view.

Rosy pink feathers blared on a tan hat. Cloud left off

watching Ingrid and the cockatiels and speared the hat with her gaze. Was that the evil Gregory? She leaned forward. No, that couldn't be. The feather on the end had shades of blue and green just like Cappie's tail. That had to be Mick pretending to be Gregory.

Mick wandered through the crowd. A female human Cloud recognized from the king's kitchen, the ultimate source of excellent snacks, caught Mick's arm. She passed him some white, square thing. Mick slipped the thing under his hat and pressed something small and sparkly into the woman's hand.

The two walked off in separate directions.

Gray and yellow wings fluttered past Cloud on both sides. She squawked and jumped halfway to the clouds overhead before she figured out the cockatiels had buzzed past her. The crowd laughed as Ingrid wagged her scolding finger in Cloud's direction. She made a fist and mimicked knocking on a door. Cloud flipped her crest up and nodded a few times as ordered. The audience broke into new fits of laughter, so Cloud kicked first one foot then the other and squawked.

Next time, watch Ingrid.

* * *

The red and white tent behind the stage was warmer than outdoors but lacked the somewhat chilly breeze and the heavenly direct sunlight. Cloud sat on her perch and shredded the seedy bread in her food bowl. Nearby, the six cockatiels nibbled on their own piece. Ash would have been mad at them for spooking him on stage, but really, how could Cloud blame her teeny cousins. First off, they'd only been following directions. Secondly, she should have been more focused on the show. Ingrid had clearly said, "Cloud, show time," before they'd started.

The tent's back flap flipped open, and a man with a gray beard and gray-streaked hair slipped in like he owned the place. His trousers and tunic were worn and out of date, but not too badly frayed. Cloud hissed and shrieked. The cockatiels added their chirps to the ruckus.

Ingrid darted in from the human dressing area on the far side as Frank stepped in from the stage.

"It's me! It's me, guys. It's me." Mick pulled the gray hair off before he peeled the beard away.

"Hello, 'Ick!" Cloud waved with her foot.

"Hi, Cloud." He turned to Frank and pulled the paper from his pocket. "Here's the information. You'll never believe who the spy is."

Frank nodded and frowned. "I saw the exchange. Who'd've thought such a sweet girl—Well, anyway, the sheriff's been alerted, and he's on his way to make the arrest." He pointed to the paper in Mick's hand. "What's Gregory after?"

Mick handed the paper over. "I haven't had a chance to look. I wanted to get out of sight before the real Gregory could spot me, and then I needed to change into this get-up so I could get in here without blowing our cover."

Frank flattened out the paper on the table where the cockatiels were eating. Some of the cockatiels crowded closer. Spinner stretched her neck out and opened her beak.

"No, Spinner. Bad!" Cloud hissed and narrowed her eyes.

Ingrid tapped the other side of the table. The whole cockatiel flock scrambled over to her.

"Guard rotations." Frank thwacked the paper with his finger. "Not just the stationary positions but the timing of patrols, too."

"Oh, nice." Mick opened a supply trunk and withdrew a piece of paper, a quill, and an inkwell. "That handwriting's almost school-perfect. I can reverse the information."

"No. Better to throw in some random variables. An exact reverse might be detected."

"Got it. That'll take me a few minutes, but it won't be a

problem." Mick took the paper and pulled a stool over to the table.

"Good. Once you get that finished, learn a show routine from Ingrid and brief her on the exchange with Gregory." Frank leaned closer. "Even with your disguise skills, I don't think you could pass for a scullery maid."

Mick chuckled. "No, no, haven't got the right build for it. That's for sure."

"I'm off to talk to the guard captain. If I'm not back when you're ready to go, don't wait for me. If Cloud doesn't make it back to her stand, remember, we need to get to Cloud before anyone else."

If you make that hat weigh less, I can fly further with it, silly human.

Frank ducked out of the tent.

"Think you can pull together a less interesting dress?" Mick uncorked the inkwell. "You're too pretty for a kitchen wench in that one."

Ingrid headed for the human dressing area. "I came prepared."

As Mick dipped the quill into the ink, Cloud returned to her bread. If she was going to have to carry an elephant of a hat, she'd need her energy.

The Hat

* * *

Cloud watched the cockatiels end their directed game of tag and come in for a landing on their multi-leveled perch. The audience's dim applause wasn't half of what the poor cockatiels deserved. They'd done so well. Cloud flapped her wings to add to the humans' sparse appreciation.

Determined not to make the same mistake this time, Cloud settled and watched Mick carefully. As was so typical of him, Mick didn't look the same as earlier. Now he wore a black mustache and a heavily embroidered tunic and trousers.

The crowds were less dense this afternoon, which would make the retrieval of the hat at least a little easier.

Mick pulled out a lute. He mimed knocking on a door then started to play a tune with a quick beat. Cloud flared her crest and nodded in time with the music, kicking her foot with each downbeat. When the music paused, she froze in place until Mick started playing again. She listened to the tune, matching her movements to his beat even when he sped up or slowed down. The audience laughed until Mick put the lute away. Cloud nodded faster and screeched her approval for their reaction.

Mick rushed closer and offered his hand. "Step up!"

Cloud kicked her left foot as high as she could before planting it on his fingers and moving across.

He leaned in. "Cloud, hat. Cloud, hat. Hat. Go."

She turned in place then crouched and launched from his hand. As she spiraled upward, she scanned the crowd for Ingrid and a man with a pink-feathered hat.

The brilliant, pink-dyed ostrich plume stood out in the sea of browns, greens, and grays. Ingrid in her patched dress headed away from the ostrich-plume. Cloud dove for the hat, but Gregory dropped something and crouched to get it as she passed. She hissed and flapped hard as she climbed and looped over.

Gregory hurried through the crowd.

Oh no, you don't! That hat is mine, human!

She sped after him. He spun and charged toward her, and she readied to grab the hat on his head. As he came closer, he swatted at her, and she veered aside, making a grab for the hat with her left foot. Soft fuzziness came away as she turned skyward and climbed far too easily. This hat wasn't heavy at all. She glanced down and hissed at the bright pink ostrich plume. No hat. Cloud let the feather go and scanned the crowd for Gregory.

A loose mass of yellow and gray with orange dots streaked toward a man speeding through the crowd toward the far gate of the market. The cockatiel flock? They'd never be able to get the hat. It outweighed all six of them together!

Cloud turned toward their target. Gregory took his hat

off and clutched it in his hand.

Uh-oh. Now how do I get it?

The cockatiel flock arrived first and turned into a fluttery mob right in front of Gregory. He stumbled backward and the hat went airborne. Cloud turned into a stoop, tucking her wings in close. She snatched the hat midair and flapped like mad as she banked toward the stage. The cockatiel flock zipped ahead of her and made for their perch.

Just like Mick's practice hat, this one weighed an elephant or more.

Cloud's chest muscles burned with the effort of so much hard flying. She had to land now before she turned into a cockatoo-shaped rock.

"Cloud, Cloud, here!" Ingrid called.

Tipping one wing down, Cloud turned toward the voice and spotted Ingrid a five-second flight away with her arm outstretched. A five-second flight could have been five years. Cloud locked her wings into glide position and let gravity pull her downward. Ingrid raced forward.

Cloud dropped the hat and landed before she went back and claimed her prize by flaring out her crest and shrieking loud enough to make any umbrella cockatoo proud. Ingrid arrived a second later and offered her hand. Cloud stepped up and let her pet take care of the weighted hat.

"Give me back my hat!" Gregory bellowed as he pushed

his way through the crowds.

"Is your hat, sir?" The sheriff's deputy came forward and took the hat.

Cloud reached for it, but Ingrid stepped away.

"It is mine, and I'll thank you to return it to me." Gregory stopped within arms-reach and grabbed for the hat.

The deputy twisted away, and his shiny badge sparkled in the sunlight. "What's this?" He withdrew a paper and unfolded it. "Interesting." He stuffed the hat into his waistband and drew a small knife from its sheath. "You're with me, sir, and if you have any ideas of trying to escape, I'm a deadly aim with these, and there's enough evidence here to justify deadly force."

He gripped Gregory by the arm and led him away.

"Good job, Cloud. Well done." Ingrid preened the back of Cloud's head and neck for a moment.

Cloud ruffled up all her feathers and shook, releasing a fog of feather dust into the air. "Snack? Snack?"

Ingrid chuckled. "Oh, I think you and the cockatiels have all earned a very nice snack."

Snack time was the best part of being a king's agent.

Cloud fanned out her tail, raised her crest, and screeched.

Scarheid in the Glisting
By Ian Hunter

They call this place the Hidden Valley. That part of Glen Coe where the mountains crowd together. For years letting the MacDonalds hide the cattle they had rustled, leading four-legged beasts up winding narrow paths that were treacherous at any time of year, but especially when the rain fell and the snow lay inches deep on the ground. Led them along those passes to where the land seemed to unfold and part before them, and everything here was plentiful.

But it is hidden no more.

* * *

I curse myself for our timidity, for it has been the end of us. We should have run when we heard the humans coming, should have fled when we caught their scent and the bitter tang they carried. Now it is too late for me and my brood. Tar-drenched rags have been placed all around the thorny thicket that is our home deep in the glen.

They burn the rags, and we burn too.

Branches crackle and die, the air thickens with smoke. Through the flames I see the hated humans, their faces contorted with laughter. I mark each one, consigning it to my memory, knowing even that is futile. I will never have my revenge on them.

Then comes another voice, educated, and I know it is the new Laird, come to watch the clearing of the last of the wildcats the same way he has cleared out the crofters.

My two remaining offspring cower beside me, then a branch splinters above us, raining down thorns and sparks and one bounds to the left, but is caught in a tangle of thicket and struggles to be free, ripping himself to pieces in the process. I smell blood and watch him struggle forward as more branches collapse, engulfing him in flame and he shrieks and writhes as the fire takes hold. Seeing the death of his brother, the last of my young panics and rushes forward, scurrying away from me. Too late, my outstretched paw tries to snag him back, but he disappears towards the flames.

Seconds pass, and I wonder and hope he has made it to freedom. Then I hear him whimper as he tries to return to me, little tail ablaze, flames racing up his spine, before his little striped head catches fire and soon dead eyes are staring at me accusingly.

His mother, who let him die like this.

They are all gone.

Burned to death.

My kin, my children.

I am the last of us, struggling to stand against the unbearable heat pressing in from every side. I gather all my strength and wrap it in a coat of fear and rage and leap from the burning thicket, thorns tearing at my body. A twisted, guttural growl rasping through my throat, and I emerge twisting through the air towards the hated group of men in front of me.

My body burns, but I do not care. My hate-filled heart feels as if it might explode within the cradle of my chest. In my mind is an image of the Laird's head as I clamber on top of it—my back legs clawing for purchase, ruining his cheeks and throat while I plunge my burning head into his mouth, tearing at his tongue as I move deeper down his gullet, choking him.

Then everything changes. The world changes, becomes different. The very air is different. Sweeter. Cooler, and while I am still leaping the men in front of me have vanished. A hand comes out of nowhere and seizes me by the scruff of the neck, and I kick and spit and struggle, but the fingers do not open. The arm does not drop. Merely swings round giving me a glimpse of a dark haired man, a twisted grin on his face.

Then the world tilts, and I am plunging downwards through the cold flowing surface of a burn. Things dart away from me, filled with dark and light and bones I can see through their bodies.

A vision, I am having a vision caused by pain and imminent death.

The water is so cold, I can scarcely breathe and my heart lurches within my chest, and seems to stutter, on the verge of stopping. Then I am pulled out and held high, a bedraggled trophy. Drookit, with all the fight washed out of me by the numbing power of the stream. Water drips from my body, leaving behind the returning, blossoming pain of the fire.

The man's arm bends at the elbow bringing me closer to his face. I try to scratch him, a feeble attempt, and he laughs, swinging his arm to the side and opening his fingers and I thump against the ground, rolling over and over into darkness, filled with nothing except the echoing dying shrieks of my young.

* * *

I wake, full of fear and anger. I cannot move, or at least my head cannot.

Something is around my neck: hard metal, like a thin

horseshow, wrapped around my throat and driven into the ground. The man looms above me. My body thrashes, and I swipe out with my front leg, trying to claw him—an action that almost breaks my neck as I move or would crush my throat. Better that way, a quick ending, or sorts, by my own paw. This is when he will gut me, or skin me, wearing my hide as a trophy, my bushy tail adorning his collar.

He bats my paw away. "Keep still, cat! Dammit, do ye want helped or not?"

The man reaches to the side and holds up a dish. Food, I think, my stomach grumbling, I cannot remember when I last fed, and I think I have been sleeping for a long time. The fingers of his other hand dip into the bowl and he brings them up, dripping in white gruel—porridge, perhaps. Even that would do me now, I think, if he does not have a bird or a ferret; a rabbit, even. He slaps the slop on to my side. It stings. I thrash, clawing. He grabs my leg and leans closer, teeth bared.

"I could let you die, cat. Easily, but somehow you have made it here. To the other side. Aye, you, a cat. A thing on four legs. What skill do you have to do that, eh? What powers do you possess? Well, we'll see, won't we? If you live, that is, but only if you'll let me help you."

Trust a human after what they've done to me and my kind? That'll be the day, but somehow I do and relax slightly, lowering my claw. He nods, and reaches into the bowl again, smearing my wounds with the stinging gruel, and eventually the stinging turns to a throbbing pain that fades to a cooling numbness.

"That's better," he says, reaching to the side, and holds up a round of stale-looking bread and tears a strip from it. "Eat," he orders, thrusting it towards me. It is not bird, or ferret, or rabbit, but it will have to do.

* * *

When next I wake I am no longer pinned to the ground. Worse, I am tethered to a tree — a slender, silver chain stretched from its trunk to my neck to a collar I cannot see. The chain is thin, but stronger than it looks. I try to gnaw through it, or weaken the links. Yet, despite my efforts it remains unmarked, perfect. I can walk, but only so far, though the burn is within my reach. The water flows crystal clear, babbling over stones as it comes down from the hills whose peaks are always shrouded in mist.

Deer amble across the slopes. Old males, I can tell by the span of their antlers, though something looks wrong with their bodies which seem to change colour slightly, again and again. From the red of their fur to something whiter. I think it might be a trick of the light or damage done to my eyes by the flames and the smoke. Despite their changing bodies I have the impression that they are old, but powerful. Untroubled as they stride through the long grasses.

I drink what tastes like the freshest water ever and watch fish that look like ghosts swim beneath the surface, their bones and innards shining through their scales. The spectres of fish would look like this, and despite my stealth and flashing paws I can flick none of them on to the bank to jerk and spasm. That worries me. If they are ghosts then I might be one, too.

* * *

The man is back again. Somehow, he is just…there. I do not hear him approaching, rustling the grass, cracking the odd branch. I do not smell him, or his clothes, or the weed he sometimes smokes. Worst of all, I do not see him, he appears from nowhere. A man who comes and goes like a phantom has me at his mercy.

He watches me prowl above the burn as he kneels on the ground and unpacks some items from his sack. "You will not catch them, cat. They are of this place, while we are not. We are just visitors, passing through."

I stop pacing, tilt my head and look at him.

"This is the Glisting, the world within the world, the refugee of the Seers."

I almost nod. A Seer, that explains everything. A Seer,

a witch, a warlock, are these all not names for the same thing? So he comes here to hide from his persecutors, those who would burn him at the stake, or drown him in a loch. Once, I watched from leafy shadows as one poor wretch was pressed to death. Pinned to the ground with wood placed on top of her then rocks placed on top of that. She shrieked and moaned for a long time, until the stones were removed and men rode over the wood with their cart and horses, and they left her there beneath the wood at the mercy of scavengers from the skies.

He produces a large bird from his sack, a grouse or a capercaillie. My mouth fills with juices. "Yet, not every Seer can come to this place, but it has been said that I am the most powerful of my kind. The High Seer of Scotland if I wished to claim that crown." Laughter falls from his mouth, a bitter sound. He moves forward on his knees, gathering wood together. "Yes, I know you would rather rip our meal apart and guzzle down its bloody innards, but I prefer my food to be cooked."

Later, he nestles against a tree, bones lying beside him on the grass, juices hardening on his beard. He points in my direction. "So what brought you here, cat?

"Did you and your kind attract the attention of the new Laird? I've heard he's come up from London to take his dead faither's place in the big house. Him, with his fancy new ideas, his new ways — he wouldn't like you prowling across his estate, taking whatever lambs you can. Oh no, if he can drive folk who have lived here for centuries off the land, put their crofts to the torch, and take the homes of those who are young and old and sick and infirm, then he wouldn't think twice of burning your den."

I growl. I can't help it. My back arches and my body tenses as my head fills with the memories of those last few minutes in the thicket, fire all around us, and that voice. Young and cultivated.

The man, the Seer, laughs, throwing a piece of breast in my direction, but I am too bristling with hate to go for it straight away.

"So, that's how you came through," he mutters.

* * *

One day he unties the silver chain from the tree, wraps it again and again around his hand, tightening the gleaming line between us. His other hand is raised before him, and his fingers open and close as if he is clawing at the air, and somehow he is. The air shimmers, cracks, revealing a slit of bright light that lengthens, and he walks through it, dragging me behind him. Despite my stubborn legs digging into the dirt I am no match for his strength, and I am pulled into the lights.

Through the lights and back into my world, I realise, sensations buffeting me from every direction. Sounds, smells — they are all there.

The Seer crouches and pushes at my back bone. "Down, cat!"

I spit at him but do as I am told.

We peer through the long grass at the scene below. People dragged from their crofts, clutching small children to their chests or whatever meagre possessions they can carry, if they have anything at all. Defeated, some are already walking away, taking the trail south. Others stand defiant, arguing with a man on horseback. My nostrils flare, I know the rider's scent. Without thinking, I start to trot forward. The Seer yanks me back. I spit at him. He holds up a finger to my face, and I am tempted to tear it off.

"Watch and learn, cat," he tells me, and I want to tell him that I know enough.

Three young men stand defiant, barring the Laird's men from getting to the last of the little knot of crofts, but they are outnumbered and are lucky only to be badly beaten, rather than be held and run through by a sword. We watch as they are left bloody and unconscious and dragged away by their kin to be tended among the bracken and the heather while their homes burn behind them.

"We've seen enough," the Seer says sadly, and we turn

to go as his hand flutters and words are whispered and the air begins to part before us, taking us to the place of safety, the Glisting.

* * *

Another day I wake to find that I am no longer tethered to the tree. The silver chain is gone, but there is still something wrapped around my throat. Is the collar also silver, I wonder, staring at my rippling reflection in the edges of the burn, my head still a mess even though the pain has lessened, though not gone entirely. There is more than enough pain in my heart, but it is nothing compared to the hatred that sits there, pulsing away. Angrily, I jab a paw at the water, splitting my reflection. Ghost fish dart from the calm edges of the water and are carried away downstream. A stag has wandered down from the hills. Royalty, yet when I look at it I can see through its fur to the skin below, then through what is rippling below that, right through to its bones. Its shape ripples as it moves. Deer to ghost deer to the skeletal remains of the deer. Everything that lives here is the same, only the Seer and I are different, outsiders.

That night, when stars shine strangely overhead, and the light of the Seer's fire has almost died, I slink forward as stealthily as I can manage, belly kissing the ground, a part of me glad that the old skills — part of my bones, my very essence—are returning. Still present, even in this aching, scorched body. The Seer does not stir while I move closer, eyes darting between his face and his hands, though he has never carried a weapon, except at the times he gutted something he brought back from the other place. The real place, my home, or what was left of it.

Nothing.

Except scorched wood and scorched bones, blackened, all of them.

I ghost beside his body. His legs, his groin, his belly, then slip onto his chest and nestle there, below his throat. I hesitate, wondering why he has not reacted, wondering why I have not struck. Is he not human, different, but still a man? A hated human. I open my mouth, and raise a paw. The Seer does not move. He might be a statue. He might merely be sleeping, so content he looks, so unworried. He might be dead. He soon might be.

"Are you going to kill me then, cat?" he asks softly, a wry smile on his lips.

He opens his eyes slowly and stares at me. This close, I notice that his eyes are different colours—one blue, like the sky; one green, like the land.

We look at each other for a long time, until he raises a hand. Empty, I notice, but he is strong, I remember that from our first encounter, will never forget what happened in the moments leading up to meeting him.

I snarl at him, spit.

"Easy," he breathes, turning his hand slowly, showing only fingers. No knife, no stick to beat me into submission, and then death.

The hand moves closer, closer, inch by inch by inch, and I tense, claws ready to rip and tear, wondering who would be faster.

"Easy...Scarheid," he says again, chuckling slightly, fingers brushing against my left ear, part of it tender and exposed, part of it covered by hard, burned fur, strands fused together, so the reflecting waters of the burn have shown me. I flinch away but his hand still follows, brushing my ear again, catching it between thumb and index finger and rubbing slowly. Calming. Hypnotic.

He closes his eyes. "Easy," his voice drifts away, and if there was any tension in his body, there is none now.

Then his eyes snap open, and he grins, fingers falling away from my ear. "Do you still want to kill me, Auld Scarheid? Kill me, and you'll never get home, cat. Kill me, and you'll never have your revenge."

* * *

Revenge.

The Glisting can take you anywhere. No matter how

guarded, no matter how safe, or as safe as the humans like to think they are. You can emerge anywhere, inside a castle, even.

I look through a window into the courtyard down below. The Seer is looking up at me. The Laird lies behind me in his tangled, bloodied sheets. I have tasted his eyes and his tongue and lapped at the blood from his throat. None of them will bring my children back, but it is enough for now.

Raising his hand, the Seer moves his fingers, not to open the Glisting, but only the window in front of me. I half-fall, half-scurry down the ivy on the outside of the wall.

"So, cat," he says, looking down at me. "Your business is done. We can walk the hills together or go our separate ways,. What say you?"

I hiss at him.

"Well, then," he says with a smile, and together we turn away as the air shines before us and another world opens its door.

THE MASTERLESS
BY STEVEN GRASSIE

1.

Both hunters keep low and still, their eyes locked on the deer. The young stag is foraging in a small clearing in the forest, seemingly unaware of his predicament. Kojima glances over at Shiro, who's about twenty paces to his right. This close to their quarry, the dark-brindle akita's tail is slowly lowering, uncoiling from its normal curled position high on the dog's back; he's eyeing the deer fastidiously and his triangular ears are cocked forward. A small smile tugs at the corners of Kojima's mouth — it's in such moments that the big akita looks uncannily like a wolf.

Kojima returns his gaze to the deer and is glad to find it yet oblivious. Slowly he raises his hankyū and nocks an arrow to its string. The half-bow's range is nothing like a long-bow's, although being a mere thirty paces away the deer stands little chance.

Early this morning, Shiro had been excited by a scent he picked up and Kojima had let him follow it—it has been a few days since they've eaten substantially. It had taken until the sun was almost overhead before Kojima glimpsed a flash of the deer's brown coat through the trees, and he and Shiro had edged closer and closer until a hand gesture from his master had halted the akita's progress. Kojima was pleased the deer was indeed a deer: if Shiro had been tracking a wild boar or, may the heavens forbid, a bear, then things might not be as straightforward as they were going to be.

Now Kojima levels the hankyū and draws the arrow until the hemp string brushes the stubble of his upper lip. The deer brings its head up, alert though clearly not alarmed. Even so, Kojima resolves to shoot his arrow—but from the corner of his eye he notices Shiro is distracted and has turned to look over his shoulder. This is beyond strange. Kojima keeps the arrow nocked but relaxes his draw and turns to follow Shiro's line of sight. The akita has now turned completely, the deer all but forgotten, and so Kojima does the same—years of experience has taught him to trust the dog's instincts. Sure enough, dark movement through the trees announces the arrival of men.

From behind, a flurry of sounds tells Kojima the deer has made good its escape. He also makes to flee—he is still in no mood for confrontation, with beast *or* man—but an arrow thuds into the tree beside his face, and then he spies two horsemen quickly approaching. Kojima likes to think he's still fleet of foot, but a man has his limits.

"Away," he whispers to Shiro, gesturing with a jut of his chin. The akita's posture has changed: head up, chest out, tail back in its place over his back. He looks at his master, his deep brown eyes barely discernible in his dark-streaked face, and has to be told "Away" again before he melts into the undergrowth.

Moments later, Kojima is surrounded by three men afoot and two ahorse; the former hold drawn bows, the latter drawn katana. He drops the hankyū to the ground before he's told to and spreads his arms wide. The archers relax their draws slightly.

"State your name and business," one of the riders commands.

Kojima sees no point in lying; there is no honor in it.

"Kojima Hisamasa. And I am…*was* hunting." He expects some sort of reaction to the sound of his name—he's being realistic, not arrogant—and he gets it: all their eyes widen and the horsemen exchange a glance.

They are samurai, these mounted men, retainers of

whichever daimyō owns this land; the others are huntsmen, judging by their garb and bows. There is an extended pause, during which Kojima looks at each samurai in turn, his eyebrows raised in question: *Well?*

"You have a hunting license?" And now each of the samurai has spoken — and Kojima notices one of the huntsmen actually rolling his eyes at the inane question.

Kojima looks at both warriors again: their young voices match well their young faces. Arms still spread, he has to suppress a smile as he says, "You are welcome to search me."

All eyes glance down at Kojima's swords riding high on his left hip, then move back to their owner's face. He has not shaved the front of his head for a while, and some strands have escaped his topknot; and his *clothes*...simple and unkempt, they are more suited to a peasant than a samurai. But those swords loudly betray what he is. And then there's the matter of his name....

The first samurai to have spoken pipes up again: "These are our Lord Yukimura's lands, *rōnin*." The last word is said like it tastes bad. "Hunting without permission is unlawful, as you kn—" His words trail off as something seems to occur to him; he glances around and, not without a trace of nervousness, says, "Where is...?" and although he's unsure how to finish the question, his meaning is obvious.

"He's around," Kojima replies, and he now lets a small

smile show as something dark moves soundlessly in the undergrowth a short distance behind the horses. But Shiro will do nothing unless his master signals to him otherwise — which he doesn't.

Even so, the outspoken samurai's unease is contagious, and his companions begin to glance around, half-expecting the akita to make a sudden and unwelcome appearance. The huntsmen fully draw their bows again — just about managing to keep them trained on Kojima — and both samurai quickly dismount and hold their swords ready.

Kojima hasn't moved a muscle; his arms remain outstretched to the side. If his belly wasn't rumbling so much from hunger, he'd perhaps be enjoying this episode.

"Loosen your sword belt, rōnin!"

Slowly, Kojima brings his hands down to the belt's knot, but it's tied tightly and it takes a while to unravel — during which his would-be captors divide their vigilance between Kojima and the surrounding forest. Eventually the rōnin lowers his swords to the forest floor, and the less vocal samurai sheathes his katana before carefully approaching Kojima. First, he retrieves the discarded swords and backs away from their owner; then he secures the weapons to his horse's saddle and, having produced a leather thong, he returns to the rōnin and proceeds to tie his hands together behind his back.

"I should think Lord Yukimura would very much like to make your acquaintance," the mouthy samurai says, coming to stand in front of Kojima.

"Your master and I are long-since acquainted, young warrior," Kojima replies, and the samurai narrows his eyes as he tries to decide if he has been slighted. But Kojima has already started walking in the direction from which the men had come, and the men can do nothing but follow.

* * *

They stand in a room adjacent to the daimyō's living quarter: Kojima, his two samurai captors, and Lord Yukimura's chief retainer, Shimazu Gozen. By far the daimyo's longest-serving samurai, Gozen is a short, stocky man, and has a stern countenance. The silence is as awkward as it is tense.

Kojima's hands are still tied as he stands impassively, waiting. He is wondering where Shiro might be, what he might be up to, although with little worry. On the journey to the castle of the Kitami clan, the akita had shadowed their little group without coming too close. But as forest had dissipated to open fields Kojima lost sight of the dog, knowing he would hang back out of sight before trailing his master under the cover of darkness.

Kojima is snapped from his reverie as a door slides open. A manservant steps back from the opened portal and the rōnin is urged forwards by a shove in his back. All four men move through to the adjoining room, and Kojima comes face-to-face with Lord Yukimura. The daimyō is frowning, the lines across his brow exaggerated by lantern-cast shadows. To one side of the room lurk two wizened advisers.

The newcomers incline their heads to their lord, and the two younger samurai cannot help their chests from puffing out. Lord Yukimura looks from the rōnin to his captors and then back again; the frown on his forehead deepens.

"I assume you were caught by surprise?" the daimyō asks.

Kojima does not reply. He can sense the mixture of shock and indignation coming from the young warriors.

"Leave us," Yukimura suddenly commands, and immediately the various men in the room make to depart, although Gozen requires a reassuring nod from his lord before grudgingly turning away. Quickly, the room empties of samurai and advisers; the manservant leaves last and slides the door closed behind him.

Lord Yukimura gives Kojima an appraising look and, despite the rōnin's undoubtedly un-samurai-like appearance, the leader of the Kitami clan says, "The years have been kind to you, Kojima."

"They might have been kinder."

Yukimura slowly nods in agreement. "And the Widow

Maker?"

Kojima gives a small shrug. "Shiro is...as ever."

Yukimura suddenly smiles and moves to stand in front of the rōnin. He says, "That dog's reputation is as dark as his coat. Although, from what I hear *your* reputation is darker still."

Kojima does not reply.

Yukimura's smile dissolves and he turns to walk a few paces away. Over his shoulder he says, "What were you doing in my forest?"

"Hunting—."

"I know you were hunting!" the daimyō cuts him off, and turns to face him again. "I mean, why would a man such as yourself be chasing deer among the trees instead of utilizing his talents better?" He shakes his head, adds quietly: "I am surprised that Lord Kenshin let you live and only exiled you; I am amazed that you let *yourself* live."

Kojima visibly flinches, but any emotional tumult he feels within remains otherwise hidden.

The daimyō gestures after the departed men. "Gozen would urge you to commit *seppuku;* he believes it is the only way for you to escape your disgrace. Perhaps I am inclined to agree."

The rōnin remains stoically silent, eyes cast downwards.

"But there is another way, a less...wasteful way to

regain your honor."

Kojima lifts his gaze to meet that of Lord Yukimura: *Which is?*

"There have been reports—dark tidings of a band of rōnin terrorizing the province, causing destruction and anguish to village after village, pillaging…. It is feared that they will eventually assault Kyōto. Indeed, the Shogun has tasked myself, among others, to prevent such an incident from occurring. The rōnin would fail, of course, but such an incursion on the capital would cause enormous embarrassment…at the very least."

"Perhaps the Shōgun should ask himself why there are so many dispossessed samurai roaming the land—not all of them coveted their lord's wife, I'm sure." Then Kojima shakes his head, as if confused. "Forgive me, but where might my honor—or lack of—come into all this?"

Yukimura is taken aback by Kojima's candidness; he takes three quick steps to stand directly in front of him. In a low, angry tone, the daimyō says, "You will join and infiltrate this band; you will send reports back to me of their schemes; you will help end this pathetic uprising, and then the Shōgun's eye will look very favorably upon you! And that, Kojima Hisamasa, will be how you restore your honorable status."

"I am no *spy*," the rōnin replies, fighting to keep his

voice steady. "Your logic is unsound — there is no honor to be found in spying. Hire yourself a ninja or two for such a mission."

Yukimura lifts his hand to strike the rōnin — but his loss of self-control is momentary, and he lowers his fist and turns away. "It seems to me that you —," he begins, but he suddenly moves to a door in the far wall and swiftly slides it open. A young boy of about eight years stands frozen, his expression equal parts surprised and fearful.

"Toki — how long have you been there?" The daimyō demands.

Little Toki mutedly stares up into Lord Yukimura's face.

Kojima says, "The entire time."

The daimyō glances at the rōnin, then returns his glare to the boy. "What are you up to? Why are you not abed?" Over Toki's head he calls, "Nakano!"

The boy's fright has subsided enough for his gaze to dart around the room, as if he's looking for something; he barely glances at Kojima. "I came to see Shiro, Father," he explains.

"Shiro...? Well, he's not here! Nakano!"

"Toki!" A woman hastens up behind the boy and grabs his arm, pulling him away; she appears mortified. Toki claims one last look around the room before his father slides the door closed.

THE MASTERLESS

The Lord of the Kitami clan turns to Kojima and for a moment seems at a total loss. "My son," he says, shaking his head, "headstrong and brave, if nothing else."

"Excellent qualities for a Yukimura," Kojima replies.

The daimyō fixes the rōnin with a long look, then says, "Think on what I have said. Consider your options carefully. We will talk again on the morrow."

2.

Kojima lies in his 'cell', which is really just a small room in an outbuilding of Lord Yukimura's fortified mansion. There is a small, square window above head-height on one of the walls, barred with a wooden grille; it affords a diminished view of the black night sky. The rōnin's hands have been retied in front of him, so at least he can comfortably sit and lie down. A small stool in the corner is the room's only furniture, other than the futon on which he rests. Two seasoned samurai stand guard in the corridor outside.

Kojima tests his bonds, but the leather-and-steel cuffs are absolutely unyielding. And he regrets having made the effort: the night's awful humidity makes it feel that the room is running out of air, although excluding the grille and a fine insect-net, the window is open.

The rōnin is beyond tired — the day has indeed been a long one — but sleep will not take him despite his best efforts to still his mind. His conversation with Yukimura repeats incessantly in his head. *Consider your options carefully,* the daimyō had said. Options? Commit seppuku or join a group of low-life brigands who had lost all connection with the Way, in order for the Shōgun to save face?

A noise from outside catches his attention; he sits up and cocks his head. There it is again: heavy sniffing. So Shiro has found him at last.

Quietly, Kojima climbs to his feet and moves the stool so it's beneath the window. Stepping up onto it, he stretches his neck towards the grille. "Shiro!" he whispers. "Good boy." A pause in the sniffing tells him the akita has heard him, and so he whispers a few more words of praise and then steps down and once more waits for sleep to arrive. Mercifully, he doesn't have long to wait: maybe it's because exhaustion finally overtakes him; maybe it's because Shiro lies just the other side of the wall.

* * *

He wakes. Momentary confusion as to his situation gives way to a vague sense of worry, though Kojima does not understand why. It's still full dark outside, and it feels like he's slept for only the space of twenty heartbeats — and right now his heart is beating as if trouble looms.

Baffled, the rōnin rolls from the futon and stands up. He listens and soon hears distant noises uncommon to an ordinary night: shouts and screams—of anger and fear—and the unmistakable clash of steel on steel. At first he thinks an over-abundance of saké and bravado has led to some strife among the wine-houses or brothels in the castle town beyond the walls; or perhaps some personal vendetta is being played out to a murderous conclusion among the samurai residences *within* the walls. But as Kojima once more uses the stool to get as near as possible to the window, the sounds are steadily escalating and he begins to entertain a more troubling notion.

"Shiro," the rōnin whispers, and he hears scuffing noises as the dog reacts to his voice and climbs to his feet. "Stay there. Stay!" The rōnin pictures the akita's head cocked as he, too, listens to the martial sounds cutting through the thick night air.

Kojima steps down from the stool and sits on it, then does the only thing he can do: he waits. Something like frustration begins to build in his belly as the tell-tale sounds of battle become louder and therefore nearer. Soon, a whiff of burning drifts through the window to tickle his nostrils.

Men's voices in the corridor: they are animated, although Kojima can only make out a few words. He stands and faces the door, peering gloomily down at the bonds around his wrists.

The door slides open and a man strides into the room. Kojima looks up and has to squint and blink against the lamplight flooding into the room around the bulky figure. He cannot help but shrink back as his eyes struggle to adjust, but then he's surprised to see Lord Yukimura. With the exception of his helmet, the daimyō is wearing full armor and arms. In his right hand he wields his wakizashi, and the lamplight runs a molten trail down the short sword's flawless blade. In his left hand he holds a long fabric-wrapped bundle.

"It would seem your predicament has lessened whilst mine has somewhat heightened," the daimyō says darkly. "They attack the castle town in numbers and in the dead of night!" His tone speaks volumes as to how he feels about such a brazen and dishonorable assault on his castle.

There is no need to ask who 'they' are; indeed Kojima says nothing at all.

The next words the Lord of the Kitami clan speaks are "Will you fight with us?" but what he really means is *Will you fight for me?*

After a moment, the rōnin gives a small nod and lifts his hands. There's a flash, and the leather cuffs part without protest. Yukimura sheathes his wakizashi and hands Kojima the bundle. Then he turns on his heel and leaves, calling over his shoulder, "I will spread the word amongst the men that you're with us!"

THE MASTERLESS

* * *

Kojima finds his way out of the outbuilding, having sliced off the remnants of his bonds with his own wakizashi. The moment Yukimura had left, he'd swiftly unwrapped the bundle containing his swords and belt, tied them around his waist, and then stretched out his back and shoulders. Now he emerges into the muggy night air to find men running this way and that, but on this higher ground where the daimyō's residence is located, the sounds of combat are still some way off.

Keeping close to the outbuilding's wall, he follows it around – and nearly collides with Shiro as he rounds a corner. Both are just as happy to see the other and Kojima scratches the dog where his jaw meets his powerful neck, while Shiro licks the back of his master's hand.

"Stay close!" the rōnin commands, and they set off downhill to where a large group of samurai has congregated in the courtyard before the inner wall's closed main-gate. As they reach the men—who are discussing how they'll deal with tonight's affront—some of them glance at the rōnin, while more glance at the akita. So word of Kojima's sudden affiliation with the Kitami clan has obviously spread, although few of the looks that come his way contain any regard.

Kojima spies Shimazu Gozen, Yukimura's chief retainer,

at the center of the group, and he's gesticulating harshly as he describes his plan of action. Kojima makes no real effort to listen; he is, of course, unfamiliar with the castle's layout — other than the typical concentric stone walls, of which this castle has two, and the moat — so he'll stick close to these men as they navigate the deliberately complex network of passageways designed to infuriate any invading force.

The gate is opened, and the samurai hurry through it to begin their downwards journey to the castle's main gate. As Kojima and Shiro follow the throng, the rōnin looks up at the angry orange glow and billowing smoke that can be seen along the top of the outer wall. Silhouetted against that glow are archers, but their intermittent shooting speaks of a scarcity of clear targets.

They round yet another bend, and the open main gate can be seen. Beyond the wooden bridge crossing the moat, Kitami clansmen — samurai and peasants alike — have engaged their attackers, and the clash and squeal of steel on steel fills the night. Screaming their family names and lineages, the newly-arrived samurai draw their katana as they thunder across the bridge and fall upon the rōnin scum who've dared to attack their castle.

True to his word, Kojima joins the fray and begins to deal death to those come seeking it. As Shiro lurks in shadows to one side — the akita's fur is thick indeed, but not much use against razor-sharp steel—his master parries two sword blows and then runs his attacker through with little effort. But just as he searches for a new foe, Kojima thinks he hears a scream from *behind* them; he glances at Shiro and sees that he too has heard the sound. Kojima stops pressing ahead and stands watching the battle before him. He observes that the enemy are steadily retreating, drawing the Kitami samurai away from the castle.

Another scream sounds, and without doubt it came from high up in the castle compound. Striding after the samurai, Kojima scans the melee and spots Shimazu Gozen felling yet another man foolish enough to face him. He grabs the chief retainer's armored arm and nearly takes his sword in the face for the pleasure.

"We must go back!" the rōnin says urgently, his voice almost lost in the cacophony of hand-to-hand conflict. Gozen's expression shows he thinks Kojima has taken leave of his senses, and he literally growls as he shrugs his arm away to rejoin the fight.

Kojima gives the combatants one last helpless look, then turns and begins to run back over the bridge. A dark flash overtakes him, and Shiro is back through the gate before he's even hallway across.

"Coward!" comes a shout from behind Kojima; he stops and turns to look. A samurai is staring after him, gesturing at him—it's Gozen, of course—and again he shouts "Coward!" before turning back to the fray. The word stings like a wasp, but Kojima cares not—to him, the stench of treachery is as thick in the air as the smell of burning.

He resumes his run to follow Shiro.

* * *

The akita is waiting for him in shadow as dark as his fur, just before the main gate of the inner wall. Shiro is panting, but not as heavily as his master is as he jogs up the hill. Indeed, Kojima goes down on one knee and puts a hand on the canine's sturdy back, as much for support as affection.

They both peer up into the area fronting the daimyō's mansion. Several spear-and sword-wielding men are milling around, and from their demeanor it's clear they do not belong here. The fact that they are indeed *here,* in this part of the castle, speaks volumes: they must have been allowed into the compound through one or more of its other, smaller gates; and considering these gates would be secured and well-manned, betrayal must be the only explanation for this calamity. As they watch, a few defenders emerge from the mansion but are quickly overwhelmed and put to the sword. All but two of the attackers disappear into Lord Yukimura's splendid residence.

"Let's go," Kojima whispers, and he and Shiro slip in

through the gate—passing the corpses of those men who'd been responsible for it—and make their way up towards the mansion. Without armor, Kojima knows he looks more ruffian than samurai and he strides nonchalantly towards the two lookouts. He clicks his fingers and points to the right and Shiro changes direction to trot towards a low building which his master has indicated. The rōnin's swords are sheathed and he calls out a greeting to the two men; they respond and smile but seem wary all the same.

"Just as planned, eh?" Kojima asks through a grin as he nears the men on the mansion's front steps.

The men chuckle and nod—then slump to the stone steps with looks of surprise on their faces and bloody smiles across their throats. Kojima holds his swords at the ready for a few moments, lest more invaders re-emerge from the mansion. But just as he relaxes and bends to clean his swords on one of the men, he hears footsteps behind him. Swiveling, he emits a short, high-pitched whistle while striking a fighting stance, to find three archers at full draw and two katana-wielding samurai. The scene is like some disturbing echo from the previous day... It is Lord Yukimura, however, who stands scowling up at him, accompanied by four of his men. "Kojima!" the daimyō exclaims, then urgently beckons the rōnin to come down the steps.

But Kojima calls out "No!" and points at one of the

archers, and all turn to see a snarling black shadow shooting towards the archer's back—but Shiro checks his charge at the last instant, and the man will yet retain the use of both hamstrings.

"Hurry!" Yukimura says, and Kojima runs down the steps and they all hustle away from the mansion. Soon they round an outbuilding and come to a halt, breathing heavily; they're out of sight at least for the moment. Shiro leans his bulk against his master as Kojima glances over the little group: every man has some sort of wound, excepting Yukimura.

"Treachery!" Kojima spits—this is not his clan, but just the knowledge that its downfall has come in such a fashion grates against his samurai sentiments.

"Treachery," the daimyō agrees, nodding, but he appears to be more resigned than outraged.

"Who might—."

But Yukimura cuts him off with, "It matters not, now, Kojima...."

The rōnin is at a loss for a moment, but then asks, "Why are you out here?"

"Because they're looking for me in there," Yukimura replies, jerking his head towards the mansion.

"And...your wife and son?"

"Safe, for the time being. Hiding in a secret tunnel leading from their living quarter to an exit in the mansion's foundations, at the back."

Kojima frowns, unsure how to formulate his next question. What might he say? He wants to ask, *"Why do you bother? The castle is doomed; the Kitami clan is doomed".* But what he says is, "And then what?"

Lord Yukimura stares at Kojima for a long while, and the rōnin watches the last vestiges of hope die in the daimyō's eyes.

Angry shouts can now be heard coming from the direction of the mansion; it cannot be long before they're found. Shiro emits a low rumble of a growl, more felt than heard by his master.

Yukimura shakes his head. "Funny…fighting Mongol invaders was easier than fighting these scum.…"

"We were younger then," the rōnin replies simply.

Suddenly the daimyō reaches around to grab the back of Kojima's neck, but the hold is familiar, not threatening. The rōnin feels Shiro flinch but he rests his fingertips atop the dog's head: *Wait.* The Lord of the Kitami clan's eyes begin to moisten, though he fights the tears back like it's the fiercest battle he's ever fought. Kojima is aware of the other samurai averting their eyes — it would not do for them to see their lord like this.

"My son…!" Yukimura whispers fiercely, hopelessly, pleadingly.

And although he wishes he doesn't, Kojima understands what is being asked of him; and for some unfathomable reason, he agrees to that ask. So he nods.

* * *

The daimyō and his men emerge from behind the outbuilding and stride purposefully towards the mansion, chests puffed out, their katana drawn. The attackers are buzzing around like a swarm of angry hornets, but they quickly calm as Lord Yukimura strolls into their midst. Fires have been set within the mansion and their light spills from the windows to cast hellish hues upon the tableau. Shouts of fury rise from beyond the inner gate, which has been closed and barred by the invaders: the returning Kitami samurai are now endeavoring to re-take their own castle. But it is futile.

Kojima and Shiro witness all of this from shadows at the other side of the outbuilding. As they watch, the daimyō and his men are slowly encircled by the rogue rōnin. There is a brief moment of serenity before the five Kitami samurai scream their war cries and attack these men who have brought senseless annihilation to their clan. Vastly outnumbered, it will take but moments for the defenders to go down—but Kojima and Shiro take the opportunity to sprint unseen across the square and down the mansion's length. At its end they find themselves in gardens, and Kojima draws his wakizashi and begins to hurry along the mansion's huge foundations, lightly tapping with the sword's hilt as he goes. *"There is a little wooden door, around head height,"* the daimyō had explained before going to meet his fate, *"it is expertly crafted and painted to seem part of the stonework. Tap on it five times."*

Shiro seems to understand what his master is up to and closely follows him, vigorously sniffing the air near to the wall. About a third of the way along, there's a hollow *thunk* and Kojima stops. Lord Yukimura had been right: even allowing for the dark, the door is seamlessly incorporated into the foundation. He taps the wood five times, waits, but nothing happens.

Five more taps — nothing.

"Nakano! Toki!" he whispers close to the door — which opens to reveal a dark, cramped tunnel. Nakano kneels on its floor; Toki sits beyond her, hugging his knees. Both are staring at the rōnin as if he's a demon.

"I have been sent," Kojima says, and after a moment a wide-eyed Nakano nods. Reaching back, she pulls Toki to his feet and maneuvers him in front of her, then kisses the back of his head. The rōnin reaches up into the tunnel and lifts the boy down, and Toki gasps as he notices the akita. The boy tentatively lifts his hand towards the dog, but Shiro turns his head to the side and moves a few paces away. Shaking his head at the akita's indifference, Kojima turns back to Nakano and realizes she is making no attempt to exit the tunnel. This does not surprise him.

"My lord husband?" Nakano asks, and the rōnin's expression is grim as he gives a small shake of his head. "Then it is my duty to follow him," Nakano says, and her meaning is clear; but then her tone becomes matter-of-fact. "There is a key around my son's neck — it opens an iron grate in the inner wall at the bottom of the gardens, as well as a secret wicket door in the Emperor's Gate. Toki will lead you; no-one knows the castle grounds better than my son! May the divine winds blow at your back."

And then she closes the door.

* * *

They are running through the gardens, zigzagging between cherry trees, down the slope towards the inner wall. They move hand-in-hand through the dark: Kojima drags the boy along and at the same time keeps him from falling, whereas Toki steers them in the right direction. Ahead, Shiro is already at the wall, pacing back and forth impatiently.

Toki veers towards an area of shrubbery against the wall. There, he drops to his knees and pulls a perfectly manicured bush to the side to reveal a small, square grate set into the base of the thick stonework.

"The key!" Kojima demands in a whisper, and the boy extracts it from beneath his kimono. The large key is on a thong and he lifts it over his head, gives it to the rōnin. Kojima bends to unlock the grate, and winces at the squeal of its hinges as he pushes it open.

"Shiro!" the rōnin says, gesturing for the dog to go through the hole. "You first, boy! Go!" The akita does as bid, though he has to half-crawl to get through.

"Me next; you follow," Kojima says and lies on his front—but then he notices Toki looking back up towards the mansion.

"What about Mother?" the boy asks worriedly.

"Gone to find your father," the rōnin replies, and he's not being entirely untruthful. He quickly crawls through the hole before any more questions can be asked.

But he has simply moved from one awkward situation to another: three men approach, emerging from around the wall's curve. Kojima quickly glances around, but Shiro is nowhere to be seen. He draws both of his swords.

Just as Toki crawls through the hole and climbs to his feet, the men falter to a stop—but they are close enough for Kojima and the boy to make out who stands before them.

It is Shimazu Gozen. And the samurai with him are not of the Kitami clan; they are rōnin.

"I must admit," Lord Yukimura's former chief retainer

says, "I could not have guessed it would be *you* I found with young Toki here." The boy makes to go to Gozen, but Kojima bars his way — he clearly doesn't understand what is transpiring.

"I am just as surprised to see *you*, believe me," Kojima returns.

Gozen gives a mirthless laugh, then draws his katana; the others unsheathe their own blades. "Cut him down!" Gozen shouts and hangs back as the two samurai attack.

One of Kojima's attackers holds a nodachi, and the oversized sword immediately seeks out his head. He easily ducks the swing, however, and dances away to swipe at the second man, whose katana deflects the blow. The three rōnin gauge each other after this initial exchange —.

Suddenly Gozen lets out a scream and Kojima takes advantage of nodachi-man's momentary distraction, slicing first at his knee and then cutting up across his face as the unwieldy sword lowers. The man falls to the ground, writhes for a moment, and then stills.

"Good boy!" Kojima says, smiling. A glance at Gozen tells him that the akita must have peeled from the shadows to sink his teeth into the man's ankle, but has now hopped away from the arc of the chief retainer's katana. With a last scowl at Kojima, Gozen begins to hobble back in the direction he came from, although Shiro follows him, snarling, snapping at his heels, but mindful of the sharp steel being swung back at him.

Meanwhile, Kojima faces the last remaining samurai, knowing he has to make short work of him—Gozen will be back, and no doubt with reinforcements. But his opponent has barely reached manhood, and he cannot help but regret what he must now do.

"Get the key and go to the Emperor's Gate!" he tells Toki; but when the boy fails to move, he says, "Now!" which does the trick.

Kojima warily eyes his opponent as Toki retrieves the key from the grate and runs off between two storehouses. He sheathes his wakizashi and changes his grip on the katana to a double-handed one. The younger man nervously licks his lips and then screams as he attacks, but his body cut is over-extended and his balance poor. Kojima has shuffled back out of the sword's arc; now he darts to the side and flashes his katana at the back of his opponent's neck.

He is running after Toki before the young samurai's head hits the ground.

* * *

Kojima is unsurprised to find that Shiro has somehow managed to get ahead of them, and he's sitting before the Emperor's Gate as if he's been waiting there all night.

This area of the castle compound is the least frequented due to its mainly ceremonial function. The Emperor's Gate is exactly that: the gate the Imperial ruler uses whenever he might deign to visit the castle, if ever. Nevertheless the extravagantly designed gate is meticulously well-maintained and permanently manned — although those men have been killed at some point in the night's heinous activities.

"Don't look at them, boy," Kojima says, noticing Toki looking at the corpses strewn in the road as they reach the closed gate. "Find the door."

Shiro's pink tongue is hanging out the side of his panting mouth, and he's looking almost accusingly up at his master. "I know, boy, I'm thirsty too," the rōnin mutters and pats the top of the akita's broad skull.

Toki has located the concealed wicket door. Kojima watches as the boy thumbs a small wood panel to the side, inserts and turns the key. The door is stiff, however, and needs a little encouragement from the rōnin before it swings outwards.

The three of them cross the exquisitely-formed bridge across the moat, and leave the castle behind.

THE MASTERLESS

3.

They finally get some rest at dawn. As colors begin to seep back into the world and birds serenade the returning sun, Kojima sits with his back against a tree. On his left side, Toki is curled up; on his right side, Shiro is similarly comfortable. They both sleep a restless sleep.

The rōnin would give his *swords* for any sort of sleep at all—he is utterly exhausted. After escaping the castle, they had raced through meadows of thick grass and eventually found their way into the forest. For speed, Kojima had carried the tired boy on his back most of the way, and his knee suffered terribly; even now the old battle wound throbs like it never has before.

Shiro makes a small noise, and the rōnin looks down at him. The dog's face is twitching and so are his front paws— Kojima hopes the akita catches whichever dream animal he's chasing.

"Now what?" he mouths down at his friend. He finds it beyond belief that just yesterday their only care in the world was catching their next meal, and now they find themselves having made enemies of a marauding band of rōnin, and responsible for a young boy who happens to be the orphan of a slain daimyo.

Kojima bumps his head back on the tree and closes his

eyes, but only to rest them. He knows that even if he tries to get some sleep, it will evade him. Although he thinks they are relatively safe for the time being, he has no doubt whatsoever that Shimazu Gozen and his new 'clan' are already seeking them.

The rōnin considers Lord Yukimura's very last words to him, before he died the glorious death of a true warrior: *"Go west, to the lands of the Musashi clan. Demand an audience with Lord Nobunaga and let my son's presence in his castle be the most dire warning to him and all others of this evil stalking the land...."*

Kojima opens his gritty eyes and again looks down at the sleepers flanking him, trying not to be envious of their peace. He will let them slumber until the sun has climbed the sky a little, and no more. And then they shall go west.

* * *

They are trudging through the forest, their tongues parched and their bellies grumbling. Kojima occasionally carries young Toki for the sake of making any serious progress, although his knee is on the brink of giving way. For a while the boy persists with questions — *"What of Mother and Father? Where are we going?"* — and the rōnin firmly tells him to save his energy for walking, not talking, that there will be time for words later. Sweating, toiling, Kojima does not bother to look back as he negotiates as straight a path as he can:

Shiro's heightened senses will most definitely pick up any signs of pursuit long before his own. A few times the akita makes to wander off into the woods, most probably to hunt something, *any*thing, but Kojima says "No!" and the canine grudgingly stays close.

In the afternoon they stumble upon a gurgling stream and gratefully quench their thirst. They need to rest, too, although Kojima leads them away from the noise of the stream before allowing them to do so. The rōnin sits facing east, his back against a tree, and Toki uses the adjacent tree to do the same. A few paces away, Shiro circles several times before sinking to the ground; he sighs contentedly through his nose, lowers his chin onto a front paw, then shuts his eyes.

"I'm hungry," Toki moans, and Shiro's head snaps up to look at him.

"As am I," Kojima replies, adding, "as is he," and nods at the akita. Shiro is frowning at the boy as if annoyed that the word has reminded him how empty his belly is, but after a moment he rests his chin back down and re-closes his eyes.

"Did my mother commit seppuku?"

Kojima looks sidelong at the boy. "I assume so; her honor was strong."

"Which means my father is dead." It was not a question.

"Yes."

The boy looks more shocked than mournful, then,

"Where are we going?"

I know where we're going; I just don't know how close we'll get. "To the Musashi clan."

There is a long pause, during which the rōnin cannot stop his eyes from closing over.

"Why did *you* not take your own life?"

It's Kojima's turn to snap his eyes open and stare at the boy—the little delinquent! He shakes his head and gives no answer, but as he looks away Toki sees his eyes flicker towards Shiro.

The boy points at the dog. "For him?" he asks, surprised.

Kojima suppresses his ire—*anger is beneath the superior man*—although he takes his time in replying. "Unlike me, *he* did not fail his master." The rōnin settles his gaze on the boy. "Should we not do everything we can to protect those closest to us, what family we have? That you sit here with me is evidence of such—that was your father's doing."

Toki is blessedly quiet for a while. Then he asks, "What did you do that was so wrong?"

"I...I tried to take something that was not mine to take."

"What?"

Kojima abruptly stands and brushes himself down. "Enough rest, let's go," he mutters. "Shiro!"

The akita hauls himself to his feet, yawns expansively, and gives himself a half-hearted shake. Then his dark brown, triangular eyes consider Toki with a cool detachment before he trails after his fast-walking master.

* * *

Dusk finds the three fugitives huddled together in the lee of a moss-covered outcropping of rock. Kojima says nothing to the boy, but he is beyond surprised they have not yet been chased down. And he is trying not to entertain even for an instant the notion that Gozen and any who might be with him have given up the chase, or even neglected to start it in the first place....

As if reading his thoughts, the boy asks, "What will become of me—when we reach the Musashi, I mean?"

If....

"You will be safe, first and foremost," the rōnin answers.

"And then?"

Kojima glances around the twilit forest, searching for something to say to distract the boy. His eyes are pulled down to his left-hand side as Shiro begins to lightly snore. The akita is lying on his side, his head close to his master's leg; the rōnin's hand rests on the dog's thick neck. *To the rescue again, boy?*

Kojima turns his head to Toki, who's leaning against his right-hand side. "Do you know what is said about this breed of dog?"

Toki shakes his head.

"It is said by some that if a samurai dies a dishonorable death, he might be given a second chance by being reborn as an akita, so that he has the opportunity to die defending the life of his master, and thus regain his honor."

Toki is quiet as he absorbs this. "Is that what *you*'d like?"

He blinks a few times. "Yes."

"Me too."

Kojima raises his eyebrows as Toki reaches his small hand over to tentatively touch the top of Shiro's head. He rubs the fur there for a while, but when his fingers begin to caress the dog's ear and he says in wonder "So soft!" the akita moves his head away and emits a low growl. "Oh— he doesn't like his ears being touched?" Toki asks the rōnin, disappointment vying with surprise in his voice.

The rōnin snorts a laugh and replies, "I think it might just be that you called him soft."

* * *

Kojima stops suddenly and lifts his arm to the side so that Toki and Shiro do the same. He has spotted movement through the trees…but up ahead, not behind.

Without being asked, Shiro silently veers away into the undergrowth; his master knows he'll circle around whoever they happen to have stumbled upon. As they stand listening, the feint sound of singing floats through the forest: a masculine voice, but it holds the tone of an older man. Kojima gestures Toki forward and soon they find themselves creeping towards what turns out to be a road. The rōnin turns to Toki, gestures *stay,* and puts a finger over his lips. The boy nods.

"Good day, farmer," Kojima calls, stepping out of the woods.

The man jumps with fright and his warble catches in his throat, choking him, and he coughs and sputters for a moment. His only companion is an old ox, and the ox is pulling an even older cart, which is small and mostly empty. Much as Kojima's captors did two short days ago, the farmer is trying to decide exactly what it is he is dealing with. His expression shows he has decided on 'brigand'.

"And where might you be coming from?" the rōnin asks.

The farmer gestures backwards. "The m-monastery," he answers, as if it should be obvious. "Trading with the monks."

"How far is this monastery?"

"A quarter-day's walk by road."

"Tell me, farmer — where are you headed?"

"Home," the man replies nervously and gestures up the road. "The next village."

Kojima points at the forest on the opposite side of the road from which he'd emerged. "Whose land is that?"

The farmer narrows his eyes, thinking he's being fooled with. He answers anyway. "Lord Nobunaga's."

The rōnin slowly nods; he's now resting his hand on the hilt of his katana. "Farmer, if later you are asked by anyone if you have seen us, my friend and I should be grateful if you'd lie."

"Your fr...?" The farmer squints nervously into the trees — then jumps in fright as Shiro walks past him from behind. The big canine briefly sniffs the scared man's leg as he goes, and even the ox shuffles its feet uneasily.

The old man looks back at Kojima and gives a quick but emphatic nod.

The rōnin steps to the side and the farmer yanks hard on the ox's harness, and the beast starts forward again. "Careful journey to 'the next village'!" the rōnin calls after the farmer. The man casts a nervous glance back and redoubles his pace.

A moment later, Toki darts across the road at a signal from the rōnin. "Why were you so horrible to that old man?" the boy asks.

"For everyone's sake," Kojima replies, and they enter Musashi clan lands.

THE MASTERLESS

* * *

It was Shiro, of course, who first registered the pursuit. Twice he stopped and turned to listen, his head cocked to one side; twice Kojima strained his ears and heard nothing but the occasional bird's chirp. But there was no reason to doubt the akita. So they ran.

And still they run. A sense of hopelessness begins to grow in the rōnin's belly: he knows they will be run down soon. He has Toki on his back now—the boy fell twice as they ran, the second time badly—and the rōnin's breathing is ragged. Moreover, it feels like a blade is stabbing his knee with every stride he takes, and it seems as if he's carrying the old ox on his back and not the boy.

Their only real hope, Kojima knows, is to stumble across a patrol of Musashi samurai—even a hunting party might come to their aid, especially if it were escorted by warrior clansmen—but it's a hope born of desperation, and he shakes his head to rid it of such fancies. And then there's this horrible recurring thought that he can't stop himself from thinking that if he drops the boy to the forest floor, if he just shakes him off his back, then he and Shiro might have a chance of escape....

No! Even then he is sure Gozen would keep coming for him—him and Shiro.

High pitched yelping from behind them. "Dogs!" Toki

331

says into the rōnin's ear. "Will they have akitas?"

"Hope not!" Kojima gasps when he can.

The rōnin is vaguely aware of Shiro suddenly peeling away from them. To distract himself from the fire in his lungs he listens for the inevitable scream of a savaged dog as the akita begins the battle—and there it is! The sound is horrible and Toki's arms squeeze him tighter.

When Kojima hears hoof-beats, he stops.

"What…what are you *doing?*" Toki asks, terrified, as the rōnin lowers him to the ground. "What's happening?"

Kojima sinks to his knees and grabs the boy's face between the palms of his hands. "Listen, Toki, listen! Run that way." He points south. "You hear me? That way, and keep a straight path! There is a monastery south of here, the farmer said—remember?" Toki is trembling, but he nods. "Shiro will come for you—you won't be alone."

"Wait! Where're you—?"

"*Go!*" the rōnin says, spins the boy around and pushes him forward. Toki begins to run. "Keep a straight path!"

Kojima stands and waits long enough for the horsemen to catch sight of him—they are many, too numerous to count through the trees. He has caught his breath now, and he sets off northwards. Without the boy on his back he makes better progress, but all the same the sounds of pursuit quickly intensify, and he thinks he hears Shiro putting down another of the dogs.

Soon the rōnin bursts into a small clearing, then slows to a walk until he reaches its center. He turns to see Shiro bounding up to him, tongue lolling, dark blood staining his muzzle. Kojima falls to his knees, rests his forehead against the dog's. They breathe hoarse breaths into each other's face.

"Go get Toki, boy," Kojima says urgently, but Shiro doesn't move. "Go, please!"

Hoof-beats rumble like approaching thunder and Shiro turns to face Shimazu Gozen and several other mounted men, head high, chest out, hackles up, tail curled over his back—and his master sees the ferocious warrior that he is. Two other dogs—one indeed an akita—slink around the edges of the clearing, loathe to come near the big canine. But then Kojima notices one of the rōnin preparing to nock an arrow to his bow and he leans forward and says *"Go!"* into his friend's ear and Shiro propels himself from the clearing before the archer can even raise his bow.

Gozen scowls as he watches Shiro go, then waves a dismissive hand. "Ach, forget the mutt! He won't go far, anyway—not when you're around," he adds, turning to Kojima. He gingerly slides down off his mount and, as he limps towards the kneeling rōnin, he draws his katana. The other men do the same and soon Kojima is surrounded by eight well-armed samurai. He sits back so that his weight is resting on his heels.

Lord Yukimura's betrayer stops just beyond Kojima's sword-range. "Not tempted to join us?" he asks with a black smile, indicating the other men, and his words elicit a few chuckles.

"There is nothing to join — you imply order where there is only chaos."

"Long I served, and *well,*" Gozen says, slightly defensive. "But should a man not be his own master?"

The rōnin replies with a question of his own: "I'm curious — do you see yourself when you look at me?"

Gozen snorts a laugh. "I am nothing like you!"

"On that we agree, rōnin." Kojima has begun to remove his upper garments.

Gozen flinches like he's been slapped on the face. "Do not call me that!"

"Would you prefer 'traitor'?" Kojima asks, and now he is naked to his waist.

Gozen's fury threatens to overwhelm him, but he cannot strike the object of his anger — not now. "Where is the boy?"

"In the forest."

"Where is the boy?"

Kojima is carefully tucking his sleeves tightly under his knees. Eventually he looks up at Gozen, asks softly, "Is it that with every moment that passes his being alive reminds you of your shame?"

The samurai surrounding Kojima begin to sheathe their weapons. "No matter," one of them says to Gozen, "the dogs will pick up the scent."

And then they all watch in something approaching a respectful silence — even Gozen, despite his scowl — as Kojima unsheathes his wakizashi. He lifts the blade and gazes at it wistfully, almost affectionately — then stabs himself below the waist in his left-hand side, slowly drags the blade across to the right side, turns the blade inside the wound, and gives a slight cut upwards.

The rōnin's tucked-under sleeves prevent him from slumping to the side or falling backwards — no ways for a samurai to die — and as he begins to topple forwards he fancies he sees a flash of brindle fur streaking between the trees.

4.

Toki is running through the forest, being extra careful not to trip on any exposed roots or stones. His breath is wheezing in and out of his heaving chest, and from time to time an upwelling of fear clogs his throat and brings tears to his eyes.

A sudden rustling noise from behind makes him yelp in

fright, and he turns to see Shiro loping towards him. The dog gives him a quick sniff but then continues several paces past the boy, although he stops to look back over his shoulder.

"Where's your master?" the boy gasps out as he approaches the dog; but Shiro sets off again, and in a slightly different direction than Toki was going. The boy takes a quick glance behind — he doesn't see anyone — and follows.

"There is a monastery south of here…" Kojima had said. A monastery? That's where monks live — however could a bunch of soft Buddhists help him? But despite his misgivings, Toki steals glances through the trees whenever he's brave enough to look up from his footing, fervently hoping to see any sign at all of the monastery.

Trees, trees, and more trees….

There! Up ahead, the forest seems to be thinning…yes, it definitely is. And there, beyond a grassy field, buildings can be seen — and a pagoda! The monastery!

But just as Toki experiences a hope-fueled burst of energy, Shiro comes running back to him and steps his front paws up onto a fallen branch to better survey the forest behind them. The boy stops to follow the dog's line of sight — he knows he should be *running* — but now fear has rooted him to the spot.

And then Toki sees them: horsemen, mounted samurai. Shiro turns and sprints towards the field, and Toki is stunned out of his immobility. He chases after the akita, pumping his arms and legs like he never has before. Soon he breaks from the trees — Shiro is already a long way ahead, pacing back and forth — but the field isn't small and the monastery still seems so far away....

He's about halfway across when he hears the thunder of the horses' hooves. He glances over his shoulder to see Gozen and the other rōnin: bad men who have destroyed his family and his home, and who are coming to take his life as well. As he struggles through the long grass, he's all the while expecting an arrow to drive into his back — but just before he catches up with Shiro that arrow hits the dog instead, and the akita screams as the projectile punches into him. Toki screams, too, and tries to run faster.

He's almost blinded by tears, but up ahead he sees a figure walking towards him, a shaven-headed old man wearing saffron-colored robes and holding a staff. The boy runs right into the old monk and wraps his arms around him like he's his father and not a stranger; but the monk pries his arms from around his waist and tells him, "Keep going," and shoves him towards a large building. Toki does as bid, and stumbles the final short distance to the building, where he collapses at the feet of another, younger monk.

As the horses approach, the old monk lifts his arms up and the rōnin rein in their horses to form a semi-circle before him. Shimazu Gozen dismounts and makes to limp towards

Toki, but the monk raises his staff to block his path.

"Step back, old man!" Gozen says angrily. "This is no concern of yours."

"They killed them!" Toki sobs. "They murdered them all, and Shiro...." but the boy becomes unintelligible as his grief breaks through the dam of shock that's been holding it at bay these last few days.

The old monk keeps his staff raised. "Nine mounted warriors to catch a boy who speaks of murder? And a need to shoot his dog in the process? This must be *someone's* concern."

Gozen begins to draw his katana, but the monk flicks his wrist and his staff strikes the top of the rōnin's sword, hammering it back into its scabbard. Gozen stumbles back, swearing. A few of the other samurai jump down from their saddles and make to draw their own weapons, but they stop as a door in the building flies open and numerous warrior-monks file out wielding a variety of bladed weapons. The monks fan out and ready themselves for action.

"It is not only samurai who fight well," the old man says. "Now begone, rōnin!"

Gozen spits. "Keep him, then!" He stalks back to his horse and awkwardly climbs into the saddle. His gaze fixes on Toki, who has now climbed to his feet. "But just make sure our paths never happen to cross."

Then he wheels his mount around and gallops away.

The Masterless

* * *

Toki sits side-by-side with Bassui, the old monk, on the steps of the three-story pagoda in the middle of the monastery complex. He is trying to tell Bassui the tale of the last few days, but he's still upset and it's a difficult task.

Now he's distracted by four warrior-monks who have emerged into view, coming from the direction of the grassy field. They move in a square, each holding a corner of a saffron robe; they are carrying something dark and heavy. Toki abruptly stands, then runs down the steps and towards them.

Shiro is lying on his side, barely conscious, his eyes half-closed. The arrow is still embedded in him, its barbed head sticking out the back of his leg. Toki gently strokes Shiro's head, and the akita's eyes flicker up to him.

"This is the Widow Maker!" the boy says to the monks, pride in his voice.

"Well, I think his days of making widows are past," one of the monks replies, "but he will live."

WIND OF CHANGE
DAVID WRIGHT

On a clear spring day in the heart of Grungea, a breeze swept across the rolling grasslands. The breeze went unnoticed by Man, for none had ever settled in this region.

But it was a wind of change.

A gentle gust briefly altered the flight of a single dove. This of itself was nothing out of the ordinary, but it was the moment that would lead three kingdoms into war and change the history of Lanis forever.

For despite the absence of Man, the dove's correcting flutter indeed caught the eye of a certain witness.

One hundred yards away, a hawk perched high in an evergreen twitched his head as he focused one alert eye on the bird. His brown and white speckled pattern hid him well against the trunk. The usual diet of rodents and hares had failed to materialize this day and he was hungry.

The hunt was on.

He launched from his roost and took wing, angling to intercept the dove. It took but a few moments to close the distance, and soon he brought up his open talons in readiness for the kill. As he dropped on the dove, he swept through empty air. His prey had eluded him at the last moment. Now the hunt fell into an inelegant chase. A bit sloppy for the hawk, who preferred efficiency, but nothing worrisome. He would catch this beautiful creature and enjoy his daily bounty.

But the dove proved elusive. The hawk snapped and clutched, repeatedly grasping nothing but air. The dove flew around him, taking advantage of its smaller size by making tighter turns than he could match.

This was why he did not like chases. It took too much effort to keep his powerful body in the air. It wasn't long before he needed a rest. The dove would live. He veered off and alighted within a nearby copse of trees.

A moment later, he sat perplexed, his avian senses on full alert. Something was wrong. Quite surprisingly, the dove had turned back and now approached him. The hawk sat still, wary of this unexpected behavior. But the dove now flew all around the space in front of him, chirping playfully, urging the hawk back to the chase.

Wind of Change

He could resist no longer. Once again he leapt to the air, and once again the dove fled. This time, however, the dove did not engage in a dance of tight maneuvers. Rather, it took a straight line. The hawk trusted his superior wingspan to win such a race and felt the rise of anticipation for his next meal.

But he could never catch the dove. No matter how hard he flew, he could not close the distance. More curiously, the hawk did not tire nor grow agitated. Instead, he calmly allowed the dove to lead him further west.

Soon, a column of smoke appeared on the horizon.

A fire usually meant an abundance of tasty prey fleeing its path. And at that moment, the hawk caught sight of a rabbit hopping through the tall grass. The hawk at last broke away from the dove's path and swooped downward. He grabbed the rabbit by the throat and turned upward again, attempting to carry his latest meal away, but the thrashing of his victim would not allow it. The hawk wrestled hard on the ground for a moment, refusing to relent his grip. The rabbit continued to fight until his neck was laid open by a pair of slashing bites.

At last the prey lay still. The hawk could now take his time and enjoy his meal. Nothing tasted as good as fresh mea—.

The hawk froze, a red chunk hanging from his beak.

Before him on the grass, stood the dove. This time, when their gazes locked something awakened inside the hawk. His mind quickened. In that moment, he rose above the base instincts of common creatures.

Awareness.

The dove turned his head to one side, chirping once. The hawk understood fully. He finished the bite of rabbit still in his beak as he looked at the distant column of smoke. When he looked back at the dove, the bird was gone.

Had it even been there at all?

It must have been. How else could he have found the rabbit? The dove had led him to food and then commanded him.

In obedience, the hawk clutched the remains of his meal firmly in his talons and took to the air in the direction of the smoke. It wasn't long before he discovered the source. In his newly awakened mind, the hawk knew the animal hide structure now below him was a crude human shelter. Smoke snaked out from a single hole at the top of the structure. Perhaps it was burning from within.

The hawk swept downward and into the open entrance of the shelter. He suddenly found himself bathed in heat, but the shelter did not burn. The human had harnessed the fire! It raged in place but failed to grow. Near the fire and dominating the small space, sat a human. Red skinned and bare chested, the man wore deerskin on his legs and adorned himself with jewelry made of tooth and claw. An axe, a bow and quiver of arrows lay nearby. Sweating heavily and with eyes shut, the man prayed to the Great Spirit.

The hawk realized all of this without wonder, already forgetting his awakened state allowed him to perceive such things that his kindred could not. He placed the rabbit silently on the ground in front of him and waited.

"Praise be to the Great Spirit!" the man exclaimed, blinking his eyes and focusing them on the hawk. "For three days I have meditated by the smoke of the spiritweed. Hunger ravishes me, and I am too weak to hunt. Yet the Great Spirit provides in the form of a most unexpected deliverer. That is for me, is it not, noble one?" The human pointed at the rabbit with an expression of honest inquiry on his face.

The hawk bent down and nudged the meat once with his beak then backed away. His duty now complete, having brought food to the sweating human.

"Many thanks." The man picked up the rabbit, tore away a small portion and tossed it to his new companion. The hawk did not hesitate to eat it.

Kindness.

"I am Jabbok, prince of the Eagle and Wolf Tribes. Do you have a name?"

Not receiving an answer, the man began preparing the

rabbit for roasting. "You are a singular creature. Any other hawk would have fled or attacked by now, if indeed they had ever entered at all." He looked pointedly at the hawk then as if expecting an answer. After placing the rabbit above the fire, he tore off one last raw bite and held it out.

"Come. Be not afraid, friend. I have forsaken the village of my fathers to seek the guidance of the Great Spirit, to beg His plan for me be revealed. This food is a much needed boon. As is your companionship, I must confess."

The hawk understood him. This human was a Whisperer. The hawk fluttered a short hop away from the fire, then walked the distance to the extended hand. The hawk snapped up the bite of meat and quickly downed it. Then the two looked at each other for a long moment until finally Jabbok smiled.

"Thank you, noble one. We must find a name for you."

Alarm!

The hawk shot upward quickly through the hole in the roof, ignoring the startled cry of the human as he forced his way out. Once in the open air, the hawk looked everywhere as he climbed.

Danger!

The hawk shrieked a warning. Loudly, for the Whisperer to hear. A score of strange creatures now charged the human's shelter. They walked on two legs and bore raiment of battle as humans would, but their heads were those of coyotes. They howled and barked as they closed in.

Jabbok emerged from the shelter in time to collide with one of the charging creatures. They both fell inside, out of the hawk's view. Two more followed. The rest began attacking the shelter itself.

The hawk screeched another warning, this time to alert the coyote-men of their own peril. Unheeded, he picked out his target, folded his wings and shot downward like an arrow.

As he dove, two of the monsters inside the shelter were hurled out, gashing wounds displaying their innards. Then the hawk hit with beak and talon, slashing chunks of meat from the coyote face. The beast howled in shock and pain, but the hawk climbed away before any possible retaliation.

The shelter finally gave way to the dozen creatures shaking it. The wooden framework covered by hides fell away, exposing Jabbok grappling with one of the attackers. Seeing more enemies closing in, Jabbok reversed his grip and flipped the coyote-man he was fighting into two others.

Gleaming battle-axe in hand, Jabbok gutted another creature, pushed him into yet another, then tucked into a roll. He came up near the edge of the animal hide. He quickly pulled it up and over three more charging monsters. As they struggled to free themselves, Jabbok ducked under the swing of one curved sword, pushed its wielder out of his way, then grabbed a piece of flaming firewood and in the same motion, set flame to the hide.

Jabbok then sought to put distance between himself and the remaining ten creatures. But he was caught in the middle. One blocked his path and others were just a heartbeat behind him.

Protect!

The hawk shrieked and dove downward. He flew past the face of the rear opponent, causing confusion and buying the Whisperer the extra moment he needed to slay the monster before him. In the next instant, the human spun around, leading with his battle-axe. The effort removed the head of his attacker, just as yet another charged him with sword held high.

The Whisperer and the creature exchanged massive blows. The coyote-man did not possess the swordsmanship to last long, but in the next moment, it grabbed the human and pulled him close. Close enough for a snap of the jaws.

Some yards away, another coyote-man readied a massive spear, poised to kill the bothersome human —

Kill!

The hawk flew right at him, raking its eyes out before it could throw the weapon. It fell to its knees, clutching its bleeding face.

Jabbok continued to wrestle his opponent. He pulled his head back in time to dodge the coyote-man's bite, but the hawk could see the creature held the advantage. As the two grappled, the hawk shot across the distance and raked that one's face as well.

The creature yelled out, clutching its face, allowing the Whisperer to deliver the killing blow unchallenged.

Now only six remained, and suddenly they seemed uncertain. Jabbok now stood by his fire, an arrow cocked back as far as his bow could bend, daring for the battle to continue. The hawk flew excitedly in circles, flashing his talons and screeching his own challenges.

One creature took a malicious step forward but in the next instant fell backward to the ground. Jabbok's arrow protruded from its throat. The others turned and fled. Jabbok felled one more with an arrow to the back before the surviving four were out of range.

The hawk gave chase, terrifying the coyote-men with his cries while diving and nipping at their heads. The Whisperer was under his protection. Any who attacked would face his wrath.

Satisfied with drawing blood from each of them, the hawk let them go and circled back to the human. He found the Whisperer stomping out the flaming hide and landed on the ground near him.

"Thank you again," Jabbok said. "Of late, those dargs have proven to be the bane of my people. Someone has armed entire packs of them with armor and weapons and set them loose in Grungea."

Jabbok nodded in the direction of the departed dargs. "Those swords they wield, they are of a design I've seen before. I believe the kingdom to the north has sent her captains into Grungea to arm and train the dargs. For the express purpose of destroying my people. I know not why. The Bear Tribe has already been destroyed. I surely would not have survived against them today if not for you."

The hawk swept over to the body of a fallen darg and poked at the exposed meat of its wound. He took one curious bite then immediately dropped it from his beak with an angry squawk.

Jabbok laughed. "I would not imagine dargs make for tasty meals."

He then shouldered his bow and held his arm out. The hawk took the offered perch.

"Kaja." The Whisperer ignored the pain of talons digging into his forearm and bore the weight of the raptor easily. "Your name shall be Kaja. It means 'loyal friend'."

Loyalty.

The hawk fluffed out his chest feathers and sounded his consent.

Wind of Change

"My time of communion with the Great Spirit has ended fruitfully," Jabbok said. "I am commanded to search for the lost Lion Tribe of my people. The *Leo Diné* disappeared years ago. It seems now the very survival of my people may depend on finding them. Will you join me on this spirit quest, Kaja?"

The hawk repeated his happy squawk of consent. Indeed, for his own duty compelled him to always protect this human. To share in the day's hunt and to join against enemies until their role in destiny was complete. The Whisperer would be his *kaja*.

* * *

And the dove was pleased.

THE EMERALD MAGE
BY RENEE CARTER HALL

We snowcats may be born for swirling blizzards and icy cliffs, but for myself, I'll take a cozy cottage hearth any day. A bellyful of roast rabbit, a fire of crimson embers, the old rug covered with layer on layer of my gray-and-white fur — *that's* comfort.

I was stretched out on that rug, dreaming of yellow butterflies, when the explosion woke me. There was no question where it had come from, and in a matter of seconds I'd already raced across the one-room cottage, shouldered open the door, and headed for Korrinth's workroom. It was actually larger than the cottage, with the same rough shutters and thatched roof. All looked well outside, and there was no smoke pouring out from anywhere, so I hoped those were good signs.

Inside, Korrinth's chair was knocked over and his worktable covered with shards of pottery, but the oil lamp was still upright, and thankfully so was the mage himself. His complexion looked a little gray, but then I realized it was just the powdery ash of whatever he'd been mixing. His curly white beard was singed and his eyebrows were gone, but otherwise he looked all right.

"Korrinth—are you hurt?"

His cloudy green eyes focused on me. "Hurt? Why would I...no, my boy, I'm perfectly fine. Just...." He looked at the shambles on the worktable as if someone else had put the mess there. "Something...didn't work right."

I took the back of his chair in my teeth and managed to get it upright. "Here. Sit down and rest a minute."

It was hard to tell if anything else in the room had been damaged. I remembered the days when everything was neatly labeled and stored away on the shelves and in the cupboards. Now half the clay jars had faded labels, bundles of herbs were lying around in piles, and stacks of books teetered next to stale bread crusts and teacups with dried leaves stuck inside.

I couldn't help wondering if the wizard's mind now looked much the same way.

I turned back to Korrinth. "I was thinking....It looks like it might rain tomorrow. Maybe we should send a message to the council and stay home this year. It's such a long journey for bad weather."

"Stay home? Nonsense! We have to be there."

"Oh, now, you said yourself last year it was just an excuse for all the high mages to get together and show off and bicker about nothing."

"Did I? Well. It's still important. I'm the emerald mage, after all. Can't have any empty chairs." His eyes lit suddenly. "Oh—I almost forgot. I have to make the tonic for Myomé's companion." He stood. "Now…Where did I put the flameroot…?"

So that's what he'd been doing. As he rummaged through the cupboards, I sniffed the remains of the bowl. Sparkweed instead of flameroot. No wonder it had gone up. We were lucky it hadn't taken the roof off. Or his head.

It was my fault, really, dozing at the fire instead of keeping an eye on him, knowing his mind wandered too much anymore for him to be safe working alone. I looked through his recipe book, as he called it, until I found the right one, and we gathered the ingredients together.

Korrinth picked up a jar, squinted at the label, put it back, and picked up another. The clay lids rattled as his hands shook. "Oh—!"

I glanced up just in time to see the jar fall. Before it hit the packed floor, I seized the jar with my mind, slowed its descent, and righted it so that it came to rest without breaking.

Korrinth gazed at it a moment, obviously puzzled, then picked it up and went on. I turned back to the recipe book, trying not to pant with the sudden exertion, the pads of my paws slick with sweat. He wouldn't put it together. Maybe he'd think he did it himself by instinct. I hated keeping secrets from him, but like so many things these days, it was for his own good.

I'd been the emerald mage's companion since he'd found me as a starving cub, lost or abandoned in the northlands. I had more memories of snuggling against his green wool cloak than I did of my mother's fur. He'd been a waywalker in those days, no settled hearth of his own, and he'd thought a fierce male snowcat would make for good protection. He named me Jiro, after a silver flower that grew in those mountains, the only one that bloomed in winter. By the time I was grown, my head came to just above his waist, he'd spelled me to speak and taught me to read, and though I saved his life a time or two in the mountains, fighting off frost-wolves and keeping him warm at night when we couldn't risk a fire, I did it not from duty or command, but out of friendship. Out of love.

Once the tonic was finished and poured into its blue glass bottle, we went back into the cottage. Korrinth sat in his chair by the fire, intending to read, but he was asleep in moments. Grateful I could use magic now instead of my teeth, I took the book from him and placed it on the side-table, drew a blanket gently over him, and went outside to finish the day's chores. A pair of leather gardening gloves, roused with a few whispered words, became my hands, and I drew water from the well, brought in a few more sticks for the fire, and milked Penelope, our goat. It had taken a little while for her to get used to me, and a good while longer to get used to being milked by a pair of enchanted gloves instead of warm human hands, but now she stood placidly by until I was done.

All through the chores, I worried. Some days he was fine, others not. It was two days' journey to the hall where the mages' council was held — would those be good days or bad? And the council itself….

When we were alone, I could help him without him noticing, but the other mages wouldn't be so easily fooled.

I put the gloves away. By now, they felt like they were made of stone, and my head ached. I wasn't born for magic, and I'd never meant to learn it, but something had had to be done. Even though it was forbidden for a mage's companion to learn, I'd had no choice — or so I told myself. I tried to ignore the fact that, tired as I was now from the chores, I was proud of how much I could do, and satisfied by how well I did it. I *liked* doing magic, but that, above all, was what I could admit to no one. Not even myself.

* * *

Dawn came rosy and fair, and we set out, Korrinth with his walking stick in one hand and the other resting between my shoulders. It looked to be a good day in more than just the weather. I'd double-checked his pack and found our supplies in good order, he hadn't forgotten the tonic, and now he was even humming an old road-song from his waywalker days. I joined in with the chorus as we walked, and he laughed and rumpled the thick fur at my nape.

"Like old times, isn't it?" he said, smiling, and happily I agreed that it was.

The second day grew cloudy. A sudden shower in the early afternoon forced us to shelter in a grove of pines. Korrinth and I gathered dry branches, but when he tried to get a fire going, he couldn't recall the name of fire and instead kept repeating variations on a word used to snuff candles, getting more and more frustrated. Finally I muttered the right word under my breath, and the flames sprang up and blazed.

"There." Korrinth crossed his arms and settled back against a log. "Must have been a bit damp."

He dozed a bit, and I relaxed, enjoying the snap of the fire and the patter of rain. Just as I was drifting off, though, Korrinth stood, looking around.

I stretched. "What is it?"

"We have to get home. It's getting late." He picked up his walking stick and looked around for his pack.

"No, it's all right. We're going to the council, remember? We'll be there tomorrow morning."

"The council." His eyes went unfocused a moment. "But Penelope--"

"Sadie has her. Sadie Cross-Creek? She's keeping her for us. She's going to make you some of that cheese you like from the milk. The kind with the herbs in it?"

"Oh." Korrinth sat back down on the log, slowly. "Yes. I suppose." He still clutched his walking stick, looking down at his hands like he wasn't sure they were his. I wondered if he expected them to look younger, stronger, the way he remembered them — the way I remembered him.

The shower passed, and we came out of the pine grove into a rainwashed meadow. Back on the road, I felt better, though I was already vowing that, one way or another, this was going to be our last council. We had walked perhaps half a mile when Korrinth slowed and stopped, leaning on his stick.

"Should we rest a bit?" I asked brightly.

Korrinth shook his head. He gazed at the horizon a moment, frowned, turned to the right, and stopped again.

"What's wrong?"

He looked back at me, and I ached at the sadness in his

eyes. "I'm sorry, Jiro. I'm…not quite certain where we are. We should be near the second marker by now, but I don't…." He looked back at the horizon. He sounded tired. "I'm afraid I don't remember."

"Hush." I nudged his hand. "All these stupid fields look alike anyway, you know that. We can't be too far off."

"We'll be late." He looked down at the road. "We'll be late, and it'll be my fault."

I pressed against him, purring. "Then they'll just have to wait for the emerald mage. It'll be good for them."

As I spoke, I tried to push aside fear and worry and sorrow to clear my mind enough to search for the second marker. The first one the day before had been a chunk of amethyst crystal wedged high up in a tree to mark the path, so suffused with magic it practically hummed. Here I felt nothing, but it was hard to clear my mind when all I could feel was Korrinth's frail hand on my back, gripping my thick fur as if it kept him from being blown away like dandelion fluff. I buried my nose in his cloak, smelling pinesmoke and a leaf of sage caught in the wool from home.

Scent. That was it. Strong, concentrated magic like the markers had its own scent, something like a cross between rosemary and the air after a storm. I whispered a spell I'd learned the week before, to increase my sense of smell tenfold, and hoped it would work.

The Emerald Mage

It was as if all the colors around me brightened as every scent grew sharper. I sneezed twice, then sniffed the next breeze. Yes — there. It was faint, but I could follow.

"Come on." I tugged gently at Korrinth's cloak. "Let's try this way." Thankfully, he followed without question, and I mock-wandered a bit, moving toward the marker's scent. I didn't know how long the spell would last, or if it would work a second time. Some seemed to be single-use only, though for some maddening reason they never told you that in the books. Maybe they didn't work the same way in nonhumans.

Finally, just as the spell seemed to be fading, Korrinth jerked a bit, as if woken up. "There it is! Clear as a bell — and there's the path." He smiled down at me. "Maybe I'm not so worn out after all."

In the old days, I might have nipped his hand playfully, but his skin was too thin for that now, so I brushed it with my whiskers instead. "You're just fine."

* * *

The council hall was actually a castle — or at least what remained of one, high on a green hill. It had been a place of ancient magic and storied battle ages ago, and now only its great hall still stood, surrounded by weathered gray stones with weeds and ivy growing between. Inside, though, the hall itself appeared untouched by time. Tapestries covered the walls, the rushes on the floor were strewn with fresh mint, and a great table of dark, gleaming wood nearly filled the room. Around that table, Korrinth and the other four mages of the council took their places.

Myomé, the crimson mage and the highest among them, took her place first. She was nearing her three hundredth year, but her dark brown skin remained unlined, though she had grandsons now who were waywalkers themselves. Her companion, a little red dragon named Reza, had already staked out a spot at the massive hearth, and when she saw me, she puffed out twin curls of smoke in greeting.

Beside her sat Sterlan, the indigo mage, with ice-blue eyes under sharp brows and glossy black hair. His companion, a silver falcon, perched on his forearm, as if they were out hunting. I'd never felt comfortable under that bird's gaze, and now that I carried my secret, I shivered a little when the falcon's dark eyes locked on mine.

Brant, the blond-haired yellow mage, was the youngest of the group in both age and appearance. His chair was empty at the moment because he was, as always, chasing after his companion, which was apparently some sort of cross between a lemur and a demon. It had already eaten half the mint out of the rushes, upset all the chalices on the table, and was now clawing its way up the largest tapestry, defecating copiously as it went. Brant's magic lay in song, and I hoped before things got started he'd take up his lute and spell the thing to sleep for the duration of the council. Or preferably forever.

The last of the company was Neely, the Beige. He was pleasant enough but had a way of fading into the background, and had he been absent, I doubt anyone would have noticed. His companion was a small rodent of some sort from its scent, though all we ever saw of it was him apparently feeding sunflower seeds to his sleeve.

Korrinth took his seat, and I settled down next to Reza by the hearth. I was glad she was there; it was good to have someone to talk to. (Technically, Brant's thing could talk, but its vocabulary was limited mostly to the words "give," "mine," and "hungry.")

"You look awful," she said, but she said it kindly.

I stretched out all the way, spreading my toes, and sighed, feeling the warmth of the fire seep through my fur. "It was a long journey. He gets tired a lot sooner now."

"And you're exhausted yourself."

"Just need a nap. I'll be fine." I could tell she wanted to say something else, but whatever it was, she let it go and curled up next to me. We rarely saw each other outside of the councils, but whenever we met, it was as if we picked up right where we'd left off.

I drifted in and out of sleep until Myomé rapped her

staff against the stones to call the council to order. Brant had managed to subdue his companion enough to have it sitting on his shoulder gnawing an apple. I hoped he had a whole bushel with him.

"Ever wonder what that thing would taste like?" Reza murmured. "Stuff it with apples, roast it nice and slow...."

I chuckled despite my worry. Maybe things would be all right. The castle's magic was deep and strong; maybe it would strengthen Korrinth somehow. Maybe it really would be like old times.

Myomé's voice rang through the hall. "I call upon each mage to bind their word to the will of this council. Sterlan, the Indigo."

"I am thus bound."

"Brant, the Yellow."

"I am—ow! You stupid little—!"

Myomé's expression looked carved into her face, though there was a hint of mirth in her eyes. "Brant, the Yellow?"

The young mage turned red enough to have been called Brant the Scarlet. "I am thus bound."

"Neely, the Beige."

Neely coughed politely. "Madame Crimson, if you please—."

"What color is it really this time, Neely?"

"I rather think it tends more toward ecru, you see,

because—."

"Very well. Neely, the Ecru."

"I am thus bound."

"Korrinth, the Emerald."

"I am thus bound."

I hadn't realized I'd been holding my breath until I released it.

"As am I, Myomé, the Crimson. So we proceed."

The first order of business was from Neely, a question about whether some sort of magic hedge had grown too tall and exactly who was responsible for pruning it. I rested my cheek against the warm stones by the hearth and sank gratefully into sleep.

* * *

"Jiro." Reza's voice, low and insistent. "Wake up."

"Mm?" I yawned. "Was I snoring?"

"No. Listen."

I turned my attention back to the table. Things had apparently gotten a bit livelier than magic horticulture while I'd been asleep. Sterlan was leaning forward, obviously irritated; Brant was frowning (at least his lemur-thing was asleep now); and Neely looked worried (though, to be fair, Neely always looked worried). Myomé was calm, but that too was no surprise; she was like the eye of a storm given human shape. But Korrinth was pale, and I didn't like that anxious look in his eyes. I growled softly and padded over to the table to sit by his chair.

"Those wards have been getting weaker by the day," Sterlan said. "Your border might as well be unwarded—any shade with more strength than a butterfly could get through by now."

The wards. My stomach lurched. I couldn't help Korrinth maintain them; only the true emerald mage could weave and hold that magic. I'd reminded him about them a few times, but apparently he either hadn't kept them up or hadn't the strength to do it as well as before.

Korrinth's gaze hardened. "I know how to protect my own border."

"Then do it. If you can."

A snarl welled in my throat. Korrinth put a hand on my head, lightly, but I felt no reassurance from it. "You have some concern regarding my abilities?"

"I have some *concern*," Sterlan said, "about this whole council. Have we all forgotten that we're guardians? That our wards keep this land safe? If any of us neglects that work"—he eyed Korrinth—"or no longer has the capacity to do it properly, we leave all our lands open to shadow. Have we forgotten the war my father fought in—was lost in—battling those forces?"

"We have not." Myomé spoke quietly, but her voice still seemed to come from the very stones of the hall. "And some of us lost as much. Or more."

I wondered if Sterlan remembered that Myomé's husband had also been lost in the Shadow War. It seemed he didn't, because he barreled on.

"These are not merely titles; these are not amusing tricks we do. Lives depend on us, and we cannot risk failing them."

"If you have a point," Myomé said, "this would be an excellent time to present it."

There was no hesitation. "I charge Korrinth the emerald mage to prove potency by ordeal."

The hall went still as ice. Only apprentices had to prove their powers; as far as I knew, it had never been asked of any mage, let alone a high mage of the council. But now it had, and if Myomé allowed it—and if he wasn't strong enough—.

I couldn't bear to finish the thought, couldn't bear to think of him so defeated. I wished I could will him some of my strength, some of my new magic's power, but that was in the realm of magical healing, and far beyond the meager skills I had.

"This is a serious charge," Myomé said. "Are you certain you wish to pursue it?"

"Absolutely."

I imagined what his bone might feel like against my

teeth.

"Maybe we should take a break," Brant said. "Have some time to rest."

"Oh, of course," Sterlan said sweetly, "because when the shadow forces creep across the border, they'll allow him some time to rest up before they attack, won't they?" He seemed to be speaking more to his falcon than to anyone else in particular. "Of course it doesn't matter that one of our high mages of fading—why, we've got minstrel boy the monkey trainer and Fruitcake the Taupe to keep us safe—"

"Ecru," Neely muttered to his sleeve.

"You've made your point," Myomé said. "Speak further, and you'll certainly dull it." She paused, and I saw pain flicker across her face before she composed herself again. "Reza, bring the testing-stone."

The little dragon gave me a sympathetic glance, then slipped out of the hall and returned a few moments later with the stone. It looked like nothing more than a cabochon of clear glass the size of my paw, set in a silver frame, but from my secret reading I knew it was a type of stone rarer and clearer than diamond, one of only seven in the world, worthless to average humans but precious to mages for its ability to perfectly reflect power without amplifying it.

Reza placed the stone on the table before Korrinth.

"A waste of valuable time," Korrinth said, "but if I

must...."

"Please," Myomé said.

All grew quiet again. Korrinth focused on the stone. Threads of pale green light danced through it, quivering, entwining. Gradually the color deepened, and the light grew brighter.

I stared at the stone as if doing so would somehow help him, as if by sheer will I could force it brighter. By now it glowed faint green throughout with deeper sparks flashing within. It would have been an impressive show for an apprentice. For a mage....

The glow intensified, as if a green flame had been lit inside the stone. Then it grew brighter still. Hope set my heart pounding. A little more, just a little more, and that would shut Sterlan's mouth and everything would be all right.

I glanced at Korrinth. His face was a blank slate, but I saw strain in the muscles around his eyes. His hands were in his lap, and from where I sat next to him, I could see them trembling. The emerald light in the testing-stone was steady, but it wasn't enough. I saw a sudden desperation in Korrinth's eyes, saw him struggling to hold even the light that was there. I couldn't bear it, couldn't bear that pain, couldn't bear to watch him on the verge of humiliation, of defeat, when he was as good as any of them had ever been —.

Something jolted through me, searing my chest like a

spear of fire. The testing-stone blazed, too bright to look at directly, and sent an emerald beam straight up to the ceiling, clear and sharp and true.

Korrinth sat back heavily, sweat shining in the lines on his pale forehead. The stone went dark.

"I hope," Korrinth said, his breaths short and wheezing, "that was enough for your satisfaction."

I stared at the rushes on the floor, heart racing. That hadn't been Korrinth at the end. Somehow that had been me. Had anyone guessed? I scanned their faces and saw no suspicion — except for Sterlan, who was in a cold fury now, fists clenched as if he were determined to fight someone but wasn't sure who. Then he snatched up his silver chalice, still half full of red wine, and threw it directly at Korrinth's head.

Korrinth put his hands up to block it but didn't have the strength to divert the object instantly and harmlessly, as any other mage would have. The chalice struck him on the temple, and I heard him cry out in pain.

I felt the roar in my chest before I heard it from my lungs, and in my rage I seized the chalice and flung it back hard at the indigo mage. He deflected it without even wincing — as simple a reflex for a mage as someone putting up their hands — and it clattered to the stone floor.

I turned back to Korrinth, purring hard, sniffing for blood, pressed against his chest, trying to climb into his lap as if I were a cub again. I wasn't sure whether I was comforting him or looking for reassurance myself. A hard welt was rising above Korrinth's eye, but that wasn't the worst. He'd passed the ordeal of the testing-stone but failed this simpler test. He knew it. They all knew it. The emerald mage sat crumpled in his chair, hand to his head, tears on his sunken cheeks. For the first time since I had known him, he looked like nothing more than an old man.

It wasn't until Myomé inspected and healed Korrinth's wound that I started to worry whether anyone knew I'd been the one to throw the chalice back at Sterlan. Certainly they wouldn't connect it to me. It could have been any of them, and it wasn't like Sterlan had been hurt. I glanced nervously at Sterlan's falcon, but it was paying no attention to me. I took a slow, deep breath and tried to relax.

And then I looked to Reza, sitting back by the hearth, and her eyes met mine, and I knew she'd seen everything.

* * *

Myomé halted the council until the next morning and went to speak with Sterlan in private, and the other mages went to the various shelters and tents they'd set up among the ruins. Myomé gave Korrinth a draught from a gold flask she carried, and only when I was sure he was sleeping soundly did I finally leave his side and look for Reza.

She was sitting at the edge of the ruins, perched on a crumbling wall of wide stones. In her claws she held the blue glass bottle of tonic we'd brought her, and when I climbed up next to her I saw it was still full. Before us, sunset glowed pink and gold in the clouds, reminding me too much of the testing-stone.

"Is Korrinth all right?" she asked.

I nodded. "He's sleeping."

"I'm sorry about...." She didn't seem to know how to finish, but I knew what she meant. Sorry your mage isn't going to be a mage anymore, whatever that would mean. I didn't know who the new emerald mage would be or how any of it worked, but I didn't care. All I wanted was to go back home with Korrinth, and take care of him, and never mind what he was or wasn't, except the closest friend I'd ever had.

"Reza...." I wasn't sure where to start. What if she really hadn't seen anything? "Back there...."

She smiled, but her eyes were sad. "How long?"

"Months. Just to help things along, that's all. I didn't mean to...." But of course I had. You didn't stay up nights reading spellbooks in secret just to help things along.

"But why can't we?" I asked. "If it can be taught, why can't we learn?"

She looked down at the bottle, tipping it gently back

and forth, watching the liquid swirl inside. "Magic's for humans."

"But *why?* There has to be some good reason."

She shrugged, still gazing at the bottle.

"Reza...." A vague suspicion teased at the edges of my mind. "What does that tonic do?"

It was a long time before she answered, and when she did, her voice was quiet and flat. "Dragons are magic. We're born with it. This...keeps things under control."

"Keeps you from being able to use magic."

She wouldn't look at me. "Yes."

"That you were born with."

"Yes. But—"

"And if you didn't take it?"

She was silent. Then she turned to face me, and her pale gold eyes held mine. A door opened in her mind, and for an instant I was able to look through it.

I gasped. I felt like I was falling, though I knew it had nothing to do with my physical body. The magic in her was a landscape, a vista of towering red cliffs, a power from within the very earth that simmered in her veins. Just trying to grasp the scope of it was overwhelming.

She closed the door. A shudder ran through me from nose to tail. If she didn't drink that tonic, she could be the crimson mage herself. Or something even greater.

"Reza...." I had no idea how to convince her. I couldn't believe she'd kept so much power pent within her for so long, hidden from everyone, maybe even from herself.

Again she gave me a sorrowful smile. "I'm not as brave as you are, Jiro."

There was nothing else to say, and it was getting dark. As I left her, I heard the soft pop of the cork being pulled.

* * *

I lay awake most of that night, exhausted but unable to sleep. When I did doze off, I dreamt of wandering the landscape I'd seen in Reza's mind, red cliffs and deep caves and tendrils of lava, with shades chasing me at every turn, creatures I could feel but never see. Dawn was a mercy, though I had no idea how I was going to get through the day. I helped Korrinth wash and dress; he was wandering badly, probably from the strain of the day before. I hated Sterlan all over again, even if what was happening to Korrinth wasn't really the indigo mage's fault.

I was taking a currant bun from our pack for Korrinth's breakfast when he spoke.

"Jiro...."

I dropped the bun and went to him. He held my face in his hands a moment, then stroked my head.

"I wanted to thank you, for what you've done. What you

tried to do."

It took a moment for me to realize what he meant. I'd never wanted him to know I was helping. I didn't want him hurt that way.

"It's all right. I'm not angry. You would have made a good apprentice." He smiled. "And you have marvelous aim."

I tried to laugh, but the sound choked in my throat. I rested my chin on his shoulder, and he stroked my fur like he had when I was little, humming the old road-song again, the words all coming back to him safe and true, and we sang it softly, for the new road, together.

* * *

When I saw Myomé's face at the council later that morning, I knew Reza had told her everything. I felt like I should be angry, or at least afraid, but all I could manage was a kind of numb resignation. I didn't know what the penalty was for companions practicing magic, but my only concern was who would look after Korrinth if I were jailed or executed. What happened to me didn't matter.

Myomé rapped her staff against the stones. "Jiro, come forward."

I went to her side. She took something from a bag on the table and laid it on the floor before me.

The testing-stone.

I looked up at her, trying to read her expression, but she was as impassive as the stone itself. I looked at Reza, but she seemed to have become a dragon statue.

I thought of the landscapes in Reza's mind, and then I saw something different. Snowy mountains. Icy crags. All the vistas in myself I longed to explore.

Whatever the cost, I wasn't going to lock them away.

I looked back at Korrinth. He smiled, and then he nodded.

I closed my eyes and cleared my mind. I could smell the snow in the air, could feel the sharp wind ruffling my fur.

I opened my eyes and focused on the stone. It glowed, then flared, then burst into a green so bright it blinded me. When my vision cleared, the beam was still there, a beacon in the stone hall, lighting the way to the path inside myself.

Myomé smiled slow and wide. "Well proven. Take your place, Jiro."

I stared at her. "Take...?" I looked back at Korrinth. He was standing behind his chair now, and though there were tears in his eyes, he was smiling, too.

I padded over to the chair and jumped up, my claws scraping the wood as I found my balance. Brant grinned at me. Neely smiled uncertainly but waved. Sterlan wouldn't look at me, but I was perfectly fine with that.

Myomé's staff struck the stones. "I call upon each mage to bind their word to the will of this council. Sterlan, the Indigo."

"I am thus bound."

"Brant, the Yellow."

"I am thus bound." The lemur-thing chittered at me. I hissed at it, and it shut up.

"Neely, the — yes, I know — Ecru."

"I am thus bound."

"Jiro, the Emerald."

I tried to speak, but nothing came out. Myomé's gaze softened, and she spoke again, slowly, kindly.

"Jiro, the Emerald."

I sat up straighter. "I am thus bound."

"As am I," Myomé said, and the council proceeded.

* * *

That evening, with my head still buzzing from a combination of magic, giddy disbelief, and sheer shock, I met Reza at the wall again. The bottle of tonic sat beside her, and when I came closer, she uncorked it and poured the contents into the weeds.

"I thought you —."

"I did take a sip," she confessed. "Just to keep it all from being so…big."

I could understand that. The world hadn't felt this huge and scary and wondrous since I was a cub.

Reza set the empty bottle aside. "Myomé says it might be hard for me to control at first, but she's going to help me."

"You must have told her a lot."

She nodded. "We talked a long time last night. Almost all night. And argued. And cried. And laughed." She sighed, sending wisps of smoke into the twilight. "And so I'm an apprentice now." She laughed. "Can you believe it?"

We sat and watched the stars come out, all the new worlds glimmering over our heads. "Actually," I said, "I can."

* * *

And now it's been almost a year since my first day as the emerald mage. I'll go to the council hall alone this year, and Sadie Cross-Creek will come to look after Korrinth as well as Penelope. Sometimes Korrinth thinks he's still the emerald mage, and I've finally had to lock the workroom door with a spell to keep him from wandering in.

There are still good days and bad days on this road, and I know soon enough the bad ones will outnumber the good. But like all the other journeys we've taken, we'll reach the end together, and as I lie before the fire in our hearth, Korrinth stroking my fur, the landscape in my mind is calm and quiet, and snow falls gently, and all is well.

THE VIOLET CURSE
BY NICK BRYAN

The sorcerer burnt away the door to Theo's home with one touch of his staff. Inside the hut, Ally could tell it was the staff, because if there was one sound she always recognised, it was the tap of a stick.

Instantly, the purple flame began, tearing into the wood, engulfing the entire plank in seconds, and the sorcerer stepped through the entrance before it even died out. He didn't seem to care about burning in the flames himself, and that only made Ally tremble more.

The sorcerer paused at the centre of the tiny hut, a small hearth in one corner, the beds of the whole family opposite. Theo's wife Mary sat up sharply in her bed, pulled their daughter to her, but not quickly enough to run. The sorcerer grinned and clicked his staff again, the purple jagged rock at its peak glowed, and cursed fire burst through into the floor.

It wasn't warm, though; it radiated cold. So freezing, it chilled Ally's feet instantly. The wooden walls and straw ceiling would have burned without any problem, but the purple flame was not natural, it didn't spread outwards. Ally was poised to run, but it didn't come towards her, simply zipped along the muddy earth like a hunting cat, straight as an arrow to engulf the beds. Mary screamed, her daughter cried, but the hissing, crackling chill was all over them, turning their skin to a dry, thin wisp and pulping the flesh below.

Ally whimpered, beside herself with her failure to even try and save them, but then the evil sorcerer whipped his purple robes around to face her too, as the flames spilled over the edge of the bed, tearing into the rest of the house.

His eyes were crackling with awful colour, face yellow and underfed, hair wispy-white beneath the hood. Surrounded, Ally could only bark forlornly and scamper on the spot as he came closer, bringing the purple flames behind him, still tapping that damn staff.

* * *

Slowly, grumbling, Ally's head stirred from between her paws, where she'd curled up in the warm darkness. Shaking and scratching at herself, tail wagging against jagged wood, she wondered what had woken her, and how long she'd been asleep. A whistle sounded outside, accompanied by the rustle of a sword dragging along the forest floor. He was back! The hero! Theo Lark, her beloved master!

When Theo had marched off to battle, Ally had pined so hard, she'd broken two leashes trying to run after him into war. Theo had explained, patiently, that they did not have any dog-sized armour, and he didn't want her going into a bloody swordfight unprotected.

But he was back now! Ally leapt upright at the sound, feeling a strange weight on her back and darkness all around her. Actually, this was a good point—why *was* she trapped under this weight of collapsed wood and grime, shifting and floating through the air when she moved?

Confused, she raised herself up, knocking the light plank above her aside and flooding her eyes with light. Immediately, Ally looked around at the wreckage of the house and remembered being afraid—remembered that sorcerer tapping his way in and destroying the building with a burst of purple fire.

And then she saw Theo, dashing into a panic as he realised what had happened. His sheathed sword was scraping along the ground in bounces, armour rattling, long brown hair flapping out behind him, mouth agape.

At that moment, she remembered what he'd said when

he'd gone away to fight. Ally had to stay home, he'd told her sincerely, and make sure nothing bad happened to his family while he was away. She looked around at the black, smoking remains, and a sad, high-pitched noise escaped her. Her head drooped with shame as Theo approached.

"Ally!" He stopped and stared, wide-eyed, at the wreckage. She went over to him slowly, and stood there, staring. She wondered if he would still want to keep her anymore.

He didn't even acknowledge her much at first—after that first pause, to look at the flattened, oddly cold remnants of their small home, he marched forward into the mess, roughly where the family beds used to be, and started lifting wreckage to get to them.

Ally couldn't help much at first, but managed to drag a few chunks away. Slowly, she became more and more excited at the thought of helping, running backwards and forwards to make a small pile nearby, trying to get it as high as her head before it fell over.

Unfortunately, the next time Ally dashed back, almost getting under Theo's feet, her jaws latched onto something soft, which resisted very slightly when she tugged it. Thankfully, he pushed her gently away before she could wrench his dead wife's hand loose.

Ally stepped back quickly, as Theo lifted the debris

away with a single flick, then gathered her body into his arms. There was no chance of her coming back—Theo didn't know the right kind of dark magic, and even if he did, she was destroyed, half-frozen and half-dissolved, blue and broken. Ally wasn't sure she still had all her fingers. They looked breakable, but she tried not to swat them with her paws.

"Oh, Mary," Theo sighed, stroking her face with a faint scraping sound, "I'm sorry. I thought I could protect you by stopping them. I know you wanted me to just wait with you, but I couldn't stand not doing anything about—."

He stopped and glanced down at his sword, before placing Mary's body gently on the ground. He looked around nearby, and found his daughter, in a similar state. He didn't say anything this time, but Ally was sure she saw a small tear trickle down his cheek, as he lay her next to her mother. She was tiny, Ally thought, and had always loved her dog. She went over and nuzzled the little girl, as Theo poked around elsewhere in the wreckage.

Her cheek was so cold.

A moment later, there was a shout from behind her. "Ally! I know who sends these cold flames! Master Venion of the Violet Ice! As soon as we've said farewell to my family, we shall find him and kill him! For vengeance!"

Theo touched his sword, as if promising it the coming

battle, and Ally barked her agreement. With that grim promise made, Theo found his shovel and began burying his family. Ally loved digging holes, but after trying to join in a few times, found that Theo preferred to do this himself, so settled for licking the dirt off her own legs and trying to finish building up that pile she'd been working on.

* * *

Ally bolted through the undergrowth, scattering leaves left and right, barking angrily at a squirrel who got in her way, chasing it a short while, changing her mind, barking again, and then finally turning around and dashing back the way she'd come.

She nosed into a pile of leaves, then clawed a tree, before running in a short circle, as if something was following her. Finally, she found what she was looking for and ran back to Theo, who was picking his way, slowly and methodically, through the undergrowth.

Ally thought she'd picked up the sorcerer's scent, and the lingering cold in the air confirmed it, so Theo had set off, using his sword to slash any undergrowth out of the way. Some of his cuts had been more vicious than was necessary, but Ally could see why he was angry.

He staggered in a couple of the muddier parts, his brown leather boots less well suited to the terrain than Ally's paws, but she had a solution to that. She ran up to him, holding a stick almost as tall as him in her mouth.

Theo eyed up the stick, as if trying to work out if she wanted to chase it, and Ally perhaps didn't help by dropping the stick on the floor and backing a few steps away, expectantly.

But happily, after the briefest of pauses, Theo worked it out, reached for the stick and used it as a staff to help him walk through the forest.

"Thanks, Ally!" he said, smiling as sincerely as she'd seen him since he came back.

Feeling she'd done a really good job, Ally bounded ahead, almost tumbling over her own legs in enthusiasm. She kept going until she found that squirrel, menaced him in a circle and barked him most of the way up a tree. Sadly, she couldn't get him to come out of the top and fall back down.

Panting heavily, Ally looked back and was disappointed to see Theo still looked quite sad. Perhaps she couldn't truly help him, she thought. Perhaps this sadness was beyond playing with his dog.

But that just made her glum, so she forgot about it a second later.

* * *

After two days of marching through the forest, Ally had almost given up on cheering Theo up by bringing him her latest findings from the ground. She eventually caught a squirrel, which he did appreciate. He speared it through the head and cooked it for dinner, throwing Ally a roasted portion of meat, but that had been it.

All the funny-coloured leaves and amusing stones left him cold. He still used her staff to pound his way forward, but only this grim pursuit of vengeance seemed to matter to him. He didn't want to have fun anymore.

At last, though, they reached a village, and Ally hoped this would cheer him up. Because much as she loved Theo spending time with her, she knew that sometimes he needed other people.

Not to mention, the village might contain someone Ally could play with! Perhaps some children, Ally loved them. They were easily amused and could be overpowered if necessary.

But her plan didn't quite work, because when they made their way into the centre of the village, Ally and Theo saw a horrifically familiar sight: the whole damn thing had been razed to the ground, ruined, *destroyed*. As Theo shuffled into the village square, stone-faced, Ally dashed away, circling the houses.

The Violet Curse

They had been burnt to cold flaking shells, walls tumbling over each other to form piles of stiff, blackened board, with chill-damaged corpses trapped underneath. In short, this was disgustingly familiar to them both. The sorcerer Venion had been here, with his cold, violet flames.

The dog whined, barking out her disgust as she failed to find anyone to play with. They were all dead, it seemed — Venion had taken his time, herding them into their homes before demolition. Ally dug at the ground with fury.

Finally, after not finding anything, she slunk back to the village square to find Theo, only to realise he was talking to a person! And not just anyone — a young boy! Wearing rags, covered in mud — this sounded like someone who Ally could share hobbies with!

She ran excitedly over to them, tongue hanging all the way out, until she got within smelling distance and veered clean away. This was not mere mud covering the child — the boy had hidden under something truly disgusting to conceal himself from Venion's fury.

"Now, lad, I'm so sorry," Theo was saying, still looking exceptionally miserable, "I half-expected Venion to come after me, but I never knew he would do this to an entire village for no reason. You must forgive me, I feel dreadful, I never realised…"

Theo broke off halfway through, because Ally was

panting so loudly that the young boy looked away. He was only a few hands taller than Ally herself, hair scruffy, face downcast, but skinny. Barely daring to hope, Ally dropped a stick in front of him and stepped a few paces back.

"Go on, lad." Theo nodded, almost smiling. "Ally's a good dog."

On hearing those words, Ally barked loudly and ran in circles around them. She hadn't entirely meant to, but it worked. The boy laughed, picked up the stick and threw it through the air. Ally gave one more triumphant woof and raced off after it. Unfortunately, she didn't quite succeed in stopping it hitting the ground.

So she tried again, and again. After six or seven attempts, Ally still hadn't managed it, but the throws were getting half-hearted, and Theo finally stepped in. Ally managed to hide her disappointment, only drooping her head and whining for a few seconds.

Kneeling down next to the still-mud-covered boy, somehow not recoiling from the smell, Theo put a hand on his shoulder.

"Lad, we're going to catch the sorcerer who did this, I promise. Can you tell us which way he went?"

There was no reply, but a clear point in one direction. Theo nodded and threw him another brief smile. "Good. Now, it's starting to get dark, and I think I know where he's going. We're going to rest here, then catch up with Master Venion and show him justice."

* * *

All the huts in the village were wrecked by the purple fire, but the boy showed Theo and Ally a couple of full hay carts which stood firm. He seemed keen to have one to himself, so they took the other. It was still standing upright, balanced somewhat precariously on its single set of wheels, load towards the front.

After squirming a while to get comfortable in the hay, Theo stared up at the stars. Ally, meanwhile, was suffering a severe itch from all the jabbing stalks, and after dancing around to crush them with her feet, decided to try biting them instead.

However, after a few minutes of snarling, gnashing fury, Theo reached over to stroke the scruff of her neck.

"Ally, Ally, come on." He sighed. "Be calm."

She couldn't be calm, the sharp stalks wouldn't stop jabbing her, but Ally knew this wasn't the time. She whined, but managed to lie still.

"Shame about the lad, eh? I remember when I was young, all my family were killed by the big ogre war. I got left alone, too. Just me and a dog, I always had a dog."

Ally woofed at the mention of dogs.

"Hopefully he'll find a way to survive. He seems strong."

Another bark, brief lick of the face.

"Anyway," Theo gave another of his sad smiles, "goodnight, Ally."

He turned over and curled up, cocooning himself within his limbs. Ally herself considered going for a run, but decided to stay near Theo, in case he needed her to bite something. She began rolling herself up too, but as she shuffled round, she found herself next to Theo's neck. His skin, still and unprotected for the first time, glistening in the gap between his hair and armour.

Ally stared, mesmerised for some reason. Some throbbing, pained feeling started up in her mind—at first, perhaps a headache, but it was more like a whole other brain in there. It spread out, grew and became a purple haze falling across her vision.

As the purple flames began to dance behind her eyes, and back through her mind, Ally remembered the last time she'd felt this. Back in Theo's hut, when Master Venion had killed Theo's family and licked their home with cold flames.

As Mary and her daughter screamed and shivered to death, Venion loomed down on the yelping dog, and reached a skinny, spotted hand out. It poked from beneath the bottomless purple robes, and as it got close to Ally, she snapped at it instinctively. She wasn't normally the sort to bite people, but doubted the evil sorcerer counted as a person.

Venion just sniggered, drew his hand back and tapped the staff on the ground even harder. A purple smoke rushed up around him, and the arm lunged down. Before Ally could move out of the way, the hand reached inside her, drifting apart into smoke.

But the fingers inside her were real and solid and clutched around her heart. He left the violet haze there, and it told her that no matter what happened, she had to keep going until she knew Theo was dead. That if the slightest moment of weakness arose, the purple smoke would make sure she killed him.

She barked at Venion angrily, but he just smiled, pulled the hand out and, with one last burst of flame, brought the house down around them. He moved the staff in a pattern around the two of them, directing the destruction, making sure he and his new doggy puppet were unharmed by the crumbling wood.

Ally just lay down, whimpered, and tried very hard to forget the whole thing and think about sticks.

* * *

After a roar of resistance, Ally opened her jaws wide and lunged for Theo's neck as he slept. The coldness behind her eyes spread to her brain, roaring in her head like a freezing sun.

It was numb, dead, empty matter, and she found herself observing from the outside as this other, drifting purple controlled her.

The hay in the cart cracked and tumbled around Ally's sudden movement, and Theo opened his eyes a second before she struck. Of course, he had hours of battle experience behind him, so one dog would've been easy. His instincts sent him rolling away towards the back of the cart.

Which meant they didn't even get to fight, as the quick tumble sent the cart rolling over its single axle, floating atop the wheels for a second, before falling back down, tilting the opposite way.

The bales of hay tipped towards the rear, and so did Theo, caught in the middle of his evasive movement, coughing and spluttering as both strands of hay and his own hair floated into his mouth. Ally dashed with all her legs, running on the spot, trying to stay on the cart, whereas Theo rolled away.

There was an unpleasant crash as he hit the ground, and the cart finally levelled out. Ally heard no sound—had she done it? Had Master Venion's curse successfully made her kill Theo?

As that possibility spread through her mind, she raced

down the cart in a panic and jumped to the floor. The purple chill had evaporated from her head, she realised, no doubt happy the job was done. Theo was lying still, covered in hay, some of it sticking out of his nose and mouth, arm askew. She poked him with a paw, and he still didn't move.

She tried barking. No response.

Was this it? Had she failed the entire family? She let out a sad moan, and rubbed Theo's face with her muzzle. Finally, probably because her nose was cold, Theo jerked and rolled over, coughing out hay as he went.

Ally barked gleefully and ran round to lick him in the face, only stopping when he pushed her away. "Ally, be careful, you nearly killed us both in that cart." Theo shook his head at her, although didn't really look angry. "Bad dog."

She just woofed agreeably, happy that Theo would never know his faithful companion had been cursed into attacking him. But at least it was over now, she thought, until the familiar hazy chill settled at the back of her skull once more.

As Theo crawled back into the hay on the floor to sleep, Ally raced around the other side of the cart to curl up, hoping she wouldn't be a danger if she kept her distance. But still — what could she do now? Placing her head sadly between her front paws, Ally fell asleep listening to the faint, angry commands of Master Venion in her mind.

* * *

When she woke the next morning, Ally wondered if Theo secretly realised what happened last night. Maybe he'd run off while she slept, to avoid his cursed dog getting another chance to kill him?

Part of her hoped he had. She could stay here forever, play with that little boy, chase dozens of sticks, never worry about the risk of committing violent murder thanks to Master Venion's mind control. She unfurled herself and padded around the cart, seeing no sign of Theo anywhere. The village looked even more wrecked and empty in the cold morning light.

Her hopes were dashed, though, when she heard voices in the village square. She briefly considered running into the woods, removing herself from the risk of harming Theo, but before she completed the thought, Ally was off, dashing back to the village square to sit in front of the boy and bark.

"Okay lad, I'll come back for you if I can," Theo was saying to him, raising his voice slightly to be heard over the woofing, "but if you don't see us by tomorrow morning, head for a bigger town."

The boy nodded, still not saying anything. Theo gave him one last sad look, before turning his attention to Ally.

"Come on, girl. We must set off. Master Venion's cave

of power isn't far from here."

Ally whined slightly.

"I know, Ally, but it's important for the safety of the realm, as well as my own vengeance. This must be done."

She gave a loud bark and sauntered off in the same direction Theo was headed.

"Good girl. We can beat him."

And in the back of Ally's mind, Master Venion laughed deep and long.

* * *

Even though she couldn't bring herself to leave Theo, Ally kept her distance from him as they made their way through the forest to the cave where Master Venion hid.

She ran off, ducked, weaved, tried to seem like she was playing, but in reality, all the sticks she brushed past held little interest for her anymore. What she wanted, truth be told, was to plough into Theo, teeth bared. Now that the curse had come upon her once, it never seemed far from her mind. She had hated not being able to help him before, now she had to worry about stopping herself killing him too.

So she dashed through the woods, chasing other animals. Whereas before she rarely caught anything, now she managed to savage two rabbits and three squirrels.

As the trees began to thin out and they approached the

mountainside, Theo stopped to cook one of the rabbits, and for a moment, Ally forgot herself and ran over to him, rather than keeping her distance. She went to sniff his feet, nearly biting three toes off on instinct.

This time, Theo noticed the snapping of her jaws. "Ally, are you alright? You've been angry since we left the village."

He rubbed the space between her ears.

"I know, I want to get Venion too. Together, we'll avenge them. Then, after that, who knows?"

She shivered and backed away from his hand, before she could attack it. Why wouldn't he notice something was wrong with her, see some purple haze in her eyes maybe, and chase her away, or chain her up until after the evil sorcerer was dead? Was he just not really here with her anymore? Had her playmate died when his family did?

She gave Theo a stare, as if daring him to see the evil planted within her, but he just smiled again and looked up at the rocks, where Master Venion's cave lurked.

"Come on then, Ally. Time to face him."

And he marched bravely forwards, Ally slinking along behind. She knew she should run away, but couldn't desert him for this final battle. She just kept walking.

THE VIOLET CURSE

* * *

As Theo explained it, the cave was the source of Master Venion's powers. He went there to fill his staff with cold flames, the mauve force flowed outwards into his body, where he used it for wicked magic.

And this scared the hell out of Ally, because how would she resist him this close to the source? Maybe that was the reason she wasn't turning back: at this proximity, her will was not her own. She tried to run away at last, got as far as four large rocks from her master, chased a small cave mouse around for a while, tried to lick her own tail, then ran back to Theo to show him a smooth pebble, before realising she'd failed to desert him. This evil curse was devious.

For his part, Theo had nodded approvingly at the stone, pocketed it, and then continued to crunch his way through the landscape of smooth, cold gravel that dotted the mountainside.

At the end of the trail was the clear entrance into the cave. Inside, even clearer as evening began to fall, was a light purple glow. He was still in there, energising the staff for evil deeds.

Rearing up, Ally yowled, but Theo gestured firmly towards the mountain one more time, gave her a small smile and put his hand on his sword hilt. Somehow, they had arrived. It was so close, blowing wicked cold air at them, a smell which chilled the inside of Ally's head. She couldn't work out why Theo wasn't afraid.

"This is it, Ally," he whispered, shivering, "we're going to make them proud, aren't we girl? We'll make sure the people we loved didn't die for nothing. And no bad magic will stop us."

She whimpered. Theo didn't take it as the dire warning she'd intended, he simply rubbed her head again.

"And afterwards, I don't know." He shook his head. "Maybe we'll go travelling, seek out evil together, keep it at bay. Just like old times when I was growing up, just me and my dog." He cried a little. "Had my chance at something bigger and I didn't protect it. It's only fools who think I'm a hero."

She reached up to lick his face, but he just pulled away, wiped it himself, leaving dirty smears, and placed his hand firmly on his sword once more.

"Now, Ally, forward. Good girl."

* * *

As they entered, the cave walls felt like ice. Ally shuddered, yipped again and moved in closer to Theo's legs, trying to stay warm. He, in turn, gently pushed her away, no doubt determined to keep space free in case he needed to move.

The air might be chilly, but the centre was alight with

flame. A perfectly spherical purple inferno roared in the heart of the cave, enough to melt them alive if it had been hot, hurling shadows towards the walls. Standing in front of it, holding the jagged jewel of his staff to the fire, was Master Venion.

His hood was thrown back, the pale, pointed face beneath rolling back in ecstasy. He didn't seem to know they were there. Ally padded slowly towards him, and Theo glanced at her, as if he knew she'd do the right thing.

Little did he know, this close to the purple flame, all she wanted to do was lunge for his blood. Her hackles were up, she was growling, advancing towards Theo, until he unsheathed his sword in a single, smooth movement. The slicing noise reverberated around the cave, sending Ally jumping back for a second, and shocking Venion off his feet.

He was off balance, the staff clattered to the ground, and Theo advanced, sword out. Ally knew exactly what she wanted to do most of all.

"Venion!" Theo called out, as the purple hood went back up. "You killed my family! You killed everyone in that village!"

The sorcerer didn't answer at first, still shaking his head as he emerged from the reverie. But, finally, he looked up at Theo and growled through gritted teeth. "You had to be distracted, then disposed of."

"You did a poor job of it, Master. I am still here."

"Not for much longer. I shall burn you into frozen atoms with a single tap of my…."

He took one step back, bent his knees gently under the robe and grasped downwards where he'd dropped his staff. It was a smooth movement, and as Theo's eyes widened, Venion clutched the wooden shaft in one hand, cackled loudly and thrust it towards the hero. "Die, you filthy —!"

Venion's nasty, sunken eyes widened. The spiked, purple gem at the top of his staff was missing, the length of the wooden pole no longer scraped to a smooth curve. In fact, it was just a stick. The same stick Ally had brought to Theo in the woods earlier; she'd left it behind Venion while Theo had distracted him.

She woofed triumphantly, and Theo reached back and down, much the same movement Venion had attempted earlier, only he came back with the real purple staff. "I believe you were looking for this?"

He nodded, smiled, then whipped his hand to one side before Venion could move. The jewel atop the staff crashed into the wall of the cavern and shattered immediately into a shower of fragments. Theo snapped the pole over his knee for good measure, whilst Ally looked on proudly and woofed them both deaf.

"Well." Venion glared at the noisy dog. "I don't need

the staff for spells I've already cast. Animal," he kept looking at Ally, "the Mauve Curse commands you."

She was so close, the cold sun froze her mind dead, her head a block of ice.

"Dog, *kill* your master. Do not rest until you know him dead."

* * *

Ally threw her head back and howled, partly in agony, but mostly hoping Theo would seize the opportunity and kill her. He had an enormous blade, after all.

But when she opened her eyes, she was still alive. Venion was cackling and she was advancing on her master, eyes staring and teeth bared, completely against her will.

Rather than raising his weapon to defend himself, Theo's arms were spread wide, sword limply pointing towards the ground. She lunged for his legs and he leapt aside, pinning himself against the cave wall. Venion's shadow was rubbing its hands with glee. She couldn't see the sorcerer himself, his curse had robbed her of the power to even turn her own head.

She simply stared, like some wild forest beast, licking her lips and gnashing her teeth. She stalked past a chunk of discarded stick on the floor without even looking twice.

The purple sphere behind them burnt brighter, casting a sickly light. Theo looked small as he dashed up against the cave wall, back pressed against it. Master Venion, suddenly remembering the stick they'd stupidly given him, took a swing at Theo, forcing the hero to duck back towards his dog, as the huge branch scraped and cracked behind his head.

Finally, unable to keep her feet slow any longer, Ally took a lunge at Theo, but didn't make a sound. Simply leapt, crashing into him and knocking him backwards, snapping and biting for his face. Her claws caught Theo deep in the thigh, he cried out, and she smelt the blood instantly.

Normally, to be honest, this would repel her. She didn't have those instincts, but right now, it drove her on, swinging for the same area to press the advantage.

Master Venion, breathing heavier, took another whack at Theo with the staff, shouting vague curses. Ally's vision was closing into a red and purple haze, as her master's hands pressed into her midriff, trying to keep her away. Suddenly, one of those hands released, and grabbed hold of the stick. He yelled in pain as her claws went into his skin again, but still smashed the wood backwards into Venion's face.

Bleeding from the nose, yelling more obscenities in the name of his Mauve Master, the sorcerer staggered backwards, only to catch his head on the purple sphere and fall forward again, screaming as his skull froze.

Ally was still slashing and biting for Theo's face, leaping up from the ground and trying to bring him down, when he grabbed firm hold of her with both hands and threw her bodily at Master Venion.

And because her claws were out and his face was gaunt and defenceless, the back of his head already half-dissolved into mush, that was all it took. Maybe she managed to get a shred of control back to push down on him a little, maybe, rake them into his eyes. Because when she looked up again, Venion was definitely dead.

He was gone, and with its disciple dead and staff shrinking, the purple heart was dissolving quickly into the air. Relief was visible on Theo's face, and it almost reached Ally too, until she realised her need to gut him hadn't diminished. Venion's death would not stop the curse — it was forever.

And Theo realised a moment later too, as he dashed for the entrance, hobbling on his injured leg, Ally dashing after him.

* * *

Despite hobbling and mumbling with pain, Theo led her on one hell of a run. From the empty cave, where Venion's body lay, surrounded by shattered purple shards, out into the dark, grunting all the way. She leapt over rocks, willing herself to lose energy, but never slowing.

She hoped Venion's death or the disappearance of the purple sphere might cause the curse to weaken, but it didn't stop. She hoped Theo would finally realise he had no choice and turn his sword on her, but he never even reached for it. The chase simply went on.

Up they climbed, around the mountain, off the ground. She tried to cut him off, but he was always just slightly too quick. Once, just before the path rose up, Theo turned around and called back to her: "Ally! Come on, girl, fight! You can do it."

But another flash of her glassy eyes and sharp teeth convinced him otherwise, and he ran higher, perhaps hoping her trance would leave her off-balance? She hoped so too, but no. Nothing interested her except catching him, and she came close once, so near he had to kick her in the stomach to get away.

The drip of blood down his leg was turning into a flow, though, and she could see him slowing. The second time she caught him would be the last.

So instead of letting her get him, Theo swerved towards a cliff edge. They weren't too high up, but the slope below was covered with small, jagged rocks. He stared down at them, clearly considering the jump, then turned back to face her. Hobbling like a cripple, perhaps he didn't like his chances.

He turned, and finally drew his sword, holding her back with the point. Instinctively, she stopped, crouched down, waiting for a chance to spring.

"Ally. Enough. Maybe this is the right way."

He took a look behind him, then waved the blade at her again as she took a bite forwards.

"I won justice for my family. I have nowhere else to go. Perhaps this is what was meant to happen." The sword trembled. "Perhaps after avenging their murder, the great plan is that you help me see them again."

Something stirred, and her legs lost their tension for a moment. Her tongue lolled looser and she whined.

"Don't worry, girl. I know this isn't your fault. But I still won't allow one of Venion's instruments to take me."

Another glance back, over the spiked rocks below. At long last, Theo threw the sword down.

"Good dog. Thank you for coming with me."

Finally, Theo spread his hands wide and let himself fall backwards over the cliff, crashing down along the slope without even a shout. Ally shook her head, the curse clearing out again, and by the time she'd rushed to the edge and looked over, his body had disappeared into the rocks, darkness and dust.

* * *

Dashing over the rocks so fast it hurt her paws, Ally raced away. Her tongue flicked out backwards, legs grew sore, eyes dried out, but she didn't slow down.

Ignoring all her surroundings, barely reacting when the stones turned to forest, emitting only the softest of whines, Ally ran as fast as possible, away from the cliff where Theo had died. She would find something to distract herself, she thought. That had always worked before. She would find a pine cone, and the pain would fade away.

The curse was gone, she could feel it, so eventually she might forget him too.

She rustled through the bushes head-on, crushing insects as she slammed her body through them, catching her foot in a plant and simply ripping it out from the root.

Finally, as the sun rose over her, she crashed out of the undergrowth, tired and exhausted, into the wrecked village. The cart where she'd first tried to kill Theo was still there, all askew, hay spilt everywhere.

Ally was close to turning and running, when she heard someone calling her name.

Her head turned, and it was the boy. The same boy from before, slightly cleaned up, clothes damp and face streaked from recent scrubbing, but definitely him. He'd enjoyed playing, she remembered.

"Ally! Are you well? What happened? Where's Theo?"

She barked, dejectedly.

"Oh." He looked down at her. "Well, do you want to come with me? We have to keep going, Theo said that.

Besides, he grew up with just a dog and turned out to be a big hero."

The boy looked enraptured, so Ally broke the pause by rushing off, fetching a stick and bringing it back. He looked down at it, grinned and threw it away again. Her tail wagging, Ally chased it furiously past the wrecked houses.

As she carried it back to the boy for another throw, she thought she saw a shadow in the bushes watching them, but soon forgot about it.

The Restless Armadillo

By Lillian Csernica &
Kevin Andrew Murphy

Nettle hurried in with the Final Edition. He shoved aside the coffee mugs, skinning knives, and the remains of Ivy's veggie burger, then dropped the papers on the kitchen table.

"Front page!" The power surged through him, leaving him lean and dark and potent, just like the powers he served.

Wasp and Ivy came over to stare down at the blurry photo of a Ford pickup and a Honda sprawled across the highway, their bumpers locked in the mother of all head on collisions.

"It says one of them lived." Ivy pouted, twisting a strand of love beads around her finger. "'Software engineer Dave

Carlson was heard to say, 'Deer! Biggest buck I ever saw! Ten points!'" She stomped off to her corner of the living room and sulked. "Points! Always points! The jerk is bleeding to death, and he's still talking about points!"

"He means the points on its antlers." Wasp ran one hand back through his yellow zebra-cut hair. "This is bad, Nettle. Even if everybody thinks he's stoned on painkillers, you said it had to be a complete kill. The spirits might rebound on us."

Nettle took a bottle of Odwalla algae mix out of the fridge. "One, they won't believe him." He pulled off the cap and drank. "Two, the guys we wanted were in the Ford. They're so much Jello in the coroner's body bags." He drank again, leaving a slimy mustache. "Three, we're protected. That's always the first consideration, and it's been taken care of."

"I don't like it." Wasp shook his head. "The possums worked. The skunks worked. But a deer? One that big? That's a lot of life force to control."

Nettle let out an exaggerated sigh. "Fine. You want to go through the whole Sealing Ritual again? We'll need fresh supplies. I took highway duty last time, so it's you or Ivy."

"You know I can't stand that!" Ivy shuddered. "Those poor little animals, all burst open and flattened out! And the smell!" She swayed, clapped a hand to her mouth, then ran for the bathroom.

Nettle snorted. "Some necromancer she is. She likes it well enough when we cut open something a little higher up the food chain."

"I came across something fresh when I biked over. See what the bastards killed today?" Wasp unzipped his backpack and pulled out a clear plastic bag wrapped around something brown and bloody. "Let's call her Laura."

Nettle drained his Odwalla and flung it into the recycling bin. "What is she?"

Wasp smiled and walked over to the corner of the living room where his ritual sand painting sat. He unrolled the plastic and spilled the partially crushed remains of a pointy-nosed, hard-shelled mammal into the middle of the painting.

"An armadillo!" shrieked Ivy, just stepping out of the bathroom. "A poor little armadillo!" She spun around and slammed the door behind her. The sound of dry heaves filtered through the wood.

Wasp grinned. "So, you'll think she'll do?"

Nettle nodded. "Definitely. We've got Ivy worked up for the pain and grief. You've already cast the blood into the sand painting, so all we need is my Dr. Dee."

"Do you really have to do that Enochian crap?"

Nettle looked grave. "Are you really going to do Hopi rip off surfer boy sand paintings? Are we really going to let Ivy play New Age hippie girl with her love beads and crystals? Hell yeah, my friend. The rituals work. We've got the papers to prove it."

"I'll get Ivy. Get your Dr. Dee stuff, dude."

Nettle fetched his Enochian grimoire and ceremonial rod from the bedroom closet where he'd hidden them behind Wasp's stash of puffed rice cakes. By the time he got back, Ivy was out of the bathroom and down on her knees before the armadillo.

"Oh poor, poor little Laura." She wailed, tears running down her cheeks as she caressed the armadillo's bloody ears. "Please, come back to us. I know it hurts, but we need you. We need you to come back and help us stop the bad men who did this to you."

"Great Spirits!" Wasp boomed, shaking his rattle and his medicine stick. "Mighty Kachinas! We beg your aid! Vulture, set free the spirit of one of those in your keeping! Let this armadillo walk the roads again!"

"Oh Azrael, kind and just, let this be so!" Nettle held the grimoire over his head. "Let this one free for just one day and just one night. By the power of God do I implore you, and by the Names written herein!"

Nettle opened the grimoire and began the long invocation, walking around the others, chanting and marking the floor with the chalked tip of the rod. The surfer boy shaman screamed to the Kachinas and threw sand from his medicine bag. The New Age girl wept and begged and rent her necklaces in grief.

The sand and chalk and Ivy's scattered beads began to glow. The armadillo twitched, slowly at first, then faster and faster. With a jerk and a shudder, Laura convulsed and rolled over onto her feet.

"Oh Laura!" Ivy prostrated herself before the armadillo. "You are back! You are back!"

Blood bubbled from the armadillo's lips.

"Oh merciful Azrael!" Nettle touched Laura's shell with the chalk, marking it with the Sigil of Azrael. "Let us understand the spirit's tongue so we may know thy wisdom."

The chalk glowed white. Laura's bubbling gave way to a cartoon animal's squeak. "Oh, it hurts! It hurts! What do you want, shaman people?"

"Sister Armadillo," Wasp said. "We, like, need you to go track down the car that hit you. Scare the crap out of them, make 'em go off the road."

"Aiiii!" lamented the armadillo. "It is far! It is far! Across the desert and beyond the hills, into the land where the plants grow lush and tall and beyond! Too far! Too far! Have mercy and let me rest!"

Wasp looked at Nettle. "Tourists."

Ivy kept stroking the armadillo's bloody ears. "Poor little Laura. Yes, that is too far. We have another task that you could do, one much easier, one that would allow you to rest. There is a man named Dave Carlson, not very far from here at all, at the place of healing and death. Go talk to him. Tell him about the awful way you died, so he'll know what he has done wrong by driving a car and by eating meat."

"It is far, and I am tired," Laura said. "Could I just go visit my babies instead? Tell them what has happened to their mother?"

"Go find Dave Carlson," Ivy said. "Go find him, little Laura. If there is any goodness left in him, he will find your babies and raise them as his own."

"Yeah," said Wasp. "Tell him he has to. Or the spirits will be angry and send other messengers."

"He will help my babies? Let me go, shaman people!"

"Go, then," Nettle said. "Return here afterward so we can be assured of your success." He chalked two more sigils on the armadillo's shell. "Mighty Azrael! Speed thy creature's way!"

A light so dark it was more than darkness rose out of the glowing sand and swallowed the armadillo. It faded, leaving the sand painting empty.

* * *

That evening Nettle sat in front of the TV, channel surfing among the various news broadcasts. Ivy sat in her corner, humming to herself, stringing her spilled beads. The rising edge on her humming forced Nettle to keep turning up the volume.

"What's your problem?" he snapped. "Do you have to keep making that noise?"

The hum stopped. Nettle turned back to the TV, settled more comfortably in the chair, turned the volume back down to a bearable level. Minutes later another sound penetrated his consciousness. Total silence from Ivy's corner. No humming, no click of beads. Nettle turned to look at her, then leaped up out of his chair.

"Ivy!" He grabbed her shoulders and shook her. "Wake up!"

Her eyes were wide open, rolled so far back in her head only the whites showed. Nettle dug around in her work basket, throwing aside thread, needles, more beads, feathers, and crystals. One pink crayon lay on the bottom. Scowling, he spat on it, then pressed the crayon to Ivy's forehead. The crayon flaked and broke, but he got the sigil mostly drawn.

"Child of Earth and Air, return!"

Amy's eyes rolled back down. She stared at him, then flung her arms around his waist and sobbed against his stomach. The door opened. Wasp came in carrying a large pizza box.

"Where the hell have you been?" Nettle yelled. "She freaked again! Get her straight, man, now!"

Wasp dropped the box on the cluttered table and ran over to Ivy. "Come on, babe. I'm here now. Tell me what you saw."

"Laura!" Ivy wailed, burying her face against Wasp's chest. "Poor little Laura! So cold! The lights, it smells so bad — ."

Nettle knelt down and took Ivy's face between his hands. "Talk to me, Ivy. Tell me exactly what you saw."

Ivy shook her head, tried to push him away. "The light, all nasty and hard. It smelled bad! Death, rotting, cold ugly medicine...."

Nettle looked at Wasp. "Medicine. That's your gig. Figure it out."

Wasp shrugged. "Sounds to me like something went wrong. Divination is your gig, dude. You figure it out."

Nettle glared at Ivy's bent head. "One of these days I'm going to jam an antenna in her ear and wire her for clearer reception."

"Hey! Lay off Ivy. It's not her fault you couldn't draw that sigil straight!"

"Watch your mouth, surfer boy." Nettle reached behind him to pick up his wand and rest its tip right between Wasp's eyes. "One more word out of you and you'll make Laura look like nothing ever touched her."

He stalked off to the bedroom and came back with his Crowley deck, then shoved the clutter off the kitchen table. He laid the Tarot cards out in the Celtic Cross. No time for anything fancy now. Wasp half-dragged, half-carried Ivy over to watch as Nettle turned over one card after another.

Ivy wiped her eyes and pulled her stringy blonde hair back behind her ears. "Magus inverted. Bad Significator. Crossed by Death! Behind us, the Four of Wands. Beside us, the Five of Swords. Crowning, the Ten of Cups."

Nettle laid the next card down. "Before us, the Ten of Swords." His hand shook as he turned over the next three cards, lining them up in a column from bottom to top. "Fool. High Priestess inverted. Ace of Swords." He touched the last card, licked his lips.

"Go on, dude," Wasp said. "Let's see it!"

Nettle glanced at the card. His mouth went dry. His heart thumped painfully against his ribs. He threw it down. It fluttered over to land against Ivy's arm.

"The World! Inverted!" Ivy screamed, scrambling backward from the card.

"Ivy!" Wasp yelled. "Don't—!"

Ivy tripped over her spilled work basket and staggered up against the sand painting, kicking it hard enough to knock sand out the far side. Its glow flickered, worms of light racing back and forth, spilling out into the dumped sand.

"Oh no!" Wasp grabbed his backpack and upended it, flinging everything in it onto the floor. He hefted a white leather pouch, then yanked it open and sprinkled a handful over the painting. The flickering light faded. He turned his stricken face to Nettle. "The pattern's broken!"

"Tell me about it." Nettle gathered up the cards, hands shaking so much they kept falling out of his grasp. He flung away the rest of the deck. Cards whirled through the air, raining down around Ivy. She screamed and slapped at them as though they were insects.

"What happens now?" Wasp asked.

Nettle turned to stare at the front door. Whose turn had it been to renew the wards, and how long ago had that been done?

"We'll just have to wait and see."

* * *

At sunset the next evening someone knocked at the back door. Ivy nearly jumped out of her skin.

"No! No!" She pointed to the door, cowering against Wasp.

Nettle got up, exasperated. "Calm down, Ivy. It's only the pizza."

"No car...."

Nettle sighed. "They use bike delivery, remember? Enviro-friendly pizza?"

He went to the door and opened it. On the back step stood a corpse, naked and sunburned. The vulture perched on its shoulder kept pecking at its chest. The eyes were already gone. In the corpse's arms were four live baby armadillos, all of them wiggling around and making noises like human babies.

"Laura couldn't make it," the zombie croaked, "but she told me. Here are her babies."

The zombie pushed the baby armadillos against Nettle's chest, folding Nettle's stiff arms around the tiny creatures. He shambled in past Nettle and grinned at Wasp and Ivy. Ivy's face turned a bilious green. Wasp started screaming.

"Hi, I'm Dave," the zombie said. "The vulture here explained everything to me. You got a computer?"

"Nuh-nuh-nuh—." Ivy pointed across the room to where Nettle's laptop sat.

"HP Pavilion, huh?" Dave asked. "Not bad." He started poking around at the desktop icons. "Oh man. Don't you people do your updates?"

The vulture tore another strip of flesh off Dave, then squawked at Wasp. Wasp stopped screaming. The vulture squawked again. Wasp nodded.

"What did it say?" Nettle asked. "It's your totem, right? What did it say?"

"Uh—Vulture's pleased, dude. He likes what we've been doing." Wasp licked his lips and swallowed. "We, uh, like, we've been promoted. Dave's, like, a gift."

Nettle looked at Dave, who was dripping sand and worse

onto the keyboard and muttering snide remarks about the state of the software.

"And it would be bad manners to send him back?"

"Real bad," Ivy whispered.

The vulture stared at Nettle with its beady little black eyes. Nettle shook his head, then shut the door and put the baby armadillos in a laundry basket lined with an old T-shirt. What did they eat? Bugs? Nettle walked over to stand with Ivy and Wasp. They watched Dave in frozen silence broken only by the pecking of the vulture and the clicking of the keyboard.

"Hey," Dave said, "Remember when that BP oil rig exploded? That pretty much trashed sea life in the Gulf of Mexico. Want to send all those critters after the Board of Directors?"

"S-s-s—," Wasp gulped, eyes still wide with horror, "Sounds like a plan."

There came another knock on the door. Ivy grabbed Wasp, whimpering.

"I think," Nettle said at last, "that's our pizza."

"Pizza?" Dave looked up. "You got a pizza? Cool. Last thing I ate was hospital food. I'm starving."

The vulture pecked at Dave while the pizza man kept knocking.

STUCK ON THE SQUIGGLYBOUNCE

BY DOUGLAS J. OGUREK

I stopped bouncing. It was no use: the squigglybounce was stuck. My vacation day was off to a bad start. I made transparent the divider between my chamber and the ish chamber.

In there, a multicolored ice cream puddle of a man sitting on the trampoline leaned against his safety bars and clutched a shapeless lunch pail. His shirt looked like a tangle of colorful ropes, and the yellow glitter all over his face revealed his addiction to NewNewSoNew.

I pressed the intercom button. "My husband and I find you to be a real inspiration."

He belched and clapped lightly. "Glashy. Look at you, dink lady."

Yourkidsabrat flapped down from the wall I'd set to beige. He looked into the ish chamber and whistled. The few remaining scent pods on his head rose. He recognized the bastard in there. So did I: he was the disgraced kids' hero Wedge Medge. And Yourkidsabrat was one of the many gilpans he'd marred to get his once distinctive voice.

Wedge Medge's trademark hair wedge had collapsed into a tangled heap, and his lean frame had bloated from repeated NewNewSoNew applications.

I petted Yourkidsabrat. "Recognize him?"

Wedge Medge, breathing heavily, paid no attention. He goggled down at the swirling, shining, writhing, jelly bean apocalypse that was Tummygrowl Town. Then he reached longingly toward the Miroom Tummygrowl statue—its sparkling stomach swelled with dink toll payments—that looped and swerved along another sky scribble as it made its way to other squigglybounces. Squigglybounces that weren't stuck.

"You should recognize him." I waved my hand over the scent pods that Wedge Medge had ripped off when Yourkidsabrat was a fledgling. He'd mix the pods with cotton candy milk then drink the concoction to get the voice that made him famous. If I let Yourkidsabrat into the ish chamber, that would be the end of Wedge Medge.

Wedge Medge belched. "Look. Miroom Tummygrowl

sparkles. Sparkly! Yeah!" The slicing quality of his voice had toned down.

In minutes, the statue would stop at our squigglybounce to collect the dink toll from me. If Wedge Medge, high on NewNewSoNew, reached through the safety bars and touched the statue's huge sparkling stomach, he would suffer the drug's worst side effect: gradual transformation into whatever sparkling material the user touched. In this case, it would be that squishy stuff. A slow, painful, squishy death. Good, but not good enough; Yourkidsabrat deserved some retribution. I pressed the button to open the divider. It didn't work. I tried the divider slot, which would have left a gap large enough for Yourkidsabrat to fit through. But that didn't work, either. Whoever was in the kiddyup chamber had locked my control panel.

The divider darkened again. Yourkidsabrat made puffing sounds. My husband, Smackbrat, and I adopted him just after Wedge Medge's gilpan farm was discovered. Yourkidsabrat, like the hundreds of other gilpans there, was emaciated, dirty, and mutilated.

* * *

The kiddyup chamber became visible through the other divider. A woman faced away from me and bounced. An annoying doodle design covered her skin-tight fitness suit.

One of her butt cheek screens showed a boy who, with skinny body and painted face, resembled a lollipop. Her son, no doubt. The other cheek read, "First place: Iwinalot Piano Recital."

She'd taken over all the squigglybounce controls. I asked her to please open the dink/ish divider slot. That would allow Yourkidsabrat to exact his revenge.

"Priorities." She continued bouncing and facing outside. "Where's your monster poo, dink?"

I removed the obnoxious glowing thing from inside my shirt. "*Tramp*oline."

"Gilpans are banned in my city."

"Lollipops are banned in mine."

She didn't get it. "Gilpans are banned in Iwinalot."

"Revealing."

The right butt screen then showed the boy's acceptance letter to the esteemed Wiggly Scissors Academy. "Where did you get clear water?"

I rested my water sack on my head.

"Let me bring it in for you: clear water is yucky, and you need to start bouncing."

"It's stalled."

"Because you're not bouncing."

"Bah-huh, bah-huh."

The left butt screen changed to a girl whose face was

smudged with ravenous shades of red and yellow. The right screen said, "Perfect grades: Sospecial School."

I tried again. "I'm not asking you to open the whole divider. Just the slot."

"We don't condone clear water. It's probably flavorless too. Priorities."

I wondered if Smackbrat or I would ever have to make architectural plans for one of the sketches this woman's kids slopped out.

The right butt screen said, "All-color ribbon winner: Ripaper Dance Competition."

I withheld the praise her butt demanded. "That's Wedge Medge in there. The guy who snipped the scent orbs off all those gilpans? Including my boy here."

She changed my beige wall to bright green and purple.

"It's very painful to them."

"A gilpan dropped an eeyuck orb in Iwinalot."

"Bah-huh, bah-huh."

"It killed a kiddyup mother."

"What did she do?" The mother had to have done something. Gilpans don't just drop eeyuck orbs unless they've been harmed. I took a sip of my water—clear, flavorless—and made a loud "Ahhh." Just a sip, though. I wanted to save it for Beige Place. If the squigglybounce ever got going.

Cheeks darkened the divider between us. Then she

made a purple and green screen to block my view of Tummygrowl Town, and a purple and green ribbed pattern on the trampoline. My water no longer appeared clear.

* * *

Cheeks made transparent the divider between Wedge Medge and me. Probably just to irritate me. He reached out toward the Miroom Tummygrowl statue. "Oh, look at that. Sparkly sparkling glashy yes!" It was getting closer.

NewNewSoNew's most deadly side effect only had one antidote: water. And it had to be applied *before* the user touched something that sparkled. He didn't have any water. I took a sip of mine. "Yes, he is sparkly. I wonder what that big sparkly tummy feels like."

Wedge Medge, his breaths voracious, opened his lunch pail then applied more NewNewSoNew.

Again I held up Yourkidsabrat. "This guy's missing a lot of scent orbs. You know anything about that?"

Ignoring me, Wedge Medge reached through his bars and up toward the statue as it looped over us. "It shines. It's so shiny, and colorful."

Yourkidsabrat whistled: he recognized his tormentor. If he got into the ish chamber, surely he'd drop an eeyuck orb. One whiff of that and everything would taste like vomit to Wedge Medge. He'd starve. That, coupled with his transformation into squish, would be a horrible death. Horrible, and just.

Wedge Medge was transfixed with the statue. Pretty soon, it would bring sparkling, potbellied justice to our squigglybounce. The divider darkened.

Yourkidsabrat nudged against me. His eyes reflected the sickly purple and green that dominated our chamber. When Smackbrat and I lost our dog Iknowyourchildsagenious, Yourkidsabrat dropped an oonice orb. I've never heard of a gilpan releasing one of those heavenly-scented orbs for a species other than its own. But when Yourkidsabrat saw how distraught we were, he released one. It made us feel clean.

* * *

Cheeks allowed me to see her again. She still bounced, and she faced me. Her face paint and the purple and green lights gave her the appearance of a malnourished parrot. And her fitness suit had breast screens. No wonder we were stuck: her breasts and butt cheeks were extracting all the energy from the squigglybounce.

She looked at her chest, across which stretched an image of a huge house. It looked like a silo knocked over then ripped open by giant claws. The left breast screen said, "My home" and the right said, "Size ranking: woweebig."

I tapped the slot between Wedge Medge and me.

"Would you kindly open this?"

Words scrolled across her chest: "Funnest Bestest Mommy Wifey."

"Revealing."

She kept looking at her chest. "Where's your face paint?"

"I haven't had the great satisfaction of encountering any children who demanded to paint my face today."

"Priorities. Where are you going?"

"Beige Place." The question was: where was Mommy Wifey going? Dressed like that. Probably nowhere. Probably just showing off a figure sliced and sucked and puttied to kiddyup perfection.

"Beige Place is boring."

"Would you mind opening that slot now?"

"You should be bouncing." One breast screen showed her, and the other said, "Highest grades: mothering and wifing. Wiggly Scissors Academy."

Must have been nice to aimlessly ride a squigglybounce in the middle of the morning. The view through her bars showed the Miroom Tummygrowl statue transfer to a sky scribble track that swooped toward our squigglybounce... and passed right next to Wedge Medge's chamber.

Wifey Mommy bounced over to block my view. "Why aren't you at work?"

"We must both have a vacation day."

STUCK ON THE SQUIGGLYBOUNCE

"You should be bouncing."

"A vacation day. From our jobs?" There was no way she worked.

"Let me bring it in for you: if you were bouncing, then we'd start moving."

We'd start moving if she turned off her breast and butt screens.

"Your monster poo's not showing again."

I held up my sparkling badge of dishonor and Yourkidsabrat nudged against it. "This is a fitting symbol for the kids' drawings I have to make buildable."

"Priorities." She turned around and kept bouncing. The left butt screen showed lollipop boy and the word "Designer," and the right one showed the Echo Building, which resembled an emaciated torso with a bloated belly.

Just once, I wanted to design a building, rather than figure out how to build some kid's fecal smear of a drawing. I'd do something to infuriate the kiddyups. Something with straight lines. Something that didn't move. Something brown, or beige. The opposite of the building on her bouncing butt.

Still, I refused to acknowledge her kids' "genius." To spite my purple and green surroundings, I took a sip. "Ahhh. Flavorless."

My chamber hissed. She filled it with kiddyup scents: popcorn, cinnamon, chocolate. No longer would my water taste flavorless.

The statue moved closer, and the Miroom Tummygrowl theme song, a jumble of twastyum tooting and boombung banging, reached the squigglybounce. I took a toy from my backpack for the dink toll.

Mommy Wifey's left butt screen showed her daughter, along with a crayon the color of tantrum. The right cheek said, "Inventor of the color Candy Cave."

I told Mommy Wifey that I invented the clear crayon.

"I've never seen that."

"Right."

She turned around mid-bounce. Her chest showed a man whose face looked like melted gumballs and whose neck looked floppy enough to raise on a pole. It also showed his yearly income: 350,000 stickers. Her husband made seven times as much as me. And her chest was seven times as large as mine.

The Tummygrowl statue spiraled and its shimmering stomach swung out.

Mommy Wifey and her bragging breasts bounced closer to the divider. "Why do you keep rubbing your stomach?"

I knocked the divider between Wedge Medge and me. "Seeing him makes me sick."

So she made the divider transparent.

Stuck on the Squigglybounce

*　*　*

Wedge Medge, his face covered in the yellow glitter, clutched his bars, and gazed up at the Miroom Tummygrowl statue. "Look at that. Sparkly glash!" Soon, the statue would be close enough for him to touch. It would take a week for him to turn into the same squishy stuff that composed the statue. But it would be so much better if, at the same time of his excruciating transformation, everything smelled and tasted like vomit to him.

Yourkidsabrat's scent pods stood straight. He screeched at Wedge Medge.

I tried Mommy Wifey again. "Don't you hate that slicing voice? He hurt many innocent creatures. He hurt my gilpan. Please open the slot."

"It's more puttering than slicing." Her chest praised gumball face as "co-inventor of Daddysmackers."

The Tummygrowl statue came close enough to see the sawtooth pattern in its rubber hair. The opposite of the abandonment atop Wedge Medge's head.

I thought of a way to get the slot open. "Daddysmacks?"

"*Ers.* Daddysmack*ers.*"

"Daddysmackers? I never heard of Daddysmackers. What are Daddysmackers?"

"Don't you have any nieces or nephews?"

"Sure. They are the very reason for my existence."

She played a butt video. It showed a girl using a Daddysmacker—I'd seen the thing hundreds of times—to slap a man. "Let me bring it in for you: Daddysmackers are parent-training devices."

I gave her a confused look. "Oh. My nieces and nephews always use ShockMa and BopPops." I pointed at Wedge Medge's chamber. "He endorsed those."

The Tummygrowl theme song played louder. I envisioned a rainbow, made of barbed wire.

Wedge Medge clapped and breathed insatiably.

Mommy Wifey bounced higher. "Candy Cave is the most popular color in Iwinalot and in Tummygrowl Town."

Wedge Medge reached toward the approaching statue, and his NewNewSoNew-smothered face glimmered. "Tummygrowl. Tummyboom!"

My plan worked: Mommy Wifey, infuriated by Wedge Medge taking away attention from her husband's invention, opened the slot between Wedge Medge and me.

Yourkidsabrat flew into his chamber. Wedge Medge cowered and clutched his shirt of colorful ropes. Yourkidsabrat dropped a scent pod, then flew back into my chamber. The slot closed.

Wedge Medge groaned and whimpered as smoke rose from the pod. The smoke surrounded him. He sniffed, and then his look of terror subsided. "Glashy. That's the oonice scent pod."

After all the pain to which Yourkidsabrat had been subjected, he chose to pay back his tormentor with an oonice pod?

Wedge Medge faced the statue. Thirty seconds away. Its "skin" looked like a cracked desert floor painted with fluorescent colors.

Mommy Wifey opened the slots between Wedge Medge and me, and between me and her. The oonice fragrance drifted in, and we both smelled it. All three of us smelled it.

I uncapped my water.

Passage
By Sheila Deeth

You don't know me. I'm a cat, or dog, or bird or fish. I can look like a human too, when I want; I'm whatever I wish. But you don't get to choose who I'm going to be. Like my sweet Sinead, you're born into your world of fact and science while I'm born into mine. If you're full-grown you've probably forgotten you ever even knew me, but Sinead won't forget. My little one keeps her feet in both our worlds, though she doesn't know it yet. That's why I'm here, to help her control it before she lets your science or her magic spoil things for her.

Look in the mirror. Sinead uses the dusty glass of a window or the surface of a pond. She has no mirrors in her world, but you, you're older; you're from a later time and I'm sure you can try. Look into your eyes. Do you see those black flecks hiding behind the blue or green or brown? Do they swim together until your center is *lost in the black of night? And can you see beyond? If you can then perhaps you really are like Sinead. Perhaps you can see through the veil to my distant place, and perhaps you can alter your facts with the breath of my magic, but be careful if you can. They'll call you a witch or a wizard; they always do, and they'll seek to destroy you. Or else they'll drown your voice and call you a liar.*

Sinead thinks I'm a cat. So does her family. But Sinead's the only one whose eyes turn black. The rest of them have forgotten how in the pain of the here and now.

I watch them pack their stuff into barrels and bags, and guess they're moving on. Who can blame them for that? Their food patch turned to slime and murk just like everyone else's. Their baby's dead like my kittens — yes, even I, like a fact-based cat, I had my litter once, and the father drowned them all. They weren't real though; they had no souls. And there's nothing here in this land for the souls I've loved, so they're moving on.

I tread behind Sinead through broken fields, past the river where my babies clawed their last and sank in their sack, and I wonder sometimes why I care. But she needs me, for all it's hard to believe the world holds anything of worth. She needs me to help her grow and guide her glowing eyes, and I can't desert her. In the town we march our private Whitsuntide parade on cobbled streets. The family makes a line from Da down to the littlest one. I pad behind on delicate paws; the tarry mud on my claws will taste foul when I wash myself tonight.

Da stoops under the weight of a wood-sided box. His arms ripple with dead muscles worn to rope. The look of hope on his face reminds me how he carried Sinead's baby sister before they lost her. She got more care than my babes at least and she wasn't dumped in water; they buried her under the rotting potato patch.

Sean carries the next crate, so big in his arms that he has to walk on tip-toe just to see where he's going. And Sinead, hair like dead grass and kitten eyes half-closed, hugs an old wooden barrel to her stomach, wrapped under in her cloak. I'm guessing she's still got her ragdoll trapped inside — that doll and I are her only comforters. Ma holds Declan in her arms while his little legs rest. Two years old he is. And no one holds me, for all that my legs are shortest.

We leave the roads and cut through fields again, eating grains and grass stems from fingers and paws, chewing as if it might fill our stomachs up or still our pangs. But then I hear a rustle off to the side. My legs spring up before I have time for thought and I catch me a field mouse which I'd share with her because I love her, but she stares like blood's the last thing on her mind.

Da fills a bucket from the stinking river and drinks. Ma wipes their faces when they've taken turns, scrubbing with spit on the corner of her coat. I lick my paws of blood's last sweetness, tasting barren soil underneath. But soon the green of countryside fades to sticky brown again and another town. Thick scents of baking, old, dry and burned, hang over us.

When the family gets too far ahead I make like a bird and fly. I mustn't stay in the air too long though—can't let them spot I'm gone. I watch the silver light wash leaden gray over an ocean's swell. Long waves lap against the coast like memories. Clouds waft like taters rotten and waiting to fall. And a ship waits at the dock. I know it's a ship because I've seen them before, long long ago. I didn't think to be near them again though, not in this life, not in this time. She was meant to be a farmer's daughter.

Raven, I remind myself. I think I was a raven back then, and the Vikings hailed me for luck when I perched on their mast, and ages passed, but that's another tale.

They're slowing, entering the port's dark slimy streets. I rush to ground, feeling feathers slacken and slide into fur again as the wide breeze leaves me. Two legs maneuver back to four and I skid around the corner, stopping right in front of her, seeing my bright black eyes reflected in the flickering green of hers.

They must have decided to live by the docks I guess. I wonder what sort of house they'll find. We'll fix it up wherever it is, me and my magical Sinead, and they'll all be okay. She'll be a dockhand's daughter instead of a farmer. And I think how she's come a long way since Ma lost the babe. Just as long she never forgets death's beyond our fixing.

The dockhands stand thickly muscled and brown with red faces frowning. Da will fill out soon I guess when he starts to work with them. He'll load the ships, exercising arms and legs until he can hold his own without me. But I don't know what the youngsters will do or how their ma will cope.

Water slips and slaps against the ship's long wooden side. The sound is redolent with the weight of waves. The whispered rhythm saps my strength as if the fish are calling, but I'd rather stick to streams, not the open sea. Salt stings my eyes.

"Stores for the trip," yells a young-old voice from shadows at the side of the road. I can't tell if the speaker's a boy or old man, all bent and crooked with blue eyes peering cloudily under his cap. "Come buy your tack and tackle now. Stores for the trip."

Da pulls us out the way of a horse and cart as we drift mesmerized into the street. Sinead almost falls. The horse almost hits her but I dance my magic by his feet. She should be doing these things for herself I think, but she's weary from the walk and I'll forgive her.

"Careful," says Da, balancing his load so he can take her hand. Sinead smiles sweetly and I'm tail over ears in love with her again. Then we head to the store with its wide dusty door hiding shadows that threaten to open and swallow us whole. A tattered awning flaps in the wind, dripping rain or sea-salt spray. I shelter, shaking wetness from fur and padding my paws to free the mud. Then I sit to wash myself. Slick black stuff sticks between my toes but my teeth are strong and neat as I nibble it away. Meanwhile the family spends its last precious pence on whatever can be found. I catch a mouse again, still slurping its wet goodness when Sinead comes to sit by me.

"Yuk," she says, turning dinner and the evidence to dust. Her eyes shine black as mine and her magic's growing. Good for her.

The wooden ship creaks and rocks scant feet from us. Water slaps against its planks. Feet thunder and echo on the ramp as passengers climb and feed themselves into its belly. I hear men shout but can't make out the words. Then roars of laughter explode even louder than the tide.

"This way folks. Check your tickets here. All aboard."

I remember Da packed tickets in his jacket pocket. He checks them a hundred times a day. Treasure from heaven they are, or a gift from Uncle Tam, who's gone to live with Uncle Sam. That's what they say. I wonder what it means.

Salty tastes of fear and excitement creep through the crowd. Some people cry. Some snatch hurried goodbyes on the shore with vapid hugs and waving arms. Others walk stiffly, eyes to the dirt, holding grimly to flimsy strips of paper and children's hands. A girl the same age as Sinead stops halfway up the ramp with a cat walking behind her. Not a cat like me, but a pretty feline thing. Then a hulking sailor stands in her way and lifts his boot in the air. "Not you little-un. Ain't got no rats, don't need no cats on our ship." He laughs and the leg moves out in a swiftly vicious kick. The kitten flies.

Sinead tenses beside me and I wish I could convince her I'll be okay. I'll fly on wings but, of course, she doesn't know the things I do. There are lots of lessons my Sinead has yet to learn.

Da comes out the shop with a bale of hay tucked under his straining arms. He's carrying a huge great barrel as well. And he's got the tickets out, flapping from the grip of hands clasped tight in front of him. Ma's got Declan hanging on her skirt while she staggers forward carrying Da's old box. It's time to move on, and the realization dawns on me:

We're not staying. We're sailing.

Sinead rocks to her feet then leans over her barrel as if to be sick. Pushing up the lid, she slips me inside where I make myself smaller than me. The doll's good company and smells of her. Then she swings her load like a cradle and moves on.

Footsteps clatter and skip on broken cobbles. Wood

thumps hollowly. I guess we must be climbing the plank. I think of the sailor kicking the cat and hope he won't notice me. But voices argue and we stop. My stomach lurches as Sinead turns the barrel over and around. I clinch my paws tight against the doll then hear Declan crying for me. "Cat. Cat. Want Shinny's cat."

Da tells Ma to carry him but I know she can't, not with her arms already full. They're all carrying stuff. I hear the boy's feet dance a jig on the planks as his voice sings out, "Want Shinny's cat!" Sinead mumbles that she can't imagine where I've got to and Da says she's lying. His hand slaps her, so now she cries as well. Then they tip the lid off my barrel to see what's inside.

Sinead's sweet magic pours like honey—clever girl—and I know I can't be seen. She's getting good. But Da tamps the lid down so solid afterward that we'll need more magic or a hammer to get me out. I mew in silent complaint, knowing only Sinead can hear me.

The barrel suddenly tumbles end over end. I sense I'm far from my sweet girl's grasp and guess she must have dropped me as she stumbled on a ladder. I can't help, but turning into a spider at least lets me hold tight until the barrel lies still. It even lets me crawl through a gap in the wood, so now I've solved the problem of how I'll get out. My spider legs feel awkward though—there are just too many of them.

But I skitter away over mountains of dirt, slip under straw, and pray no-one squashes me.

I should have prayed no spiders would prey on me. One crawls with thick black body, almost shiny, a bright red splash on her belly. But I shake out my fur and gobble her up as a treat.

Of course, the family has moved on. Dogs follow scents better than cats I suppose, but I'll wander awhile in my feline form, sure they can't have gone far. I hear Sinead crying over her barrel but refusing to confess what she's lost. The doll's fabric releases its scent of wetness with her tears, and I follow the trail. Even halfway across the floor I can savor Sinead's precious salt.

Da spreads hay. "This is our bed," he says lugubriously. "Lay you down." So they squash themselves head to toe and side to side, like kittens on a rug. I crawl into Sinead's trembling arms, displacing the doll while she dribbles delight over me. Then Declan grabs the scruff of my neck and laughs.

"How on earth?" asks Da.

"Well, it can't really be my cat," says Sinead, improvising admirably. "There's no way she could be here 'cause she ran away. But it'll keep Declan happy if we keep it."

I purr, keeping Sinead happy too.

There are mice on the ship, and rats, despite what the sailor said. And there are cats. So I'm fine for food though it's hard to chase things down in the crush of the hold. So many bodies press in and the air is thick with smells, the crumbling dryness of hard-baked biscuits mixed with salty sweat and sweet body odors, with sickness, and over it all the moans and groans of timbers and families wailing as the ship rocks on the waves. We're on our way. Insects crawl through the straw where passengers lie, but there's no meat on them. Water sloshes in huge wooden barrels, shared out each day and slopping over the sides 'til the floor's slick and slimy — water they pour over sickness as if they think they can wash it away.

A stranger hauls me up as a woman lies dying. "Cats. They're bad as rats. They carry plague." He's wrong of course, but he holds me by one paw and my claws can't reach him. Sinead's green eyes turn black with magic and I hiss a warning at her. Not here. Not where she can be seen. Then I leap from my captor's grip as he catches his hand on the top of the ladder. I tap him gently with wings when I change into a seagull, and he almost falls — honor satisfied I think. Then I soar in delight — the air's much fresher up here.

Flying up the rigging, I balance precariously on cords that hold the billowing sails in place. Black clouds flood the horizon with fear. Gulls flock together, squawking and rising in balls of flapping wings then swooping low. A storm's brewing outside as well as in.

PASSAGE

Rainwater thunders and pours off the wings on my back. Salt sea soars. Brave sailors lower their acres of flapping cloth while timbers rock. I need to land but the deck keeps swaying and I rather think I'll fall. Foamy and frothing with sloshing waves, the timbers are slick as winter's ice and slimy as Irish potatoes. Bird claws can't grip, and I fail to change in time then slide over the side. But for the magic I'd drown.

Down here the fish are calm as if the weather belongs to another world. I follow the ship in smooth dolphin skin, snack on trails of salty green, and wait in peace until it's safe to reappear. When a long parcel wrapped in canvas falls over the side I wonder who's died and rock my head to sense the touch of power riding the waves. My Sinead's still alright.

The weather turns again at last and hot sun pours over the water, warming a layer to comfort just below the rocking mirrors of the waves. I swim up, spread my wings and fly again, then swoop to land in the hold and turn back into a cat.

"Stupid ca—" A booted foot leaps out, and I shift into spider then spin my web. It feels soothingly free—a peaceful way to descend into the hold with no leaping and bounding, just drifting like silk on the air, but it's fragile, scary too.

The woman's still ill who was crying before so I know the dead body wasn't hers. Sinead sits beside her, eyes shading to black and bleeding back health into her. Oh, this girl is good. She dribbles her power like an expert so no one will know. She was surely born for this. Then a child starts crying, and Sinead turns hard-baked biscuit into warm soft bread. *Be careful they don't find you out.* Crumbs fall to the murky deck, and I slurp them up before anyone can see. Sinead's black eyes peer magically into mine and the bond's growing strong between us. Me and my girl, we'll conquer this new world, if I can just persuade her not to be discovered before we get there.

My next seagull flight reveals the shore's approach at last, Uncle's Tam's beloved America. But the weather's turned again. Sinead climbs on deck, and together we blow the rising storm out to sea. Now a gentle breeze slides us toward the dock. We've got the hang of this. Sailors are pleased at the ease of our approach and so are we. Come, my Sinead.

Sun shines, a foreign sun, soft light, and warm. A proud bright statue stands with stars behind her head and a flame in her hand. Come, my Sinead.

Then I hide in her barrel again. Nobody knows. No one will see. Officials will pass us through to this New World where the uncles wait and we'll start over. Who knows, she may still end up a farmer's daughter and I'll live at her side, catching mice in the barn, chasing chickens, and sitting on her lap, my black-eyed magic growing into hers until she knows, until she's safe.

My Sinead will make a powerful American witch, and then... *When I'm done with being this witch's familiar I think I'll try for something further in the future — your time perhaps. Have you tried looking into that mirror yet?*

About the Editor

Scott M. Sandridge is a writer, editor, freedom fighter, and all-around trouble-maker. His latest works as an editor include the Seventh Star Press anthologies *Hero's Best Friend: An Anthology of Animal Companions*, and the two volumes of *A Chimerical World, Tales of the Seelie Court* and *Tales of the Unseelie Court*.

For more on Scott and his work, please visit:
http://smsand.wordpress.com

Check out the following pages
to see more from

 SEVENTH STAR PRESS

All Seventh Star Press titles available in
print and an array of specially priced
eBook formats.

Visit www.seventhstarpress.com for
further information

Connect with Seventh Star Press at
www.seventhstarpress.com
seventhstarpress.blogspot.com
www.facebook.com/seventhstarpress
www.twitter.com/7thstarpress

Transcend Reality!

Explore post-apocalyptic fantasy worlds!
Read the Seventh Star Press anthology *The End
Was Not the End*, from editor Joshua H. Leet!

softcover ISBN: 978-1-937929-07-7
eBook ISBN: 978-1-937929-15-2

Want Sword and Sorcery?
Pick up the anthologies *Thunder on the Battlefield:
Sword*, and *Thunder on the Battlefield: Sorcery,*
from editor James R. Tuck!
(author of the Deacon Chalk novels)
Available in print and eBook!

Thunder on the Battlefield: Sword
Softcover: 978-1-937929-24-4
eBook: 978-1-937929-25-1

Thunder on the Battlefield: Sorcery
Softcover: 978-1-937929-26-8
eBook: 978-1-937929-27-5

Now available from Seventh Star Press! A series that fuses the digital realms with those of the supernatural, in a world where in the beginning... evil gained the upper hand.

H. David Blalock

The Angelkiller Triad

Featuring cover art and interior illustrations by the award-winning Matthew Perry

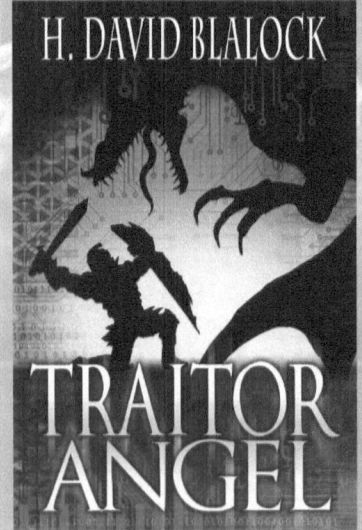

Softcover ISBN:

9781937929732

eBook ISBN: 9781937929749

Softcover ISBN:

9780983740230

eBook ISBN: 9780983740285

Gorias La Gaul adventures from Steven Shrewsbury!
Enter an ancient world of heroes, blood, and steel in the
tales of Gorias La Gaul! Hard-hitting Sword & Sorcery in
the vein of Robert E. Howard!.

Softcover ISBN: 9781937929800   Softcover ISBN: 9780983108634

eBook ISBN: 9781937929831   eBook ISBN: 9780983108641

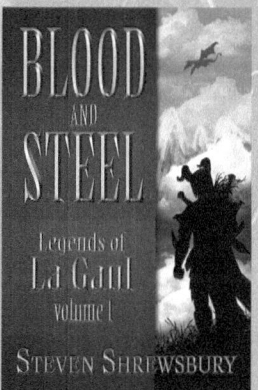

Softcover: 978-1-937929-28-2

eBook: 978-1-937929-29-9

Chronicles of Ave Now Available!
Be sure to check out the novella-sized single-author collections of short stories from Seventh Star Press!

Now Available!

Have many action-driven fantasy adventures in the world of Ave in Stephen Zimmer's *Chronicles of Ave, Volume 1*.

Softcover: 978-1-937929-30-5
eBook: 978-1-937929-31-2

Grand Epic Fantasy from Stephen Zimmer!
Explore the world of Ave in the Fires in Eden Series from
Stephen Zimmer! Epic Fantasy for those who enjoy authors
like George R.R. Martin and Steven Erikson!

Softcover ISBN: 9780982565612

eBook ISBN: 9780982565698

Softcover ISBN: 9780983108627   Softcover ISBN 9781937929855

eBook ISBN: 9780983108610   eBook ISBN 9781937929862

Action-driven Fantasy from D.A. Adams!
Begin your journey into The Brotherhood of Dwarves, the
popular YA Fantasy series from D.A. Adams. An action-
filled saga where the dwarves are not just sidekicks!

Softcover ISBN: 9781937929916   Softcover ISBN: 9781937929923

eBook ISBN: 9781937929930   eBook ISBN: 9781937929-947

YA Fantasy From Jackie Gamber!
The highly-acclaimed Leland Dragon Series from Jackie
Gamber! Strong character-driven YA Fantasy for those
who enjoy authors such as Christopher Paolini.

Softcover ISBN: 9780983108672

eBook ISBN: 9780983108696

Softcover ISBN: 9781937929893

eBook ISBN: 9781937929817